BY MARY MAXWELL
BY MAX MERRIWELL

PAT MURPHY

A TOM DOHERTY ASSOCIATES BOOK
NEW YORK

This is a work of fiction. All the characters and events portrayed in this book are either products of the author's imagination or are used fictitiously.

WILD ANGEL

A Tor Book
Published by Tom Doherty Associates, LLC
175 Fifth Avenue
New York, NY 10010

www.tor.com

Tor® is a registered trademark of Tom Doherty Associates, LLC.

ISBN: 0-812-59042-2
Library of Congress Catalog Card Number: 00-027729

First edition: August 2000
First mass market edition: September 2001

Printed in the United States of America

0 9 8 7 6 5 4 3 2 1

Praise for WILD ANGEL

"Murphy's previous foray in the fiction of Max Merriwell, THERE AND BACK AGAIN, turned Tolkien into space opera. This new tale of an orphaned girl adopted by wolves in mid-19th century California is an even wilder mix, with elements of mystery, western, and fantasy/adventure, as filtered through the feminine sensibility of Mary Maxwell. Sound like an author on holiday, just out to have some fun? For that one could just use one pseudonym—this is something rather different. . . . There's a lot going on here. But along the way, Maxwell/Merriwell/Murphy also provides the reader with a rip-roaring good time." —*Locus*

"Murphy's latest novel forms the middle part of a triptych of tales paying homage to classic works of the imagination. Faithful to the spirit of Edgar Rice Burrough's *Tarzan* tales, and Rudyard Kipling's *Jungle Book*, this story of a young girl's courage and resourcefulness belongs in most fantasy and YA collections."

—*Library Journal*

Praise for THERE AND BACK AGAIN

"A delight!" —*The New York Times Book Review*

"A very good book and a remarkable achievement."
—*Aboriginal Science Fiction* on *There and Back Again*

"There are many reasons to recommend this novel, but the main pleasure of THERE AND BACK AGAIN lies in the sly way Murphy weaves together elements of fantasy and science fiction, blending the classic with the modern to create a tale which, despite its derivative nature, stands effortlessly on its own. . . . All in all, it's a delightful romp which does justice to its source material. THERE AND BACK AGAIN is wise, knowing, respectful, and, in its less self-conscious moments, fascinating in its own right." —*Nova Express*

ALSO BY PAT MURPHY

The Falling Woman

Nadya: The Wolf Chronicles

There and Back Again

FOR EDGAR RICE BURROUGHS

—MARY MAXWELL

FOR MARK TWAIN

—MAX MERRIWELL

FOR OFFICER DAVE

—PAT MURPHY

CONTENTS

PART FOUR: 1863

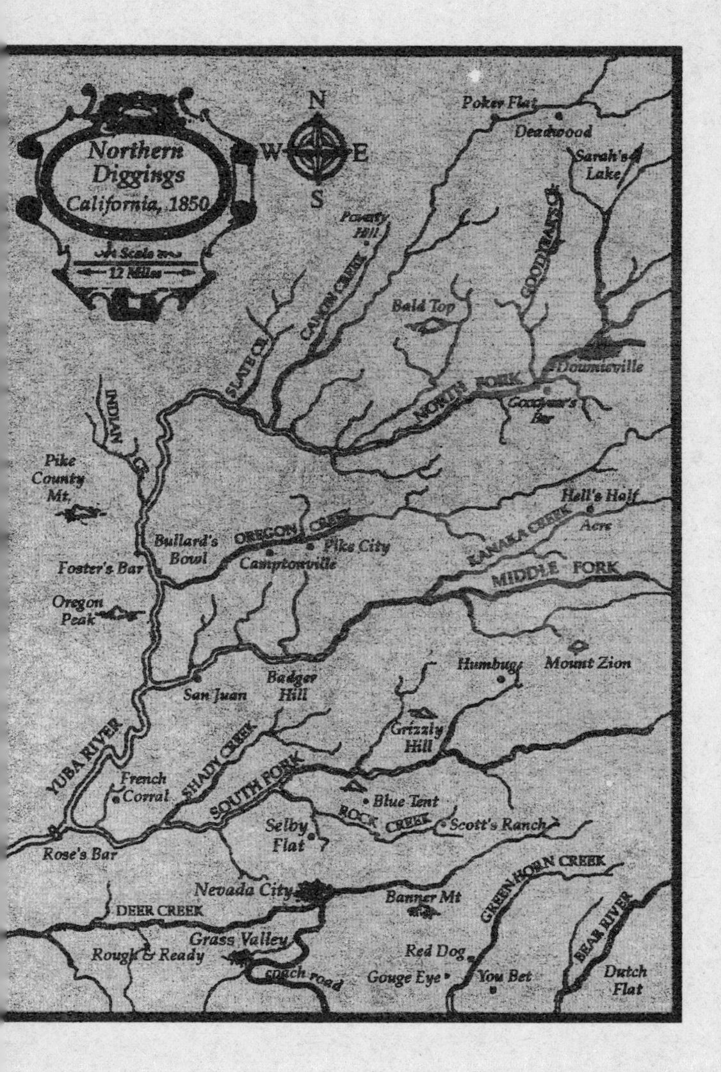
Northern
Diggings
California, 1850
Scale
12 Miles
N
W
E
S
Poker Flat
Deadwood
Sarah's
Lake
Poverty
Hill
CANON CREEK
SLATE CR.
Bald Top
Downieville
NORTH FORK
INDIAN
CR.
Pike
County
Mt.
Hell's Half
Acre
KANAKA CREEK
OREGON CREEK
Bullard's
Bowl
Pike City
Camptonville
Foster's Bar
MIDDLE FORK
Oregon
Peak
Humbug
Mount Zion
San Juan
Badger
Hill
YUBA RIVER
SHADY CREEK
Grizzly
Hill
SOUTH FORK
French
Corral
Blue Tent
ROCK CREEK
Scott's Ranch
Selby
Flat
Rose's Bar
GREENHORN CREEK
Nevada City
Banner Mt
DEER CREEK
BEAR RIVER
Grass Valley
Rough & Ready
Red Dog
coach road
Gouge Eye
You Bet
Dutch
Flat

PART ONE

1850

Oh, what was your name in the States?
Was it Thompson or Johnson or Bates?
Did you murder your wife
And fly for your life?
Say, what was your name in the States?

—Popular song of the 1850s

1

MURDER IN THE WILDERNESS

"Persons attempting to find a motive in this narrative will be prosecuted; persons attempting to find a moral in it will be banished; persons attempting to find a plot in it will be shot."

—*The Adventures of Huckleberry Finn;* Mark Twain

RACHEL MCKENSIE SAT ON THE GROUND BESIDE THE CANVAS TENT that was her temporary home. She was writing a letter to her sister, using a flat-topped granite boulder as a writing desk. For just a moment, she had paused to appreciate the beauty of the California foothills.

The spring air carried the sharp scent of the pines and the sweet green smell of new leaves. A few feet from the tent, a brook flowed through a tumble of boulders. Her daughter Sarah stood by the water, playing with pebbles. Barely a toddler when Rachel and her husband William had started the long overland journey west, Sarah was walking confidently now. She was three years old—small for her age, but bright and alert, fearless in her acceptance of the wilderness world through which they traveled. As Rachel watched, the child laughed and held her hands out, showing her mother a white pebble that she had found in the streambed. "Mama!" she said. "Mama, look!"

William was farther downstream. The shallow metal dish that he used to pan for gold was leaning against a boulder and his broad-brimmed hat was pushed back on his head. He was talking with a blond man who had just ridden down the trail that led out of the mountains. It was, Rachel thought, the same man they had seen riding up that mountain trail with a companion earlier that day. The man had his friend's horse tied behind his own. Rachel wondered idly if the man and his friend had a claim higher in the hills.

William was asking the man about gold—Rachel was sure of that. The year was 1850, just after that precious metal had been discovered at Sutter's Mill. In the California foothills, men always talked of gold. Rachel and her husband, like so many others, had come west to find their fortune.

Rachel shook her head, chiding herself for her idleness. It was time that she stopped daydreaming and prepared the midday meal. She corked her bottle of ink and set it and the pen on top of the letter to keep the paper from blowing away. Then she stood and shook out her long skirts. Just as she turned her head toward the tent, a gunshot echoed up the valley.

William lay on the ground at the blond man's feet. William's hat had fallen beside him and a dark stain was spreading across his blue-cotton shirt. Rachel froze, staring at her fallen husband. In that moment, the blond man turned toward her, lifted his rifle, and fired.

The bullet caught Rachel in the chest and sent her staggering. As she fell, she cried out—a wail of pain and surprise. On the long journey west, she had worried about Indians and wolves, about stampedes that would trample them and flooding rivers that would carry their wagon away. But now that they were in California, she had thought her worries were over. How could this be happening now?

She could feel hot blood seeping from the wound in her shoulder, wetting the rocky ground beneath her. The sunlight was warm on her face; the world seemed unnaturally bright and clear. In the distance, the blond man left his horse and began climbing the slope toward her. She could see her daughter, standing by the stream. The little girl was gazing up at her, eyes round in sudden fear.

"Mama?" Sarah said, her voice barely audible over the roar of the stream.

"Run, Sarah," Rachel gasped. "Run and hide."

Sarah knew how to run and hide. It was a game they had played together often. On the long journey across the prairie, the Indians that they met had admired the child for her coppery hair. More than one chief had wanted to trade for her—offering William buffalo robes and ponies. That was when Rachel had taught Sarah to run and hide, to find a place that was out of sight and come out only when her mother called.

"Run and hide, Sarah," Rachel gasped and prayed the good Lord would protect her daughter. "Run and hide. Hurry." She closed her eyes against the sunlight.

Sarah scrambled among the boulders, searching for a place to hide. She squeezed between two boulders and found a slab of granite leaning against a rocky patch of hillside, making a tiny cave. She slid through the opening, which was just big enough to admit her, and crouched in the cool shadows, her heart pounding with fear. Through the opening, she could see the tent, see her mother lying on the ground.

The man had a knife in his hand and a rifle under his arm. Sarah sat very still, motionless in the darkness. As she watched, the man bent over her mother with his back to Sarah. When he stood, a few minutes later, he held a handful of bloody hair. He glanced around then, as if he felt her eyes upon him, as if he feared someone had witnessed his crimes. For a moment, his eyes rested on the mouth of the cave where Sarah hid.

Sarah did not move. She was crying, but she did not make a sound. Her mother had told her that she must be silent when she hid, as quiet as a mouse. She squeezed her eyes shut, not wanting to watch, not wanting to see what the man would do next.

When she opened her eyes, he had yanked her mother's quilts from the tent. Boxes of food were open, spilling flour and beans onto the ground. He held up the feather bed, her mother's precious feather bed, and slashed it with his bloody knife. The wind caught the feathers, and they swirled and danced above the boulders, flying away into the mountains.

The man tossed the feather bed aside and turned away. Silent and motionless in the safety of the cave, Sarah watched him go.

She stayed in the cave, hugging her knees for warmth and waiting for her mother to call her. She waited. She was very young. It seemed strange that her mother had fallen to the ground, but the world was filled with events that she could not explain.

She could not come out until her mother called. Those were the rules. She closed her eyes and waited, her mind drifting like a feather on the wind. She listened to the roar of the stream as it flowed over the rocks, and the sound filled her head, washing away the sight of the man standing over her fallen mother. For a time, she slept.

WHEN SHE WOKE, it was cold in the cave, and she was hungry. She squeezed through the opening into late-afternoon sunshine and made her way to the tent. The spring air smelled of new leaves, pines, and freshly spilled blood.

Her mother's body lay in front of the tent. Her scalp

had been torn away and the rocky ground beneath her head was dark and sticky with blood. The wound in her chest had bled freely as well, and a dark stain had spread across her dress.

Sarah stood a few feet away, unwilling to approach too close. "Mama?" she said. In the past, when she made that sound, her mother had smiled and responded. But now the magic sound failed her.

"Mama," she said again, louder this time. "Mama!" A shout that echoed from the valley walls. "Mama!"

She ran to her mother's side and tugged on her hand. The skin was cold to the touch; the hand was stiff and unyielding. As the shadows grew long, Sarah crouched beside her mother's body, her small fists clutching the faded calico dress, her face wet with tears.

The hill to the west cast a shadow that engulfed the weeping girl. Sarah, chilled in the evening air, huddled by her mother's side, shivering in the cold.

THE SUN SET, and the full moon rose, illuminating the valley with its cold silver light. In a clearing up the hill from where Sarah waited, a she-wolf named Wauna sat on her haunches and lifted her head to howl at the rising moon. Her voice rose on a mournful note, stretched thin by the wind. The other members of the pack joined in, their voices singing in harmony.

Wauna's teats were heavy with milk. Early that day, she had gone hunting with the pack, leaving her pups in the care of a younger she-wolf. The hunt had gone well. The pack had brought down a young deer, and Wauna had eaten her fill. But when they returned to the den, the wind was scented with gunpowder and blood.

The young she-wolf that they had left to guard the pups was dead by the mouth of the den, shot in the head. The pups lay beside her. They had been hauled from the den and their throats had been slit.

All her pups were dead on the ground. While the pack milled about in confusion, Wauna had licked the pups, trying to wash away the blood and bring them back to life. They were so young, their eyes barely open. She smoothed their soft fur with her tongue, cleaning them, trying to warm their cold bodies. Perhaps they only slept. If she tried, she might wake them.

Her mate Rolon and the other members of the pack milled around her. Buried in the den, where the pups had been hidden, was a wooden box that stank of man sweat. In the bushes below the den, there was a dead man, one of the two men who had carried that box. The dead man had been shot, and he had fallen facedown in the bushes. The other man—the man who had left the scent of his hands on the bodies of her dead pups—had ridden away. The smell of horses lingered in the bushes where the animals had been tied.

Rolon had begun to follow the killer, but Wauna would not go with him. She had stayed with her pups, lying beside them and offering her teats so that they might suckle. She nudged the largest one with her head—a black male, the color of Rolon. She whimpered to them, a low plaintive sound, but they did not respond. There was no life in them. Despite her efforts, the pups lay still.

Now night had come and the moon had risen. Wauna knew that the pups would not wake from their terrible sleep. She had followed Rolon away from the den and up a small trail that stank of man scent. In a clearing by the dead trunk of a lightning-struck pine, Wauna had stopped, raised her muzzle to the moon, and howled, a mournful cry that echoed through the valley.

When she paused to take a breath, she caught a scent on the wind. Gunpowder and blood—human blood this time—and the same stink of man sweat that lingered by the den and on the trail. She stood for a moment, growling low in her throat, then set off in the direction of the scent. Rolon and the other members of the pack followed.

Less than a mile from the den, she saw the tent, a flapping white thing on the side of the hill. That's where the scent of man sweat was strongest. The man scent was old—the man was gone. But mixed with the scent of blood was the warm smell of another human.

Rolon and the others headed downstream, following the man smell, but Wauna stalked toward the tent and found Sarah, still clinging to her mother's body.

When the wolf approached, Sarah looked up. She knew dogs—one of the other families on the wagon train had brought their old farm dog, a tolerant animal that let Sarah pull his ears and ride on his back. That dog had been her friend.

When Wauna sniffed her, Sarah released her grip on her mother's dress and reached out to stroke the animal's soft ears. Wauna licked the child's face, tasting the salt of her tears. The child hugged the animal's neck, drawn to the warmth and comfort she offered.

Such a helpless human, so small. Wauna let the child pull on the fur at the ruff of her neck. The tugging of the tiny hands reminded her of how her pups had wrestled with her, biting at her fur, tumbling over one another clumsily in their battles. So small and helpless.

What is it about a nursing mother that lets her recognize a hungry child? Mother cats have adopted puppies and baby rabbits. Mother dogs have nursed kittens with their own litters. What silent message passes between mother and child, cutting across species lines, communicating without words?

The child whimpered as the wolf licked her. She was tired and hungry, and she had no words to express her sorrow. She made baby noises, and Wauna responded, recognizing the note of hunger. The wolf turned on her side, exposing her nipples. With her head, she nudged the child toward her nipples just as she would have directed a wayward pup.

Sarah snuggled closer to the wolf's warm body, her hands gripping the animal's fur. The child was old enough to eat solid food, but young enough to remember suckling at her mother's breast. Wauna's nipples had a warm, milky scent that drew her.

By the time Rolon and the others had returned from investigating William's body farther downstream, Sarah was suckling at the wolf's teat, clinging to Wauna's thick fur just as she had clung to her mother's dress. When Rolon came near to sniff the child, Wauna growled, warning the male to keep his distance, just as she had warned packmates away from her own pups when they were first born.

Later, when Sarah had drunk her fill of the wolf's rich milk, Rolon's restless pacing indicated that the pack was ready to move. Wauna, not wanting to leave the child behind, nudged the sleepy girl, whining low in her throat. Sarah put her arms around the wolf's neck, embracing her as she had the old dog on the wagon train. When Wauna whined again, Sarah swung her leg over the wolf's back, still holding tight to the animal's neck. Moving carefully, aware of the fragile burden she carried, Wauna followed the pack, carrying Sarah away into the mountains.

2

IN THE MOUNTAINS WITH THE BEASTS

"The proverb says that Providence protects children and idiots. This is really true. I know because I have tested it."

—*Autobiography of Mark Twain;* Mark Twain

MAX PHILLIPS TUGGED ON HIS MULE'S LEAD. "COME ALONG, Wordsworth," he said conversationally. "You're a lazy, good-for-nothing beast and an overrated poet. Let's move along, or we won't make Selby Flat by nightfall."

Max was eager to reach town, where he could sleep on a lumpy strawtick mattress, rather than on the cold, hard ground. He was thirty-three, older than many of the gold-seekers. After three weeks in the hills, he missed the comfort of a bed, however lumpy.

Max had been wandering the hills, panning gold from the mountain streams and sketching the scenery in his notebook. He was a self-trained artist—he could capture the likeness of a man or a mountain in a quick pencil sketch, a handy talent to have. Down in the mining camps, he drew portraits of miners, earning more gold from that occupation than he ever found in the California hills. Men asked him to draw their portraits, then bought the sketches to send home to their loved ones.

But sometimes Max grew tired of the company of miners, tired of all the talk of gold, tired of the drinking and gambling and endless conversations about women back home. When that happened, he struck out on his own, prospecting for gold and lingering to capture the beauty of the landscape. Now he had a notebook filled with sketches, a poke full of gold dust, and a hankering for the finest meal that Selby Flat had to offer.

The trail curved out of the pines and headed downward, following the creek into the valley. Max could see the white canvas of a tent. Someone had staked a claim beside the creek. A greenhorn, Max suspected. The spot didn't look promising.

Max made his way toward the tent. "Hallo!" he called. "Hallo!" No answer.

Quilts were spilled in a tangle beside the tent's front flap. Boxes of food, some burst open, littered the slope. As he approached, three jays flew squawking from the body that lay in front of the tent.

Max knelt beside the body to examine it. A woman, dead for a few days, by the look of it. Shot and scalped and left unburied.

Max closed her staring eyes. The wind blew up the valley, carrying white feathers from the torn feather bed that lay among the rocks. He felt cold and empty and suddenly lonely. He hadn't felt lonely in all the time he had been in the mountains. He liked being alone. He had come to California from Chicago, and he preferred the wide-open spaces to the crowded urban streets. He had been happy, wandering the hills. But now, kneeling by this dead stranger, he felt sad and abandoned.

He did what he could. He wrapped the woman's body in a quilt to protect her from the jays and the coyotes until he could bury her. He murmured a prayer over the body, asking God to look out for her, to take her to a happier place. He glanced inside the tent. In the clutter in front of the tent, wedged by the wind beneath a broken box, he found a letter and sat in the sunshine to read it.

Dear Audrey,
After all of the hardships of the trail, California is a paradise indeed. The land is wild, that is true, but it is beautiful as well. As I pen this letter, I am sitting in front of our snug tent. Higher in the mountains, snow lingers far into the spring, but here in the foothills the sun is warm and the grass is green.

From where I sit, I can look across a verdant valley. William is panning for gold in the stream. Little Sarah stands by the stream nearby, fingering pebbles as if she, too, is looking for gold. The sunlight glistens on her red-gold curls, and that's all the gold that I need. She has grown so much in the last year. She's bright and alert and sharp as a tack, a laughing child who even now holds her hands out to show me a pretty white stone that she has found.

William and I are well. The mountain air is sweet and healthy and the water is fresh and pure. I think this place will be good to us. I just know that we will find a rich claim here, and I'll send you gold nuggets the size of goose eggs. I hope

The letter ended there, obviously incomplete. No one would ever know what she had hoped.

Max stood and slipped the letter into his pocket, wondering what had happened to William and little Sarah. In the debris scattered beside the tent, he found three letters from the States, all of them addressed to Rachel McKensie, which he assumed was the woman's name.

He expanded his search and found William's body beside the stream below the tent. Like the woman,

William had been shot and scalped. Still no sign of a child.

Long ago, in another life, Max had had a daughter. He did not like to think of that time. But now, as he searched for the lost child, he could not help imagining his own daughter, lost in the wilderness. She would be weeping; she would be frightened.

"Sarah!" he called. "Sarah! Where are you?"

After an hour of searching, he shook his head. There were so many places a child could hide. Alone, he could search this wild countryside for hours without covering it all. He needed help. At last, he took the mule's lead and headed down to Selby Flat.

IN 1850, SELBY Flat was inhabited by three hundred or so men and three women. For about a mile along the shores of Rock Creek, miners had built cabins and shelters and shacks, constructing them of canvas, of logs, of brush, of stones yanked from the hillsides.

The path that meandered among the shacks was muddy when it rained and dusty when it didn't. At night, it was a dangerous place to stroll. On either side of the path were so-called coyote holes—some of them ten feet deep—remaining from mining operations. Drunken miners regularly tumbled into these pits as they wandered in search of their cabins. The hills on either side of the creek were riddled with long burrows dug by miners in search of gold.

That Sunday afternoon, a dozen miners lounged on a patch of gravel and sand beside Rock Creek. The surrounding boulders were draped with cotton shirts and canvas trousers, washed in the rushing water and now drying in the sun. For the past hour, the men had been sitting around in their underdrawers, idly discussing the latest excitement in the town. Four days before, two armed men had held up the stage, shot the driver, and stolen a shipment of gold headed for San Francisco.

A fellow named Arno had gone missing at about the same time. Most of the miners figured that Arno, with the aid of a confederate, had stolen the gold. The identity of the confederate was a mystery.

There was no sheriff in Selby Flat. No sheriff, no judge, no official representative of the law. A jury of miners dispensed a rough sort of justice, subject to the consent of the general population. Stealing was punished by whipping and banishment. Murder—unless it was in self-defense—was punished by hanging. A posse of miners had set out to look for the stagecoach robbers, but they'd lost the trail and given up after two days, returning to their claims.

"I'd guess Arno's halfway to Mexico now," suggested Jasper Davis, a tall blond miner. "He and his partner took that gold and headed south."

"I reckon you could be right, Jasper," allowed Johnny Barker. "If he were holed up around here, folks would have seen him for sure."

"I was riding down the trail from Grizzly Hill at about the time they were holding up the stage," Jasper continued. "I suppose I'd have seen them if they went up that way."

"I just keep on wondering who his partner was," a third man said. "Arno wasn't bright enough to plan a robbery on his own. And he didn't seem to have any good pals."

"I saw you and him drinking together one time," Johnny said, looking at Jasper. "A couple of weeks ago, at Selby's Hotel. Did he say anything about a partner?"

The blond man frowned. "You know, now that you mention it, he did mention that he had a partner down Hangtown way, where he was mining before. He said something about him going prospecting and his partner following along after."

"Prospecting?" Johnny snorted. "Checking out the stage, more likely. Prospecting for a good time to rob it."

It was then that Max came down the dusty trail from Grizzly Hill, leading his mule. "Hallo," he called to the men by the creek. "A man and a woman have been murdered up the trail a piece. Their little girl is lost in the mountains. I'm going to Selby's barroom to gather a search party. Pass the word."

"A woman? Murdered?" Jasper said, but Max had already moved on, tugging on the mule's lead. The men dressed and followed.

Several buildings in Selby Flat offered lodgings for transient miners: a log cabin with a bunkroom had beds for a dollar a night; a large canvas tent provided space on a dirt floor for half that price. Selby's Hotel, located at the center of the encampment, was the biggest and best of the miners' hotels.

Selby's was a sprawling structure built of logs and roofed with thick brown canvas. It was a palatial establishment by the standards of the area. First-time visitors, stepping off the dusty (or muddy) path into Selby's barroom, had been known to stop dead in their tracks, frozen in place by its unexpected opulence.

The walls were hung with pale pink calico that had been printed with roses of every size and variety, ranging from delicate blossoms smaller than a baby's thumb to cabbagelike blooms the size of a man's head. The cloth draped elegantly around a massive mirror, brought all the way from New York to San Francisco by ship, and from San Francisco to Selby Flat on the back of a mule.

Mrs. Selby took very good care of that mirror. Every morning she wiped away the dust and polished the glass. Then she polished the cut-glass decanters and the jars of brandied fruit that stood on the shelf in front of the mirror. The floor was dirt, of course, but that dirt was hard-packed and Mrs. Selby swept it each morning. The room was furnished with benches and tables constructed from rough-cut planks. Mrs. Selby had wanted nicer furniture, but she made do by draping the tables in bright red calico to hide the rough wood.

By the time Max reached Selby's, word had spread, and the room was crowded with men who wanted to know what had happened. When Mr. Selby called for quiet, Max stood by the grand mirror and described what he had found up by Grizzly Hill.

Death was common enough in the mining camps. Men got drunk and fell in the creek and drowned. Men didn't hear the warning rattle of a sidewinder, got snakebit, and died of the poison. Men got into fights and sometimes killed each other for gold. Mexicans killed white men and white men killed Mexicans and both killed Indians and Chinamen. A man's murder was unfortunate, but nothing to make anyone hurry down the trail.

A woman's murder, however, was something else. There were few women in California—three in Selby Flat, half a dozen in Nevada City. There were more down in Sacramento and San Francisco, but those cities were a long way off. Men would travel fifty miles on foot to eat an apple pie made by Mrs. Selby, a matronly woman with a broad pleasant face that no one would call beautiful. Women were precious; women were rare. A woman's murder demanded action.

It was a rough crowd that filled Selby's barroom. Men from every walk of life had come to California in search of gold—farmers who had abandoned the plow, husbands who had abandoned their wives, sailors who had abandoned their ships. Rascals and heroes, wise men and drunkards. All of them sat silent as Max told of the dead woman who lay by the side of the creek. He read Rachel's letter aloud: "I think this place will be good to us. I just know that we will find a rich claim here, and I'll send you gold nuggets the size of goose eggs. I hope . . ."

Rachel's last words hung in the air as Max put the letter down. For a moment, each man in the room thought of his own hopes and dreams. I hope I'll be rich. I hope I'll be happy. I hope that my sweetheart will still be waiting when I get back to the States. I hope that I get out of these mountains alive.

A moment later, the miners were all talking at once—shouting about finding the murderers, about justice, about honor. One man was sure that Indians killed the woman. He'd seen some Diggers up that way not a month ago. It must have been Mexicans, shouted another. You couldn't trust Mexicans around a white woman. They had to form a posse and catch the killers and string them up, showing them that this was a civilized place.

Then Mrs. Selby's voice cut through the babble. "That poor little girl," she said, her voice breaking. Her hands were knotted in her apron; her broad face was wet with tears. "She's in the mountains with the wild beasts. You've got to find her."

"We'll find her, ma'am," called Jasper Davis. He had climbed onto a bench and was standing above the crowd. "I'll lead a search party. We'll start tonight. Who's with me?"

Max stood at the back of the room with Mr. Selby, watching the miners crowd around the man, ready to rescue the poor little girl and bring her to Mrs. Selby's motherly arms. "Who is that fellow?" he asked Mr. Selby, gesturing at the blond man.

"His name's Jasper Davis," Mr. Selby said. "He came here a month ago from Sacramento. A few days back, he struck a rich streak up the creek a piece. He's a good fellow."

Max nodded, accepting the information but reserving judgment on whether Davis was a good fellow or not. Mr. Selby's estimation of a fellow's goodness depended more on the man's financial stability than on any other characteristic.

Outside, the sky had grown overcast. The clouds had darkened from the pale gray of granite to an ominous gray-black. As the miners shouted about how they would find the little girl and hang the killers, the first drops of rain began to fall.

SARAH WAS, AS Mrs. Selby had said, in the mountains with the wild beasts. The wolf pack had taken shelter in a grove of pines. Wauna lay down close to the trunk of a tree, and the girl sat on the carpet of pine needles beside her, surrounded by wolves.

"Dog," she said to Wauna, testing one of the sounds that her parents had taught her. The wolf made a low whining noise in her throat, and Sarah responded with a whimper of her own.

Wauna leaned close to sniff the girl's face. Sarah grabbed the ruff of fur at the wolf's neck and used it to pull herself to her feet. When Wauna licked Sarah's face, the girl lost her grip on the wolf's fur. She fell into a sitting position, still holding her hands out to the wolf.

After two days of suckling at Wauna's teats and sleeping beside the female wolf, Sarah smelled of milk and wolf, just like any wolf pup. While the girl sat in the litter of pine needles that covered the ground, Wauna licked her face, washing her clean. Sarah closed her eyes. Her memories were vague and muddled, but the touch of Wauna's warm, wet tongue was like the cloth her mother had used to wipe her face each night, rubbing away the dirt with water warmed on the campfire. "Mama," she murmured, and Wauna responded with a whimper, licking away the salty tears that rolled down the little girl's face.

Thunder rumbled, a warning of the storm to come. Overhead, the branches of the pines lashed in the cold wind that blew down the mountains, where winter snow still lingered. Sarah shivered and Yepa, a young female wolf, moved to sit close beside her, blocking the wind. Yepa, Wauna's daughter from the year before, had helped her mother care for the litter of pups, watching over the youngsters, letting them chew on her ears and pounce on her tail. This new youngster was strange, but when Wauna accepted her as a pup, Yepa did the same. She tolerated this pup's behavior, just as she had indulged the pups that now lay dead in the valley.

Seeking warmth, Sarah huddled between Wauna and Yepa, snuggling against their warm fur. Lightning flashed, illuminating the snowcapped mountains that surrounded them. The thunder rumbled again, and Wauna cocked her ears, listening to the mighty growls from the sky. Lightning flashed white, like sharp teeth in a dark mouth. Thunder growled and barked. Wauna nuzzled Sarah's ear, whimpering low in her throat.

A few feet away from Wauna, Rolon answered the thunder with a low bark and a whimpering growl. Then he lifted his head and howled, a long, lonely wail that echoed from the mountains. Wauna joined in, singing on a higher note that blended with Rolon's. Then Yepa and Duman and Ruana and Dur, all Wauna's children from the previous litters, joined in. Omuso, an older male, came in late, joining the chorus.

Mountain men say that wolves howl like devils, like banshees, like the lost souls in hell. They say the sound is dreadful, terrifying, unimaginably frightening. They shiver when they hear the wailing of the wolves, touched by a chill of the spirit. These men huddle by their fires, fearing the darkness of the mountains that surround them, fearing the wilderness that they hope to tame.

Surrounded by howling wolves, Sarah stared up at the night sky, mesmerized by the flashing lightning. The song of the wolves filled her with a strange feeling, a sense of urgency that made her heart pound faster. This feeling did not come with words—she had few words. But she remembered the touch of a wet cloth on her face, her mother's hand stroking her hair, her father's low voice singing her a lullaby, wordless memories that filled her with sorrow and passion.

When Wauna lifted her head to howl again, Sarah turned her face skyward and joined in with a wild young cry, a high note that rose above the others. If any mountain men had been listening, they might have wondered what new terror had joined the pack, a frightening creature with the shrill voice of a child. But there were no men to hear. Sarah clutched the neck of her adopted mother and howled, her face wet with tears and rain.

3

A CLEVER VILLAIN

"The calamity that comes is never the one we had prepared ourselves for."

—Mark Twain

THE MINERS FROM SELBY FLAT WERE DELAYED BY THE STORM. BY the time the pounding rain let up, night had fallen. They left town at first light, but it was a long and muddy trail from Selby Flat to the McKensie's camp on Grizzly Hill. Beside the South Fork of the Yuba River, the rain had washed out the trail, and the men had to climb high on the riverbank to make a new one.

Late in the afternoon, they reached the canvas tent where Rachel lay. Her body was still wrapped in the quilt, as Max had left her. The men stood beside the creek, surveying the wreckage that surrounded the tent. Now that they had reached their goal, they were uncomfortable and uncertain of how to proceed.

"I came through here last Friday," Jasper said. "I must have seen them just before the Injuns got them." He frowned down at the quilt-wrapped body, his jaw set in a grim line. "I talked to her husband; I didn't talk to her, didn't see the girl. If I'd been a little later, maybe I could have helped."

Henry Johnson, a beardless youngster of eighteen, awkwardly patted Jasper's shoulder. "We'll do what we can for them now."

Jasper shook his head, as if shaking off his sorrowful thoughts, then glanced up at the hills, down at the valley. "We can divide into teams," he suggested. "Each team can take an area and search for the girl."

"Her body, more likely," murmured Johnny Barker. "Or what's left of it." He'd been a trapper in the Rockies before coming to California, and he had no illusions about the child's chances.

"If we find her body, we'll give her a Christian burial, along with her mama and papa," Jasper said solemnly.

"If it was Injuns, they might have taken her captive," suggested Henry. "I've read about that." Henry had arrived in Selby Flat just a month before, having come to California by ship from Boston. Before taking that voyage, he had bought every book about California and the West that he could find, compiling a library that included scholarly accounts of exploratory expeditions, practical advice for travelers, matter-of-fact descriptions of military campaigns, and lurid novels that abounded with Indian captives and beauteous Indian maidens. On the ship, he read them all, amassing a storehouse of information and misinformation. "Many Western tribes take captives and raise them as slaves."

"Never heard of the Diggers doing that," Barker observed. Like most of the miners, he held the tribes native to California in contempt, regarding them as dirty beggars and savages. "If they didn't kill her, then the weather and the wolves did."

"Enough jawing," Jasper said. "I'll search that way." He waved a hand up the trail. "Max, why don't you give me a hand? We can rendezvous back here."

The men split up, each taking a different area to search. Max followed Jasper up Grizzly Hill, on the trail that led to the town of Humbug. Where the slope leveled off a bit, Jasper stopped and let Max catch up.

"I just couldn't keep talking about the little girl like that," Jasper said. He was looking out over the valley. "I keep thinking about her being lost out here, all by herself." He shook his head. "By the sound of her mama's letter, she's too young to get far. Too young to talk, most likely."

"Probably knows a few words," Max said. "She can walk, so it's likely she can talk some."

Jasper shot him a curious look. "You have children?"

Max shook his head, denying the past.

Jasper shrugged. "She'll know her name, then."

Max nodded. "She'll know her name."

From some reason, Max did not like this man. It was nothing he could put his finger on; the man had done nothing wrong. In fact, he had done many admirable things—rallying the miners to form a search party, encouraging the men as they made their way on the muddy trail, insisting that they search the area carefully, though the odds that the child had survived were slim. But there was something shifty about Jasper—he stared into space rather than meeting Max's eyes.

But perhaps it was nothing. Max was a short man, small-boned and wiry, and Jasper was tall and broad-shouldered. Max felt ill at ease in crowds and Jasper seemed to be a natural leader. He was younger and stronger than Max. Perhaps it was a touch of envy, Max thought, the simple jealousy that the weak feel for the strong, the timid feel for the confident.

"Let's call her name as we look," Jasper suggested, turning to continue up the trail. "Maybe she'll hear us and come out."

Max followed the big man up the mountain. "Sarah," Jasper called as he walked. "Sarah, come out."

After an hour of searching, they stopped to rest in a small clearing, where a lightning-struck pine raised its blasted branches to the sky. The sun was low in the west, and Max was weary. For two days, he had been traveling without much rest.

"She couldn't have come this far," Jasper said. "We'd best head back."

From the clearing, the main trail continued to the northeast, but a small trail, worn by deer, most likely, branched off to the east. "We should check down there," Max said.

"You're tired. I'll take a look, while you rest a spell," Jasper suggested.

Max leaned back against the trunk of the pine, closing his eyes for a moment. He listened to Jasper's footsteps as the man made his way down the trail. "Sarah," Jasper called. "Sarah. Are you there?" Jasper's voice faded in the distance.

Out of Max's sight, Jasper Davis smiled, happy to leave the other man behind. "Sarah," he called. "Come here, Sarah."

He had been hard-hit when Max had read Rachel's letter. What bad luck that he had missed the child.

He reached the wolf den where he had hidden the gold. "Sarah," he called again, just in case Max could still hear him. "Where are you, Sarah?"

He glanced behind him to make sure that Max had not followed him, then lay on the rocky ledge in front of the den and reached inside to feel a corner of the strongbox. He stood and dusted himself off, glancing at the bushes where he had hidden Arno's body. The bodies of the wolf pups and the wolf that had been guarding them still lay by the den. Everything was just as it should be.

Jasper smiled, thinking of how cleverly he had set up the stagecoach robbery. Over a bottle of whiskey, he had made a deal with the stagecoach guard, a man who was unhappy with his job and his salary. The bargain was simple: When Arno and Jasper appeared in the stage road, demanding the gold shipment, the guard would make sure that his shots went wild. In return, he'd get a fifth of the loot and Arno and Jasper would split the remainder.

The guard had kept his part of the bargain. Arno and Jasper appeared in the stagecoach road, blocking the way with their horses and demanding the gold shipment. The guard's shot missed the two of them—just as they had agreed. But Jasper's aim was accurate: He hit the guard in the heart and killed him instantly. And he and Arno got away clean with fifty thousand dollars in gold.

Jasper smiled down at the bushes that hid Arno's body. Not a very bright man, Arno.

"You nailed that guard good and proper," Arno had said cheerfully as they rode away. "He sure looked surprised."

"He certainly did," Jasper agreed. "That he did."

Together, they rode into the mountains, to the wolf den that Jasper had located earlier. Jasper shot the wolf that guarded the den, pulled the squirming pups from the safety of the den and slit their throats. Arno helped Jasper lift the strongbox of gold from his horse.

"I'll be hiding my share of the gold here," Jasper had said. Arno had laughed at that. All the way up the trail, he'd been talking about how he would spend his share of the money, about the fine whiskey he would drink and the fancy women he would buy.

Jasper had known all along that he couldn't let Arno have any of the money. Arno was a fool at the best of times, and a drunken fool, more often than not. Arno would lead the law back to Jasper, just as surely as he'd squander his share of the gold. He would start bragging to the first bartender who poured him a drink, to the first dance-hall girl he slept with.

Jasper was squatting beside the strongbox when Arno said, "I reckon I'll take my share now." Without a word of warning, Jasper had lifted his pistol and shot Arno through the heart. Arno barely had time to look surprised before he tumbled over dead.

Then Jasper had opened the box and transferred a few handfuls of gold dust from one of the big bags into his own pouch. It would be unsafe to take more—any man who suddenly started spending freely would be suspected of the robbery. He closed the strongbox and shoved it into the den, where it would be safely hidden. He tumbled Arno's body into the bushes.

Now, standing on the rocky ledge in front of the wolf den, Jasper felt happy and secure. No one had disturbed his gold, and no one would. Sarah McKensie was surely dead. The odds of a child surviving one night in the wilderness were slim—and it had been four days since he did her parents in. That child would be no trouble to him. She couldn't tell the miners that Jasper Davis had gone up the mountain with Arno and a box of gold—and he had come back alone. She could not tell them that he had murdered her parents so that they could not betray his secret.

He was smiling when he turned his back on the wolf den, heading back up the trail to where he had left Max. "Sarah," he called as he walked. "Come out, little Sarah." By the time he reached the clearing where Max waited, his face was set in a grim expression.

MAX OPENED HIS eyes and saw Jasper coming up the trail. "You found nothing?" Max asked.

"Nothing. Let's go back to camp. Maybe someone else has found her."

The other men had been equally unlucky. No sign of the child or her body. By the light of the setting sun, the miners used William's shovel to dig a grave. They buried Rachel and her husband together in the valley and marked the spot with a cross constructed of two oak branches lashed together with rope. Over the grave, Henry murmured a few words from the Bible.

They had done what they could, Max thought. The child was gone. Johnny Barker thought she had been devoured by wolves; Henry held to his theory of Indian capture. One way or the other, she had vanished.

As the sun set, Max sat beside a boulder—the very same boulder that Rachel had used as a writing desk—and sketched the valley, the creek running through the meadow, the oak trees and grasses. Henry Johnson had gathered a bouquet of poppies and placed it by the cross. The orange flowers caught the golden light of the setting sun and seemed to glow, as if illuminated from within. The cross at the head of the grave cast a long shadow in the grass. An acorn woodpecker flitted from an oak tree to the upright of the cross, paused for a moment, then flew away in a flash of black-and-white wings.

Max penned the sketch in careful detail. He would send a letter to Audrey North, the woman to whom Rachel McKensie had been writing. From Audrey North's letters to Rachel, he had gathered that the women had been sisters. Perhaps, he thought, Rachel McKensie's sister would take some comfort in knowing that Rachel had been buried in a beautiful place.

The others made camp on the far side of the valley at a goodly distance from the grave and the McKensies' camp. When the sun set, Max joined the others by the campfire.

IT WAS LATE the next day when they reached Selby Flat.

Rain had begun falling in the morning, a persistent

drizzle that soaked through Max's wool felt hat in the first hour and his coat in the second. The trails were slick with mud and treacherous, and it was a long, slow journey back to town.

Mrs. Selby met them at the entrance to the hotel. Drenched from the rain and chilled to the bone, the men trooped into the bar, long-faced and weary. Max was among the first to enter.

"No sign of the little girl," Max told Mrs. Selby. He described their search, then shook his head despondently. "All we could do was to give her mother and father a decent burial, then come on back."

"You did your best," Mrs. Selby said. "No one can ask for more than that." She patted Max's shoulder.

"I thought I'd write a letter," he said. "To her sister back home. Let her know what happened."

Max hung his hat and coat by the fire that burned at one end of the hall. The space in front of the fire was crowded with boots, and the room stank of steam and sweat and drying socks.

He found a table at the back of the room near one of the gaps in the walls that served as windows. The dreary late-afternoon light that shone through the calico curtain gave that table the best lighting of any table in the house. Turning his collar up against the cold draft that blew through the opening, he settled down with his notepad and pencil to compose a letter to Mrs. Audrey North of New Bedford, Massachusetts. He had the address from letters he had found by the tent. It was difficult, but he knew that it had to be done. Since he had discovered the bodies, he felt that it was his place to do it.

Dear Mrs. North,
It is with a sorrowful heart that I must write to tell you that a tragedy has befallen your sister and her family.

There is no way to soften this news, and so I will state the facts directly. Your sister and her husband have been murdered by unknown assailants and their daughter Sarah is missing and most likely dead in the mountains.

I was returning from prospecting on Grizzly Hill when I passed the place where your sister's family had camped. There I found a terrible scene of destruction. Unknown persons had shot your sister and her husband and had wantonly destroyed much of their property. There was no sign of the child, Sarah, that your sister mentions in her letter.

A group of miners from the nearby encampment of Selby Flat have thoroughly searched the area, hoping that divine providence had somehow protected the innocent child from harm. Alas, we have found nothing. Some have suggested that Indians might have carried the child away, but that seems unlikely. I believe that the child is dead and that her body has been carried off by wolves.

I can give you no information about who perpetrated this terrible crime. Some suspect Indians, but there is no proof that the savages were involved. We have done our best to give your sister and her husband a Christian burial and we have said a prayer for Sarah, that she, too, may rest in peace.

It might comfort you to know that your sister's last thoughts were of you. I enclose a letter that I found beside her tent. I also enclose a sketch that I made of the valley where your sister died.

He was finishing this line when Mrs. Selby returned to the table, having bustled about and made sure that all the miners were cared for. While she read the letter, Max took out his sketch of the gravesite.

Mrs. Selby wiped away a tear with a corner of her apron. She returned the letter to him and peered over his shoulder at the sketch. "That's lovely," she said.

Accepting the letter from Mrs. Selby, he wrote a final line. "You have all my sympathy at this time of sorrow." He could think of nothing more to say, no words that could make this tragedy any less painful to Rachel's sister. He signed his name and folded the note and his sketch of the valley around Rachel's half-written letter.

"I'll send it with the next stage," Mrs. Selby said. "Such sad news for a sister to hear. But I'm sure your sketch will be a comfort to her."

4

WANTED

"A man should not be without morals;
it is better to have bad morals than none at all."

—*Mark Twain's Notebook;* Mark Twain

FOR THE NEXT FEW WEEKS, THE MINERS OF SELBY FLAT CONTINued speculating about the robbers who had held up the stage and about the villains who had killed Rachel McKensie and her family. The murders were generally blamed on Indians or Mexicans. Arno's continued absence made him a favorite for the robbery. The stage company offered a reward for the recovery of the gold, but no one came forward to claim it.

Without a hint of shame, Jasper Davis speculated and discussed the murders with the others. He felt no guilt, no remorse.

Jasper Davis was an extremely intelligent man with no conscience. The youngest of six boys, he had been born on a hard-scrabble dirt farm in the hills of Tennessee. His mother, exhausted by the needs of the farm and the demands of her boys, had died two years after his birth, leaving the toddler to the indifferent care of his older brothers and drunken father.

Jasper had grown up hungry. His father was an indifferent farmer; his brothers were wild boys who helped on the farm only when threatened with beating. There was never enough food for everyone. At mealtime, he got what was left when his brothers were done—never enough to satisfy his growling stomach.

Jasper had grown up dirty. His face was always grimy. He wore clothes that his older brothers had outgrown, all well-worn and stained before he got them. He had no cause to wash, no cause to dress up. After his mother died, he never went to church. He never went to school—his father saw no need for schooling. "Waste of time," he said. "He don't need no schooling. Don't want him to think he's smarter than his pappy."

Jasper had grown up mean. The runt of the litter, his father called him, the smallest of a family of tall, lanky, rawboned men. His father cuffed him, his brothers beat him up, and he kicked the dog when he could get away with it, which was rarely. His father treated his coon hound with more care than his children.

At age sixteen, Jasper killed his father. He waited until his brothers were out somewhere raising hell, then he hit the old man in the head with the same hatchet they used to butcher the hogs. He burned the house, stayed for a time to watch the flames, then took the mule and headed west.

That was back in 1843. On his way west, he had held many jobs—he wasn't lazy and he could work hard when it suited him. America was a big country, with many opportunities for a young man in the process of transforming himself. Jasper worked for a year as a deckhand on a Mississippi stern-wheeler. On board, he made the acquaintance of Gentleman Jack, a lawyer from New Orleans who had, after a series of shady dealings, found it wise to leave town and take up life as a riverboat gambler and con artist.

One night, standing outside the gambling salon and having a smoke, Jasper had looked through the window and watched Gentleman Jack cheat at cards.

He saw exactly how the man palmed the cards and exactly how much he took from his fellow swells.

When Jack stepped out on the deck, Jasper hailed him. Standing at the rail while the brown waters of the Mississippi flowed past, Jasper explained, in a low, soft, reasonable voice, exactly what he had seen.

"How much do you want?" the gambler asked, ready to pay for Jasper's silence. His fellow cardplayers would have been quite happy for an opportunity to beat him senseless and take their money back.

Jasper shook his head. "That ain't it. I don't want money. I want you to teach me."

"Teach you what?"

"How to gamble. How to act like a gentleman."

The gambler laughed—then saw the dangerous glint in the young man's eyes and stopped. "That will take a while."

"I'll travel with you," Jasper said.

They traveled together, and Jasper learned a few things. He got a better suit of clothes, a better haircut. He learned that "ain't" wasn't proper English and that a gentleman blew his nose on a kerchief, rather than wiping the snot on his sleeve. He watched and he listened and he learned.

Though the association was forced upon him, Gentleman Jack enjoyed teaching the young man. Jasper was a quick study. He learned to say "please" and "thank you." He learned how to flatter a lady. He learned to gamble and he learned to palm cards. He helped Gentleman Jack work out some new methods of cheating.

Jasper improved himself. By the end of his first year with Gentleman Jack, he might have been taken for a pleasant young man raised on a proper family farm—still a bit rough about the edges, but well-meaning and polite.

Then one night, after Gentleman Jack had done particularly well at cards, Jasper strangled his mentor, took the profits, and headed west once again. It was time for him to move on, and he needed money to do that.

There is not space here to detail all of Jasper's exploits. Suffice it to say that he came to California in 1849, like so many men, to make his fortune and remake himself. He thought it was time for him to adopt the veneer of respectability.

For that, he needed money. That was where the stagecoach came in. He robbed the stage to get the money he needed, then covered his tracks by killing all witnesses. Except for Sarah, but surely she was dead in the wilderness.

He was smart enough not to spend the money he had stolen all at once. He would spend it gradually, establishing himself as a successful miner, a respectable man of means.

MAX STAYED IN Selby's Hotel for a time, happy to have a bed to sleep in and a roof over his head. He staked a claim a mile or so north of town, on a gravel bar that looked promising, and worked it just often enough to keep his hand in. He'd been staying at Selby's for a week or so when Mr. Selby mentioned some past business.

"I still have that sketch of yours," Mr. Selby said. Max was eating a late breakfast at the bar and the barroom was empty. "That Arno fellow never stopped by for it." Mr. Selby waved toward the mirror. Max could see a sketch tucked behind one corner, held up by the weight of the framed glass against the rough wall. Arno's grinning face, captured in pen and ink.

Just before Max had left on his prospecting trip, Arno had begged Max to complete a sketch of him.

Arno, a short, tough man with a high opinion of himself, had posed by the fireplace at the end of the barroom, grinning to reveal his gold front tooth. Bandoleers crossed his chest and a bowie knife of impressive proportions was sheathed at his belt.

It had been a long, wet, spring afternoon, and Max had been reluctant to leave the warmth of the barroom. So he had lingered over the portrait, shading it carefully and including details that he might ordinarily leave out. The handle of Arno's knife, for example, had caught Max's attention: the polished wood was decorated with silver inlay depicting a running wolf with black-onyx eyes. Max had included this detail in the sketch. The portrait was, Max thought, one of his best.

It was only after Max completed the portrait that Arno had told him that he couldn't pay for it right away. "I'll be getting the money soon," Arno had said. "A fellow owes me some money, and he's coming to town. I'll pay you then."

Max had frowned, feeling that Arno had taken advantage of him. "When you pay me, that's when you'll get the picture."

Arno had argued. "But I might be gone by the time you come back."

"My point exactly," Max had said. "You'll be gone and so will my payment."

Still grinning, Arno had pulled his knife, leaning back in his chair and using the point of the blade to clean his fingernails. The blade glinted in the dim light of the bar. A running wolf, twin to the one on the handle, had been etched on the knife's blade.

Easily twelve inches in length, the blade was an inch and a half wide at the handle, tapering only slightly for the first eight inches, then curving to a saber point. Both edges of the curving section were sharp, giving the weapon a ripping edge on the back as well as a foot of cutting edge on the front. Below the curving section, the back of the blade was sheathed in brass, a metal softer than steel. In a knife fight, an opponent's blade could catch in the brass, which kept it from sliding down the blade to cut the hand of the knife fighter. At the handle, a broad guard offered further protection. Patterned on the famous knife of James Bowie, this was a knife fighter's blade.

Max glared at Arno, refusing to be intimidated. "You'll get the picture when I get my payment," he said.

It was just then that Mr. Selby had come up to join them. "What the hell are you doing with your knife out, Arno. I can't imagine why you need that in here."

"We were having a business discussion," Arno said sheepishly, and slid the blade back into its sheath. A man who angered Mr. Selby would be banned from the best bar in town. Arno clearly wasn't willing to risk that.

Max took advantage of the interruption. "I'm sure Mr. Selby could help us out here. Arno wants to pay me for this portrait when he gets the money, but I'm leaving town. Do you suppose you could hold the picture and take payment for me when he has it?"

For a share of the proceeds, Mr. Selby agreed to hold the portrait for Arno's payment. Max left town the next day. But Arno, it seemed, had never returned with the money.

Mr. Selby frowned at the portrait. "What do you want to do with it?"

Max shrugged. "If you're willing to keep it for a time, then let's just see if Arno shows up to claim it."

"And if he robbed the stagecoach like some of the boys think, it'll make a fine wanted poster," Mr. Selby said.

Max laughed. "For now, let's just leave it where it is and see if Arno comes back for it."

JUST A FEW days later, Patrick Murphy, an agent of the recently formed Pinkerton National Detective Agency came to Selby Flat. "I've been engaged by the stage company and the bank to investigate the robbery," he explained to Mrs. Selby. "I confess I'm startled to find such a fine establishment so far from civilization."

Mrs. Selby regarded Mr. Murphy with approval. He had, she thought, an intelligent face and a discerning eye. He was dressed far better than the miners, in a fine sack coat and vest. She gave him her best room, an alcove that Mr. Selby had partitioned off from the general dormitory with a calico curtain.

Over lunch in the barroom, Mr. Murphy asked Mrs. Selby a good many questions about the town, about the stagecoach robbery, about the speculations surrounding it. She was happy to answer his questions, tell him about suspicions regarding Arno and the robbery, and fill him in on things that he hadn't thought to ask about, such as the murders on Grizzly Hill, the price of eggs, and the difficulty getting dried apples so far from Sacramento. She asked some questions of her own, mostly about women's fashions back in the States, a subject on which she found Mr. Murphy's knowledge less than satisfactory. Even so, Mrs. Selby enjoyed their chat and promised to introduce him to some miners who might be able to answer questions that she couldn't.

Late that afternoon, she spotted Max in the doorway and rushed out to meet him. "Max!" she called. "There's someone I'd like you to meet. He's here to investigate the stagecoach robbery. I've been telling him about the murders, and he had some questions." She took his arm and led the way to Patrick Murphy's table by the kitchen—her best table. Late-afternoon light shone through an open window beside the table, illuminating the detective's face.

"This is Patrick Murphy," she said. Max's expression was one of shock and recognition.

"Max," said Patrick. "Who would think that two old friends would meet again like this?" He grinned at Max.

"You know each other!" Mrs. Selby was delighted. She glanced at Max again to see if her delight was shared. Max wore a worried frown; he did not look happy to see Patrick Murphy.

"We certainly do!" Patrick was saying. "Max and I met in Chicago years ago, back when I was a policeman. Isn't that so, Max?" He did not give Max time to answer. "But there's no need to get into that now. I have a new job these days, Max. I'm a detective with the Pinkerton National Detective Agency. Sit down, sit down. I wanted to talk to you about the robbery of the stage."

Mrs. Selby left the men together. It was a busy evening. She brought their supper, but could not linger to chat. There were hungry men to feed, and she had no time to waste. She noticed that they drank together, making considerable inroads on the bottle of whiskey that Mr. Murphy had purchased. Mr. Murphy smoked one of his fine cigars, nine-inch panetella supers of an East Coast make, far better than the pipes and foul-smelling, six-inch stogies that most of the miners smoked.

She was serving dinner to a tableful of miners when Max asked her if he might take the portrait of Arno from behind the mirror. She nodded her consent

Business didn't slow down until after sunset, when she looked over and noticed that Max was gone. She checked on Mr. Murphy then.

"Did you have a good chat with Max?" she asked.

"Indeed I did."

"He's such a gentleman, Max is," she said. She sat down in the chair that Max had vacated. "He's a cut above most of the miners. He reads books and he draws so well. He is really an artist."

Patrick nodded. "He mentioned this fellow, Arno, who never came back for his portrait." He tapped on the portrait, which was spread on the table. "With Max's permission, I'll be using this to make a wanted poster."

Mrs. Selby nodded. She was less interested in Arno than she was in Patrick's opinion of Max.

Max was, in Mrs. Selby's mind, a bit of a mystery. He was a cultured man, an artist, and he did not seem to be motivated by gold fever, as so many of the miners were. She wondered what had brought him to the gold country. Max had brushed off her questions about his past, saying that he didn't like to think about all that.

"You mentioned that you were a policeman when you met Max. Was Max a policeman?"

Patrick smiled, as if at a private joke. "No, not at all. But our work did bring us together."

"An artist and a policeman." Mrs. Selby raised her eyebrows. "Sounds like an interesting story there."

"That may be, but you won't hear it from me." Patrick put down his whiskey glass.

Mrs. Selby shook her head in frustration. "You are being far too mysterious, Mr. Murphy."

"My good Mrs. Selby, without mystery, life would be dull indeed." Still smiling, he refused to answer another question.

THE NEXT TIME she saw Max, Mrs. Selby asked about how he knew Patrick Murphy, but Max said, "We met in

Chicago," and would say no more. Mrs. Selby's curiosity remained unsatisfied.

In the hills, the wooden trunk remained safe in Wauna's den. The jays pecked out Arno's eyes; the coyotes gnawed his bones. And far from the questionable civilization of Selby Flats, Sarah lived among the wolves.

5

FIRST HILL

"All you need is ignorance and confidence; then success is sure."

—Mark Twain

WAUNA CARED FOR SARAH AS SHE WOULD HAVE CARED FOR HER own pup. She suckled Sarah when the child was hungry, washed her face and hands with a warm wet tongue, kept close watch over her.

Wauna took the girl to a sheltered hollow on the side of a hill, protected on two sides by rocky outcroppings that offered small caves and crevices where wolf pups could hide. On the third side was a mixed stand of oak, incense cedar, and yellow pine. The fourth side was open to a wide forested valley.

There, under Wauna's watchful eyes, Sarah played in the sunshine. By day, squirrels scampered and scolded in the oak trees; woodpeckers and jays foraged among the fallen leaves, searching for acorns left over from autumn. At night, Sarah listened to the quavering call of the screech owl, the chirping of the crickets. Sarah learned about the world around her—and she learned about the wolves.

A wolf pack is an extended family, connected by blood relationships and bonds of affection. The leaders of the pack are the alpha male and alpha female, patriarch and matriarch. All other members of the pack have positions on a social hierarchy, a complex network of relationships that dictate each animal's behavior. In Sarah's pack, Rolon and Wauna were the alpha pair.

In a pack, all the wolves—from the highest to the lowest—help care for the pups. When Wauna, the pack's alpha female, took Sarah as her pup, the other wolves accepted her as such.

At first, the wolves let Sarah play as any pup plays. But gradually, they began teaching her that some things were not appropriate. When she tugged on Ruana's ears, the young female nipped her softly until she let go. Then Ruana nuzzled Sarah's face softly to reward the proper action. When Sarah stared at Rolon with an expression that offered a challenge, the male wolf growled softly and bowled her over. Then he stood over her and nudged her face until she looked away. From these lessons, Sarah learned the proper way to behave.

Wolves do not communicate with words, as humans do. They speak to each other in subtler ways. A movement of the ears can communicate anger; a shift in the angle at which the tail is held can indicate distrust; a lowering of the head can suggest an apology; a direct stare presents a challenge.

A wolf that is greeting a friend wags his tail, rubs against his friend, and maybe licks his friend's muzzle or nudges his friend's nose with his own. A friendly wolf signals his goodwill with his ears, pricking them up in interest or laying them back in a submissive gesture that indicates he has no interest in fighting. He may grin a wolfish grin, with lips pulled back and turned up at the corners. He may whine or make a sound that's a little like humming, a cross between a moan and a whine that rises and falls in pitch. He may rear up to place his paws on his friend's back or indulge in a wolfish hug, embracing his friend with one or both paws. In the ecstasies of greeting, he may softly grab his friend's muzzle in his jaws in an affectionate love bite.

Sarah learned to read the body language of the wolves, becoming attentive to subtle signals that most humans would overlook. She could tell when Omuso would be glad to have her scratch his ragged right ear, torn in a fight long ago—and when it would be better to leave the old male alone. She played with Dur and Duman and Yepa, rolling on the ground and growling puppy growls. She joined in the chorus each morning, when the wolves howled to greet the dawn. She howled with Wauna when the alpha female called to her packmates, summoning them to rendezvous.

Though she had no tail to wag, and her ears were useless for signaling her intentions, she learned to communicate her own feelings, adapting the signals used by the wolves to make herself understood. She could sniff noses, she could grin, she could whine and hum. Where a wolf might lick or use his jaws, she used her hands—grabbing a muzzle, scratching an ear, rubbing a chin. She could indicate that she wanted to play or solicit attention and grooming or warn a wolf away. Her packmates came to accept her gestures, reading her intentions as easily as they read each others'.

As a pup, Sarah was the lowest-ranking member of the pack—but she was also its most indulged member. Recognizing her frailty, the wolves treated her more gently than they would one of their own, nipping softly where they would have chastised a wolf pup more severely. Still, she learned to submit to a higher-ranking wolf, trustingly exposing her neck to the beast's sharp teeth, whining low in her throat to communicate her surrender.

Like any child, Sarah explored her environment. In

a moist, shady place, she found the plant known to some as miner's lettuce, and feasted on the soft green leaves. She ate tender shoots of young clover. When Wauna brought her the remains of a kill, she teethed on scraps of dried meat and hide. But she preferred Wauna's milk to the tough meat, and continued to suckle.

Over the passing weeks, Sarah gradually shed her clothing. She pulled off her underpants when she squatted to pee, then abandoned them where they fell. Inspired by the squirrels, she scrambled up into the low branches of one of the oaks. Once, when Dur was in a temper, she escaped the wolf by climbing higher than she ever had before. When her frock caught on a branch, she scrambled out of the garment and left it hanging in the tree. After a month in the wilderness, she wore only a tattered white petticoat that grew dingier with each passing day, and a pair of leather moccasins that her human mother had purchased from a friendly squaw on the trail westward.

Wauna worried about Sarah. This strange pup seemed healthy, but she was slow to develop, lacking the endurance and speed of a young wolf.

What worried Wauna more than anything else was Sarah's lack of interest in meat. The first food that wolf pups eat is partially digested meat, regurgitated by wolves who have returned from the hunt. Pups beg for food by licking at the muzzles of adult members of the pack. Wolves also carry meat back from the hunt—for the pups and the adult wolf who stayed behind.

Unlike a wolf pup, Sarah did not beg for food. She ignored the meat that Wauna dragged to the sheltered hollow. Instead, Sarah continued to suckle, growing strong on the milk that would have nourished half a dozen wolf pups. For a time, Wauna was tolerant, indulging the strange pup and letting her continue to get her sustenance from milk. Having lost her own pups, Wauna was determined to keep this one healthy and strong.

Eventually, game grew scarce in the area around the hollow where Sarah stayed. The pack moved, and Sarah moved with it. Wauna stayed with the girl, trailing behind the rest of the pack. The little girl walked as far as she could. When she tired, she draped herself over the mother wolf, lying on Wauna's back with her arms locked around the wolf's neck. Each day, Wauna would find a safe place to leave the girl while the pack hunted. Sometimes, Wauna stayed with her. Sometimes Yepa stayed.

One sunny, summer day, Sarah waited in a high Sierra meadow for the pack to return. Yepa was napping in the shade while Sarah explored the meadow.

She was hungry. The girl had suckled long after pups would have been weaned, and Wauna's milk was drying up. That morning, when Sarah had tried to suckle, Wauna had curled up, hiding her tender nipples from the girl. When Sarah had persisted, Wauna growled softly and nipped at the child's hand, gently warning her away. Wauna had little milk and little patience left.

In the meadow, Sarah found some tender clover and plantain leaves to eat. She devoured the leaves, but they did little to assuage her hunger. She was searching vainly for something to eat, when she noticed birds flitting among the branches of a blackberry bush on the edge of the meadow.

The birds flew away at her approach, chirping in protest at the disturbance. The birds had been feeding for some time, but a few blackberries remained on the branches. Sarah reached into the bush for a big berry. The thorns scratched her arm, but she got the berry and crammed it into her mouth. It tasted wonderful—sweet, ripe, and warm from the sun.

Thorns could not dissuade her. Patiently, carefully, she pushed her way through the branches. She found a berry that a bird had pecked and rejected, another that was only half-ripe. The little girl did not overlook any possibilities, finding and devouring the smallest and sourest of the wild berries with enthusiasm and relish.

Sarah was deep in the blackberry thicket when Wauna returned with the pack, carrying a piece of meat torn from the kill. Searching for her foster child, Wauna followed Sarah's scent across the meadow.

A young cottontail rabbit was foraging in the meadow when Wauna returned. The rabbit saw the wolves, but when they showed no interest in him, he continued grazing. He was happily occupied in a patch of clover when Wauna suddenly appeared, bearing down on him.

Foolishly, the rabbit panicked and bolted from cover right under the mother wolf's nose. Wauna dropped the meat that she carried and lunged for the fleeing cottontail. Instinctively, the rabbit fled toward the protective cover of the blackberry thicket.

Just as the cottontail was about to dive into the cover of the bramble patch, Sarah emerged from the bushes, scratched and grimy. She was still hungry, having been rewarded for her diligent search with just a few small berries. When the child stepped directly into the path of the fleeing rabbit, the animal changed direction abruptly. Fearing the human as much as the wolf, the panicked rabbit turned to one side.

Wauna was on him, her jaws closing on his neck. Still running, she snatched the rabbit off his feet, breaking his neck.

Sarah ran after Wauna, her childish squeals of excitement blending with the mother wolf's growls. Wauna jerked her head and opened her jaws, tossing the cottontail to her foster child. Sarah, running on two legs as her human parents had taught her, snatched at the rabbit with both hands. She caught the carcass (more by luck than by skill) in a tight embrace. Throwing herself down on the meadow grass, she bit at the cottontail's neck as she had seen Wauna do.

Sarah's teeth were not sharp enough to penetrate the animal's hide, but Wauna's fangs had already torn the rabbit's fur and bitten deep into the artery that carried blood to the animal's brain. The rabbit's heart, beating its last, pumped warm, salty blood into Sarah's mouth. The girl swallowed, hungry for nourishment, sucking at the wound as she had at Wauna's teat.

She growled like a young wolf then, pulling at the still warm carcass with her hands and teeth. A young girl is not equipped to rend and tear a carcass like a young wolf, but Wauna helped, nudging Sarah aside with her muzzle. Planting a paw on the carcass to hold it in place, Wauna ripped open the rabbit's belly, exposing the soft internal organs.

Sarah plunged a tiny hand into the warm viscera and pulled out the liver. Cramming the organ into her mouth, she chewed happily as blood ran down her chin. She feasted on the heart and lungs, then licked rich blood from her hands. Finally, sated and smeared with blood, she curled up in the grass with her foster mother.

Wauna was happy that this strange pup had fed. Now she would grow strong. The mother wolf licked the girl clean, washing away the blood of the cottontail and cleaning the bramble scratches. Sarah laughed happily, warm in the sun and well fed at last.

Meanwhile, back in Selby Flat, Mrs. Selby was polishing her mirror. That morning, she had received a letter addressed to Max, sent care of Selby's Hotel. From the return address Mrs. Selby knew that the letter came from Audrey North.

As she polished the mirror, Mrs. Selby thought sorrowfully of little Sarah. Without stopping her work, Mrs. Selby muttered a prayer for the little girl, a plea that she find happiness in her mother's arms in heaven. Little did Mrs. Selby know that Sarah was far from heaven. Smeared with blood and dirt, in a wilderness meadow, Sarah had indeed found happiness and a mother's love.

AN HOUR LATER, Sarah woke from her sleep and licked blood from her lips. She was not a young wolf—no, she could not be that—but she had taken a step toward savagery and survival. She had eaten raw meat and relished it. She wanted more.

Wauna was a patient teacher. Under her tutelage, little Sarah learned to flush rabbits and mice and ground squirrels and quail from cover and send them running into Wauna's jaws. Once, when a young quail was slow to escape, Sarah snatched up the bird and broke its neck, her first kill.

Hunting and killing became a part of her life. Like her savage ancestors, she ate her meat raw, licking blood from her hands and relishing the salty taste of it.

Having learned to eat the fresh meat from these kills, Sarah began supplementing that diet with meat from the pack's kills, which Yepa and Wauna brought her. She could not bite through the hide of a downed deer as her packmates could, but she could pick at the scraps of flesh once the hide was torn away by the teeth of the wolves.

In the afternoons, while the pack rested and played,

she foraged for other foods. She competed with the birds for the fruits of a variety of plants, snacking on wild strawberries, gooseberries, thimbleberries, and Sierra plums. Craving greens, she ate the leaves of miner's lettuce and clover.

She had the face of a cherub—sweet blue eyes and delicate features surrounded by a halo of red-gold hair—but she was as dirty as any child could ever hope to be. Her hair was a glorious tangle; her face, smeared with berry juice; her arms and legs tanned from the sun. But she was happy for all of that. She hunted, and she thrived in her new family.

6

ROMULUS AND REMUS

"Get your facts first, and then you can distort them as much as you please."

—Mark Twain

MICHAEL DAY, A MAN GENERALLY KNOWN AS SOCKS, WASN'T looking for a lost child. He wasn't looking for gold either, though he wouldn't have complained if he had stumbled across a rich pocket. But he wasn't a miner—he had spent a few days working a rocker and the work didn't appeal to him. He wasn't inclined to spend his time standing in mud, shoveling mud, staring at mud, and hoping to spot a glimmer of gold.

No, Socks was hunting for deer and packing the venison down to the mining towns, where hungry miners would pay a handsome price for fresh meat. There were many ways to strike it rich in California, and Socks figured it was easier to take the gold from men who had dug it up than to go prospecting for gold himself. So he'd bought a pair of pack mules and he was hunting.

Socks was used to hunting alone. In 1835, when he was eighteen years of age, he had drifted westward to St. Louis. There he joined an expedition of trappers heading into the Rocky Mountains. For the next decade, he'd lived in the mountains, wearing buckskins, living with the Indians, and sporting the fur cap that was the mark of the mountain man. In 1845, when beaver was just about trapped out, Socks had headed west, going along on an exploratory expedition to California. Then in 1849 he'd guided a wagon train full of emigrants along the trail west. After that, having had his fill of nursemaiding greenhorns and city folks, he reckoned he'd just stay in California for a time.

That's how he'd come to be camping high in the hills, beside a lake with water as clear as the air. Hunting had been good. With his Hawkens rifle, he'd brought down three deer. He'd butchered them and hung the carcasses to bleed. That evening, as he lay in his bedroll, he listened to wolves howling.

On the way across the plains, the fools who had hired him shivered like women when the wolves howled, terrified by the wailing voices that sang to the moon. Socks didn't mind the wolves. He'd shoot 'em if they came prowling around his camp, but otherwise he didn't pay them no mind. He pulled his fur cap low over his ears and fell asleep listening to their singing.

THE WOLVES KNEW Socks was there, of course. They could smell the smoke of his fire, the biscuits that he had made for dinner, the reek of his tobacco, the dried blood of the deer he had killed. But the pack had brought down a young doe that evening, and they were well fed. They had no reason to nose around the mountain man's camp.

But Sarah was intrigued. The smells of his camp awakened memories. The woodsmoke and aroma of baked biscuits lured her close. Those were smells that reminded her of her mother, of camping with her family on the trail west.

Before dawn, when the pack was stirring, while Socks still slept, Sarah crept to the edge of his camp, drawn by curiosity. She prowled through the camp, moving as silently as any wild creature frightened by the presence of man. She had been with the wolves for four months, and she had come to move as quietly as they did, her moccasined feet noiseless on the pine needles that covered the ground. Beside the mountain man's fire pit, she found a tin where he had put two biscuits away for breakfast, sealing them in the tin so the varmints wouldn't get them.

Sarah could smell the biscuits inside the tin, but she could not get to them. Still moving quietly, she carried the tin away from the camp to the shore of the lake. Among the wolves, she had learned that it was best to take your food to a secluded spot and eat alone. Beside the still water of the lake, she pried open the tin.

These were biscuits that her mother would have scorned. Rather than baking them properly in a cast-iron Dutch oven, the mountain man had toasted them on a stone by the fire. They were burned on the outside, half-raw on the inside, tasting of woodsmoke and ash. As the sun rose, Sarah crouched by the lake and devoured them with gusto, eating even the blackened bits.

SOCKS WOKE AT dawn. A thin mist hung over the lake water. The air was cold; the first sunlight touched the water with a glimmer of silver. As he watched, a fish jumped, and Socks smiled without moving in his bedroll. He might catch a mess of fish for breakfast, before packing up and heading down to the mining camps.

A movement on the shore of the lake caught his eye. Something grayish white, moving along the shore, where the way was flat and easy. He squinted at the shape, not quite believing his eyes.

A little girl was making her way along the lakeshore. She wore only a pair of moccasins and a grimy petticoat that had once been white. Her hair was a tangle of coppery curls. By the color of her hair, he knew that she wasn't an Indian child.

As he watched, she crouched by the lake and put her head down to drink. She lifted a dripping face and wiped the water away with a careless hand. Then she bent her head to the water again, her eyes fixed on something in the shallows.

Socks was not a man given to flights of the imagination. It made no sense to him that a little white girl would be wandering alone in the wilderness, but he accepted the evidence of his eyes.

As she sat up, Socks saw a movement in the brush behind her. He kept his eyes focused on that spot, until he saw the movement again. What he saw made him reach for the rifle that he kept, always ready, alongside his bedroll.

A grizzled, old wolf was crouching in the alpine laurel beside the lake. Ears up, the animal watched the little girl splashing in the water. Not ready to pounce just yet, Socks thought. In no hurry for his breakfast. The old villain had no reason to rush. Breakfast was there whenever he wanted it. The child was unprotected—easy prey.

No, Socks thought. She was not unprotected. Sitting up in his mess of blankets, smelling of deer blood, tobacco, and sweat, his fur cap on his matted hair, Socks was an unlikely hero. But he saw himself as a hero, as the child's savior, rescuing her from the perils of the wilderness. Moving slowly to avoid drawing the eye of the wolf, he carefully loaded his rifle. The wolf did not move as Socks sighted on its head—a clear shot, an easy shot.

SARAH KNEW OMUSO was behind her: she heard the wolf moving through the bushes and smelled his scent on the breeze. The others were on higher ground, away from the man's camp.

Sarah was happy. Her stomach was full, and the first rays of the morning sun were warm on her head. On the lake bottom, she had found a pretty white-quartz stone. She was going to show it to Omuso just as she had shown pretty pebbles to her mama, so long ago.

She was turning from the water when she heard the crack of a rifle shot. She smelled gun smoke and saw Omuso fall, his right eye suddenly gone, replaced by a bloody hole. She looked in the direction of the sound and saw the man, his rifle at his shoulder.

A memory—sudden, sharp and clear. She was holding a white pebble out to her mother when she heard the crack of gunfire. She looked toward the sound and saw a man with a rifle. Her mother fell, whispering to her: "Run. Run and hide."

Sarah ran. Her heart pounding, her legs pumping, she fled without looking back, through the brush and up into the trees, running to Wauna, to the pack, to safety. She took with her a valuable lesson. Men were dangerous; men killed without warning; men killed at a distance. She had seen this happen twice. She understood it now.

She got away for one simple reason: Socks did not sleep with his boots on. He had learned, in his first year of trapping, that his feet stayed warmer at night if he took off his boots, took off the socks that he had worn all day, and put on a pair of wool socks. His mother had knit those socks for him before he had left for St. Louis, and he had promised to wear them to keep his feet warm at night.

He had kept his promise, and when the socks his mother had lovingly knit for him wore out, he purchased another pair and continued the same routine. This routine was, of course, the reason for his nickname. In the community of mountain men, where bathing more than twice a year could get you a reputation as a dandy, Michael Day's nightly changing of socks seemed the ultimate in fastidiousness. Each night, he put on sleeping socks; each morning, he put on his ordinary socks, which he washed every few weeks.

When Socks crawled from his bedroll to go to the rescue (or so he thought) of the little girl, he stopped to change his socks and pull his boots on, giving Sarah a significant head start. There wasn't a terrible rush, he reckoned. The wolf was dead. The little girl would recognize him as her savior and come when he called. So he could take a moment to put on his boots.

But the little girl didn't come when he called. The wolf was dead, sure enough. A clean shot through the eye; a damn fine shot, he thought. But the little girl was gone. Vanished, leaving behind the prints of her moccasined feet in the sand by the lake.

Socks followed the little girl's trail up the slope for a bit. He found sign of other wolves: tracks, tufts of fur in the grass where wolves had been sleeping, the gnawed bones of a deer kill. It looked like the little girl had run right to where the wolves were sleeping, but there was no indication that the animals had attacked her.

He followed her trail a little farther, calling as he went. "Hallo! Hallo! Little girl! Come back!"

She didn't come back. He lost her trail on a granite slope and could not find it again. He spent a day by the lake, searching for the little girl without success. Then he packed the venison on his two mules and headed to Downieville, the nearest large town, to sell his meat and tell his tale.

JASPER DAVIS WAS having lunch at Downieville's Lucky Dog Saloon. The primary purpose of this thriving establishment was to relieve miners of their gold while providing them with food, alcoholic beverages, and entertainment (in the form of gambling).

Jasper had provided half the capital for the establishment of the saloon and now he was entitled to half the profits. For Jasper, this had proven an extremely profitable investment. He was well on the way to becoming a prosperous businessman, and that was quite useful. Once he was known to have a successful business, no one would question his free-spending ways.

"I'd recommend the venison steak." Samuel, Jasper's partner and the man who managed the saloon's day-to-day operation, pulled up a chair and sat down at Jasper's table. "A mountain man just came down from the high country. Had venison to sell and a crazy story to tell."

"What sort of story?"

"Claims he saw a little white girl romping around by a lake in the high country. Just a slip of a girl, wearing nothing but a petticoat. Claims he saw a wolf stalking her. He shot the wolf—has the skin to prove that—but the little girl ran away and vanished in the woods."

Jasper frowned. He didn't like the sound of this. "Probably just an Indian brat."

Samuel shrugged. "That's what I said. But he says this child had a head of curly red hair and the face of an angel. He swears that she was no Indian. I think maybe he's been in the hills too long." Samuel jerked his head toward the bar. "That's the fellow. Goes by the name of Socks."

Jasper eyed the man who was leaning on the bar. Jasper thought it was unlikely that the daughter of Rachel McKensie had somehow survived for months in the wilderness and had made her way to a lake many miles from Grizzly Hill. But the story made him uneasy. This hunter claimed he had seen a redheaded child. Rachel McKensie had been a redhead. Jasper remembered Rachel's hair quite vividly; he had thought as he scalped her that those curly locks would have made quite a prize for an Indian brave.

Jasper was a thorough man. He disliked having any loose ends. He wished that he had found the child when he had murdered Rachel and her husband. If he had, he would have made a clean sweep of it. No loose ends; no unfinished business. But perhaps luck had presented him with an opportunity to take care of this loose end.

"Is he going hunting again?" Jasper asked.

"He didn't say."

"Might be nice to have a regular supply of fresh venison," Jasper said. "If he were willing . . ."

"I reckon that would be good," Samuel agreed.

"Let me talk to the fellow and see what I can work out." Jasper got to his feet slowly and strolled over to the bar.

A few hours later, after several drinks and a couple of fine venison steaks, Jasper and Socks were the very best of friends. Jasper had heard the story of the angel child in the forest several times in its entirety—from the moment Socks spotted the child to the moment he lost her trail on the granite slopes beyond the lake.

"Poor little girl," the mountain man repeated. "All alone out there. I called and called." He shook his head, made melancholy by the memory and the whiskey.

Jasper nodded sympathetically, though he thought

the man was taking the matter far too much to heart. Like many of the men who had left civilization behind, Socks was excessively tenderhearted on matters related to home and family. The sight—or the imagined sight—of this girl child had awakened in him a wistful longing, as if by saving this little lost girl he could somehow redeem himself.

Socks drained his glass. "I reckon when I go hunting again, I'll go back to the lake. Maybe I'll find her." He brightened at that prospect.

"Would you mind if I came along?" Jasper asked. "It touches my heart to think of that little girl out there alone. I'd sure like to help."

By the end of the evening, after finishing a bottle of whiskey together, Jasper and Socks were partners, dedicated to finding the lost angel child and bringing her back to civilization. Two days later, Socks led Jasper to the lake, where they made camp and began their search.

For the next two weeks, they searched the area surrounding the lake. While he was looking for the little girl, Socks hunted for deer. In that time, Socks found only one indication of the little girl's presence. On a manzanita bush not far from the lake, he found a tiny scrap of white lace. "I reckon it's a bit torn from her little petticoat," Socks said. He held the delicate lacework pinched between grimy, callused fingers. "I reckon that proves she was here."

Finally, when it was clear that they would find nothing more, Socks packed the deer carcasses back to Downieville. Jasper left the mountain man there. "If you find that little girl, let me know," Jasper told Socks when he bid the mountain man farewell. "I know folks who would take her in, raise her proper."

The mountain man nodded, convinced that Jasper was a fine fellow, with the child's best interest at heart.

"I'll sure do that," he told Jasper. Jasper rode back to Selby Flat, still plagued by that niggling doubt, the uneasy possibility that someone might know his secret.

AT THAT TIME, Max was working a claim on the North Fork of the Yuba River with Henry Johnson, the earnest young New Englander who had thought that Sarah had been adopted by Indians. Max and Henry had a canvas tent for a shelter, and they cooked over a fire by the creek. Their camp was far from any other miners, and Max liked it that way.

As long as the weather held and the claim kept paying, it wasn't a bad life. They woke up with the sun, ate a breakfast of cold pork and biscuits, then set to work shoveling dirt into their long tom, a wooden cradle through which the creek flowed. The moving water washed away lighter sediments, leaving gold dust caught in the riffles of the cradle.

At midday, they stopped for another bite to eat and a bit of a rest, then they got back to work. When the sun reached the top of the ridge, they quit for the day and measured their take.

While Henry occupied himself with the gold, Max made dinner. After dinner, Max would lean back against a boulder that retained the heat of the afternoon sun and sketch. He sketched the river, striving to capture the way the light played on the water's surface. He sketched the hills with their rich texture of pines and aspen. He sketched Henry, head tilted back, a haze of pipe smoke around him, writing a letter to the folks back home. It was a fine way to relax.

Sometimes, inspired by Henry's example, Max wrote in his notebook. If he'd had anyone back home to write to, he would have written a letter. But he had no family, so he wrote for himself, describing the clean air, the golden afternoons, the soothing rush of water past the door of their tent.

It was peaceful there in the mountains. Each Sunday afternoon, Henry went to the trader at Downieville for supplies, that being the nearest outpost of civilization. Max, having little use for civilization, stayed in camp.

One Sunday afternoon, Henry returned from his weekly trip with a melancholy expression.

"What's the trouble, partner?" Max asked. He was lounging in the shade of a yellow pine, having passed the afternoon sketching. As a rule, the weekly visit to Downieville left Henry broke, but cheerfully drunk. "Why the frown?"

Before he answered, Henry unstrapped the supplies from the mule's back. He set the pack on the flat boulder that served as their kitchen table, as it was situated right next to the fire pit that served as their stove. Then he took a seat on a boulder not far from Max.

"I got to drinking with a fellow," Henry said in a low voice.

Max nodded. "I see. That's usually not the sort of thing that gets you down."

Henry shook his head. "This fellow had been hunting and he saw the strangest thing." Then Henry told Max about Socks and what he had seen. "A little girl, alone in the woods," Henry said. "He knew she wasn't an Indian, by her curly red hair."

Max put down his notebook and sat up, giving Henry his full attention. "A little white girl with curly red hair?" he asked.

Henry nodded. "I wondered if it might be the daughter of the woman who was murdered."

"Sarah McKensie." Max frowned. The lake Henry had described was many miles from Grizzly Hill, where Rachel and William McKensie had been killed. But it seemed strange that this phantom child had red-gold curls. Rachel McKensie had mentioned her daughter's red-gold curls in her letter.

"That's it. Sarah McKensie. Maybe she was adopted by Indians and they took her up there. But he said he didn't see any sign of Indians."

"He looked?"

"Looked high and low. Then he went back a second time with that fellow from Selby Flat, Jasper Davis. They both looked, and they couldn't find hide nor hair of her." Henry sighed. "Maybe it was just his imagination. A man can get to imagining things up there alone. A dream, maybe."

"Maybe," Max said. "Now you say that he shot a wolf that was stalking her?"

"That's right. Then he tracked her up into the hills, where he found the tracks of other wolves. Poor little girl, surrounded by beasts."

"Well, there's another theory for you," Max said. "Romulus and Remus."

"What's that?"

"The legendary founders of Rome. As infants, they were left to die in the wilderness. But they were adopted by a she-wolf who had lost her cubs."

"They were left to die!" Henry was outraged. "Where was this?"

"Ancient Rome."

"Foreigners," Henry said angrily. "You never know what they'll do." And he was off on a rant about the Chinamen who had staked a claim down the creek a ways. The miners in town were talking about running them off the land, but figured there was no need just yet.

Max wasn't listening. He was wondering about little

Sarah McKensie. Could the savage heart of a wolf have been touched by the little girl's plight?

The next Sunday he went to Downieville with Henry. He found Socks in the local saloon, drinking up the last of his profits and planning another hunting trip. When he asked the mountain man about the little girl, Socks told the same story that Henry had related—a little girl running wild, a wolf nearby, a heroic mountain man, attempting to save the girl. Socks told also of his return to the lake, with Jasper Davis's assistance.

Miners who had come into town for supplies gathered around the mountain man, buying him drinks and talking about the little girl in the mountains. There was a wistfulness about their talk, a sweet melancholy, as if the little lost girl reminded them of all that they had left behind. One man talked of his wife back home, another of his younger sister.

While they talked, Max sketched, capturing the faces of these hard-bitten men in a moment of sentimental longing. A man with a banjo played a few sad songs—about lost love, about going home, about the ones who were left behind. It was a sweet, sad, maudlin evening.

The next day, Max had a notebook filled with sketches and a head full of sadness. He told Henry that he couldn't work that day, and he sat beneath the yellow pine tree and wrote about the night before, managing to be both sentimental and humorous as he told of how a lost child had touched the hearts of the hard-bitten miners and traders. He sent his writings, with the sketches of the men in the saloon, to the *Nevada City Gazette.*

7

THE BEGINNING OF A CORRESPONDENCE

"The reason I dread writing letters is because I am so apt to get to slinging wisdom and forget to let up. Thus much precious time is lost."

—Mark Twain

"PICK UP YOUR FEET, WORDSWORTH," MAX TOLD HIS MULE. "NO need to raise such a cloud of dust." The beast paid him no mind, continuing to scuff its hooves through the trail dust.

The summer sunshine was warm on Max's back as he came over the top of the ridge and headed down toward the trail that ran along the creek to Selby Flat. Just a couple more miles to go. The creekside trail was broad and flat, a pleasant change. For the past few days, he'd been climbing up and down ridges along ill-marked trails and bushwhacking through the chaparral.

The claim he'd been mining with Henry Johnson had played out a few weeks back. Though Henry had elected to stay in the northern diggings, Max decided to return to Selby Flat.

He followed the switchbacks down to the creek with a sense of relief. Soon, he could get a fine dinner and a good night's sleep at Selby's Hotel. Below him, he could see a mining camp—a tent by the creek, a long tom in the water, a trio of miners lounging on the rocks, enjoying an afternoon break.

"Hey, Max! Max—is that you?" One of the miners was waving. Max recognized Johnny Barker and returned his wave.

"Hello, Johnny. Working hard, I see."

"Come on and join us," Johnny called. "Tell me where you've been."

Max stopped for a time, letting Wordsworth have a long drink while he chatted with Johnny. The miner introduced Max to his companions and they asked the usual questions and touched on the usual topics. How good were the diggings up north? Max said he had done well there. He and his partner had taken two thousand dollars out of the ground between them. Not the richest diggings, but not bad.

How rich was the ground here? Not bad; not bad. The miners were careful, not wanting to encourage him to stake a claim nearby. Nothing to complain about.

Then Johnny allowed as how he'd read Max's article in the *Nevada City Gazette*. "You had half these boys weeping and the other half looking out for wolves and little girls," Johnny said. "Was a sight to behold. You've got a way with words, partner."

Max smiled, acknowledging the compliment.

"You reckon that little girl could really be living with wolves?" Johnny asked.

Max shrugged. "It could happen. It's a strange world."

"That it is. Hey, when you get to Selby Flat, you'd best go to Selby's Hotel, first thing. Mrs. Selby has a letter for you. I reckon she's burning with curiosity about what's in it. She asks about you all the time."

"Maybe she just misses my charming smile," Max said.

Johnny laughed.

The miners invited Max to stay to dinner, but he continued down the trail, curious to see what was in the letter. It was late in the afternoon when he reached Selby's Hotel. He noticed that a wanted poster with his portrait of Arno was tacked to the outside wall of the hotel. It had already started to tatter and fade. Max put Wordsworth in the corral and stepped into Selby's.

The sweet smell of warm apples and cinnamon filled the room, which was crowded with miners. Max spotted Jasper Davis on the far side of the room. Jasper waved Max over to the table where he sat alone. "Hallo, Max," Jasper called. "I reckon you came all the way from Downieville for a piece of Mrs. Selby's apple pie."

Max sat down at Jasper's table. Socks had told Max of how concerned Jasper had been for the little lost girl, leading Max to think he must have misjudged the man. "That Pinkerton fellow's been here," Max said. "Saw the wanted poster outside."

Jasper nodded. "No one's seen hide nor hair of Arno since the robbery. I figure he headed to Mexico."

Max nodded. "Maybe that Pinkerton fellow will go after him."

Jasper laughed and shook his head. "No, that fellow plans to stick around. Told me he was thinking Nevada City might be a nice place to settle down. They're looking to appoint a town marshal, and he figures on applying for the job." Jasper leaned toward Max. "You know, I saw that piece you wrote for the newspaper. Real nice what you had to say about that little girl. Do you really reckon she could have been taken in by a pack of wolves?"

Max shrugged. "Could be." He had been asked many times about Romulus and Remus; he was used to the question.

"So when she ran away, she ran off with the wolves," Jasper continued.

"I suppose so."

Jasper nodded thoughtfully. "So if a man tracked the wolves, he might find the little girl."

"Why yes, that could be." Max studied Jasper's face. Surely the man's interest in rescuing Sarah was admirable. But there was still something about Jasper that struck Max wrong. Something about him reminded Max of acquaintances back in Chicago who were on the shady side of the law, individuals who were humbugs and frauds and always on the dodge.

Max did not have an opportunity to analyze Jasper's interest in Sarah any further just then. Mrs. Selby had emerged from the kitchen and spotted him. "Max!" she called, bustling across the room while drying her hands on her apron. "Oh, Max, I'm so glad you're back. I have a letter for you." She pulled a battered envelope from where she had tucked it behind the mirror and brought it across the room to him. "It's from Audrey North, the sister of that poor murdered woman."

Max tore open the envelope and read the enclosed letter, written in a bold hand.

I am grateful to you and to the men of Selby Flat for all your efforts on behalf of my sister and her husband. I thank you for writing to tell me of my sister's fate. Were it not for your kind letter, I would never have known what happened to her. I would wait for news of her, always hoping, always disappointed.

I find it comforting that my sister's last letter was so

optimistic and hopeful. My sister had an adventurous spirit. I take comfort in knowing that she was happy before her death.

In my heart, I cannot believe that little Sarah has perished. I cannot imagine that anyone, however depraved, could murder a child so sweet and innocent. You say it is unlikely, but I choose to believe that little Sarah is alive. I picture her living with some savage tribe, adopted as their daughter, her curly hair tamed with bear grease, her pale face standing out in a clan of ruddy faces. Perhaps I am being foolish, but I trust my heart and my heart tells me that she cannot be dead.

I have a request to make of you. I have no right to ask—you have already been so kind—but I will ask, even so. Please write again, if you are moved to do so. Tell me of California, so that I might understand the strange place to which my sister traveled. If you hear any news of my niece, please let me know.

I have framed your drawing of the valley where my sister died. It hangs on my parlor wall, where I can see it as I drink my tea each morning. I thank you for sending the drawing and wonder what I might do to repay you. I understand that some items are in short supply, there in the West. Please let me know if there is anything that I might send that could gladden your heart as your lovely rendering gladdens mine.

Max looked up to find Mrs. Selby reading over his shoulder. "Such a sweet letter," she said. "You must write to her immediately and tell her about what that mountain man saw."

"I don't know," Max said slowly. "It might be cruel to raise her hopes."

Mrs. Selby frowned, considering that. A miner sitting at a nearby table, a burly, bald-headed man named Ned, leaned over and took advantage of the pause to ask Mrs. Selby about the pies. "How long afore they'll be done, ma'am?" he inquired politely.

"In just a bit," she said, barely glancing in Ned's direction. Her attention was on Max. "She wants you to offer her hope," Mrs. Selby said. "That seems quite clear."

Max glanced at Ned, who was staring in the direction of the kitchen. "Do you suppose you ought to check on that pie?" Max asked. "It smells just grand."

Mrs. Selby waved a hand, dismissing the pie. "Yes, yes. I will. But you must write to Mrs. North and tell her about what that hunter said."

Max shrugged, still reluctant.

"Mrs. Selby?" It was Ned again. "Don't you think those pies might burn?"

"You must write," Mrs. Selby said to Max. "You must write and tell her about the wolves."

Ned stood up then, looming over Max. "I think that's a fine idea, Mrs. Selby. I'll make sure he writes. You go check on those pies." Ned smiled down at Max. "You'd best start writing, or we'll never get any pie," he said softly.

Max nodded in resignation. He opened his travel bag and took out pen, ink, and paper. "You check that pie, and I'll get started," he told Mrs. Selby.

Under Ned's watchful gaze, he began a letter to Audrey North. By the end of the evening, he had not finished it. He promised Mrs. Selby, when she served him apple pie, that he would.

The letter, which began as a simple report on what Max had learned from Socks, became something more. He described the town of Downieville and the tavern where he met Socks. He explained that the world of the mining camps was not the civilized world she knew. He described Mrs. Selby and Selby Flat, an oasis of civilization. He wrote of himself and his life.

"The men of Selby Flat were happy to do all they could for your sister," he wrote. "There are so few women here. We are a company of men, which leads to great camaraderie and great loneliness. I do a excellent business in portraits, capturing miners in all their bearded glory so that they might send the likeness to their wives.

"I sympathize with this sentiment. I was once a married man, but my wife died of a fever long since. Were she still alive, I cannot imagine how hard it would have been to leave her and seek my fortune in California. But that is what so many good men have done—leave their loved ones safe at home while they endure the dangers of the wilderness."

Several days later, he finished the letter, sealed it in an envelope that Mrs. Selby provided, and addressed it to Audrey North. After some thought, Max included with the letter a copy of the piece he had written for the Nevada City paper.

AS SUMMER TURNED to autumn and the days grew colder, the wolves moved down into the foothills, following the deer but staying clear of settlements, where miners were tearing up the hillsides in search of precious metal. One autumn afternoon when the sky was dark and threatened rain, Wauna led the pack to the den where her pups had been killed.

Sarah explored the den, squeezing into the narrow opening and feeling the corner of a rough wooden box. Sheltered by the den, the box retained a faint smell of man sweat, and the scent made Sarah anxious and unhappy.

She was naked now. She had lost her petticoat and moccasins somewhere along the way. But her skin had tanned in the California sun, and the soles of her feet had grown tough. She was as healthy as a savage child could be.

The pack wandered down the hill to the campsite where her parents had died. The tent was still there. No one had troubled to clean up the area, though passing Indians and miners had searched the wreckage for valuables. The quilts and boxes that Jasper had scattered on the slope were still there—washed by the rain and dried by the sun. The fabric had faded, and the wooden boxes had begun to warp and split. Grasses had taken root on her parents' graves, softening the raw earth with greenery.

Sarah wandered in the wreckage, drawn by feelings that she could not name. She was restless, nervous, ready to bolt at the slightest sound. There was something here that drew her—and something that made her wish to flee. But the attraction was stronger than the fear.

She pulled at the boxes, examining what she found. In one box, overlooked by Indians and scavenging miners, she found a hunting knife in a leather sheath. The rivets in the handle were touched with rust, but the blade was still shiny when she pulled off the sheath. Holding the knife, she ran a finger along the edge, marveling at how it glittered in the sun. Cut by the sharp steel, she yelped in pain and dropped the knife.

For a long moment, she stood on the slope, sucking her injured finger and staring at the blade that lay among the rocks at her feet. She was struggling with a memory that came to her from far away. She remembered that same sharp blade, or one just like it. She had reached out to touch it, and someone had snatched her up and said, "No, Sarah," in a deep, warm voice. Papa, she remembered. That was

Papa. She remembered sitting on a lap—Mama's lap—and watching Papa use a knife like this one to skin a rabbit.

She squinted at the knife. She could use something that could cut a rabbit skin. Focusing on that memory, she reached out and took the knife by the handle, holding it as she remembered Papa had. She pushed the sheath onto the blade. The sheath was attached to a belt. Clumsily, carefully, she looped the belt over her shoulder so that the knife dangled at her side. Then she continued to explore.

She found a child's sweater caught beneath a wooden keg. One sleeve was unraveling. The wool was grimy with dust. But for all of that the sweater was intact. It had been knit by Aunt Audrey and sent along with the wagon, but Sarah did not know that. She knew only that the wool was warm against her skin and the air was cool. She pulled the sweater over her head (remembering her Mama's voice saying "Let me help, Sarah," as she struggled to pull on her clothing).

A dirty child, armed with a hunting knife and clad in a ragged sweater, she wandered. She found a pair of mocassins, just a little larger than the ones she had discarded that summer. Her mother had traded for them on the trip across the plains, knowing that her daughter's feet would grow and thinking that children's shoes would be in short supply. Sarah pulled them onto her feet.

She touched a scrap of fabric, torn from a quilt, admiring its patches of color and struggling to remember a sound she had once known. "Mama," she muttered, fingering the fabric.

As the sun set, Wauna went searching for her adopted daughter, and found her huddled in a wool sweater, sheltering beneath the canvas of the collapsed tent. She was weeping quietly, caught by memories that she could not understand.

THE WINTER WAS mild that year, with no snow in the foothills. Wauna and Yepa watched out for Sarah. At night, she slept between them, kept warm by their body heat. On days when the pack traveled great distances in the hunt, Wauna or Yepa stayed with the girl, joining the pack only after the hunt was over. Sarah howled with the pack at night, her high-pitched cry joining the deeper howls of her packmates.

As winter edged toward spring and the days grew longer, Wauna's attention wandered from her foster pup. Rolon was always close by Wauna's side—grooming her, following her. The other males in the pack—young Dur and Duman—also followed Wauna when they could, but Rolon warned them away, with stares and growls. Once, when Dur ignored Rolon's warning and came too close, the two males fought, a short and savage conflict that ended with Dur on his back, his tail between his legs, and Rolon standing over him.

Sarah was puzzled by the change in her foster mother's behavior. She did not understand that it was the mating season.

During mating season, a wolf pack is in turmoil. The younger males are eager to supplant their father, the alpha male. Often, a brash young male will challenge the alpha male and get himself thrashed as a result. The younger females are on edge, their hormones in a state of flux. Sometimes the alpha pair will leave the pack, seeking seclusion while they mate.

Yepa did her best to reassure Sarah. If her communications had been formed into words, she might have said, "Be calm, little one. This is a season of change, but it is nothing to worry you. Stay with me and be safe."

And so it was in the early spring that Wauna and

Rolon disappeared from the pack for a few days. Yepa cared for Sarah while Wauna was gone, keeping the child close by her side. When the alpha pair returned, life resumed its normal course.

Two months later, Sarah woke up feeling cold. When she had gone to sleep, Wauna had been on one side of her and Yepa on the other. Yepa was still at her side, but Wauna was gone.

Sarah got up and stretched in the sunshine. She squatted to pee on the edge of the clearing where the pack had spent the night, lifting the hem of her sweater out of the way of the stream of urine.

Though the air was chilly, it was warmer than it had been for many weeks. Sarah pushed up the sleeves of the grimy sweater that had been her only garment through the winter. Aunt Audrey would have been shocked at how filthy it had become—marked with pine tar and river mud and the blood of Sarah's kills. It had been soaked by the winter rains and dried in the sunshine. The wool had stretched and lost its shape. Grimy, disreputable, baggy—but still a warm substitute for the fur coats of her packmates.

The clearing where the pack rested was on the side of a hill. Halfway up the hill was an old fox den. For the past few days, Wauna had been digging in that den, excavating a tunnel and a chamber large enough for her to curl up in. Sarah had explored the den when Wauna had taken a break from digging, but could not understand why this underground chamber held such fascination for her mother. Why crawl underground when the spring sunshine was so warm?

That particular morning, Rolon crouched outside the den, as if standing guard. Sarah stood beside him, listening to strange whimpering and mewling sounds that came from the underground chamber. She caught a familiar scent—mother's milk.

When she moved toward the mouth of the den, Rolon warned her away with a growl. It wasn't until the next day that he allowed her to creep into the passage to meet her new brothers and sisters, four fat pups that crawled blindly over one another to reach their mother's teats.

For the next three weeks, Wauna stayed in the den with the pups. The pack hunted as usual, bringing meat back for Wauna. Sarah waited at the entrance to the den, standing guard with Rolon or Yepa.

One morning, Sarah was drowsing in the sun at the entrance to the den. Yepa was asleep, not far away. The rest of the pack was off hunting.

Sarah woke when something warm nudged her side. When she opened her eyes, she found a pup leaning up against her. It was Beka, the first pup to venture from the den. She leaned against Sarah's leg and stared out at the world with wide eyes. When Sarah reached down and fondled the pup's ears, Beka licked Sarah's hand and gazed up at her.

A tiny puppy growl made Sarah look up from the pup at her side. Marek, the largest of the pups, stood in the entrance of the den. His other sisters, Istas and Luyu, were just behind him. He was a sturdy pup with jet-black fur, unmarked by gray or white.

Marek's ears were a little back. His head was tilted to one side; his tail, level—neither wagging nor tucked between his legs. In his posture, Sarah read embarrassment and uncertainty. He was a little afraid of the outside world, which is why Beka had been the first one out. He was a little embarrassed by his fear, wanting to appear to be the strongest in all things.

His dark brown eyes focused on Beka, the pup at Sarah's side. Without hesitation, Marek pounced on her. While Sarah watched, the male pup wrestled his sister to the ground, dominating her with tiny puppy growls.

WAUNA'S PUPS GREW up, playing and learning in the way of wolves. Sarah watched them grow, helping Yepa with baby-sitting duties. As the pups grew, so did the rivalry between Beka and Marek.

Bullies exist among wolves as they do among people. Marek was a bully. He dominated his sisters, always claiming the sunniest place to sleep, the largest portion of food, the place closest to Wauna's side.

Luyu was almost as large as Marek, but she was a shy, good-natured pup, unwilling to fight. She let her brother have his way, content to make do with second-best in order to avoid trouble. Istas was equally accommodating.

Of the pups, Beka was the only one to challenge Marek. Though she was the smallest of the pups, the runt of the litter, she fought for her rights. In a fair fight on level ground, Marek always won. Though Beka snarled and fought, Marek could bowl her over and pin her to the ground, dominating by virtue of his superior size and strength.

But Beka knew how to pick her fights. Once, Sarah watched as the pup scrambled to the top of a boulder. Patiently, Beka waited, motionless, until her brother wandered below. Then she launched herself from the boulder top and landed on Marek, knocking him down. Once she had the advantage, Beka did not give an inch, fighting with determination and ferocity. On that occasion, she won, forcing her brother to submit. More often, she lost, but never without a fight.

When Beka was six weeks old, Sarah noticed that the pup was limping. Marek had just forced Beka away from a place in the sun, and, for the first time, Beka gave way without a fight.

Sarah followed the limping pup into the shade and sat down beside her. Gently, Sarah took Beka's paw in her hand. The pad of the pup's paw was hot and inflamed. Beka had stepped on a branch of whitethorn bush, and a barb had embedded itself in the tender pad of her paw.

The pup whimpered as Sarah touched the injury. The girl stroked Beka's ears and murmured to her, making sounds like the ones Wauna made to soothe the pups. Beka remained still while the girl pinched the thorn between her fingers and pulled it from the inflamed flesh, leaving the wound clean so that it could heal.

Sarah cuddled Beka in her lap, keeping the pup warm. Later that day, when the pack brought down a deer, Sarah brought some scraps of meat to Beka, keeping Marek and the others away while Beka ate. That night, Beka slept with Sarah and Yepa, kept warm by the girl's body heat. Until Beka's paw healed, Sarah took care of the pup.

Why? Perhaps Sarah recognized a kindred soul, small in body but large in spirit. Whatever the reason, Sarah cared for Beka, and Beka returned that attention with affection. When her paw had healed, Beka followed Sarah wherever she went, a loyal companion.

The pups matured quickly, as wolf pups do. By the time they were six months old, they were traveling with the pack, assisting in the hunt.

8

AN AMAZING YOUNG SAVAGE

"It is better to take what does not belong to you than to let it lie around neglected."

—Mark Twain

THE SUN SPARKLED ON THE ROCKS BY BEAR RIVER. SOON THE snows would come, but now the air was balmy, warmed by the late-autumn sunlight. The river was little more than a stream now, a trickle that placidly meandered among the boulders of the riverbed, spreading to form a pool where the rocks formed a natural dam, then wandering on.

Sarah crouched beside the pool. With both hands, she splashed water on her face, washing away the smudges of blood on her chin. A few steps downstream, the rest of the pack was drinking. The pups were six months old, already traveling with the pack. Not two hours before, the pack had killed a young doe, born just that spring. The wolves were well fed, ready to nap in the sun for a time.

Sarah still wore her grimy sweater. The garment was filthy; it was unraveling at the hem, where Beka had chewed it during one of their play fights, and at the end of one sleeve, where Sarah had caught the yarn on a bush and pulled it loose. But though the sweater was unraveling around her, it still kept her warm at night.

Sarah stood up. Rolon was lounging beside a granite boulder, where sunlight reflecting from the stone and sunlight from above combined to warm a patch of sand. Marek and Istas were wrestling nearby, with Istas getting the worst of the match. Luyu watched, obviously glad that she was not part of the game. Wauna and Yepa had settled down on a patch of sand, napping comfortably. The other wolves were drinking, wandering among the boulders, relaxing after the hunt.

Beka came up beside Sarah, wagging her tail. The young wolf nuzzled Sarah's cheek, then yawned an enormous, gaping yawn. It was an invitation to curl up for a nap together.

A jay squawked in the bushes, then took flight. Beka pricked up her ears and Sarah stared in the direction from which the bird had flown. The air was still.

"Robby, come back here," a young girl's voice called in the silence.

A little boy, not more than five years old, emerged from the brush beside the river. He was overdressed for the weather. He wore a bright red flannel shirt, a wool sweater, sturdy canvas trousers, and leather boots. He marched toward the water with great determination, a child with a mission, ignoring the wolves, ignoring Sarah.

Sarah watched with great interest. Pausing at the edge of the water, the little boy yanked his sweater over his head and dropped it on the rocks. The shirt followed. He sat on a rock by the pool and tugged one boot off and then the other.

"Robby, where are you?" The girl was close, but still hidden by the bushes.

Robby did not reply. He had finished with the boots and was busy yanking down his canvas trousers, exposing his pale bottom to the autumn sun. He saw Beka and Sarah staring at him—they were nearer than the other wolves—and he stared back.

"Doggie," he said to Beka, in a tone of accusation.

He was naked now, and Sarah stared at him in fascination. She had never seen such a small, naked human before. He was hairless, like her. He had hands, rather than paws—not so good for running but better for grooming and picking up rocks and such. As she studied him, she noticed that he wasn't exactly like her—he had an extra bit of flesh dangling between his legs. But on the whole, he was more similar than different.

Beka was already standing beside Robby, sniffing his face. The other wolves were watching, ears up, alert and curious. Marek and Istas and Luyu were heading over, and Rolon had gotten up. Sarah stepped over to meet this strange creature. He was so small and soft-looking; she wasn't afraid of him as she was of other humans.

AT THAT MOMENT, Robby's sister Martha stepped from the bushes. Their wagon train had stopped for the day in a meadow a short distance downriver. Her mother was washing clothes; her father was trying his hand at panning for gold in a small stream that flowed into the river.

Martha was supposed to be watching Robby, but she had been distracted by a school of minnows swimming in a shallow pool. She had splashed in the water, trying unsuccessfully to catch the fish in her hands. When she finally gave up, she realized that Robby had wandered off, following the trail that ran alongside the river.

She had pursued him, hurrying to catch up. "Robby, you come back here. Mama said we shouldn't go too far. . . ." She had left the shelter of the bushes behind before she realized that Robby was not alone. A pack of wolves and a little girl in a dirty sweater watched her with great curiosity.

To Martha's credit, she did not scream. She stood very still, returning Sarah's stare.

"Robby, come here," she said, her voice a perfect imitation of her mother's commanding tone. "Right now. Not another word."

But Robby was laughing as Beka sniffed his face. He stayed where he was.

SARAH WATCHED AS Martha hurried to her brother's side and grabbed his hand. Marek was just a few feet from the boy now, pushing Beka aside so that he could examine these strange creatures. Sarah could see the tension in Martha's body, smell the fear in the girl's sweat—Martha was ready to run, which would have been a terrible mistake.

At the moment, the wolves were curious. They had fed recently and weren't hungry. But if Martha ran, they would chase her—that was an instinctive reaction, triggered by the sight of a fleeing animal.

Sarah stepped between Marek and Martha, taking hold of the girl's hand, just as Martha held her brother's. Martha stared at her, eyes wide and fearful. Martha said something—"Who are you?"—but Sarah didn't understand the words, funny noises that reminded her of the past.

As she gripped Martha's hand tightly, Sarah stared at Marek, warning him off. She growled and bared her childish teeth. She never used her teeth in her play fights with the young wolves, but snarling and showing her teeth communicated her intentions. Her knife, the weapon that substituted for her teeth, was already in her hand.

Beka turned to face Marek, standing beside Robby. She added her growls to Sarah's, warning her brother to back off.

Marek hesitated, uncertain. Like any bully, he preferred situations where he could gain the upper hand with no risk to himself.

Taking advantage of his uncertainty, Sarah tugged on Martha's hand, leading her back to the path through the bushes. The girl followed willingly, dragging Robby with her. Beka lagged behind, watching Marek to make sure he didn't attack.

Sarah led the two children along the river, until she could smell the smoke of a campfire. As they walked, Martha asked her questions: "Who are you? What are you doing here? Where is your mama?"

So many strange sounds. Sarah remembered that long ago time when she had talked to her mama and papa. She had known several dozen words, which she strung into sentences and questions of a sort. "Hungry now." "Mama eat?" "We go now?" Old memories.

She stood by the river, sniffing the breeze. Campfire smoke and coffee and corn bread baking by the fire.

"Robby! Martha! Where are you?" A woman's voice calling.

Sarah hesitated, still holding Martha's hand.

"It's Mama," Martha said. "Come on."

"Martha! Robby!" A man's voice.

Sarah stiffened, remembering the crack of a rifle shot, Omuso falling, a man's voice calling.

She released Martha's hand and stepped away. "We go now," she said, shaping the old words. "We go."

She turned and ran, with Beka at her heels.

MARTHA'S MOTHER WAS dubious about Martha's account of the encounter with the wolves and very upset about the loss of Robby's clothes. Martha's father threatened her with a switching for telling lies, but she stuck to her story and led them to where she had seen the wolves.

Sarah and the wolves were gone, along with Robby's clothes. Martha found the grimy sweater that Sarah had been wearing, tossed in the bushes beside the river.

Sarah wore Robby's clothes through the winter. In the spring, she cached the sweater and shirt and boots in a rocky cave. The wolves cached food, burying kills for later consumption, and Sarah had, even at her young age, recognized the value of saving something for later.

SARAH REMAINED WEAKER and slower than her packmates, but she compensated for her physical lacks with her keen intelligence. She learned from observing the creatures in the world around her. Seeing raccoons hunt for frogs in the marshy meadows, she tried it herself—and discovered that spring peepers can be tasty. Watching a spotted skunk raid the nest of a quail, she learned to search out nests and devour the eggs. Observing squirrels feasting on the seeds of the sugar pine, she took to harvesting the cones herself, cracking the nuts between two stones and eating the tasty meat inside.

From the cougar, the golden lion of the California mountains, she learned stealth. When she lay still, she became one with the land beneath her. From the badger, she learned the value of putting up a fierce appearance. From the black bear, she learned to look beneath the surface. After watching a bear turn over logs and find tasty grubs, she added these insects to her diet.

Though she lacked the strength and stamina of a young wolf, Sarah had abilities that the wolves lacked.

When a burr got caught in Rolon's ear, Sarah's clever hands yanked it free. She could climb up oak trees and scramble up rocky faces too steep for the wolves to ascend. She could snatch a choice bit of meat from a kill, then escape into a tree to eat in peace, out of reach of her hungry packmates.

After Omuso's death, she had been careful to stay out of sight of any humans—but she observed people without being observed. The brown-skinned people who had lived in these hills long before the settlers had come from the east knew what plants could be eaten. Sarah watched them from hiding and followed their example, harvesting the bulbs of wild onions and quamish plants that grew in wet meadows, eating the sweet flowers and leaves of wild mountain violets, the tender shoots of bracken ferns, and the spicy leaves of wild mint.

White people both frightened and fascinated her. One of the trails that emigrants to California followed down to the Sacramento Valley ran through the southern edge of the wolf pack's territory. When the pack was traveling in that area, Sarah often hid near the trail to watch wagon trains of emigrants pass, marveling at the lumbering oxen and the creaking wagons.

Once, Sarah saw two boys playing by the riverside. The older of the two, a lad of twelve, was skipping stones in a wide pool. That had been a valuable lesson. Later that day, Sarah had tried throwing rocks herself. Her first attempts were weak, but she persisted until she could lob a stone with considerable accuracy and power. It was a glorious day when a stone she threw struck a fat quail squarely in the head, bringing the bird down.

She was still wearing Robby's trousers when she learned to throw stones. She took to carrying rounded stones in the pockets, ready for use at any time.

When the weather grew warm, she used her knife to cut off the trouser legs, but continued wearing the rest, unwilling to give up the convenience of pockets.

Another time, she spied on a man who sat by the river and sharpened his knife, honing the blade on a stone worn smooth by the river. That, too, she had imitated, using a river rock to sharpen the blade that she wore at her side, honing the steel to a razor-sharp edge.

Sometimes, she stole from the emigrants, snatching clothing that had been spread to dry on rocks by the river. When she outgrew Robby's trousers, she stole another pair. More than once, she slipped silently into emigrant camps at night, wandering among the sleeping travelers, looking for items that she could use: a pair of wool socks, a new pair of moccasins, suspenders to hold up her trousers, a hunting knife that was stronger and sharper than hers.

By the time she was seven years of age, she was an amazing young savage. From her youngest days, she had done her best to keep up with the pack. As she grew older, her stamina increased until she could run for hours without tiring, eating up the miles with an effortless loping pace.

She could climb like a squirrel, scrambling up rocky faces and sprawling oak trees with ease. She could sit quietly in the forest while a covey of quail walked within a few feet of her, unaware that the motionless figure beneath the trees was a human being. She knew every rock and tree in the pack's territory—the best time and place to find berries and birds' nests and edible greens, the best hunting grounds, the best places to hide.

Her life among the wolves was happy. Wauna and Yepa were her mentors; Beka was her friend. She remembered her true parents only dimly; they were vague figures that appeared in her dreams. Mama was a soft voice and a comforting lap, a memory that blended with her memory of cuddling up to Wauna's warm fur. Papa was a rough voice and a pair of hands that lifted her high above the earth.

She knew that she was different from her pack-mates. Their bodies were covered with warm fur, while hers was smooth and hairless. Their teeth were strong and sharp, while hers were small and blunt. She had a flat face and a tiny nose and she ran upright, rather than on all fours.

Even so, she thought of herself as a wolf. She watched people—the Indians and the miners—but she did not think of herself as one of them. No, she belonged to the pack. She watched people; she stole from people, but she was not one of them.

PART TWO

1855

STONE WOLF

"There are many humorous things in the world; among them, the white man's notion that he is less savage than the other savages."

—*Following the Equator;* Mark Twain

STANDING ANKLE DEEP IN MUDDY WATER, MALILA DUG FOR NETTLE roots. The village chief was suffering from aches and pains in his joints. Malila's grandfather, Hatawa, was the village healer. He said that bathing in water in which nettle roots had steeped would soothe the chief.

A short distance up the creek, Hatawa was gathering the shoots of the horsetail plant. A tea brewed from these plants would ease a feverish patient. Malila could hear him chanting, giving thanks to the horsetail and the nettle for their help. A shaman and healer, Hatawa knew the proper way to behave. In a world that was changing, it was his duty to strive to maintain the balance between the people and the spirits, a task that had become more difficult since the coming of the strange people who seemed so intent on destroying the world.

The snows had melted in the high country, and the streams were full. The air was cool and carried the scent of green, growing plants.

Before the white men came, Malila's people had

lived on Rock Creek. It had been a rich land, abundant with deer in the hills and fish in the streams. A few white men came, then more, and still more. Then many, many white men, as numerous as ants on an anthill. The white men were as busy as ants, busy destroying the world. Tearing down the hills and throwing dirt into the streams to poison the fish. Cutting down trees and building dirty, crowded villages to which more white men came. Poisoning themselves with their own powerful firewater and letting the visions tempt them to fight and kill their fellow white men—and any others who strayed into their path.

Malila's people grew sick with diseases—fevers and poxes that killed without mercy. Her mother died of a fever, though her grandfather treated her with herbal medicines and chanted over her sweating body. Against Hatawa's wishes, Malila's father went to work in the white men's mines, saying that he would return with food and clothing and an understanding of the ways of these strange people. But his friends returned without him and told Hatawa that the riverbank had collapsed in an avalanche of rocks and dirt, burying Malila's father.

When Malila was twelve years old, her village had moved away from the place where their ancestors had lived, building a new village higher in the hills, where the winters were colder but the streams still ran clear. That same year, Malila had been visited by powerful dreams that convinced her grandfather that she had the potential to become a shaman.

High in the mountains, Malila had gone on a vision quest. For three days, she had fasted and prayed. Alone beside a creek, she had drunk a tea that Hatawa had brewed, a sacred drink that brought visions. As she sat in the sunshine, she listened to the creek whisper and babble as it flowed among granite boulders.

One boulder drew her eye. Mottled gray granite, worn smooth by flowing water and blowing wind, it resembled a wolf that had curled up to sleep. Sunlight reflecting from the flowing water played on the boulder's surface, making the stone look like fur, rippling in the breeze. Malila squinted at the stone, surprised by how much it looked like a sleeping wolf. A shadow formed an ear; two dark streaks marked the animal's eyes.

As she watched, the stone that was a sleeping wolf opened her eyes, pricked up her ears, and lifted her head to look at Malila. The wolf's eyes shone in the sun like the gold that the white men sought. Malila closed her eyes, startled at the vision.

She felt hot breath on her face and opened her eyes. A great gray wolf stood before her. The animal's nose was just inches from Malila's face. Golden eyes stared into hers. In the pupil of each eye, she could see her own reflection: dark hair, dark eyes wide with excitement.

The wolf spoke to her. "I am glad you have come, my daughter. You will join my pack."

Malila saw that the other stones were moving, too. A black boulder shook itself and became a black wolf with green-gold eyes. A mica-streaked stone was a silver-gray wolf with pale blue eyes. The landscape shifted around her as the wolves came to sniff her face.

"You will come with us," the first wolf said.

Once, as a child, her cousin had jumped from a high cliff into a deep pool in the river. Not to be outdone, Malila had followed him, launching herself into space. In that moment of falling, there was joy and terror, an exhilarating rush ending in a splash of ice-cold water.

As she stared into the eyes of the wolf, Malila felt

that sensation again. She was falling, dizzy, tumbling through space with a rush of joy and terror. Then the rush changed to the headlong rush of running—she was running on all fours. All around her were wolves, great beasts with sharp teeth, grinning and running in pursuit of a deer. The terrified deer stumbled, and the lead wolf, the great wolf who had come to Malila first, leapt up to grab the animal's nose and pull her head down. The pack was on the deer then, ripping at her haunches and tearing at her throat. Malila was attacking with the others, her teeth bared, her heart burning with a fierce joy.

She came back to her body in the woods with the taste of blood in her mouth. The great wolf still stood beside her. The others surrounded them.

"You are one of us," the great wolf told her. "You are a wolf. Listen." Malila listened, and the great wolf sang a song that ebbed and flowed like the voice of the river, a sweet meandering tune like the lullaby a mother sings to comfort her child.

"Remember this," the wolf said. Then the animal curled up beside the creek, closing her eyes. She became a gray stone beside the water, nothing more.

Malila laid her hand on the stone, and it was warm—perhaps from the sun, perhaps from the wolf within. There by the flowing water Malila sang the song the wolf had taught her.

Strong magic, her grandfather had said when she told him of her vision. She had to be strong to contain such a powerful spirit. He worked with her over the years—teaching her to channel her power and use it for healing, teaching her the ways of the shaman.

Now, four years after the wolf had visited her in a vision, she was a self-assured woman of sixteen. She helped her grandfather in ceremonies. When they needed medicinal plants that grew in the lower altitudes, she went with him down the mountain.

THE SUN WAS low in the sky when Malila waded out of the water and walked up the creek to where her grandfather was working. "Grandfather! If you stand in the water too long, you'll need this nettle root as much as the chief. I will make a fire and cook dinner."

That night, they sat by the fire, eating acorn mush. Malila was tired. It had been a long day's journey from the village to the swampy ground where the horsetails grew, followed by hours of digging to unearth the nettle roots.

Her grandfather must have been tired, but he didn't show it. He sat by the fire, placidly eating the acorn mush she had prepared. She had seen him in rituals, dancing and calling on the spirits, and she knew his power. But that power was hidden now. The firelight revealed only a tough old man, as enduring as the manzanita bushes that clung to the mountainside. The flames danced in his dark eyes; his skin shone in the firelight like burnished leather.

Somewhere in the distance, a wolf howled. Another joined in, and then a chorus. From another direction came an answering howl. Malila glanced at her grandfather, then added her voice to the chorus, letting the wolves know, in their own language, that she was passing through their territory, that she meant no harm.

"They call to me," she told her grandfather. "Sometimes, I dream about running with them and never coming back."

He nodded. "You have the wolf in you. But you belong to the people, too."

She nodded, smiling because she knew what he would say next. "I must find the balance between the wolf and the woman," she said.

He returned her smile, nodding. "You know it all now. You don't need my advice anymore."

The wolves howled again and Malila responded.

WHEN MALILA HOWLED, Sarah was not with the rest of the pack. She and Beka had been wandering along the edge of the creek—Sarah was foraging for greens while Beka hunted for mice and rabbits and other small game. Beka was four years old, an adult wolf. When Sarah strayed from the pack, Beka came along, more often than not.

That day, their trail had crossed that of three white men, traveling up the mountain. Sarah had followed them for a time, out of curiosity. Beka had tagged along.

Sarah didn't like the smell of the men: they reeked of tobacco and gunpowder. When the men had made camp on the creek, she had lost interest. When Rolon howled, summoning the pack, she and Beka were heading back to rejoin them for the evening hunt. She and Beka had responded to the pack's howl—and then Malila had responded as well.

Beka had headed straight back to where the pack waited. She had spent the day exploring with Sarah and was eager for the hunt. But Sarah had delayed, following the sound of Malila's voice until she could see the light of the campfire. There, she hesitated, testing the breeze. She knew by the scent that a man and a woman sat by the fire. No tobacco, coffee, or whiskey—scents that predominated at the camp of the miners. Just the warm aroma of acorn mush.

She crept closer, curious about the pair of Indians. She could hear their voices, soft and guttural, blending with the croaking of frogs in the swamp. The moon had not yet risen and darkness hid her as she moved silently through the trees. Crouching behind a low shrub, she listened to the Indians' voices, though she could make no sense of the sounds they made. From her hiding place, she could see the man's back and the woman's face. She watched as the woman lifted her head to howl again.

Miners sometimes howled to the wolves, but their howls would not have fooled the most simple-minded wolf. They sounded like wolves to no one but themselves.

But this woman truly howled like a wolf. Her voice was rich and low, carrying a wealth of meaning. I am here, she was saying. I am resting, not hunting. I will not interfere with you, but I am here.

While Sarah watched, the woman stood up, said something to the man, then walked away from the fire, into the darkness. She was walking toward Sarah, her head up, her eyes wide, staring into the darkness.

Sarah stayed where she was, confident that the woman could not see her, wondering what the woman would do. She posed no threat; she had no weapon that Sarah could see.

The woman stopped just a few yards away from Sarah. For a moment, she stood motionless. Then she began to sing.

Sarah had heard miners singing around their campfires. She had heard Indians chanting and singing as they gathered acorns in the fall. But she had never heard a song like this. It rose and fell like a mother's lullaby, like the whimpers with which a mother wolf comforts her pups in the den. A human voice, singing like a mother wolf.

Sarah lay in the shadows, listening to Malila sing.

THE GOLD RUSH brought all kinds to California. There were good men who were willing to work hard and hoped to get rich from their labors. And there were bad men—gamblers, swindlers, cutthroats, and thieves—who hoped to get rich without working quite so hard.

The men that Sarah had observed earlier were of the second variety. Joseph, Andrew, and Frank, three brothers from Missouri, had traveled overland to California. Unlike most emigrants, they had profited by their journey, stealing horses from one wagon train and mules from another.

The brothers thought California was a fine place. There were plenty of men with money in the gold country, just waiting to have that money taken away. That night, the brothers were particularly cheerful. Along a lonely trail, they had found a man prospecting alone. Without a pang of conscience, they had whacked him on the head, taken his gold, his grub, and his pack mule, then tumbled his body into a gully, leaving him for the coyotes to dispose of. Among his provisions, they had found two bottles of whiskey, and that had made them quite jolly. That night, they drank themselves to sleep.

In the morning, they did not feel nearly so cheerful. "Where is that mule?" Joseph snarled. He was the oldest brother and, as such, he had claimed more than his share of the whiskey. That had been very well the night before, but now his head was aching. His temper was not at its best (and truth be told, his temper was never very good). "I told you to tie it up last night, Frank."

"I reckon it pulled up its stake and wandered off." Frank, the youngest brother, could not remember whether he had ever tied up the mule, but he suspected that he hadn't. If he had gone off to tie the mule, he would have missed his turn at the whiskey bottle.

"Well, I reckon you'd better go find it," drawled Andrew, the middle brother. He was the smallest and the smartest of the three. Joseph was a large-framed man, tall and broad-shouldered, with hands large and strong enough to strangle a bear. Frank was shorter and softer, a big-bellied youngster with a hint of a whine in his voice. Andrew was shorter than either of them, a slender man who made up for his lack of size with cleverness, a sharp customer who cheated at cards.

"You'd best help him," Joseph said. "That boy can't find his own arse with both hands."

Andrew grinned. Frank wasn't the sharpest lad, particularly after a night of drinking. Besides, Andrew thought it would be wise to avoid Joseph's company until he downed a few cups of the poisonous brew he called coffee. "Sure enough," Andrew agreed.

While Frank and Andrew were saddling their horses, the mule announced its whereabouts. From up the creek came a great braying noise, the sort of ruckus that only a mule in trouble can make. As Frank and Andrew rode toward the noise, the ground grew swampy; their horses splashed through muddy water, and the air stank of rotting vegetation.

Andrew caught a glimpse of the mule up ahead. An old Indian man was holding the animal's bridle, urging the animal forward. The old man was muddy; Andrew reckoned he'd been in the mud with the mule. An Indian girl was swatting the mule's rump with a switch. Andrew could hear the Indians talking to the mule, jabbering in that incomprehensible language of theirs. As Andrew watched, the mule lunged forward, pulling itself from the mud. The old man shouted something; it sounded triumphant to Andrew.

Then a rifle cracked and the old man fell, collapsing into the mud. Blood spread across the rabbit-skin cloak that covered his chest.

Andrew glanced at Frank, who was lowering his rifle. "That Injun was stealing our mule," Frank said.

Andrew nodded. He thought it was more likely that the Indians were just freeing the mule from the mud, rather than actively stealing it, but Frank wasn't in a good mood and it made no sense to argue. At least he'd waited until the Indians got the mule out of the mud. Andrew didn't like to get dirty.

The Indian girl was cradling the old man's head, jabbering away. Her eyes were wide; her face was wet with tears.

Andrew watched as Frank rode up beside her. For an Injun, she was pretty, Andrew thought. She wore a rabbit-skin cloak that hid her breasts. That was too bad. The Injun gals down in the valley didn't bother to cover their breasts at all, and that was nice. But her skirt was barely down to her knees, showing off muscular legs. Nice. It didn't leave too much to the imagination, and Andrew had a good imagination.

"Might as well save your breath," Frank was telling the girl. "I reckon he's dead. He should never have tried to steal our mule."

She stared at Frank as he swung down from his horse, took the mule's lead, and tied it to the back of his saddle. She said something in the Indian language, then she was on her feet, pulling a knife from her belt, lunging for Frank.

Frank sidestepped her lunge and grabbed her knife hand, twisting it around behind her back. Andrew smiled. His little brother was big and dumb, but he had years of experience in barroom fights. This little lady would be no match for him.

Frank took the knife away, twisting her arm cruelly, then pushed her, adding to her momentum so that she tumbled forward into the mud. As she fell, her skirt rode up, giving Andrew an even better view of her legs. Very nice. It had been months since he'd had a woman.

Then she was rolling, fast as a cat, and going for Frank again. Lots of spunk, but not much sense. Frank sidestepped her charge and caught her with a backhand that sent her reeling into the mud again.

"Go get her, little brother," Andrew called, urging his brother on. When Frank went after her, she rolled to one side. He turned to follow. His feet slipped on the slick mud, and he fell, landing in the mud with a splash.

The woman was going for Frank then, her knife ready. Andrew lifted his rifle. A pity to shoot her—a waste—but he had to save his fool of a brother.

SARAH WATCHED FROM her hiding place in the branches of an oak tree. She had rejoined the pack the night before, but had returned to the Indian camp before dawn, drawn by curiosity.

Sarah had watched the Indians drag the mule from the mud, had seen Frank shoot Hatawa and fight Malila. It was very puzzling. She could not understand the relationships among these people. She did not understand what was going on.

The mule, she supposed, belonged to the pack of men. She understood possession. If a wolf had torn a piece of meat from a deer carcass and run away with it, the meat belonged to that wolf, and that wolf would fight to keep it. Maybe the mule belonged to the men, and they wanted it back.

But the men had not indicated their desire. Frank had attacked without warning. As he rode up, he had been smiling, showing no signs of anger. He did not growl to warn the Indians away from the mule. He just lifted his rifle, the stick that killed at a distance, and the old man fell dead.

The woman's attack on Frank made more sense to her. The woman's anger was clear on her face before she attacked. She was defending the old man, who had been part of her pack. Though Sarah had not understood the words Malila said, her feelings were clear. Anger and hatred and pain.

She watched the fight between Frank and Malila. The man was big and slow and powerful, like the grizzly bear. The woman had to be fast. She had to keep out of his reach until she was ready to strike. Sarah liked this woman.

The woman was doing well—then Sarah saw Andrew raise his rifle. She had seen what rifles could do. Her reflexes were those of a wild creature; she saw the movement and acted, snatching a stone from her pocket and hurling it at Andrew's head.

Years of hunting had given her a strong arm and a good aim. The stone struck Andrew in the temple, causing him to lurch in the saddle. He fired, but missed Malila. His horse, startled, reared back, throwing him from the saddle.

Sarah did not hesitate; her time with the wolves had taught her the virtues of immediate action. A hunter who hesitated went hungry. She sprang from her hiding place in the tree to land on Andrew's back. Her knife blade glittered in the rising sun as she held it ready, baring her teeth and snarling to communicate her dominance.

If Andrew had indicated his submission by lying still and exposing his throat, she would have spared him. Wolves established their positions by fighting, but rarely fought to kill.

But Andrew did not know the rules. He knew only

that the sport with the Indian girl had gone wrong; that he was being attacked by a growling savage child. He struggled, turning beneath his attacker, trying to shake her off. He reached upward, his thumbs ready to gouge out her eyes, his hands eager to throttle her senseless. But before he could reach Sarah's face, her knife had slashed deep into his neck.

Her hands red with blood, Sarah stared down at Andrew's body. She was hungry—she had not hunted that morning. But she did not lick the blood from her blade, as she would have if she had butchered a rabbit or a deer. The body reeked of tobacco and whiskey, bad smells that turned her stomach.

Still alert to possible danger, she looked to Frank. The big man lay still. Malila crouched in the mud beside his body. Her hands were covered in crimson blood.

While Sarah watched, Malila cleaned her knife on a tuft of grass. Sarah approved, knowing that Malila had also decided that the flesh was too tainted to eat.

Malila studied Sarah and said something that Sarah did not understand.

"WHO ARE YOU?" Malila asked again. The savage girl watched her, but did not speak.

Such a strange child. Not an Indian and surely not a white girl. Her hair was a mass of red-gold curls, not the hair of any Indian. Her skin was bronzed from the sun. She carried herself with natural grace and dignity. Her eyes were bright and alert, shining with the spark of intelligence. She wore only a pair of white man's trousers, raggedly cut off at the knees and held up with suspenders. On a belt, she carried a knife in a leather sheath.

The girl was watching Malila intently. Gracefully,

she rose from her crouch and closed the distance that separated her from Malila with a few swift steps.

The girl was whining low in her throat. Malila stood frozen as the girl paced around her. She felt hot breath on her neck as the girl sniffed her, inhaling her scent. As the girl prowled around her, the sound became a humming, a song without words. Malila recognized the tune—the song that the wolf in her vision had taught her.

"The wolves," Malila said. "You have come from the wolves."

The girl stopped singing and stared into the swamp, in the direction of the men's camp. Glancing at Malila, she started away through the swamp, leaving the mule and the horses. Malila hesitated, looking down at her grandfather's body. The girl looked back at her and whimpered entreatingly, clearly asking Malila to follow, to hurry.

"Andrew! Frank! Where the hell are you?"

Frightened by the angry shout in the distance, Malila hurried after the savage girl. In shock, still reeling from her grandfather's death, Malila followed the girl through the swamp.

The ground was treacherous, pocked with mudholes like the one that had captured the mule. But the wild girl knew her way. She followed a circuitous route, leaping with confidence from one patch of solid ground to the next. Once, she climbed an oak and made her way along the spreading branches to another patch of firm ground. The shouting of the white man faded in the distance.

HOURS LATER, MALILA collapsed beside a creek. The wild girl crouched beside the running water. She drank like an animal, lowering her mouth to the water.

"Where are we going?" Malila asked the wild girl. The girl studied her with an expression of intelligent concentration, but said nothing.

"What is your name?" Malila asked. No answer. She pointed at herself. "Malila," she said. "That's my name. Malila."

Sarah tilted her head, watching Malila.

"Malila," the Indian woman repeated.

Sarah listened to the sounds that the Indian woman made, then tried to shape her lips to make the same sounds. "Ma," she said, a sound she remembered from long, long ago, when the one called Mama had taken care of her. "Ma."

The woman nodded. "Malila," she repeated.

Sarah struggled with the second sound, a sweet, high sound like the cheeping of the finches in the brush. "Ma . . . li," she managed. "Mali."

Again the woman nodded.

The third syllable came easily—it was a combination of the first one and the second one. "Ma . . . li . . . la," Sarah said triumphantly, a strange collection of sounds. Sarah grinned. "Malila," she repeated.

Then the woman pointed to Sarah and asked something. Sarah did not understand the words, but she understood the question. "What is your name?" the woman was asking.

Her name among the wolves was not just a collection of sounds, but something more comprehensive than that. She was identified by her scent, by her position in the hierarchy, and all of that could not be contained in a sound.

What was her name? What sound was her own? Speaking with Malila reminded Sarah of that time long ago when she lived with the woman she called Mama and the man she called Papa. Those people had a name for her. They called her by a collection of sounds that began with a hiss like a snake and ended with the same sound that ended Malila's name.

"What's your name?" Mama had asked her long, long ago. "What's your name?"

"Sarah," she told Mama.

Mama had laughed and clapped her hands. Sarah. That, Sarah thought, was her name among people.

Slowly, with great care, Sarah pronounced the syllables that had delighted Mama so long ago.

"Sarah," Malila repeated, studying the savage girl and remembering the stone that had become a wolf in her vision quest.

In the language of Malila's people, the word "sara" meant "stone." Sometimes, the word was used as a name, and it was a name of great power. The spirits that lived in stones were powerful and generous. When stones were struck together in the proper way, the spirits provided sparks which gave to the tribe fire. Other stones, treated differently, became arrowheads and knives and other tools.

This savage girl was a wolf and a stone, and she had come to Malila when she needed help. Malila bowed her head, overwhelmed by all that the name implied.

Sarah studied Malila for a moment. The Indian woman was tired, she recognized that. It did not make sense to her; their travels that day had not been particularly strenuous when compared with the travels of the pack. But she could tell that Malila was tired.

Sarah herself was hungry. She had not fed that day, except for a few bites of miner's lettuce, picked on the run. It was midday. As they traveled, she had seen many fat marmots among the rocks. These animals, common on the rocky slopes of the Sierras, were similar to woodchucks, living in burrows in the rocks. They made good eating.

With gestures, she made Malila understand that she was to stay there, in the rocky grotto by the creek. Sarah scrambled up the rock face. Before Malila could speak a word, she was gone.

Malila waited by the stream, listening to the water babble over the boulders. The wild girl had taken her by unfamiliar ways, but Malila knew that they were heading in the general direction of her village. She recognized the sloping mountain that her tribe called Eagle's Head. The village was tucked into a valley at the foot of that mountain.

At rest for the first time in hours, she washed in the stream, using tufts of the hardy grass that grew among the boulders to scrub her hands, washing away the blood that darkened her fingernails. The white man's blood, she thought with a shudder. She cleaned her knife and brushed dried blood from her rabbit-skin cape.

In solitude, she wept and prayed for her grandfather, who lay dead in the swamp. She thanked the great wolf for sending Sarah to save her. She prayed for her people, who hid in the mountains, asking that the mountains keep them safe from white men who might come for revenge.

She was finishing her prayers when she heard a sound behind her. The wild girl stood beside the creek. The carcass of a dead marmot, slain by a well-aimed stone, dangled from her hand.

The marmot had been gutted; Sarah had eaten her fill of the tender internal organs. Among the wolves, eating was not a social activity, but something that was best done alone. She had brought the remainder of the carcass to the Indian woman as a wolf might bring meat to a puppy.

Malila's actions when Sarah gave her the carcass puzzled the wild girl. Rather than eating her fill of the fresh meat, Malila first gathered bits of wood. A tough old pine tree that clung between two boulders just up the stream offered a few dead branches.

Malila made a small pile of kindling in a wind-sheltered hollow. With flint and steel from the pouch at her belt, she made sparks that fell on the dry kindling. She blew on the tiny flame, building it up into a small fire, over which she roasted the marmot meat.

Sarah watched the flames in amazement. She had seen fire before. She remembered when a rapidly burning wildfire set by lightning had swept through the foothills, burning the grass and dry foliage and leaving the trees untouched. Sarah had learned to avoid the leaping flames of wildfires. She had also seen distant campfires, but she had never been so close to one.

The scent of the roasting meat tickled her nose. The Indian woman sliced a piece of meat from the carcass and offered it to Sarah. Startled, Sarah accepted the meat.

Malila cut another piece of meat for herself. Rather than turning away to eat her meal in solitude, Malila ate in front of Sarah, as if certain that Sarah would not challenge her and take the food. She ate with her knife, slicing off bits of meat that she could pick up and eat with her hands. Sarah followed her example, relishing the unfamiliar flavor of cooked meat.

While they ate, Malila studied Sarah. "You are a very powerful spirit," Malila said, "and you are also a young girl." She frowned. "Your hair is like a white man's hair. Did the white men bring you here?" Sarah looked up from the leg she was gnawing, listening intently. "I wish I could talk to you," Malila said.

"Talk," Sarah repeated after Malila. "Talk to you." She smiled happily, obviously pleased to be making sounds.

Malila leaned forward. She could teach this wild spirit to speak. Her eyes on Sarah's face, Malila pointed at the meat roasting on the fire, then at the meat in the girl's hand. "Meat," she said in the language of her people. "Meat."

Sarah's smile broadened, and a look of understanding brightened her eyes. She repeated the word after Malila.

For the next hour, they sat by the fire and Malila taught Sarah words, simple nouns. Fire. Tree. Leaf. Grass. Sand. Water.

For Sarah, this was more than a language lesson. It was a new world, a world in which sounds—sounds alone without gestures or scents—could mean things. Making these sounds awakened old memories. Long, long ago, she had learned other word sounds from Mama and Papa.

Sarah laughed and repeated the strange sounds that Malila made. She waved a hand at the fire and called out its name. Fire. Rock. Sand. Grass. Tree. Leaf. Water. She could name them all.

As the fire died down, Malila stared in the direction of Eagle's Head. "I must go back to the village," she said, not because she thought the girl would understand, but because it seemed right to speak with her.

Of course Sarah knew where the Indian village was. It was in the pack's territory, where she knew every tree and every rock. She knew where the deer grazed and where the grizzly bear had her den. She knew of the path that rabbits followed in the brush and the trails that humans followed through the mountains. Of course she knew where the Indians lived.

She had always intended to take Malila back to her village, but now she felt a strange reluctance to do so. For the first time, she had experienced the pleasure of human companionship.

But she knew that the Indian woman could not live among the wolves. She knew that she had to take Malila back to her own people.

Sarah led Malila up the mountain, following the stream at first, then cutting across an area where a rockfall had cleared the slope of brush. Though she could smell the Indians' cooking fires, she continued on her way, taking Malila to the edge of the meadow where her village stood. They could see the bark lodges of the Indians, the smoke rising from cooking fires.

"Come with me," Malila said, taking Sarah's hand in hers.

Sarah pulled her hand away. Though she had spent the day with Malila, she was a wild thing still, wary of humans.

"You will go back to the mountains," Malila said. "Back to the wolves."

Sarah listened to the words, understanding none of them.

"You will come back to see me," Malila said. "You must."

Still Sarah listened without understanding.

"Here." Malila lifted the necklace of bone and shell from around her neck and placed it around Sarah's. "This is to thank you and keep you safe and bring you back."

Sarah touched the necklace and smiled. Then she turned without a word and vanished into the forest.

THAT EVENING, JOSEPH rode into the mining town of Hell's Half Acre, burning with the desire for justice.

"Injuns! Injuns killed my brothers," he shouted as he rode up to the log cabin that served as bar and boardinghouse. His brothers' bodies were slung over their horses; he had not stopped to bury them. "Murdering Injuns!"

A man stepped from the cabin, lifting a lantern high. "Injuns?" He squinted at Joseph, glanced at the bodies, then frowned at the mule. He stared at Joseph, still frowning. "You take that mule from the Injuns?"

"That's my mule," Joseph said impatiently, swinging down from his saddle. "The Injuns were stealing it when they killed my brothers."

The man with the lantern glanced at the bar. Three other men stood by the door, staring at Joseph. One of them had a bandaged head. "That your mule, Nathan?" he asked.

"Sure is. And that's the fellow who took it."

Nathan had a hard head. He had survived the brothers' attack and climbed out of the gully. Just by luck, a miner heading back to Hell's Half Acre had found him lying on the trail and had taken him to town.

Joseph never did get a posse up to pursue his brothers' murderers. In the town of Hell's Half Acre, he was hung for a mule thief and buried with his brothers.

AFTER SARAH LEFT Malila, she returned to the pack. But she was restless. She hunted with the wolves, but she thought often of Malila.

Sometimes, she repeated the words that Malila had taught her. "Tree," she told Beka. "Leaf. Grass." The wolf responded with affection—licking Sarah's face, rubbing against her hand—but that was no longer enough for the girl. She wanted more.

Her mind buzzed with new thoughts. She still wore the necklace that Malila had given her. Sometimes, she touched the beads and wondered what Malila was doing.

A few weeks later, the pack's travels brought them near the Indian village. It was early in the afternoon, and the pack was resting in a shady hollow, having brought down a deer in the early dawn hours.

Sarah left the pack for a time. She was drawn to the village. Her meeting with Malila had awakened something in her. She wanted to talk with Malila again; she wanted to learn more words. A young girl, raised without human contact, she also longed for friendship. She burned with a desire to figure out the world and discover her place in it.

She was just to the south of the village when she caught Malila's scent on the breeze. She followed the trail of that scent to a thick patch of deer brush on a dry hillside.

Sarah heard Malila before she saw her. The Indian woman was singing softly to herself, a wandering tune that blended with the humming of bees in the deer brush. Silently, Sarah made her way toward the sound, following a rabbit trail through the bushes. Breathing deeply, Sarah inhaled the minty scent of bruised yerba santa leaves and the warm aroma of Malila herself.

Through the branches, she caught a glimpse of Malila and stopped where she was. Malila's back was to Sarah. The woman was gathering leaves from a yerba santa bush and dropping them in the basket at her feet. For a moment, Sarah simply watched her.

Sarah was wild, and she was shy as wild creatures are shy. For a moment she thought about slipping quietly away through the brush and returning to the pack. Beka would lick her face; she could curl up in the shade beside Wauna. Her heart was beating quickly, as if she had been running. She hesitated, watching the slim Indian woman pluck leaves from the bush, listening to her song of gratitude, as she thanked the plant for giving its leaves to help the tribe.

As Sarah watched, Malila stopped humming and lifted her head, as if she had heard something that caught her attention. She turned away from the bush, and spoke. "Is someone there?" She saw Sarah, staring through the bushes, and she smiled. "Sarah," she said.

Sarah stepped from the shelter of the bush, her hesitation forgotten when the young woman smiled. "Malila," she said softly, each syllable separate and distinct. She enjoyed pronouncing the strange sounds.

She circled the woman, as she would have circled a member of her pack, grinning, stroking Malila's hair.

"I knew you would come," Malila said, though she knew that the words meant nothing to Sarah. "I knew you would come and find me."

Malila still held a yerba santa leaf in her hand. Playfully, Sarah snatched the leaf from Malila. "Leaf," she said. "Leaf." Such a strange sound.

Malila smiled and held out her hand. "Hand," she said to the wild child. She took Sarah's hand in hers. "Hand."

Malila taught Sarah more words, all through that long summer afternoon and many afternoons after that. All through the summer, Sarah came to the village when the pack was nearby.

At first, Sarah only approached Malila when she was walking outside the village. But one sunny afternoon, Malila persuaded the wild girl to go to the village. She walked with Malila among the bark lodges, staring back at the wide-eyed children, growling at the skinny dogs that came to sniff at her legs.

Malila led her to a lodge that smelled of drying herbs. "This is my home, Sarah," Malila told her. "You are always welcome here."

SARAH WAS INTRIGUED by the Indian village and the people who lived there. With Malila, she learned to weave baskets from reeds, to braid rope from plant fibers, to cure animal skins to make leather, to make a fire with the sparks that leapt from stones.

She noticed that the people in the village treated Malila with deference and respect. The young woman was high in the hierarchy of this pack.

The summer days were growing shorter when Sarah asked Malila to show her how to make arrows.

"I don't know how to do that," Malila told her. "That's men's work."

Sarah frowned.

"I will see if I can find someone to teach you," Malila said.

And so Sarah met Notaku, the tribe's best stone worker and weapon maker. On a summer afternoon, he showed her how to shape an arrowhead from obsidian.

"Press hard," Notaku said. "Like this." He laid his hands on top of hers and pressed down, pushing the deer antler tool against the roughly shaped obsidian arrowhead. With a high-pitched cracking noise, a circular flake of obsidian broke free, leaving a razor-sharp edge. "Again," he said, repositioning the tool on the arrowhead. "You do it, this time."

He sat back on his heels, watching as Sarah pressed against the tool. Another flake, a circular flake no bigger than the fingernail on her littlest finger, broke free, extending the sharp edge. Sarah looked up at him, smiling, and he nodded, returning her smile. "Again," he said.

He glanced at Malila, who sat on the ground beside him. The young woman had become the village's shaman and healer, a position that set her somewhat apart from the rest of the village. She lived alone in the bark house that she had once shared with Hatawa. She spent many hours gathering medicinal herbs, walking in the hills alone. And often, she spoke of the white man's spirit, the spirit called Sarah, who came to her when she was alone.

Malila had asked Notaku to teach this spirit to make arrows, and he had agreed—from friendship for Malila. Sarah was, Malila said, a powerful and playful spirit. She wanted to understand the ways of the people, and Malila was teaching her.

"Why would a spirit need to know how to make arrows?" Notaku had asked her.

"She is a white spirit," Malila said. "And she is very young. She does not know how to make arrows. I think it would be good for a spirit of the white people to understand our ways." She spoke of balance—of how the white man was out of balance with the world. She thought, perhaps, that this wild spirit, who took the form of a child, might help bring balance back to the white man.

Notaku had agreed to meet this Sarah. He was a brave man. A man less certain of himself might have refused, unwilling to put himself in the way of such power.

When he met the spirit called Sarah, he knew he had made the right decision. She was quick to learn, more patient than the boys he had taught, more careful with her hands. She watched him with uncanny concentration, devoting her full attention to his words. She had the bright eyes of an animal who is thinking of nothing but what she sees in front of her.

Such a strange spirit, he thought, looking down at her curly red-gold hair. Like a child in so many ways. Malila said that she hunted with the wolves, that she fought like a wolf. Legends told of children who lived with the wolves and learned to become wolves.

Another flake broke free, and another. Under Sarah's patient hands, the arrowhead was taking shape. Next, he would teach her to shape a shaft from the wood of the wild currant bush, to bind the arrowhead to the shaft with sinew, to feather the arrow with split hawk feathers, to make a sturdy bow of juniper wood.

He smiled at Malila, the smile of a teacher who is watching a pupil do well. This wild spirit, this Sarah, would understand the ways of the people. Beneath Notaku's deft hands, something new was taking shape.

10

THE CAPTAIN'S WIFE

"Circumstances make man,
not man circumstances."

—*Mark Twain's Notebook;* Mark Twain

ONE SUNNY DAY EARLY IN AUTUMN, SARAH LAY ATOP A BOULDER that she had climbed. From that vantage point, she could see a cow that had grown tired of traveling, a bony beast worn thin by the long journey across the plains. The cow seemed to think that the South Yuba River valley might be a nice place to settle down. The animal ambled along the rocky river bottom. The frayed end of a rope dangled from her neck; she had gotten loose from the back of the wagon she had been following for a few thousand miles.

The cow would have been easy prey, but Sarah was not hungry just then. She had, with a well-thrown stone, killed a rabbit that morning, and her stomach was full. It was a warm afternoon, and the pack was resting, about a mile to the north. Sarah was not interested in hunting, but she was always curious. So she had come to where the trail passed, so that she could spy on any passing emigrants.

A man on a horse rode along the trail, in pursuit of the straying cow. On his saddle, he carried a lariat made of four strands of braided rawhide. Frankly, it was a better lariat than the man was a cowboy. He'd purchased the rope from a Mexican cowboy who was down on his luck. The cowboy thought he needed a drink more than he needed a lariat. So the man bought the lariat and the Mexican cowboy bought the drink and everyone did well on the deal except of course for the cow. The man who bought the rope had, from that day on, persisted in trying to rope that cow, whether she needed it or not.

He was bringing the cow to California because he had heard that milk was in short supply there. A practical man, he figured if he didn't strike it rich in the gold mines, he could always sell milk to the other miners. On the long journey across the plains, he had grown reasonably adept with the lariat, much to the cow's dismay.

As Sarah watched, the man took the lariat from his saddle and tossed the loop over the head of the wayward cow. The cow kept moving until the loop tightened around her neck. Then she stopped, having been through this before. The man kicked his horse into a trot and the cow followed.

Sarah stared after them. That lariat seemed like a very handy thing to have.

That night, while the pack was hunting, Sarah crept into a copse of trees not far from where the man with the cow had stopped for the night. The man and his traveling companions had made camp in a grassy valley by a small stream. The livestock was tethered in the meadow, grazing contentedly. Enticing smells drifted across the meadow: baking biscuits and frying bacon. The men's voices carried across the open valley. They were talking about finding gold and making their fortunes and such.

Sarah waited, listening to their voices without understanding. Among the wolves, she had learned to wait patiently until the time was right. While she waited, she thought about what she might do with that lariat, once she had it.

The wolves lived in the here and now. They did not plan for the future. They remembered the past, but only as far as it was useful to do so. Rolon remembered places where the hunting was good, places where there was danger from humans or other packs. But he did not think on the past and consider how he might have done differently; he did not imagine the future and plan for it. Sarah had grown up among the wolves, hunting with them, running with the pack. But she had a human imagination, a capacity for planning, an innate cunning that her packmates lacked.

When Sarah was just a toddler, her human mother had told her stories. The stories always began the same way. "Once upon a time, there was a little girl named Sarah who was brave and bold and beautiful." In her mother's stories, little Sarah went on great adventures—some of which paralleled the real little Sarah's life. In her mother's stories, little Sarah had said good-bye to her home in Connecticut and set out across the wilderness on a great journey to California. Of course, in the stories little Sarah had ridden her own pony and had saved her mother and father from a savage band of Indians (who turned out to be quite friendly), from a fierce pack of wolves (little Sarah had tamed them with bacon and kindness), and from numerous other dangers along the way.

Sarah did not remember the stories that her mother had told her. But she had inherited her mother's imagination and willingness to spin a tale. Now, sitting alone in the darkness and listening to the voices of the men at the campfire, she imagined stories for herself. She imagined herself crouching in a tree, holding the lariat at her side. The pack was chasing a deer, and the animal ran beneath the tree. She tossed the loop over the deer's head and, in her imagination, stopped the deer in its tracks.

Sarah thought about the wonderful lariat and listened to the rise and fall of human voices, a strangely comforting sound. When the voices fell quiet and the fire burned low, Sarah made her way closer, ghosting between the grazing animals so quietly that they did not look up as she passed.

She paused at the edge of the camp, listening to the steady breathing of the sleeping men. Her eyes were accustomed to the dark. Unlike the emigrants, she had not spoiled her night vision by staring into the glowing coals of a fire. By the light of the rising moon, she could see clearly.

The men slept around the fire. One of them had his head resting on a saddle. Looped around the horn of the saddle, inches from the man's head, was the lariat Sarah coveted.

For a time, she stayed at the edge of the camp. The men slept soundly, weary from their day's travels. At last, she crept closer, her bare feet silent on the soft grass. The camp was dark except for the moonlight and the glowing coals of the fire. She could hear the mules cropping the grass, the soft snores of the sleeping men, the chirping of crickets in the grass. Squatting on her heels by the saddle, she reached out and put her hand on the lariat.

It wouldn't come loose from the saddle.

Sarah stared at the rawhide cord that held it in place. She had never encountered a knot before, and it puzzled her for a moment. She had seen the man easily take the lariat from his saddle, yet now the rope seemed to be attached to the saddle. Gently, she tugged at the lariat, but the knot held.

Carefully, she pulled at the rawhide cord, trying to work it loose. Her first efforts pulled the knot tighter, but then she began to pick at the knot itself. This puzzle intrigued her. She had never encountered anything quite like this knot. The tendrils of the wild grapevines twined around the oak trees, but that was just a tangle. She knew, from watching the man take the lariat from his saddle, that this twisted cord could be untangled and freed.

JEFFREY WOKE WHEN he felt something tugging on his pillow. A half-naked savage crouched by his head—a young girl, wearing nothing but a pair of cut-off trousers and a belt that held a sheath knife.

A dream, he thought. This wild creature could not be real. The moonlight glittered on her curly hair, unlike the hair of any Indian he had seen in his travels across the prairie. Her features were delicate—a thin, aristocratic nose; wide, blue eyes focused on his saddle.

At that moment, the savage smiled—such a sweet and innocent smile. The lariat came free of the saddle and Jeffrey saw it in the savage's hand. And then she was gone, melting into the darkness like a ghost.

Jeffrey closed his eyes and slept. In the morning, he woke to find his lariat gone. His companions laughed when he told them that it had been stolen by a half-naked white girl, and teased him about being away from his wife for too long. Nothing in the camp had been disturbed, except for Jeffrey's lariat, and the others claimed he must have lost that somewhere along the trail.

IN THE FOLLOWING days, Sarah carried the lariat with her wherever she went. She played with it, experimenting with knots like the ones that had held it to the saddle, with sliding loops like the one she had seen the man use to rope the cow.

In the long afternoons, while the pack rested in the heat of the day, she practiced throwing a sliding loop over boulders or bushes or trees. Beka often watched her as she played with the rope.

One afternoon in the pine forest, she succeeded in tossing the loop over the broken stub of a high branch. Pressing her feet against the tree's broad trunk and pulling herself upward with the rope, she climbed up to the branch she had lassoed. Beka watched from the ground, her eyes wide with disbelief, as Sarah perched in the tree, higher than she had ever climbed before.

Just a few days later she had occasion to use her new skill. It was just before dawn. The pack was coming down the mountain, trotting in single file after Rolon. Through the long night, the pack had been hunting without success. Rolon led them through the pine forest into a valley filled with ancient oaks. The air was cool. The first light of the rising sun illuminated the mist that drifted among the thick branches of the trees.

Rolon stopped, staring into the woodland, his head high as he sniffed the air. In the distance, Sarah could see a mature buck, standing among the oaks. The deer had seen the wolves. His head was up; he was ready to fight or run.

A powerful buck in his prime is not easy prey, even for a pack of wolves. A large buck can outrun wolves easily. If cornered, he can fight back, delivering kicks that can disable or kill an attacking wolf. Earlier that year, Luyu had been kicked in the head by a buck. Though the pack eventually brought the animal down, Luyu had died of the injury. Now, watching the buck, Rolon hesitated.

Sarah was hungry. She eyed the buck, judging its distance from the pack. If the pack gave chase, the deer would escape. But perhaps there was another way.

She leapt onto the lowest limb of a nearby oak. Agile as a monkey, surefooted as a tightrope walker, she ran up the branch to the trunk of the tree, then stepped over to another branch that led toward the buck. From the end of that branch, she leapt to another tree, making her way through the branches toward the deer.

In the meantime, Rolon had begun stalking his prey. His eyes fixed on the deer, he walked toward the animal, moving slowly. His goal was to close the distance without frightening the buck enough to make it run.

The buck's attention was focused on the wolves. He ignored the rustling in the branches overhead, keeping his eye on the immediate danger of the approaching pack.

Sarah slowly made her way through the branches until she was about ten feet from the buck, on a low limb six feet over the animal's head. She loosened the noose on the end of the lariat, wrapped the free end of the rope tightly around her hand, and then tossed the rope over the buck's head.

Luck was with her. The noose cleared the buck's antlers and fell neatly into place around his neck. As the deer felt the rope touch him, he bolted. Sarah laughed as the noose pulled tight around the buck's neck, but her laughter was cut short when the taut rope yanked on her arm, pulling her from her perch. She fell to the ground below.

Fortunately, she was on a low branch. Years of experience in climbing and falling had taught her to relax with a fall, catching herself with bent legs, ready to leap in any direction. But the pull of the rope yanked her forward, so that she fell awkwardly, landing half on her feet, but stumbling forward as she hit and falling full length on the grassy ground.

The buck, whirling to face his attacker, saw the girl

land and charged. Sarah rolled, barely escaping the trampling hooves. The buck reared to strike again, but Sarah was already moving, scrambling to her feet. Still clinging to the end of her precious lariat, she dodged behind the thick trunk of the oak. As she ran around the tree, she inadvertently snubbed the rope around the trunk, just as a sailor takes a wrap around a cleat to hold a line fast.

From a distance, Sarah's packmates had watched the rope tighten around the buck's neck, had seen the girl fall from the tree. How strange it was. Strange enough that the girl climbed a tree, but stranger still that she had fallen from the tree, pulled by something as thin and brown as the rattlesnake that dwelled in the rocks. And now the snake-thing held the buck, keeping it from running, but not preventing it from attacking the girl.

Beka started the attack, running to Sarah's assistance, her teeth bared in a snarl. The others were right behind her, rushing forward to set upon the buck. Wauna and Yepa leapt at the buck's head, snapping at his soft muzzle. Rolon, Beka, Marek, and the others circled behind, tearing at the buck's flanks.

When the buck turned to face these attackers, Wauna and Yepa renewed the attack on the animal's rump, biting and tearing at the hind legs. The buck lowered his head to threaten Rolon with his antlers, but the male wolf dodged and savagely bit the buck's muzzle, holding fast when the buck tried to raise his head.

The buck was fighting for air. The rope choked him; the wolf held a death grip on his muzzle. On all side, enemies attacked him. In that moment, Sarah sprang into action, pushing her way through the growling wolves to reach the animal's head. There, she attacked with her knife, the sharp blade that served her where her teeth could not. With a swipe of the keen blade, she slit the buck's throat.

The buck's blood gushed over her legs and feet. The end came quickly then. The buck collapsed to his knees, then fell to his side. Rolon and Wauna ripped at the animal's belly, gorging themselves on the soft organ meats, while the others tore at the wounds, stripping away the tough hide to reach the muscle underneath.

Sarah stood still for a moment, watching the wolves feed. When it comes to food, wolves have no manners. Each wolf fights for a share of the carcass, snarling and threatening its packmates. Any wolf who succeeds in tearing off a chunk of meat takes it away from the others, retreating to eat in solitude before returning to fight for more food.

The savagery of the pack when feeding was familiar to Sarah. What held her still, what startled and amazed her, was her own role in bringing the buck down. She had killed small game, but never an animal the size of this buck. She stared down at the rope in her hands, the wonderful lariat. Such a powerful weapon. If it could stop the mighty buck, what else could it do?

A pang of hunger interrupted her reverie. She dropped the rope and pulled her knife from her belt. Usually, she hung back while the other animals fed, but not today. This was her kill, and she would take her share of it.

In the midst of the snarling beasts, she pushed between Marek and Dur to grab one of the buck's forelegs, twisting the limb while pulling on it. With her knife, she stabbed at the buck's shoulder, severing the connective tissue that held the leg to the body. With a mighty effort, she pulled the leg free.

Dur lunged for the leg, but she snatched it away, already leaping for the branch above her. She grabbed the branch in one hand, clinging to the leg of the buck in the other. Marek leapt after her, snapping at the meat even as she lifted it out of reach, then snapping at her feet. Too late. She swung her feet up to lock her legs around the branch.

Laughing, she perched on the branch, the buck's leg across her lap. While Marek stared at her from below, his eyes hot with envy, she used her knife to strip away the deer hide, feasting on meat.

Long after Dur had returned to the carcass, fighting with the others for the choicest bits, Marek watched Sarah devour her prize, savoring the meat, gnawing on the bone.

WHILE SARAH PERCHED in an oak tree, gnawing on a bone and laughing at the black wolf that watched her from below, Max was sitting on the porch at Selby's Hotel writing a letter to Sarah's aunt. Over the years, Max and Audrey North had corresponded steadily. He had told Audrey of his life and he had learned of hers. She lived in New Bedford, the wife of the captain of a whaling ship.

"I know something of loneliness," she had written to him early in their correspondence, "as I spend many months each year watching for sails on the horizon, praying that my husband is well, wishing that he were safe at home. More than once, I have wished that I could go with him. However hard the journey, I think I would find it preferable to waiting at home—so dull, so comfortable, so safe."

Audrey North wrote poetry and published it in magazines like *The Ladies Repository* and *Appleton's Journal of Literature, Science, and Art.* Max had read the work of a few women poets—like Mrs. Felicia Hemans (known in the press as the British nightingale) and Mrs. Lydia

Howard Sigourney (know as the sweet singer of Hartford). He did not care for their poetry, finding it cloyingly sentimental. He had written to Audrey North, expressing this opinion, and he had been startled when she wrote to tell him that she agreed. Her favorite poet was a newcomer named Walt Whitman.

At Max's request, Audrey sent him a poem that had been published in *Appleton's.* The poem, titled *The Captain's Wife,* described a woman walking on the beach. That morning, when the weather had been fair and clear, her husband's ship had put out to sea. But as she paced along the shore, a storm was brewing. The wind swept in dark clouds, the waves lashed the shore, and as the storm built, so did the woman's feelings.

Unlike the women in the poems of Mrs. Hemans and Mrs. Sigourney, the captain's wife shed no tears. The bell in the village tolled, calling her to church, but she did not go. The rumble of thunder drowned out the bell. Lightning split the western sky. As rain lashed her face, she raged with the stormy sea.

Max found the poem both impressive and unsettling. In a return letter, he praised the poem for its lack of sentimentality and revised his mental image of Audrey. Initially, he had pictured her as a sweet and delicate New England lady. After reading *The Captain's Wife,* he imagined her as stout and courageous—a broad, no-nonsense woman built rather like Mrs. Selby.

Recently, a Boston publisher had published a collection of her poems. "I have met with some small success," she had written. "I find that rather gratifying."

She had taken the liberty of showing Max's sketch of the miners and his story about Socks and the lost child to the editor of *The Ladies Repository.* The editor had published the story, sent him a bank draft for twenty dollars, and clamored for more. Every now and again, he would send another sketch and another story about life in the mines.

When Max's work was published back in the States, the San Francisco newspapers had taken notice. As a result, the demand for his work had increased and he regularly published sketches and short essays in several newspapers. It was, as Audrey would put it, "rather gratifying."

Over the years, he and Audrey had corresponded very honestly about all manner of things. At that moment, he was writing to her about the civilizing influence of women.

"Take, for example, Mrs. Selby," he wrote. "Before a miner goes to Selby's Hotel, he combs his hair, washes his face, perhaps trims his beard. He cleans up his language as well, banishing blasphemies. Under her benign influence, Selby Flat is a far more civilized place.

"Compare Selby Flat to other towns, like Humbug or Hell's Half Acre or Rough and Ready. There is no comparison. Consider, if you will, dozens of men camped along a river for months on end, digging in the mud each day, cooking their own grub each evening. There is no laundry, no proper latrine, no facilities for bathing other than the river itself. The men wash their clothes primarily to reduce the insect population before the itching drives them mad. Under these conditions, men—even the best of men—become shaggy and grimy and far more aromatic than the polite society of women would allow."

Max heard footsteps behind him and looked up from his letter. Mr. Selby had stepped from the barroom. He sat down on the bench beside Max, opened his tobacco pouch, and began to fill his pipe. "Care for a smoke?" he asked.

Max set aside his letter, leaned back against the sun-warmed wall, and settled in to catch up on the news.

He'd been up on the North Fork, visiting Downieville and the mining camps along the river for an article that would appear in the *Nevada City Gazette.* Max accepted the pouch and filled his pipe.

"I hear that you're about to elect a sheriff," Max said.

Mr. Selby nodded. "That's so," he said. "Election will be next week. I reckon we'll be electing Jasper Davis. He's been buying drinks for the past week, and everyone figures him to be a fine fellow."

Max puffed his pipe thoughtfully. "He's done well for himself, has he?"

"No question about it. He's a smart man and he's a lucky man and he's done very well."

"Lucky? How's that?" Max asked.

"You hear about the big fire in Grass Valley?"

Max nodded. A fire had swept through the city, leaping from one wood-frame structure to the next, burning stores, saloons, hotels, and homes, leaving the city in ruins.

"Jasper was building a new hotel in Grass Valley when the city burned. Handsome place, made of fieldstone rather than wood. Said he liked stone 'cause it was solid. It was out on the edge of town, a ways from the nearest building."

"So it survived the fire?"

Mr. Selby nodded. "Didn't even get singed. After the fire, he was the only hotel still in business. Everybody went to Jasper's place to do their drinking and gambling and such. He did all right."

Max nodded again. Some men, he thought, made their own luck. He wondered if Jasper happened to be one of those. But he kept those thoughts to himself.

PART THREE

1859

11

A YOUNG MAN'S GUIDE

"Authorship is not a trade, it is an inspiration; authorship does not keep an office, its habitation is all out under the sky, and everywhere the winds are blowing and the sun is shining and the creatures of God are free."

—Mark Twain

FROM THE TOP OF A SUN-WARMED GRANITE BOULDER, SARAH watched the man who sat by the lake. She had been watching him, on and off, for the past two days, leaving only to hunt, and returning to find the man still there. He puzzled and intrigued her.

Most people that she had followed over the years were very busy. The Indians hunted, fished, and gathered plants for food. The miners scratched holes in the dirt and mucked about in the streams and rivers. She did not know why they did the strange things that they did, but they were always busy, always doing something. Though this man looked like a miner, dressed like a miner, smelled like a miner, he seemed to spend most of his time sitting in the sun, doing just about nothing. Sometimes he stared at a small rectangular object for hours at a time; sometimes he seemed to be moving a stick, as if making marks on a different rectangular object. And sometimes he just sat and stared, watching his mule graze in the meadow, studying the surface of the lake, the mountains that surrounded it.

Once, early in the morning, she watched him sit quietly, staring at a doe and fawn that grazed in the meadow. At first, she thought he was stalking the deer, but he did not move, did not approach the animals. At last, when the wind shifted, the deer caught his scent and bounded away. He made no move to chase them.

At night, he slept in a canvas tent beside the lake. In the early morning, he fished in the lake's cool waters. Sometimes he cooked biscuits—she could smell the tantalizing aroma drifting across the lake. On the second night he was there, she sneaked into his camp. By the remains of his campfire, she found a few broken and burned pieces of biscuit, which she devoured. Bread was a rare treat, and she relished it when she found it. The rectangular things that the man stared at each day were hidden inside the canvas tent, protected from her curiosity. She slipped away, still curious.

Sarah was twelve years old, a well-armed, young savage. She wore a knife at her belt and carried her lariat, her bow, and a quiver filled with arrows slung over one shoulder. In warm weather, she wore moccasins and a pair of men's trousers, cut off at the knee and held up with suspenders. She liked the trousers because she could carry stones in the pockets. In cold weather, she wore moccasins, long trousers, and a rabbit-skin cape, a gift from Malila.

She knew the ways of the wolves. She knew something of the ways of Indians, for she had continued to visit Malila over the years. Learning to speak the Miwok language had satisfied some urge within her that the language of the wolves had not. But though she visited the Indians and watched the white men, she always returned to the wolf pack. They were her family. Beka remained her frequent companion, following the girl on many of her long journeys away from the pack.

Sarah stretched in the sun, lazy and warm. She and Beka had gone hunting at dawn. One of her arrows had brought down a fat marmot. She and Beka had breakfasted on its warm flesh. Then Sarah had come to the lake to see what the man was doing. Beka, not sharing Sarah's fascination with the human who camped by the lake, had wandered off to explore, while Sarah continued to watch the man.

He was moving the stick again—for most of the morning he had alternated periods of staring at the lake with bouts of scribbling.

MAX SAT ON a broad granite slab beside the lake, writing a letter to Audrey North. "I have fled to the mountains," he wrote, "escaping the eager, young men who come to the gold fields with copies of my book tucked under their arms. Everywhere I go, I see young men dressed in sensible canvas trousers and cotton shirts, carrying precisely the make of shovel and pick and canteen I recommended, with their scarves tied just like the miner in the sketch on page 5 of *A Young Man's Guide to Gold Fields.* I know that if I were to look in their packs, I would find all the items from the checklist on page 45 of *A Young Man's Guide to Gold Fields.*

"They are all dreadfully earnest young men. They make me feel quite ancient and creaky. I feel quite spry for my advanced age of forty-one, but they treat me with such deference, asking my advice on any number of things that I have no business advising them on. I confess, they bring out the worst in me. A sweet-faced young fellow asked me the other day which hotel I would recommend, and I sent him to one right next to the lodge of E Clampus Vitus, where the sound of the Clampers' drunken hilarity was sure to keep him up all hours. Damned if he didn't come back the next day to thank me. He had, it seemed, joined the Clampers and had a fabulous time. Ah, for the stamina of youth.

"How strange it is to have struck paydirt in a profession I would have thought even chancier than mining. In your last letter, you protested that my book would have succeeded without your assistance. Though I hesitate to question your expertise in the area of publishing, I beg to differ. Without your encouragement and assistance, I would still be writing an occasional article for the *Nevada City Gazette.* If you hadn't shown my essay to your editor, I would certainly never have written a book that has garnered me more gold than all my mining efforts.

"I have begun work on my next book—at least that is the excuse I have given for fleeing the questionable civilization of Selby Flat and camping at this remote lake. It is a beautiful spot. The other morning, I sketched a doe and her fawn, grazing not one hundred yards from my tent. So far, I have spent more time fishing and sketching than I have writing, but I have great hopes. It seems to me that writing is a bit like prospecting in that regard: One must always have great hopes."

Max stopped there, putting his pen down. He leaned back on the sun-warmed granite, contemplating the play of light on the water of the lake. The morning mist had burned away while he had been writing. The still blue waters of the lake reflected the mountains and the pines. It was time to be moving.

He had decided to hike around the lake to reach the bare granite slopes on the far side. From that location, he wanted to sketch his camp, a lonely tent beneath towering pines. Besides, he thought that the fishing might be better there. So he packed his fishing pole and his notebook in a rucksack, put on his hat, and set out around the lake.

Halfway around the lake, the granite slope rose to a sheer cliff. Here and there on the cliff face, bushes and trees clung to cracks and ledges, forming patches of green and brown against the gray of the stone.

A dense thicket of thorny bushes grew at the base of the cliff, leaving a narrow patch of marshy ground at the edge of the lake. Max had the choice of picking his way through the brambles or squelching through the mud. He chose the mud near his chosen path was a patch of broken branches where some large animal had blundered through the bushes.

His boots sank in the mud and he could feel cold lake water seeping in through the seams. The bushes leaned out toward the water and he had to step carefully over the branches. It was slow and unpleasant and he was wondering if he had made the right choice when he reached a dead end. There, the bushes grew down to the water's edge, forming a thorny barrier to further progress. He could try to hack his way through brambles, he could go for a swim, or he could turn back. He was considering these options when he heard the sound of a large animal crashing through the brush behind him.

Startled, he turned to face the sound. A grizzly, a beast with a reputation for a ferocious and unpredictable nature, burst from the bushes and glared at Max with angry, red-rimmed eyes. The animal stood by the lakeshore, blocking Max's retreat to his campsite.

Max backed away until the barrier of bushes made further retreat impossible. There, he froze, hoping the bear would return to the bushes from which it had come. He had no rifle, no pistol at his side.

Staring at the bear, he remembered what he had

written in the *Young Man's Guide.* He had advised would-be miners against carrying firearms. "A pistol seems like a useful weapon," he had written. "That is, it seems useful until you bet your life on it. Then the persnickety thing misses fire, blows up in your hand, or sends its bullet a country mile to one side of target. A beginning marksman can hit a target with a pistol—as long as the target is at least the size of a barn and the marksman is no more than ten paces away. As for the rifle, it can be a fine weapon in the right hands. If you're handy with a rifle, you already know that. Mine aren't the right hands. If you're a city-bred fellow, yours may not be the right hands either. More greenhorns end up shooting themselves in the foot with their newly acquired rifle than ever hold off a ravaging wolf or a charging bear."

It was good advice, he thought. He stood by that advice. It was fine advice for all the young men who were coming west. But as a man who had been in the West for some time, he wished he had not followed that advice.

The bear reared onto its hind legs, roaring a challenge to the puny man who had disturbed its rest. As the beast moved, Max saw the dark slash of an unhealed wound in its powerful shoulder. The animal had been injured. Probably, Max thought, by some fool of a greenhorn who had armed himself, not following Max's advice. Now the animal was wounded and angry, and Max had, unwittingly, disturbed its rest.

FROM A LEDGE no more than fifteen feet above Max's head, Sarah watched the man with interest. She stood on the leaning, twisted trunk of a pine tree that had managed to take root in a crack in the granite. Her back was braced against the rock. She had followed

Max around the lake, taking cover behind boulders and brush, moving as silently as a mountain cat.

From this vantage point, Sarah had watched with amazement as Max blundered past the sleeping grizzly. The man was as foolish as a pup just out of the den. How could he be unaware that a wounded bear was sleeping nearby? The air reeked of bear and of blood. The bushes had been broken where the bear had barged through them. Was he half-asleep to miss these warning signs?

In the wilderness, such inattention usually resulted in death. But Sarah was curious about Max. If she did not rescue him, that curiosity would never be satisfied.

When the bear reared, he was just below Sarah. Before the animal could drop to all fours and charge the man, Sarah tossed her lariat. The loop of rope settled over the grizzly's mighty shoulders, tightening as the bear pulled against it. Sarah had looped the end of the lariat around the trunk of the pine tree, knotting it securely in place.

Feeling the pressure of the rope around his shoulders, the bear roared again and lunged against the restraint. The pine creaked, but held for the moment. The lariat, a stout cord braided of seven strands of buckskin, held firm for a moment.

The bear lunged again, throwing the entire weight of his body against the rope. The rope held, but the pine tree to which it was secured did not. The tree's roots were shallow, and the bear's lunge pulled it free of the cliff and sent it crashing down into the bushes below.

Sarah, feeling the trunk give way beneath her feet in the instant before it fell, leapt to one side, finding a foothold on another ledge. From there, she took in the situation at a glance. The grizzly was facing away from her, offering no good targets for her arrows.

The man was staring up at her. His hands were empty. It was that, in the end, that saved him. If he had lifted a rifle to fire at the bear, she would have left him to his fate. She did not like white men and their killing sticks. But he had no rifle.

The bear was biting at the rope that bound him. As Sarah watched, the strands of leather parted, giving way beneath his jaws. In a moment, the bear would be free. Then he would reach the man and crush him with a single blow.

Before that could happen, Sarah called to the bear in the language of Malila's people. "Hey, Grandfather, you foolish bear, leave that man." From her pocket, she snatched up a stone and hurled it at the bear, striking the animal square in the head. "Fight me. I am the mightiest of the wolves. I am here to do battle with you."

The bear shook his head, angered by the blow. He turned away from Max, searching for the source of the rock and the shouting. Sarah waved her arms.

MAX WATCHED IN awe. A slip of a girl, no more than a dozen years old, taunted the grizzly. An extraordinary girl—lithe and graceful, was dancing on a ledge so small that many men would have found it a terrifying place to stand still. Sunlight glistened on her golden skin, revealing well-developed muscles. Her hair was a halo of red-gold curls, a burst of glory against the gray granite.

As Max stared, she hurled another stone at the bear, laughing and shouting as the beast clawed at the cliff face, reaching up with powerful paws to swat at this pest. His blows fell just inches below her dancing feet.

The pine tree had fallen at the foot of the cliff. Scrambling with his hind feet, the grizzly gained a foothold on the fallen tree and lunged upward, reaching the ledge where the girl stood. But she was no longer there. An instant before the bear's paw swept across the ledge, she had stepped upward to a tiny foothold a few feet higher than the ledge. With one foot on the rock and one arm hooked around the branch of a bush that clung to the cliff, she was lifting her bow, stringing an arrow. At the same time, the bear was gathering himself to lunge again.

The girl released her arrow, which embedded itself in the animal's shoulder. The bear roared, biting at the arrow, then swatting at the cliff with its mighty paws. The girl, standing just beyond the bear's reach, calmly strung another arrow.

Again, she lifted her bow and made a clean shot to the animal's right eye from a distance of a few feet. The bear roared again. Pawing at its eye, the beast fell backward away from the cliff.

Max heard bushes snap as the bear's body crashed into the thicket. The sound of the crash echoed from the cliff face.

Then there was silence. In the sudden hush, Max stared up at the girl on the cliff. She met his eyes, regarding him with steady confidence.

"Hello," Max called, his voice uncertain. "Who are you?"

Still, the girl regarded him steadily, her brow furrowed slightly as if trying to make sense of his words. Then she glanced downward and made a growling, barking noise. Without looking at Max, she stepped down to the lower ledge, then dropped from his view behind the bushes.

A warbler trilled in the sudden silence. In the lake, a fish jumped, landing with a splash. Insects buzzed in the bushes. Max took a deep breath, drawing sweet air into his lungs. For a moment, he wondered if the whole incident could have been his imagination. Had he somehow dreamed of a savage girl who had rescued him from death? Moving slowly, Max made his way through the bushes to the foot of the cliff.

SARAH CLIMBED DOWN from the cliff to meet Beka, who had returned to the lake in time to see the grizzly fall. Now, Sarah thought, she and Beka would feast on grizzly meat. They could summon the pack to join the feast, for this carcass could provide enough meat for all.

She heard the man coming through the bushes toward the fallen bear, as clumsy as a bear himself. Would the man fight for a possession of the carcass? She didn't think so. He would not, she thought, stand a chance against the weakest member of the pack.

She dropped to the ground by the great body of the bear. Matter-of-factly, she strode to the animal's head to reclaim the arrows that were buried deep in the animal's shoulder and eye. She tugged them free, then joined Beka, who was ripping at the bear's exposed belly. Sarah drew her knife and used the sharp blade to slit open the abdominal cavity. She would skin the beast later and take the hide to Malila. The Indian woman would like that. While Beka chewed on the intestines, Sarah sliced off a fist-sized piece of the bear's liver.

When Max came through the bushes, that is how he found his rescuing angel. She was sitting on the bear's shaggy haunch, happily gnawing on a piece of liver. Her face and hands and naked chest were smeared with fresh blood. At her feet, a wolf was tearing at intestines dragged from the bear's belly. The air reeked of blood and death.

As Max stepped into sight, both the girl and the wolf stopped their feeding. The wolf stared at him.

Sarah dropped her free hand to her knife and studied him with eyes as blue as the mountain lake.

Max stood very still. He had to find out who this girl was. "I'm Max," he said to Sarah. "Who are you?"

Sarah stared at the man. She didn't understand his words, but she knew that he was speaking in words. Rather than growling to warn him off, she spoke to him in Malila's language. "This kill is mine. If you are hungry, you may eat, but you may not carry any meat away. The kill belongs to my pack."

Beka had risen to her feet, her eyes fixed on the man. She began to growl low in her throat, warning the man to leave now. Sarah slid off her perch on the boulder and squatted by the wolf, placing a hand on the animal's head. The growling subsided.

"I'll go back to camp," Max said, feeling foolish. "Why don't you stop by? I'll make biscuits." He backed away, keeping his face to the strange pair until the bushes hid them from sight.

BACK AT CAMP, the incident seemed like a nightmare. A terrifying bear, a rescuing angel, a savage wolf. But it was a dream that echoed Socks's vision of many years before. A savage girl and her wolf companion, living far from civilization.

Max washed the cuts and scratches he had gotten from the bushes. He felt cold, even after he took off his wet boots, pulled on dry socks, put on his buckskin jacket. He sat on the granite slab beside the lake, warming himself in the sun. When his hands finally stopped shaking, he took up his pencil and drew the image that had burned itself into his mind.

He drew a young girl, dancing on a tiny ledge. Her face was beautiful, the features delicate and aristocratic. She was on the edge of puberty, her naked breasts just beginning to bud, her youthful body starting to take on a woman's curves. A smiling girl, innocent and free. Below her, a snarling bear reached up, striving to swat the girl from her perch, to crush that young body. The beast's curving claws glinted in the sun. The finished picture made Max shiver again, remembering that moment when it all seemed hopeless.

He turned the page and drew again. This time, the bear lay fallen in the bushes. He drew the savage bear's claws, harmless now. The mighty paws were still; the beast had been conquered. The girl sat on the beast's shaggy side, as comfortable as a lady in her drawing room. Her ragged trousers showed her muscular legs. The dark liver in her hand dripped blood onto her naked chest. But she was not concerned with her lack of clothing; she was not bothered by the blood. She was smiling. Innocent and triumphant.

He looked up from his second sketch and saw the wild girl, silently watching him from a few feet away. Her wolf sat at her feet.

"Hello," Max said, setting the notebook down on the rock. She stepped up onto the granite slab and came closer, studying his face. When she was just a foot away, she squatted beside him, still staring at his face. Her nostrils flared as she inhaled his scent.

He was fighting the urge to get up and move away from her intense scrutiny when she looked down at the notebook. She picked it up, squinting at the sketch.

"That's you," he said, feeling foolish but knowing he had to say something.

For the next hour, Max was subjected to a thorough inspection. The girl examined his notebook, his pencil, his wet boots, his socks, his clothing. When he showed her how the buttons on his shirt worked, she was delighted and spent several minutes buttoning and unbuttoning his cuffs. She tugged on his hair, comparing the color and texture to her own.

Throughout all this, the wolf watched, lounging at ease at the base of the granite slab while Max was poked and prodded. The girl had no sense of personal boundaries. She tugged on his hair and collar, sniffed his hands, and stood entirely too close for Max's comfort. But he put up with these indignities.

And he studied her in return. Though he felt some qualms about being quite so close to a nearly naked girl, he put them aside. She seemed so comfortable that after a time he almost forgot her lack of clothes.

While she inspected his person and his possessions, he talked with her. She talked back in some kind of guttural babble. An Indian language, he thought. At first, she seemed frustrated that he could not understand her. Finally, she accepted that he did not and seemed willing—perhaps even eager—to learn his language.

She reached out a grimy hand and touched his bearded cheek. She frowned, then touched her own cheek. In her guttural language, she asked something.

"This is my beard," he said. "You don't have a beard."

"Beard," she repeated, stroking his cheek again. "Beard."

"That's right." He smiled and nodded. Then he touched his hair. "Hair." He stroked her curls. "Hair."

"Hair," she repeated, touching her curls, his hair.

Then he tapped his chest. "Max," he said. "I'm Max."

She patted his chest. "Max," she said. She patted her own chest. "Max," she said.

"No. I'm Max." He touched his chest again. "Max."

He tapped his head, his arm, his foot, repeating each time. "Max." Then he pointed at her. "What is your name?"

SARAH STARED AT the man called Max. She pointed to herself. "Sarah," she said. That was what her Mama had called her, what Malila called her now. Malila told her it was a name of great power.

The man's eyes widened. "Sarah," he said. "Sarah McKensie." He said a great many words then, too fast for her to repeat. He was smiling and yet his eyes were wet with tears. He took her hand and held it tightly.

After talking for some time, he released her hand. He said something she didn't understand and beckoned to her. She understood his gesture and followed him to his campsite. Beka hung back, licking her lips nervously, but Sarah encouraged her to follow. After a time, she did, making sure that Sarah was always between her and the man.

Sarah watched Max build a fire and make dinner. She wasn't hungry—she had eaten her fill of bear meat that afternoon. But the strange foods intrigued her. She would not eat the salt pork, but she ate three biscuits with great enthusiasm. She gave the salt pork to Beka, who devoured it, keeping a watchful eye on Max while she ate.

As Sarah ate her fourth biscuit, Beka snuffled in her ear, then moved away. She returned a moment later, then moved away again. Her motions indicated that she was leaving, going to find the pack. Sarah rubbed Beka's ears, an acknowledgment that she understood. The she-wolf left, but Sarah stayed with Max. She was interested in this man, unwilling to leave just yet.

As the sun set, the air grew chilly. Max went to his tent and came back with a red shirt that had seen better days. He handed it to her and demonstrated in pantomime how to put it on. She took the garment and studied it. She rubbed the cloth against her cheek. Soft and warm—she liked that.

With his help, she put her hands into the sleeves. He pulled the collar around her neck and buttoned a few buttons. The sleeves were far too long, and the shirt billowed around her, with enough space inside for another girl her size.

She shook her arms, watching the loose ends of the sleeves flop around, and laughed. She stood and spun around, letting the sleeves fly and the shirt billow. Such a silly garment. When she stopped spinning, Max beckoned her to him and rolled up the sleeves so they did not get in her way. He fastened her belt on top of the shirt. Sarah stroked the worn flannel, enjoying its warmth against her skin.

It was dark when Sarah heard Rolon's voice, leading a chorus of howls. Beka had led the pack to the bear's carcass. Sarah stood up and responded with a howl that echoed across the lake.

Max shivered, staring at the girl. The firelight touched the delicate features of her face with crimson; her voice was that of a wild animal. She smiled at him and said something in the guttural language she had spoken when he met her at the bear carcass.

He gazed into the darkness, where the wolves howled. She touched his shoulder as if to reassure him, to tell him there was no cause to worry. And she left him, running into the night.

Max leapt to his feet, starting after her. But she had disappeared into the darkness before he could take two steps. "Sarah!" he called after her. "Sarah! Come back!"

The banshee chorus of wolves was the only answer he received.

12

THE SAVAGE LIFE

"Training is everything. The peach was once a bitter almond; cauliflower is nothing but a cabbage with a college education."

—Mark Twain

MAX STAYED UP BY THE FIRE FOR HOURS, FEEDING THE FLAMES and listening in the darkness, hoping that Sarah would return. The frogs sang in the marsh by the lake. Bats swooped low over the water, feeding on insects. At last, the half-moon rose, casting a glowing path of silver on the surface of the lake.

The girl had not come back. Max retired to his tent, where he spent a restless night.

He was frying flapjacks for breakfast when the girl returned, carrying a haunch of bear meat. She greeted him with a radiant smile. The angelic beauty of her delicate features contrasted sharply with the bloody meat that she carried.

He accepted her gift of meat, motioning her to sit by the fire. She stayed with him that morning and ate his flapjacks with great gusto. When he fried up some of the bear meat, she sampled the cooked meat carefully.

Throughout breakfast—and throughout the rest of the morning—Max taught her English. She was a quick student, remembering the words he had taught her on the previous day and adding to that vocabulary eagerly.

Behind those angelic blue eyes was a sharp intelligence, Max realized, and a hunger for knowledge. In the early afternoon, she left him, indicating with gestures that she would be back. She returned in the late afternoon with a freshly killed rabbit. Her wolf trotted along behind her and shared in the rabbit, devouring the intestines while they dined on the meat, roasted over the fire. Max gave her another language lesson, during and after dinner. When the sun set, she and the wolf left him, summoned by a chorus of howls.

Over the next few weeks, this became their pattern. She arrived each morning with gifts of fresh game and edible wild plants. Sometimes her wolf was with her; sometimes she was alone. He cooked for her—she had a passion for biscuits and flapjacks, and she came to tolerate cooked meat, though she preferred to eat it raw. He taught her English, expanding her vocabulary from nouns to verbs and helping her construct short sentences. "This is a tree." "I am hungry."

He worked to teach her concepts as well as words. The knife, the lariat, Max's cooking fork—these were all tools. This is my knife; this is your knife.

He had so many questions for her. How have you survived for all these years in the wilderness? Why haven't you made contact with anyone before now? Where did you get your clothes, your weapons? She could not understand his questions yet. But given time, he was confident that she would understand him.

At first, she was wary around him, keeping an eye on his every move, always alert. Her wolf—Beka was the animal's name—was also watchful.

But after a time, both she and Beka began to relax. On the third day, Beka accepted a biscuit when he offered it, and by the end of the week she leaned her big head toward him so that he could rub her ears. Between lessons, Sarah and Beka would play in the grass, chasing one another in a game that looked very much like tag.

The first time one of their games ended in a wrestling match, Max was horrified. Sarah and the wolf were rolling in the grass, growling ferociously. Beka's teeth flashed in the sun as she snapped at the girl, but somehow, miraculously, the girl's hands were always out of reach when those cruel jaws snapped shut.

"Sarah!" Max shouted, grabbing a stick from the pile of firewood, a club that he could use to beat the wolf and drive her away from the girl. "Beka!"

The two stopped their play—for it was nothing more than that—and stared at him. He stopped where he was, holding his club and frowning.

"Oh," he said. "You're just playing."

"Playing," Sarah agreed. She was sitting beside Beka, leaning against the wolf. As Max watched, she reached under the wolf's chest and grabbed a paw. With a quick movement, Sarah flung her weight against the wolf's shoulder, toppling Beka. The game was on again.

Sometimes, when lessons were done, Max sketched Sarah. Once, on a long sunny afternoon, as she and Beka napped in the meadow, he sketched the two of them. Sarah curled up in sleep, knees drawn to forehead, arms wrapped around knees, feet tucked close to buttocks. Beside her, Beka lay at ease, her head leaning against the girl's leg, her paws twitching as if she were running in her sleep.

Sarah's hands, clasped around her knees, were so small, so delicate. There was a thin line of dirt beneath each broken fingernail. Three scars, spaced about as far apart as Beka's teeth, marked the back of her left hand—souvenirs, he suspected, from a play fight that had been too rough. An assortment of cuts and scratches decorated her knuckles, the inevitable consequences of an active life. A scrape on one hand from climbing the cliff; a cut on the other from a fish-hook (he had taught her to fish).

Max remembered a hot summer night, many years ago. He had been sitting on the porch with his wife. His daughter, just five years old, had fallen asleep, half-sprawled across his lap. Sweet Nell—awake, she was all arms and legs, elbows and knees, a noisy blur, always in motion. Asleep, she grew soft, rounded, her breath coming and going as quietly as the wind in the trees.

He wished he had drawn her then. But he had not known how precious that time was. That knowledge had come too late.

A breeze from the lake blew a strand of hair across Sarah's face. Max reached out to smooth it back. Before he could touch her face, her eyes were open, watching him. Relaxed, but always alert.

He glanced at Beka. The wolf was watching him, too.

He smiled, knowing that however small and frail she looked, Sarah was far from helpless. "Sleep," he said.

"Sleep," she repeated softly.

SARAH FOUND THE language lessons both fascinating and tiring. She was eager to learn how to communicate with this strange man named Max.

As her language skills improved, he asked her about her past. How had she come to live among the wolves?

It was difficult to communicate abstract concepts. Max managed to get across the idea of "yesterday," but for Sarah all of the past was one long yesterday. Yesterday, she killed the bear. Yesterday, she was a pup. Yesterday, she suckled at the breast of her mother, Wauna.

One warm afternoon, they sat on the granite slab, looking across the lake, talking together as best they could. "Yesterday," Max said. "You lived with the wolves."

Sarah nodded.

"Yesterday before that," he said, "you lived with the wolves."

"Yes."

"And before that?"

"Many, many yesterdays," Sarah said. "With the wolves."

"Before that," he persisted. "Where did you live then?"

She frowned then, thinking of Mama and Papa. She felt a tension in her throat and her chest, as if a great hand were squeezing her heart. She shook her head. "I don't know."

He was studying her face, and she sensed a tension in him. After all the time they had spent together, she could read him as she could read the wolves in her pack. "I think you do know," Max said. He touched her hand. "Do you remember your mama? Tell me."

She growled then, pulling her hand free. She leapt from the sun-warmed granite and ran away. When Max called after her, she did not look back. She joined the pack, where no one would ask her about times past. Yesterday, and yesterday, and yesterday—they did not matter. That was done with. That was gone.

She curled up with Wauna and Yepa that night, sleeping between them, taking comfort in their warmth. She groomed her foster mother's thick fur, trying not to think about yesterday. That was over.

SARAH DID NOT return to Max's camp until sunset of the following day, appearing beside the fire when Max had all but despaired of seeing her again. "Hello,

Sarah," he said, looking up from the fire. He had decided that he would not push her to remember if she did not want to. "Are you hungry?"

She accepted the biscuits he offered, crouching by the fire and holding them tight in her hands. For a moment, she did not eat.

"Before the wolves," she said at last, "before the wolves, there was Mama. There was Papa. Then something bad." She used a word from Malila's language that meant "wicked, evil." "And I go with the wolves."

Max nodded, imagining little Sarah running away from the scene of her parents' murder, weeping and finding comfort among the wolves. He put his arm around her shoulders. She was trembling, and Max knew it wasn't from the cold. "Here now," he said soothingly. "You don't have to talk about it. You don't have to remember."

A week later, Max left the lake and returned to civilization. He had never intended to stay in the wilderness for as long as he had. He had used the last of his flour, the last of his oil, the last of his coffee. The nights were growing cold. He shivered in his bedroll, wondering where Sarah slept, how she kept warm as the nights grew longer.

"I must go soon," he told her one morning. "I want you to come with me."

"Where do you go?" she asked.

"Back to Selby Flat." He had, over the past week, prepared for this moment by telling her about Selby Flat. He had talked about Mrs. Selby, a woman like her mama, and about the wonderful foods that Mrs. Selby would make for her. Biscuits and bread and apple pie. He had talked about her aunt Audrey, who would be so glad to learn she was alive. It had been hard to come up with any other enticements. Sarah did not like clothing; she did not trust people. But he knew she liked biscuits and he thought she'd like Mrs. Selby and her aunt. "You'll see Mrs. Selby there. And your aunt will come and get you."

Sarah studied him. "Many people in Selby Flat," she said.

"That's right. Many white people like you. Will you come with me?"

She shook her head. "No." She offered no polite excuses, no explanation. Just a simple answer.

"Why not?"

She frowned, puzzled by his need for an explanation. It seemed so obvious. She had never been in a mining town, but she had seen many miners, studying them from hiding. She could imagine a place with many miners crowded together. Why leave the mountains to go somewhere crowded and dirty? "I do not like the mining town," she said.

"You need to be with your own kind," he told her. "You need to be with other people."

She stared at him, remembering the white men she had encountered before she met him. The man who shot Omuso for no reason. The brothers who had killed Malila's grandfather and assaulted her. Crazy men, who attacked without warning. "White people are dangerous," she said.

Max bit his lip, but did not reply for a moment. Watching his face, she thought he might agree with her. After all, he had come to the mountains alone. She thought that he had his doubts about white people, too.

"No," he mumbled. "No, you can't think that way. Some people are bad—but there are many good people. You must come with me. At least for a little while. You can always come back to the wolves."

Again, she shook her head, frowning. "I stay in the mountains."

"There are many things there that you will like," he said. "Mrs. Selby makes excellent biscuits. And apple pie like you've never tasted!"

She shook her head stubbornly. "I stay here," she said.

"No. You have to come with me." He talked a great deal then—about Selby Flat and her aunt and civilization. She did not understand all of the words he used, but she understood enough to know that he wanted her to go.

"Later," she told him.

She left not long after sunset. For a time, Max sat by the fire, watching the flames die to coals. Then he went to bed, where he tossed and turned, unable to sleep for wrestling with his conscience. He could not leave the child in the mountains alone. Yes, she thought she was happy, but it wasn't right. He would not be able to explain to Audrey that he had found Sarah and lost her again. She had to come with him. If he had to hog-tie her and sling her over the back of his mule, he'd take her back.

From a sheltered hollow by a granite boulder on the far side of the lake, Sarah watched Max's campfire die down. She leaned against the stone. It retained the heat it had absorbed during the day, warming her as it cooled in the night air.

She had sensed a change in Max when she refused to go with him. As he talked about Selby Flat, he had grown more and more tense. If he had been a wolf, she would have prepared for an attack.

In the morning, Max woke from uneasy dreams and crawled from his tent. Usually, Sarah was waiting for him, sitting on the granite slab by the lake. Today, there was no sign of her.

He spent the day waiting, alone. He wondered if something had happened to the girl. Or had she somehow guessed that he planned to take her against her will? After all, she had the wisdom of a wild creature.

The next day, he waited again. Sarah did not make an appearance. That second night, the weather turned cold. He woke to snow flurries. The meadow was dusted with white; the air was cold and crisp. Inside wool socks and leather boots, his feet were icy. He knew he could stay in the high altitudes no longer.

With a heavy heart, he loaded his gear onto the mule. "You know, Longfellow," he said to the mule. "I'd be happy if I could just see her again. That would be enough."

He left his camp, leading the mule. By the granite slab where he had spent many an afternoon, he paused, looking out over the lake. On the bare granite slopes of the distant shore stood a figure, a human figure. He recognized the red shirt he had given Sarah. As he watched, the figure waved, a gesture of farewell.

He waved back, his heart lightening. "Good-bye, Sarah!" he called across the lake. "I'll be back."

The mountains echoed his voice. "Good-bye . . . good-bye . . . good-bye." Smiling, he headed down the mountain.

SARAH WATCHED HIM go. She thought about what it would have been like to go with him, to travel among white men as one of them. She shook her head. Max told her that there were many good men, but she knew from experience that there were many bad men as well.

So she watched Max go, then turned away from the lake. She would rejoin the pack, return to her life among the wolves.

The pack had spent the summer ranging through its territory, hunting and raising the most recent litter of pups. When their travels took them near the lake,

Sarah had rejoined them for an evening's hunt. But when they had ranged far from the lake, she had hunted alone.

The wolves accepted Sarah's absence and welcomed her when she returned. Sometimes, wolves craved solitude. It was not unusual for a wolf to withdraw from its pack, traveling and hunting alone and then rejoining the group at a later date.

After Max returned to Selby Flat, Sarah traveled eastward, climbing higher into the mountains. On the second day, she picked up the pack's trail. Not far from the edge of the pack's territory, she found a boulder that had been scent-marked by several wolves. She recognized the scents of her packmates. By the intensity of the scents, she knew that they were less than a day's travel away.

She followed the trail, covering the ground at an easy lope and coming upon the pack while they rested in a sheltered hollow. There, her old friends greeted her with great enthusiasm. Wauna and Yepa wagged their tails furiously, grinning to show their pleasure. Wauna reared up and placed her front paws on Sarah's shoulders, bathing her foster daughter's face with a warm tongue. Dur, Ruana, and Istas romped around her like pups.

Wauna's latest litter—a trio of gangly pups—hung back at first. Sarah had spent so little time with the pack of late that they were shy with her as they would have been with any stranger. But she scratched their ears and played chase with them until they accepted her as a friend.

After the excitement of the first meeting was over, Sarah settled down with the pack. Within the hour, she noticed that relationships among some of the wolves were not as relaxed as they had been when she left. Dur, the beta male, was grooming a wound on his right paw—a small cut in the pad of his foot had become infected, inflamed.

Wolves, when stalking deer, select the weakest members of the herd for their prey. They are alert to any behavior that indicates weakness, and they exploit that weakness without mercy. The pack's survival depends on it.

Within the pack, wolves use that same awareness of weakness to determine when to challenge their packmates. A wolf that wants to move up in the pack hierarchy watches for the moment to attack, waiting until the wolf who is superior to him is ill or injured.

Sarah noticed that Marek was watching Dur bathe his injured paw. Marek was smiling the relaxed grin of a confident wolf, when he stood and stretched, his black fur shimmering in the sunshine. He strolled over to where Dur lay and stood so that his shadow fell across Dur's face, blocking the sun that warmed the beta wolf. From this position, Marek stared at Dur.

Dur lifted his head from his paw and growled at the lower-ranking wolf, pulling his lips back to show his teeth. The fur on the back of his neck rose, an indication that he was irritated by Marek's behavior. His message was clear: I'm warning you nicely. Back off.

But Marek did not look away. He continued to stare at Dur, taking a step closer so that he was looking down on the beta wolf.

The other members of the pack gathered, watching the confrontation. Sarah crouched beside Wauna, her hand on the she-wolf's back. Wauna licked her lips nervously, distressed by the inevitability of the battle. Marek would not back down, Sarah knew that. And she knew that Dur would not give up his position without a fight.

Dur snarled and shifted his weight, ready to stand up. At that moment, Marek lunged, knocking the beta wolf back down and snapping at Dur's throat. Dur, a seasoned fighter, met Marek's jaws with his own, and for a moment the two wolves fenced with open jaws, teeth clashing against teeth as each fought for the advantage. Dur moved quickly, and his teeth closed on Marek's right paw, a sharp bite intended to punish but not injure.

Marek jumped back, still facing Dur, angry but unhurt. Dur was on his feet, glaring at the younger wolf as Marek circled, seeking to attack from another angle. For a moment, Dur hesitated. He licked his lips. His gums were bleeding where Marek's teeth had cut them.

In the wolf pack, most battles for dominance were won and lost without bloodshed. It was to the pack's advantage to minimize bloody battles among its members. A family cannot survive if the members are constantly battling. An injury to a member weakens the pack as a whole. The pack needs its members to be healthy and strong, ready to hunt so that the pack can thrive.

A subordinate wolf tests the will of the wolf above him in the hierarchy in many ways. If the dominant wolf is not confident and strong, the rivalry will intensify until the subordinate wolf is constantly testing the dominant animal. By the time the challenge escalates to a battle, both wolves know who will win. The wolves fight, but the fight is quickly over. The combatants may be bitten and bruised, but the injuries are rarely serious. The loser submits to the winner, acknowledging the victor's supremacy. And the pack hierarchy is established once again.

Dur had chosen to warn the younger wolf, failing to recognize how serious the threat to his position had become. Dur could have broken the younger wolf's leg, but he had chosen not to weaken the pack. The beta wolf had made a choice. This choice, Sarah realized, would not serve him well.

It was not fair—but the wolf pack did not recognize the human concept of fair play. Two wolves would fight and one would win. The winner might be stronger or faster or smarter or simply more ruthless. The reason did not matter. One wolf lost; one wolf won.

Marek rushed in without warning, striking with his shoulder to Dur's left side. To stay on his feet, Dur had to take the full force of the charge on his injured foot. The first time that black wolf tried this maneuver, Dur met the charging wolf with snapping teeth. He got a grip on Marek's neck, but the black wolf tore free.

Marek circled. Sarah could smell blood, could see blood wetting the fur at Marek's neck. But the black wolf ignored the injury, circling to Dur's left side. The beta wolf turned as Marek circled, but his injured foot made him slow, too slow to keep up.

Marek lunged again, striking with his shoulder. Dur stumbled, but recovered, snapping as the black wolf leapt away.

Both animals were growling, their hackles bristling. Their eyes were locked in the intimate gaze of battle, neither willing to surrender, neither willing to acknowledge weakness. Sarah caught a flicker of fear in Dur's eyes, the realization that he had made a mistake.

A third time Marek lunged, as if he planned to strike Dur with his shoulder again. Dur braced himself for the impact. But Marek, for all his bullying ways, was a clever fighter. At the last moment, he darted in low, snapping at Dur's uninjured leg, connecting with a brutal bite that tore the flesh to the bone.

Marek jumped away, then charged again, bowling Dur over and pinning him, jaws on his throat, choking him. The black wolf shook his opponent, tearing the fur and skin. Sarah felt a spray of hot blood on her cheek.

Dur shrieked in pain. His tail was between his legs. His ears were flattened to his head, a signal of submission. His lips, no longer snarling, were pulled back in a fear face, a grinning mask of submission.

At last, Marek stopped his punishment. He stood over the fallen wolf, glaring down at him. Then, turning away, Marek shook himself. He settled down in the sunny spot where Dur had been sleeping and made himself comfortable.

Dur lay where he had fallen, whining low in his throat with each breath. Wauna went to him, touching her muzzle to his in a gesture of greeting, then grooming his face with a comforting tongue. Sarah joined her foster mother, stroking the fallen wolf, comforting him. From his place in the sun, Marek, the new beta wolf, grinned.

13

LITTLE LOST LAMB

"Always acknowledge a fault frankly. This will throw those in authority off their guard and give you opportunity to commit more."

—Mark Twain

"EAT UP, MAX," MRS. SELBY URGED. "YOU NEED SOME MEAT ON those bones of yours."

Max accepted another helping of potatoes and grilled onions, another pickle, another slice of fresh-baked bread—all foods he had sorely missed during his time in the mountains. He washed down a salty bite of pickle with beer and considered his heaping plate. He would have to be careful, or he wouldn't have room for dessert. Mrs. Selby had promised him apple pie.

It was a weekday afternoon, and the dining room was nearly empty. Most men were out working their claims. Max had arrived just a few hours before, and Mrs. Selby had insisted on feeding him right away, not waiting for dinnertime to roll around.

"Where have you been all this time, Max?" Mrs. Selby asked. "Mr. Selby and I were wondering where you'd gotten to."

Max glanced across the room at Mr. Selby. He rather doubted that Mr. Selby had given Max's whereabouts a moment's thought. Mr. Selby had been very busy. Over the summer, he had built a fine addition to the hotel, a dining room with a wooden floor and real glass windows, transported from Sacramento at great expense.

Selby's was the finest hotel this side of Nevada City. The Selbys brewed their own beer, grew fresh vegetables in an extensive kitchen garden, brought cattle in from the ranches near Sacramento, and generally did their best to bring civilization to the gold fields.

Businesses in the hills of California usually didn't last long. The gold fields were a place of rapid change; the get-rich-quick mentality of the miners affected the surrounding businessmen. Towns burned in a night and were rebuilt in a month. The average hotel was thrown together in a week or so, remained in business for a month or two, maybe even a year, then folded when the owner left for richer pickings.

Thanks to Mrs. Selby's influence, Selby's Hotel was an exception, a rock in shifting sands. Max was delighted to be able to return to the calico-draped barroom, to admire the new dining room.

"I was up in the mountains, sketching, camping beside a lake," he said. "Looking for solitude and a good place to fish." He studied Mrs. Selby's motherly face. He hadn't told anyone of his meeting with Sarah. Now that he was back in the mining towns, the encounter seemed dreamlike, unreal. He knew that Mrs. Selby would be happy that Sarah was alive—but upset that the child had not come to her motherly arms. He hesitated, then continued. "I found a little bit more than that."

"What did you find, Max?" Mrs. Selby seated herself comfortably in the chair across from him, obviously anticipating a good story.

Max took his sketch pad from his saddlebag and opened it to a sketch of Sarah, sitting by the lake and sharpening her knife on a smooth stone. She was wearing his shirt with the cuffs rolled up and her pair of cut-off trousers. Her legs were bare.

Mrs. Selby frowned at the sketch and then at Max. "An Indian girl without enough clothing to cover herself? I thought better of you, Max."

"Look at her face," Max said quietly. "And her hair—it's the color of burnished copper. She's no Indian. She's a white girl living in the mountains with the wolves."

Mrs. Selby studied the sketch again, then stared at Max, her eyes wide. "Sarah McKensie," she murmured.

Max shrugged. "She came out of the mountains and saved me from the biggest grizzly you've ever seen. Before I started teaching her, the only words of English she knew were Mama and Papa."

"Where is she?" Mrs. Selby scrutinized him as if he might be hiding the girl in his pocket.

"Last I saw her, she was waving good-bye from the far side of the lake."

"You left her there? Alone in the mountains? The poor little lost lamb." Mrs. Selby was almost in tears.

"She didn't want to come back with me. The only way I could have brought her back was if I'd hog-tied her and dragged her back. And I suspect I would have been the one who ended up hog-tied. I tell you, she may be lost, but she's no lamb."

"Why? Why wouldn't she come back?"

"She doesn't seem to think much of people," Max said. "Can't say as I blame her, sometimes."

"I can't believe you left her up there," Mrs. Selby said again.

"Left who where?" Max glanced up. The tall man who had spoken was silhouetted in the light that shone through the open door. He stepped inside, and Max saw his face. Jasper Davis.

The man was looking quite prosperous. His boots were polished; his slouch hat was nearly new. He wore a black broadcloth vest over a clean cotton shirt that hadn't seen much wear, and a gold watch fob looped from his buttonhole to his vest pocket. Max expected that a fine gold watch was on the end of it. On Jasper's vest shone a silver star.

"Sheriff Davis!" Mrs. Selby was on her feet, holding her hands out to the man. "Max has found Sarah McKensie."

An expression flickered across Jasper's face—a mixture of fear, anger, and shock, quickly replaced by a look of determination. Max saw the determination and wondered if he'd imagined the fleeting expression that preceded it.

"You found her after all these years?" Jasper said.

"He found her and then he lost her again. He left her up in the mountains alone." Mrs. Selby shook her head, still looking at Max accusingly. "You have to save her, Sheriff. Can you get together a posse? With enough men . . ."

Jasper sat down at the table beside Max. "Tell me what happened."

Reluctantly, Max told them of his encounter with the grizzly, of meeting Sarah, of teaching her English, and of her refusal to return with him. He would not have chosen Jasper Davis as his confidant, but it seemed that he had no choice.

"We have to bring her back for her own good," Mrs. Selby insisted. "She'll freeze up there." Mrs. Selby pushed her chair away from Max, regarding him with horror. "For the life of me, I can't understand why you left her up there."

Max shook his head. He had convinced himself, during the long walk back to Selby Flat, that he had done the right thing. "You didn't see her. This is a child who can fight a grizzly and win. She's done just fine without any help for all these years."

"A child!" Mrs. Selby cried. "A little girl, alone in the wilderness."

"Not quite alone," Max said. "The wolf that followed her . . ."

"A wolf! You think that makes it better?" Mrs. Selby turned to Jasper. "Can you raise a posse?"

"A posse would scare the child so much she'll never come out of the hills." Jasper's voice was easy and soothing. "Yes, we have to rescue the child, but maybe me and Max should just mosey up there and bring her back." He glanced at Max. "What do you think?"

"She doesn't trust people," Max said.

"We can convince her," Jasper said. "We have to. I can't have it on my conscience that I left a child in the wilderness."

Max frowned. Jasper and Mrs. Selby were voicing concerns that had plagued him before he left the lake, concerns he had managed to dismiss. Looking at Mrs. Selby's sorrowful face, he felt guilty. Perhaps he had given up too soon.

"If you won't come with me, I'll go alone," Jasper said.

That decided Max. No matter what happened, it would be worse if he left Sarah to meet the sheriff alone. He was her friend; he couldn't do that. "Very well. I'll go with you."

"Maybe we can lure her out with one of Mrs. Selby's apple pies," Jasper smiled at Mrs. Selby. "Surely no child could resist that."

"The poor lamb," Mrs. Selby murmured.

AT THAT MOMENT, the poor lamb was chasing a deer. The deer was an old buck that ran slowly, favoring one leg.

Sarah ran with her packmates, glad to be with them

again, glad to join in the hunt. In the hunt, the wolf pack came together and worked as a unit, many animals with one purpose. When the pack gave chase, all disputes were forgotten. The wolves were united. Like dancers in a troupe, like musicians improvising a tune, they were working together, responding to one another, playing off each other.

Sarah ran, her nostrils filled with the scent of the deer. Yepa was at one side; Beka at the other. At a look from Rolon, Sarah fell back and took up a position by a sturdy oak, holding the loop of her lariat loosely in her hands, wrapping the other end around the tree. Like any good leader, Rolon knew how to use the strengths of his pack members. Now that Sarah was back, he was making use of a hunting strategy they had perfected together over the years. Sarah waited as Rolon and the others turned the deer, chasing the frightened animal toward her.

Panicked by the wolves at its heels, the buck did not hesitate to rush past Sarah. The hot scent of the animal's fear filled the air, mingling with the aroma of fresh blood. The buck was bleeding from many wounds, but he was running hard. Without Sarah's help, the wolves could still lose him.

As the buck passed her, she tossed the loop of the lariat neatly over his head. When he reached the end of the rope, his head jerked to a halt, but his body kept going, flipping in an ungainly somersault. His neck was broken even before the wolves closed in.

Rolon was the first wolf to tear at the fallen buck. That was his right. Wauna was behind him, and Sarah was just behind Wauna. Behind her came the others, growling beasts eager for the feast.

With her sharp knife, Sarah slit the buck's abdomen, a long deep cut that spilled a flood of blood and viscera onto the carpet of pine needles. While the wolves pulled at the mess, Sarah sliced out the liver and turned to leave the fray and eat in peace.

Marek blocked her way. Rather than tearing meat from the carcass, the black wolf had adopted a different strategy: He ambushed those who had successfully obtained choice bits of meat.

Sarah met his challenging stare with a steady gaze. She was not willing to give in to him.

Marek snarled, lips pulling back to reveal his teeth. His head was high; his ears were back; his dark eyes were fixed on her. His message was clear: I am your superior; you are my subordinate. Give me what I want, or I will punish you.

Sarah did not move, standing her ground and returning Marek's stare. In the past, she had sought to avoid conflict with him, choosing to flee rather than fight. But her time with Max had changed her in subtle ways. She knew that she was not a wolf; she was something else, something different. She did not know what she was, but she knew that she was strong; she was fierce. She had killed a grizzly. She would not submit to Marek's domination.

In her right hand, she held the coveted liver; in her left, she held her knife. When Marek sprang, she moved quickly, taking an action no wolf would have taken. Marek wanted her food. A wolf would respond to such an attack in one of two ways: abandon the food to the other wolf or fight to protect the food.

But Sarah took a third course. As Marek sprang, she threw the bloody liver, catching the black wolf full in the face. The disputed food became a weapon. The sticky organ meat clung to Marek's fur, temporarily blinding him. In that moment, Sarah jumped to one side.

Marek's leap carried him past Sarah. The black wolf collided with Rolon and Wauna while the alpha pair was feeding at the carcass. At the moment that Rolon and Wauna turned to chastise Marek for interrupting them, Sarah attacked, throwing her full weight against the blinded wolf and knocking him over. As he fell, he struck Yepa and Beka, and those wolves turned on him as well.

For just a moment, Sarah held Marek down, her knife pressed to his throat so he could feel the cold metal through his fur. Then she snatched up the liver and leapt clear of the conflict, leaving Marek facing the wrath of four wolves.

She sat in the branches of the oak and laughed as Rolon, Wauna, Yepa, and Beka trounced the black wolf.

THE NEXT DAY, Jasper and Max reached the lake where Max had met Sarah. The snow flurries had given way to cold rain and freezing sleet. The trip had been miserable, cold, and wet. Jasper didn't mind any of that. He whistled as they rode through the rain and chided Max for grumbling.

Jasper had done very well for himself over the years, using the money from the stagecoach robbery to establish legitimate businesses, to build himself up as a man of status and means. But the possibility that Sarah McKensie lived had preyed on his mind. The girl could destroy all that he had accomplished simply by identifying him as her parents' murderer. He had been so careful to eliminate anyone who could connect him with the stagecoach robbery. It seemed unfair that this child could still upset his otherwise flawless plans.

Now that Max had located the child, Jasper could settle the matter quite satisfactorily. He would kill the child—out of Max's view, if possible. If necessary, he could dispose of Max as well. Max was such a mild-mannered fellow; he didn't even carry a pistol. Jasper couldn't see the man putting up much of a fight. And he would have no trouble explaining Max's disappearance. Accidents happened in the high country. One way or the other, Jasper could settle this problem for good. So Jasper whistled and joked as they rode.

The rain had let up by the time they reached the lake. They made camp in the same spot Max had camped before. After they had set up camp, Max took Jasper to the place where Sarah had killed the grizzly.

The grizzly's bones had been scattered by the wolves, picked clean by coyotes and other scavengers. Sarah had taken the skin and the claws as gifts for Malila. Max found the bear's skull, still intact, at the bottom of the cliff.

"He was a big 'un," Jasper said in a respectful tone. "You say the girl killed him?"

"That's right. With a lariat and a bow and arrow."

Jasper nodded. "Mighty impressive," he said.

Back at camp, Max settled on the granite slab by the lake with his sketch pad. "We'd best stay here," he told Jasper. "If she comes looking for me, this is where she'll come."

"Fine. You stay put while I explore a bit," Jasper said. "Maybe I can find some sign of her." He left Max in camp and headed out around the lake.

If he spotted her when Max was out of sight, it would all be easy. Shoot her and hide the body. He would tell Max that he had shot at a deer, but missed.

Jasper picked his way carefully through the marshy meadow, heading toward the shore of the lake. Halfway to the shore, he glanced back at the camp. He had an unpleasant feeling that he was being watched, but Max was staring in the other direction, up into the mountains. Jasper shrugged and continued on his way.

SARAH WATCHED JASPER go.

She had been traveling with the pack when she had run across their camp of the previous night. She had recognized Max's scent—and she had recognized the scent of another man.

The other members of the pack sniffed the man scent and moved on, dismissing the trail as unimportant. But Sarah had lingered, and Beka lingered with her.

When Jasper had killed her parents, so long ago, Sarah had been a child, raised by human parents and no more attuned to her sense of smell than any other child. Back then, she could not have identified Jasper by his scent. But her years with the wolves had focused her attention on her sense of smell. By comparison with her packmates, her sense of smell was dull, but compared to any human's, it was remarkable. She could sniff the air and know that a doe and her yearling fawn were hiding in the brush, that a cougar was prowling nearby, that a badger was digging on the slope above the meadow (the scent of the animal mingling with the aroma of freshly dug soil).

A scent can stir memories that lie forgotten, awakening emotions associated with those memories. The scent of Jasper Davis stirred unfamiliar emotions in Sarah. She did not know why, but the scent of this man touched her with an inexplicable dread, a feeling of helplessness and terror. She was afraid; she wanted to run; she wanted to hide.

Beka nuzzled her face, puzzled by the fear that she smelled in Sarah's sweat. The she-wolf licked Sarah's face, trying to reassure the girl. Beka started away, following the pack. When Sarah did not follow, the wolf returned, circling her friend, staying close.

Sarah wanted to run, but she could not. This man, the man with the terrifying scent, was with her friend Max. Perhaps Max was his captive. Overcoming her fear, she followed their trail. Beka came with her.

At the lake, Sarah and Beka watched from concealment while the men made camp. The situation puzzled Sarah: Max did not seem to be frightened by the man; he seemed to be talking with him amiably enough. She watched them go to the place where she had killed the bear, then return to camp. When Jasper walked away from camp, she waited until he was out of sight. Then she crept to the edge of the granite slab where Max sat sketching, coming up behind him.

"Max," she said softly. Her heart was pounding. Even from there, she could smell Jasper's tobacco, catch the acrid scent of the man's sweat.

Max put down his pencil and turned to look at her. "Sarah," he said. "I came back to get you. I . . ."

"No," she said, interrupting him. "We must go. We must run away. That man . . ." She looked in the direction in which Jasper had gone. "Very bad." She searched her limited vocabulary for words that would convey her feelings. "Rotten," she said, a word that Max had applied to spoiled meat—bad-smelling and foul. She shook her head. "Dangerous." That was a word that Max had applied to rattlesnakes and cougars and grizzlies, all animals that could kill you.

"What are you talking about?" Max stared at her. "What's wrong?" He could see that her hands were trembling. Her face was pale, beneath its tan.

"Run away," she said. "Run and hide."

"Sarah, don't be afraid. You . . ."

"Run away!" she repeated. "Come." She came around the rock, reaching out. When he put his hand in hers, she grabbed it and pulled him down, so that he half jumped, half fell into the meadow beside her. Beka snuffled in his ear, greeting him properly. But Sarah had no time for that.

"Now!" She was pulling on his arm, trying to drag him away from the camp, away from the lake.

"Sarah, what are you doing? I . . ."

He and Beka followed her, not as fast as she would have liked, but at least they followed. She did not listen to his questions, did not stop to answer. She wanted him to leave this place and go with her to the safety of the hills.

They were at the edge of a stand of trees when Sarah gave his hand a mighty yank, causing him to fall full length on the grass. She fell flat beside him, just as the sharp crack of a rifle shot echoed from the granite slopes. "Hurry!" Sarah called. "Run away."

And she was gone, vanishing among the trees, faster than he could have followed if he wanted to. Beka was at her heels.

"I SAW THE WOLF," Jasper told Max that night by the campfire. "I saw you. I didn't even see the girl. You were running, and the wolf was coming right after you. I thought you were in trouble. Otherwise, I never would have fired. I was firing at the wolf."

"The wolf is Beka, Sarah's friend," Max said. His voice was flat.

Jasper studied Max's face, wondering whether the man believed him. Max was a hard fellow to read, Jasper decided.

"I know that now," Jasper muttered. "I'm glad I missed. Never thought I'd be glad to miss a wolf." He shook his head slowly, then put his head in his hands, covering his face. "The worst of it is—I've chased her away."

"You're right there," Max said slowly. "We won't be seeing her again."

Max didn't speak for a while, then Jasper felt Max's hand, patting his shoulder. "She'll be fine," Max said. "She belongs up here. She'll be fine."

Jasper nodded, dropping his hands as soon as he had composed his face into an expression of grim determination. "I'll have to tell Mrs. Selby what happened. That poor lady."

Jasper noticed that Max was watching the fire, giving Jasper a chance to compose himself. What a gentleman he was. Jasper liked that in a man. The more polite and sympathetic a man, the easier he was to fool.

"We'll just tell Mrs. Selby that we didn't find her," Max said. "That's close enough to the truth."

WHEN THEY RETURNED to Selby Flat, Max wrote a long letter to Audrey. He described Sarah, doing his best to be objective. He enclosed one of his many sketches of the girl. Sarah was healthy and smart and strong—but she ate with her hands and ran with wolves and was unlikely to be presentable in New England society anytime soon. She was a sweet-tempered child who could kill a grizzly and eat its liver raw.

"HE SAYS THAT my mother was a white woman named Rachel," Sarah told Malila. After she had left the lake, she had gone to seek out Malila's advice. They sat by the fire, sipping yerba buena tea. "He says that I have an aunt who misses me." She shook her head. "How can she miss me when I do not even know her?"

Malila watched Sarah quietly. The adolescent Indian girl that Sarah had rescued four years before had grown into a young woman, a healer in her own right. Though Malila had spent many hours with Sarah, the Indian still wondered what the girl was. A spirit of some sort? A human made of flesh and blood? Or a human touched with a powerful spirit that made her more than flesh and blood? Malila thought that the last answer might be right. She was a human girl, possessed by a powerful wild spirit.

"He came with another man." Sarah shivered. "A very bad man."

Malila nodded, accepting Sarah's assertion that the man was bad. "So you ran away."

"I had to," Sarah said. "He is too strong."

"But before that," Malila said softly. "You did not go with the white man called Max. Did you want to go?"

Sarah shrugged, a gesture she had picked up from Max. "I do not know. Part of me wanted to go."

"Why?"

Sarah looked uncomfortable, confused. "To find out . . ." She stopped, unable to say what she had wanted to find out.

"To find out who you are," Malila said, filling in the silence. "To find out where you belong."

"I belong with the pack," Sarah said.

"Sometimes," Malila said. "Sometimes you belong here with me. And sometimes, maybe you belong with these white people." Malila studied the girl, her riot of red-gold hair, her skin, pale beneath the tan.

Over the years, Malila had speculated about Sarah's relationship with the whites. Perhaps, Malila had thought, Sarah was the white people's wild spirit. When she ran away, the white people lost their connection to the wilderness. By losing her, they lost their balance, and that was why they tore up the land and poisoned the rivers and drove off the game. Perhaps if Sarah visited the whites, they would see how they fit in the world.

"I think you need to meet these white people to learn who you are," Malila said. "They are a part of you."

Sarah sipped her tea, gazing into the fire. Since she had rejoined the pack, she had been restless and uncertain. She was glad that she had not gone with Max, but she kept thinking about him. Her dreams were haunted by sights and sounds and smells of the past. She dreamed of her mama's face and her papa's hands, lifting her above his head. She dreamed of baking bread and frying bacon; of harmonica music and a woman singing lullabies. And when she woke, she was with the wolves.

Sarah shrugged again, sipping her tea and wondering what to do.

14

ANGEL IN THE WILDERNESS

"I have been on the verge of being an angel all my life, but it's never happened yet."

—Mark Twain

IN THE AUTUMN OF 1859, WAUNA WAS FOURTEEN YEARS OLD, A healthy old age for a wolf in the wild. She had been four years old, a mature wolf, when she met Rolon and formed the pack. She had reigned as alpha female for ten years, and during most of that time she had not faced a serious challenge from the lower-ranking females. There were, as in any pack, always younger wolves testing her leadership. But Wauna dealt with insubordination quickly and firmly. Consequently, insubordination was rare. The other wolves respected her. Under her guidance, the pack was stable, free of the turbulence and change found in packs where the alpha pair was constantly battling to retain dominance.

Sarah remembered her human mama as a dreamlike figure: a soft voice, a gentle touch. But the memory of her human mama wiping her face clean with a warm cloth had been overlaid by the memory of Wauna's tongue washing her. Wauna was her mother.

On a chilly night with the promise of snow in the air, Sarah fell asleep curled up between Yepa and Wauna, warm and content. Wauna had borne many pups since adopting Sarah. Those pups had grown to adulthood, becoming mature wolves. Some, like Yepa, had remained with the pack. Some had left the pack, striking out on their own. But Sarah, her little foundling, had never entirely grown up. In many ways, Sarah was still her pup. When Sarah was with the pack, she slept by her foster mother's side.

That night, Sarah woke in the darkness, feeling cold. She blinked sleepily, wondering what had woken her.

It was a cold, clear, moonless night. Overhead, the stars shone in the blackness of the night sky: brilliant, beautiful, and indifferent to the doings of the creatures who gazed up at them from the earth below. The Milky Way was a sweep of white across the center of the sky. Malila's people said that the Milky Way was a path through the sky, a trail to another world. When people died, they followed the path.

Gazing sleepily upward, Sarah snuggled closer to Wauna, seeking to share the mother wolf's warmth. Her foster mother did not move—did not shift in response to Sarah's movement, did not sigh in her sleep. The night seemed unnaturally still. Sarah could hear Yepa's soft breathing beside her, but she could not hear Wauna.

Sarah knew much of violent death—the death of deer at the fangs of the wolves, the death of wolves in battle. But this was something else: Wauna was asleep and would not wake. Sarah sat up and stroked Wauna's head. The mother wolf did not respond. Sarah whispered to Wauna, but the wolf's soft ears did not swivel to hear her.

Yepa woke when Sarah moved. The wolf watched as Sarah tried to rouse Wauna. Yepa sniffed Wauna's muzzle, washed the mother wolf's muzzle and face. When

Wauna did not respond, Yepa washed Sarah's face, tasting salty tears as the child wept for her foster mother.

YEPA BECAME THE alpha female. She had learned much from Wauna. Like Wauna, Yepa was calm and wise in her treatment of the younger females.

The wolves accepted Wauna's death quickly. They remembered the past, but they lived in the present, accepting each moment as it came. Sarah was blessed and cursed with the human propensity to remember the past and plan for the future. She mourned for Wauna, aching for the comfort the wolf had given her, grieving as she had for her human parents.

After Wauna's death, Sarah spent more time away from the pack, exploring the mountains with Beka at her side. She was restless, irritable. She was not a wolf—she knew that. But as long as Wauna was alive, she had felt as if she belonged with the pack, at her mother's side. Now she felt that she did not belong.

She was not a wolf. She spoke with the Indians, but she was not an Indian. She watched the whites—the miners and the emigrants who passed through the pack's territory—but she was not one of them, either. She had belonged with Wauna. She did not belong anywhere else. She thought about this as she and Beka roamed the mountains together.

WINTER CAME EARLY that year. Snow fell on the high peaks and in the lower elevations, catching weary emigrants who were late in crossing the Sierras. So it was that two sisters and their children huddled around a small fire. They had set out from Missouri in the spring with brave intentions, in a train of three wagons, with their husbands, their younger brother, and their three children.

On the Great Plains, Ellie's husband had died of a fever. When they were crossing the Rockies, their younger brother had died in an accident. A chain had snapped when they were hauling the wagon up a steep grade. The wagon had rolled back, crushing his legs. Despite Ellie's nursing, he had died of the wounds.

On the grueling trail down the brackish trickle known as Mary's River, Indians had attacked and stolen three oxen. Betsy's husband had intercepted an Indian arrow and had died of his wound a few painful days later. That left Betsy and Ellie and their three children.

The group had set forth from Missouri with great hope and too much baggage. They had left most of the baggage behind on the plains and in the desert, lightening the load by abandoning dishes and books and pots and pans and feather beds. Surprisingly, with their menfolk dead, the two women did not abandon hope.

Betsy and Ellie had been raised on the frontier—sturdy, stout-hearted women, disinclined to give up in the face of disaster. The two women, with their children, had abandoned all but one of their wagons. With Betsy leading the oxen and Ellie whipping them from behind, they brought that wagon across the Carson Desert and up the Truckee River canyon. At the lake where the Donner party had camped in the winter of 1846, two of the oxen had refused to go on. There, the women had abandoned their last wagon. Refusing to stay in that place of bad luck and past pain, they had packed their meager possessions on the back of the remaining two oxen.

They were at the top of Donner Pass when it started to snow. Lightly at first, dusting the tops of the trees, then harder. As they made their way down the pass, the snow covered the trail. They had walked that all day, struggling through the snow, climbing over one ridge, and then another.

Betsy, the older sister, led the way. By the time they made camp, she was no longer sure of the trail. Everywhere she looked, there were mountains and trees and snow. One ridge looked much like another. Her feet ached from the cold. Her eyes burned from staring into the snow, searching for any sign that others had passed this way.

Ellie built a fire and mixed flour to make a batch of biscuits. They had left their cooking pans behind at Donner Lake. So Ellie had wrapped bits of dough on green sticks, carved from a tree with her husband's buck knife, which she wore in a sheath at her side. Now, over the flames of a fire, she toasted the dough, cooking biscuits to feed the three children.

"What will we do tomorrow?" Ellie asked Betsy, as the biscuits toasted on the fire. "This is the last of the flour."

"I don't know," Betsy murmured.

"I wish we hadn't left the Bible behind in the desert," Ellie said. She had been fretting about the Bible ever since they abandoned it. "I'd read the passage about manna in the wilderness." She looked skyward, clasping her hands under her chin. "If only the good Lord would send one of his angels to save us. It wouldn't have to be much of an angel, just someone to show us the way."

Ellie had been talking about the good Lord and his angels for weeks. Betsy was happy to pray for the good Lord's intervention, but she was getting tired of listening to Ellie talk about it.

She poked at the fire with a stick. "We need more wood," she murmured, and started to get up.

"I'll fetch some," Tommy said. At age eight, he was the oldest of the children, a little man who tried to take care of his mother. "You stay here." Tommy stood up and trudged off to search for wood. Shivering in the cold wind, he headed for a stand of pines.

SARAH WATCHED THE boy approach the trees. Attracted by the smell of cooking biscuits, she had been watching the small group by the fire. The boy who trudged toward the pines was younger and smaller than she was.

"You need to be with your own kind," Max had told her. Was this her own kind?

She watched him search beneath the trees, picking up fallen branches and bits of wood. He looked thin and hungry. He was no threat to her, that was clear.

"Hallo," she said.

The boy stopped where he was, staring at her. His eyes were wide and frightened. "Hallo," he said. He didn't move, just stared at her. She stared back, studying the boy. "Are you an angel?" he asked.

She frowned at him. "What is an angel?" she asked. Max had not taught her that word.

"One of God's helpers," the boy said. "An angel come to rescue us. We're so hungry and so cold and my little sister, she's crying 'cause she's so hungry and so cold and my mama doesn't know the way." He was almost crying himself, blinking fast and shivering a little in the cold. "It snowed, and we lost the trail."

Sarah studied him. She had wondered why these people had strayed from the track followed by most of the emigrants.

"Please." The boy reached out and took her hand, holding it tightly in his cold fingers. "Please come help us. Tell my mama the way. Please."

She could have broken free easily enough. The boy clutched his firewood in one arm, tugged on her hand with the other. But she followed him, curious about these people by the fire.

"Mama," Tommy called. "Mama, I found an angel."

One of the women at the fire stood up, staring at her. "An angel?" she said. "Or another lost soul?" The woman held out her hand. "You poor girl. Come and get warm."

It was the tone of the woman's voice that won Sarah. Until Betsy spoke, Sarah could have still turned her back and returned to the mountains. These people were not part of her pack; they were none of her concern. But the woman's voice was warm and caring. She reached out and took Sarah's hand, pulling her into the circle of warmth around the dying fire. She put her arm around Sarah's shoulders. "Where did you come from?" the woman said.

Sarah stood for a moment in the protective circle of Betsy's arm, blinking at Ellie and the two little girls who sat beside her. "You are hungry?" she asked the little girls. They both nodded. She looked at Betsy, and said, "You stay here."

She returned to the forest, leaving the women by the fire. She had killed a marmot earlier that day, a fat animal that had put off hibernation for one day too long. The animal was too big for one meal, so she had cached half the meat in a snowbank for later retrieval.

She brought it to the hungry women, who roasted it on the fire. They ate meat while Sarah ate burned bits of their biscuits, hungry as always for bread.

"What kind of animal is it?" Ellie asked, and Betsy shrugged.

"Some kind of rabbit, I reckon. Don't ask too many questions."

When Ellie and the girls went to sleep, wrapped in

blankets by the fire, Betsy and Sarah and Tommy sat up. "Where did you come from?" Betsy asked.

"I live here," Sarah said.

"But where are your folks?" Betsy asked.

"Where's your mama?" Tommy asked.

Sarah thought of Wauna and stared at the fire, not answering.

"I think her mama is in heaven," Betsy said to Tommy. She put her arm around Sarah and hugged her close. Maybe this mysterious child was an angel, as Ellie maintained, but it seemed to Betsy that this was an angel in need of a little mothering. "You need to be fattened up," she told Sarah. "If I had you at my kitchen back home, I'd feed you apple pie until you got a little meat on those bones."

But Betsy never got the opportunity to fatten Sarah up, to add a layer of fat to her hard muscle. In the morning, at the first sign of light, Sarah woke them, waited while they packed their meager possessions on the oxen, then led them to the trail.

She walked with them all morning, setting a brisk pace and carrying the smallest of the girls when she lagged behind. "Can you smell the smoke?" she asked the little girl. The little girl shook her head.

"Can you smell the smoke of the campfires?" Sarah asked Betsy.

"Maybe." Betsy sniffed the cold air. "I think so."

"There," Sarah said, pointing down the trail. "Go down there, and you will see a cabin. They will help you."

"But what about you?" Betsy said. "You come with us. You can't . . ."

Sarah put the little girl beside her mother. "Good-bye," she said. Without another word, she disappeared into the trees.

"Come on, Betsy," Ellie said. "I can smell the smoke. Let's go."

Reluctantly, Betsy followed the others down the trail.

"THE LORD SENT an angel to save us," Ellie told the miners. The men had fed them, given up their tents for them.

"An angel," asked one miner. "What did she look like?"

Ellie frowned. "Not what you might think," she said slowly. "A dirty red-flannel shirt, moccasins. Not nearly enough clothing." Ellie wet her lips and went on. "She was beautiful, but she was very dirty. She liked biscuits. And her eyes were wild, like an animal's."

"You're sure she was an angel?" the man asked.

"Oh, yes," Ellie said. "There's no doubt."

"She sounds rather dirty for an angel," another man said dryly.

Ellie lifted her eyes from the fire. She smiled, an innocent smile that would make any man ashamed of teasing her. "Of course she was an angel," Ellie said. "But she was wild. A wild angel."

15

LEADER OF THE PACK

"When a person cannot deceive himself, the chances are against his being able to deceive other people."

—Mark Twain

THE NEXT SPRING, MAX TRAVELED TO THE LAKE WHERE HE HAD met Sarah the previous year. He camped alone. At night, he listened to the distant howling of wolves. He called Sarah's name until the mountains echoed. But Sara did not come.

He waited.

He fished in the mountain lake, standing on the shore and casting his line. More often than not, he caught fish and fried them up for supper.

He wrote to Audrey North and reread her latest letter to him, a long and thoughtful missive. She seemed undismayed by his description of Sarah's table manners, thrilled by the news that she had been dubbed the Wild Angel of the Sierras. She wrote of her desire to come west and visit the lake with him, to see her niece after all these years. "When my husband returns from sea, I will consult with him on this matter. I cannot leave without his knowledge, though I would like nothing better than to travel westward. I find myself dreaming of mountains and wolves and my heart aches when I wake to my house on the shore."

He told himself that he was working on another book. Rather than picturing the men who made their living in the mines, this one would depict the wild beauty of the land. That's what he told himself he was doing. But what he was really doing was waiting.

Sometimes he had the feeling that he was being watched. When he stood on the lakeshore, he scanned the surrounding hills, but he saw nothing.

One night, after he had been camped by the lake for almost a week, he sat by the fire, baking biscuits in a Dutch oven. Every night, he had made biscuits, hoping that the aroma of baking would lure Sarah from hiding. On this night, he had waited until dark to build a fire and cook his supper. The moon had not yet risen. Above him, the stars blazed in the sky.

Around him, the world was dark. But he knew she was there. He could feel her watching him, unwilling to reveal herself. While the biscuits baked, he lay back on the ground, looking up at the stars.

"I wonder how many stars there are. More than you could count, I wager." He spoke in a conversational tone. By the lake, the spring peepers sang. In the fire, a pine knot crackled and popped. Otherwise, the night was quiet.

He waited for a moment without speaking. A breeze stirred his hair, tickled the back of his neck.

"I'll lie here and count them," he said. "One, two, three, four . . ." He had taught her to count to one hundred. She had delighted in numbers. He could smell the biscuits baking and knew that she could smell them too. ". . . seventeen, eighteen, nineteen, twenty, twenty-one . . ." He caught the first whiff of burning biscuits. ". . . thirty-two, thirty-three, thirty-four . . ."

"The biscuits are burning," Sarah said.

He continued gazing at the stars. Her voice had

come from behind him. She was still outside the circle of firelight, he guessed.

". . . thirty-seven, thirty-eight, thirty-nine . . ."

"Max! The biscuits are burning!"

She was closer now, but he did not turn to face her. ". . . forty-two, forty-three . . ."

"Max!" She stood over him, glaring at him. "Take the biscuits off the fire."

He sat up then. Leaning over, he hooked a stick through the handle of the Dutch oven and pulled the cast-iron pot away from the fire. The biscuits were a little burned, but not too badly. "Hello, Sarah," he said.

She was a year older, a year taller. She still wore the flannel shirt he had given her, and a pair of ragged, cut-off trousers. She looked healthy.

She frowned at him. "You did not bring that man."

He shook his head. "I did not bring him."

Warily, she crouched by the fire.

"As soon as the biscuits cool, we can eat them," he said. He was afraid that she would run away again.

She was not ready to abandon the subject of Jasper Davis. "He is a bad man."

Max nodded. "Sarah, I'm sorry. He told me he thought Beka was chasing me. He was shooting at Beka."

She narrowed her eyes. "I don't think so."

"What do you think?"

"I think he is a very bad man."

Max bit his lip. He could not argue with her, in good conscience. He had never liked Jasper Davis. There was something shifty about him. Nothing that Max could put his finger on, but something not quite right.

Max shrugged. "He said he was shooting at the wolf. He said he wanted to help you. I couldn't see any reason he'd be lying."

"What is that?" she asked, frowning.

"What?"

"Lying. What does that mean?"

He blinked. He had, the previous summer, managed to introduce Sarah to a number of abstract concepts, but lying was not among them. "He didn't tell the truth."

She continued to frown.

Max scratched his head, trying to figure out how to explain. He was glad that Sarah had come to speak with him. She did not seem to hold a grudge against him for bringing Jasper to the lake, but she was puzzled.

"Look in the pan," he said. "How many biscuits are there?"

Sarah counted. "Four."

"I say there are three biscuits."

She stared at him. "You are wrong. There are four." She pointed. "One, two, three, four."

"When I say that there are three, I am lying."

"Lying means you can't count."

"I know there are four biscuits, but I say there are three. I am lying."

She stared at the biscuits. "There are four. Why would you say there are three?"

Max shook his head in frustration. "Here, would you like a biscuit?" He used a stick to poke one of the least burned biscuits to the edge of the pan, when he could pick it up with his fingers. He gave it to Sarah, who devoured it.

"Now there are three," she said. "One, two, three."

"So if I said that there were four, I would be lying."

She studied his face with a baffled frown. "That man. What is his name?"

"Jasper Davis."

Sarah repeated the name several times and nodded. Her fascination with words had extended to names. Words and names intrigued her. In the fashion of the primitive savage, she seemed to believe that knowing the name of something gave her a power over the person or thing. For some reason, the name "Jasper Davis" seemed to hold a particular interest. She frowned as she said it, as if the name itself made her uneasy. Looking thoughtful, she ate another biscuit, using the blade of her knife to scrape it from the pan.

"You do not like Jasper Davis," she said, after licking the last crumbs of the second biscuit from her palm.

"That's true." He nodded.

"You are afraid of Jasper Davis."

He frowned at that. "Afraid? Not at all. It's true that I don't like the man, but . . ."

Sarah watched him blustering about Jasper Davis. His shoulders were hunched high and stiff; his eyes blinked a little too quickly; he did not meet her eyes as he spoke. It was clear to her that he was afraid, very afraid. And yet he said that he was not. His words and his feelings did not match. How strange that was.

She laughed, interrupting his monologue. "You are lying!" she said with delight, understanding the concept at last. "You are afraid, and you say you are not. You are lying."

THE SUMMER PASSED. Max taught Sarah more English. He asked her to take him higher into the mountains with her, and she complied, taking him on long hikes away from the lake into the wild lands that she knew so well. He took his notebook and sat and sketched, while Sarah and Beka roamed and hunted or slept or played.

Once, on a sunny afternoon after a long hike, they rested for a time on a mountainside. Sitting beside Max as he sketched, she asked him a question that had been troubling her. "Max, where is your pack?"

He looked up from his drawing. "I don't have a pack. People don't travel in packs."

Sarah frowned. His answer did not match her experience. Most of the white people she had seen over the years were traveling in groups. "Ellie and Betsy were traveling in a pack." She had told him about her encounter with the emigrants.

"That's a family," Max said. "Mothers and children. Not a pack."

Sarah shrugged. "Family, pack—where is your family?"

"I don't have one." Max scowled at his drawing, then began darkening the lines with short, hard strokes of the pencil.

"Why are you angry?" she asked him.

"I'm not angry," he snapped.

She studied him, wondering why he would deny something so obvious. "You are angry," she said.

The pencil lead snapped, and he put it down, still frowning. He did not look at her. "I am not angry at you," he said softly.

She studied his face. He was angry and he was sad. She did not want him to be sad. She reached out and took his hand. "I had a family once," he said. "But that was a long time ago." She squeezed his hand, not knowing what to say. "My wife is dead. My daughter was better off without me. I did something wrong. I broke the law and went to jail."

She did not know what the law was, but she was sorry that it was broken, since that made Max sad. She did not know what jail was, but clearly it was not a good place to go.

"Can I be your family?" she asked him. "Beka and I—we will both be your family."

He nodded, squeezing her hand. "I think you already are."

AS THE DAYS grew shorter, Max tried to persuade Sarah to return with him to Selby Flat. One night, sitting by the fire, he told her, "You belong with your people."

"I belong with the wolves," she said.

"You are more human than wolf," he said.

She gazed at him. Beka lay beside her, staring into the fire. The wolf's eyes gleamed in the firelight; her tongue lolled out over sharp white teeth. "People are dangerous," Sarah said.

Max smiled. "Some people think wolves are dangerous."

Sarah nodded gravely. "Some wolves are."

"And some people are dangerous. But not all people. What did you think of Betsy and Ellie?"

"I thought I would talk to them," she said. "To see if they were dangerous."

"That's good."

She stared into the fire. "Some people are not dangerous," she said grudgingly.

"Some people are nice."

She nodded.

"Mrs. Selby wants you to come to Selby Flat," he said. "She wants to make you apple pie and biscuits. Your aunt wants to see you. She lives very far away, but I could take you there."

Sarah looked nervous. "I don't want to go far away," she said. "I belong here."

It was hard for Max to imagine what she would do if she came with him. He could not imagine her in proper clothing, hampered by skirts, sipping tea in the parlor and fussing about ribbons in her hair.

"I will come back next summer," he said.

She nodded. "I will look for you."

AFTER MAX LEFT, she returned to the pack. She had been away from the pack for more than a month, spending her time with Max by the lake while the other wolves roamed their territory, hunting wherever game was most abundant. She found them high in the mountains, far from the mining camps.

She saw Istas first, a sweet-tempered female who had been littermates with Marek. As soon as Sarah saw Istas, the girl knew that something was wrong.

Istas was an easygoing, mid-ranking wolf that avoided squabbles whenever possible. But Sarah could tell that she had been in a fight not long ago: Her right ear was torn and scabbed; she was limping, and her left front paw still bore the bloody marks of a bite. Sarah ran to greet the wolf, eagerly touching noses, stroking the wolf's soft fur.

Istas seemed glad to see her, but Sarah noticed that she was hesitant to lead the girl to join the rest of the pack. Sarah understood why as she approached.

The pack was resting in the shade of a pine. They had killed a buck and feasted on venison. Now they were sleeping and grooming each other, exhausted from the hunt and sated with meat.

As Sarah approached, Yepa stood to run and greet her, then hesitated, staring at the black wolf who crouched in the sun in the center of the pack. He returned her look, flicking his ears back to communicate his disapproval, and Yepa sank down again.

When Sarah had left the pack, Rolon had been the pack's leader. Over the years, he had grown a little slower, a little stiffer. But his minor physical decline had been offset by his wisdom. Rolon knew the mountains like no other wolf. He could find game when food was scarce; he could unify the pack in a hunt as no other wolf could.

A month later, Rolon was gone. He would never have submitted to Marek. Sarah knew that. She knew that the old wolf was dead, killed by his son in a fight for dominance. Now his son led the pack.

Marek stood and stretched, his black fur glistening in the sun. He grinned, opening his mouth and letting his scarlet tongue loll out, relishing his power.

Marek was watching Sarah, staring openly in a gaze that was both a warning and a challenge. Secure in his power, he wanted her to fight him.

Sarah dropped her gaze, acknowledging his supremacy. They would fight, she thought, but not here and not now. She needed time to prepare.

She thought about Max, and she thought about lying. She was lying to Marek, deceiving him with a gesture just as misleading as a lying word. Perhaps Max was right—maybe she was more human than wolf.

The deception had the desired effect. Marek lay down and rested his head on his paws, keeping his eyes on Sarah as she strolled to Yepa's side and greeted her sister. The other members of the pack gathered around, greeting her with gently wagging tails and covert glances at Marek. He did not interfere. He simply watched, the sunlight glittering in his yellow eyes.

Rolon had been a benevolent ruler. When the pack was hunting, he tolerated no insubordination. Each wolf had a place and a role, and he would chastise any who failed to perform. But when the pack was loafing or playing or traveling, Rolon relaxed his discipline. Confident in his power, he did not require constant acknowledgment of his position. He would let pups pounce on his tail or romp on his head without reprimand. He played with the others on occasion, chasing leaves, wrestling, and romping.

Marek was, by contrast, a petty tyrant. The slightest transgression, real or imagined, earned the offending wolf a savage beating. It was such a punishment that had left Istas bruised and limping. Whether the pack was resting or playing or traveling, the wolves kept watch on Marek, alert to changes in his mood, wary of a possible attack by the black wolf. Marek was happy, but the others were nervous, restless, ill at ease.

Game was abundant, and the pack lingered in the high country, where Sarah had found them. The snows had not yet started and the weather was crisp and cold. In the high country, trees were scarce and granite boulders lay tumbled on granite slopes like the building blocks of a giant child.

At age thirteen, Sarah was a formidable opponent in any fight. What she lacked in strength, she made up for in agility and intelligence. She knew when to fight and when to run, how to outsmart a stronger opponent. Her agility let her wiggle out from under an opponent at startling speed. Her muscles were strong from running and climbing. Her endurance was remarkable, gained from hours of running with the pack. She was indifferent to ordinary pain, ignoring the pricks and scratches of thorns, the irritation of minor bites and cuts. She was not fearless, but she was confident in her own abilities and did not waste her time on pointless anxiety.

There in the high country, Sarah laid her plans. On a rocky slope, she found a tough, old juniper tree that had been blasted by many a winter storm. One thick branch had been cracked by the previous year's heavy snowfall, and she worked it loose, breaking it from the trunk by working it back and forth. From it, she fashioned a club, breaking the branch to the length she wanted, shaping it to her hand by whittling the narrow end. She cut a leather thong from the hide of a deer that the pack brought down, she wrapped the thong around the club, and threaded the loop of the thong through her belt so that she could carry the weapon with her. She wandered the rocky slopes and canyons, searching for places that could give her an advantage in a fight. And then she waited, patience being a virtue she had learned long ago.

The time came, as she had known it must. On a clear, cool afternoon, a rabbit ran along the edge of the meadow where the pack was resting. The wolves had downed a yearling doe the day before, but most of the carcass had been consumed. The youngest wolves were gnawing on the bones, already eager to search for other prey. Rolon would have already roused the pack for the next hunt, but Marek had delayed, lazing in the sun. He had fed well, and he was content.

That was when the foolish cottontail ran by.

Sarah was harvesting sweet wild strawberries from the plants that grew in the shade at the edge of the meadow. She was hungry, but she had chosen not to leave the pack to hunt on her own. When the rabbit dashed by, she quickly nocked an arrow and let fly. The arrow found its mark, and the rabbit fell, pierced to the heart. Hungry for fresh meat, Sarah ran to snatch up the fallen rabbit.

She was crouching in the meadow, skinning the rabbit with her knife, when a shadow fell across her. She looked up to see Marek. The black wolf was staring at her, staring at the fresh meat. He was some twenty feet away, strolling toward her. Sarah growled, warning him off, but he continued toward her.

Her choice was clear. Give up the prey that she had killed for herself or fight with Marek. Sarah showed her teeth in a ferocious grin and took off running, carrying the dead rabbit.

Marek chased her. She had known that he would.

His reaction was instinctive—by running away, she had shown weakness, and any wolf would give chase.

She had a head start. She maintained it as she dodged through the scrubby trees at the edge of the meadow and onto a slope of granite, scraped clean by the passage of glaciers thousands of years before. Her bare feet pounded the smooth stone, propelling her forward as fast as she could go.

Wolves often chased one another in play, but this was no game. She heard Marek growling as he gained on her. The black wolf was at her heels as she dodged into a narrow canyon formed by a wall of granite and a tumbled granite slab some six feet high. The canyon ended where a rockfall had closed the way.

She ran to the rockfall, dropped the carcass of the rabbit, and whirled to face Marek. This was the spot she had chosen for her fight. In the narrow canyon, Marek could not circle her. Her back was protected by the walls of the canyon and the rockfall.

She faced him, a slender, blue-eyed girl clutching a club in one hand, a knife in the other, pitted against a raging wolf. It was a scene to break a human mother's heart. Compared to the black wolf Sarah seemed so tiny, so frail. How could life pit her against such an opponent? How unfair! Surely this battle was hopeless!

But Sarah had no illusions about fairness, and she did not view the battle as hopeless. She grinned at Marek, showing her teeth. Blunt-tipped human teeth, useless in this battle except to signal her willingness to fight.

Yes, she was ready and more than willing. She had waited and watched and now she faced her opponent with savage joy in her heart and a smile on her lips. She had learned from Dur's mistake—she would show no mercy, give the black wolf no second chance.

Marek charged her with a roar.

Sarah had watched Marek fight, had observed his

weaknesses. He relied on his superior size. He always began by rushing his opponent, charging in at top speed and smashing into the other wolf. More often than not, he bowled his opponent over, then went for the throat, attempting to lock his jaws around his rival's windpipe and choke the other wolf.

Marek charged as Sarah knew he would, but the girl leapt out of the way, springing up to a foothold on the granite slab that formed one wall of the canyon. She had chosen the spot because it allowed her to add a third dimension to the fight, taking advantage of her ability to climb.

Marek skidded on the slick granite. As he turned to leap at her, she jumped over him, landing behind him with her back to the rockfall. He whirled again, amazingly fast for an animal of his size. She was swinging the club as he turned, and she heard his teeth snap closed as the club connected with his muzzle.

He lunged for her, and again she sprang upward, finding a foothold on the other canyon wall, just out of his reach. She tried the same trick again, leaping behind him and swinging the club, but he was ready this time, dodging the strike to his head and taking a solid blow on his shoulder while he snapped at her legs.

His jaws slashed her right leg, penetrating the skin, but did not close quickly enough to hold her fast. She was away again, leaping up onto the rockfall. With one foot, she pushed a loose rock, sending a few rocks tumbling down. Marek dodged the falling rocks, then threw himself at the slope, struggling to reach her.

Already, she was in motion, jumping for another perch. The wound on her leg was bleeding now. She left a splash of crimson blood behind on the rock as she leapt away to another perch.

She leapt from perch to perch, swinging the club. Sometimes, she connected, but more often the black wolf dodged and darted in to slash at her legs again. Her skin glistened with sweat. Bloody footprints decorated the rockfall and the canyon floor.

Marek was relentless in his pursuit. The black devil lunged and slashed and whirled, giving her no opportunity to rest.

Marek attacked, Sarah leapt for a foothold, and her foot slipped on the blood and the sweat. She fell, landing in a crouch before the wolf. The black wolf sprang for her throat, but as fast as he moved, she was faster. She lifted the club, turning it horizontally to the ground and jamming it between his open jaws. At the same moment, she stood, swinging her leg over the wolf to straddle him, placing her full weight on his back and bearing him downward. With one hand, she pulled on the club, forcing it into Marek's mouth like a bit in the mouth of a horse. With the other hand, she drove her knife into Marek's throat, through the thick fur and into the artery that carried blood to the brain. She did not hesitate. She showed no mercy. She remembered his battle with Dur and knew that she could give him no second chance.

Marek's blood joined hers, pumping from his throat to darken his glossy fur. His blood stained the granite at her feet. The wolf struggled, his claws scrabbling weakly against the smooth rock in the struggles of a dying creature. Then he collapsed beneath her on the canyon floor.

Sarah's legs were trembling when she walked out of the canyon. She was bleeding from abrasions where she had scraped her skin against the rough granite, from places where Marek's teeth had slashed her. In one hand, she held her club, notched with the marks of Marek's teeth. In the other, she clutched the knife, dripping with his blood.

At the entrance to the canyon, Yepa and Beka

greeted Sarah with concern, circling her, licking her wounds, leaping in joy at her return. The rest of the pack gathered around, welcoming her with a frenzy of wagging tails and grinning faces and low moaning howls of excitement.

Yepa raised her head and howled in earnest, just as she would to gather the pack for the hunt. The others joined in, a joyous chorus. Sarah lifted her head and howled with the others, weary and battered, but triumphant.

SARAH HAD KILLED the pack's leader, but she did not take on that role. She had always been set apart from the others, and that situation did not change. Yepa was the alpha female. After some squabbling among the males, Duman, one of Dur's litter mates, became alpha male. He was a sturdy wolf—an excellent fighter, a skilled hunter.

With the pack under the leadership of Yepa and Duman, Sarah felt free to wander the mountains alone or in Beka's company. She was restless, no longer content to live from day to day with the pack. She did not belong with the pack; she knew that. But she did not know where she did belong.

16

HER OWN KIND

"The rain . . . falls upon the just and the unjust alike; a thing which would not happen if I were superintending the rain's affairs. No, I would rain softly and sweetly on the just, but if I caught a sample of the unjust outdoors I would drown him."

—Mark Twain

TOM MORRIS WAVED TO HIS COMPANION AS HE MADE HIS WAY across the log that served as a bridge over the creek. "Good-bye," Tom called. "I'll see you in San Francisco."

Tom and his friend Joe had been camping by the creek and working a claim. It had been a profitable summer—they had taken almost two thousand dollars' worth of gold from the creek. But when Joe decided to head for the lowlands, Tom wasn't quite ready to go. His share of the summer's earnings was nine hundred dollars—and he hoped to make a hundred more before he went to the city. He had set himself a goal of a thousand dollars, and he was determined to make it.

"Don't stay too late," Joe called back.

Tom waved back, smiling but dismissing Joe's advice. After two years in the mines, Joe considered himself an old sourdough. Though Tom had been in California for less than a year, he felt he was quite competent to do without Joe's advice.

"Don't forget—if the rains come, get to high ground."

Tom smiled and waved. Joe sometimes acted like Tom was a fool, without a bit of common sense. Of course he would get to high ground.

For the first few days after Joe's departure, the weather was cool, but clear. Tom shook his head and laughed, thinking of Joe's warnings about the winter rains. On the third day, the sky was overcast. Late in the day, drizzle dampened the soil. It was inconvenient, Tom thought, as he retired to his tent, but nothing to worry about. If it kept up, he would pack out in the morning—even if he was still short of his goal.

In the shelter of his tent, he prepared a cold dinner of ham and biscuits. As he ate, the drizzle became a downpour. He watched the water rush down the bare hillside on the far side of the creek. He and Joe had cleared the hillside of vegetation and shoveled the loose soil into their long tom in their quest for gold. Now the rain washed dirt into the creek, a torrent of silty water.

Tom eyed the rushing creek with some trepidation. The water was rising quickly. Already, it was eating at the bank that supported one end of the log bridge. He and Joe had felled the tree to make a bridge to the north side of the creek, where granite slabs formed a sheltered campsite. Tom squinted at the wet log that spanned the creek. That bridge was his path back to civilization. Surely the creek couldn't rise high enough to jeopardize the bridge.

In the morning, he would pack out, he decided. That would be the prudent thing to do.

He tried to sleep, but the pounding rain kept him awake. The roar of the creek was punctuated by falling boulders, washed from the hillside by the rushing water. At midnight, he heard a crash. Peering into the rain, he saw that the bank had collapsed beneath the log bridge. The rushing waters churned around one end of the fallen log, rolling it into the torrent.

Morning dawned, and still the rain fell—a deluge of biblical proportions. The muddy water of the creek was lapping at the granite slab beneath his tent. He packed essentials, taking his gold, his food, his knife, his rifle. The water was washing up to the door of his tent when he abandoned it.

There was no way back to the south side of the creek. Even if he could have reached the south bank, there would be no way out in that direction. From his tent, he could see that the steep trail that they had followed down into the canyon had washed out.

On the north side of the canyon, the prospects did not look much better. The north canyon wall was formed of granite slabs, slick in the rain. One slip, and a climber would fall to his death. But Tom could see no other way. The creek was rising and he had no choice.

Tom began to climb. A crack in the granite offered a series of precarious handholds. His feet found footholds, rough patches in the granite, tiny ledges. In minutes, he was chilled to the bone. His hands could barely feel the rock to grip it. He glanced down only once, and that terrifying glimpse convinced him not to look down again.

He looked up, searching for the next handhold, the next precarious foothold. He could see the top high above him, silhouetted against the sky. He decided that it would be best not to look at the top. It would be best to concentrate on where to place his feet, where to grab hold. One step at a time.

He climbed until his arms shook with fatigue. Just when he thought he could cling to the rock no longer, he reached a ledge. A little more than two feet wide, just a few feet long; big enough that he could stop and rest.

He stood with his face to the wall, unwilling to turn and look outward. He was afraid to look at the drop below him. He leaned his forehead against the cliff, ignoring the rain that dripped down the rock and splashed on his face. The rain had died back to a drizzle, just enough to wet the rock and keep him soaked.

As the trembling in his arms eased, he looked upward. The top was close, so close—maybe twelve feet above him. But the rock that separated him from the top was polished granite, a sheer expanse. He could see no handholds, no footholds, no way up. He reached up carefully and felt the rock, hoping that it was not as smooth as it appeared. His hands confirmed what his eyes had seen: slick and smooth.

No way up. And there was no way he could climb back down. He stood frozen in place, his hands stretched above him.

At that moment, looking up, he saw a movement at the top. Someone's head, popping over the edge of the cliff to look down.

"Halloo!" he called. "Is someone there? For God's sake, help a miserable soul. Halloo!"

A girl's face came into view, and Tom knew he was dreaming. A pretty girl with red-gold hair and a dirty face. A hallucination, to be sure.

A rope came snaking over the smooth rock, dangling down past the ledge. He took hold of the rope. A strong rope of braided leather. A hallucination, he knew, but a very comforting one. He was glad that his hallucinating mind believed in quality products. The rope was secured to something above; it held when he tugged on it.

He tied the rope around his waist, knotting it securely. Then he called up again. "Halloo!"

The girl's head popped back into view and took another look at him. "You climb," she said.

He climbed, trusting his hallucination and pulling himself hand over hand by the rope, using footholds where he could. At last he reached the top, pulled himself over the edge, lay at full length, eyes closed, hands on the solid ground. "Thank God," he muttered. "Thank God."

He opened his eyes when he felt a tug at his waist. The girl was untying the rope from around his waist. She had already untied the other end, which had been knotted around a sturdy pine. She wore a red-flannel shirt and a pair of men's trousers, cut off at the knees. Her legs were bare. He stared at her legs, then shook his head. It did not seem wise to ogle.

At that moment, a wolf trotted up and stood beside her, wagging its tail and looking for all the world like a big, friendly dog. Tom blinked as the hallucination began to make a kind of sense.

"You're the angel, aren't you?" Tom murmured. "I've heard about you. You saved some travelers last year. You live with the wolves."

She pushed a handful of wet hair out of her face, watching him with unnerving intensity. The wolf nudged her leg, and she turned away, as if she might leave him there.

Tom sat up. His hands were still shaking—from cold and from muscle fatigue. "Wait," he said. "Please wait. I don't know the way from here."

She looked back at him, a puzzled look on her face. "That way," she said, pointing. "You'll find a trail."

"I'll build a fire first," he said. "I have to get warm. And maybe . . ." He frowned, trying to remember what he had heard about this rescuing angel. She was dirty; she was wild; she liked biscuits. He had some flour in his pack, the last of his food. "I could make biscuits," he said.

SARAH HELPED THE man gather wood and sat with him by the fire for a time. She listened to him talk and happily ate his biscuits.

"You saved my life," he told her. "How can I thank you?"

She shrugged and ate another biscuit. He had nothing that she wanted. She had seen him climbing up from the creek—a long, hard climb—and had lingered to see if he would make it. When he stopped so close to the top, she had decided to help him. So much effort, she thought, should be rewarded. And the biscuits were good.

"You shouldn't be out here alone," he was saying. "It's a rough life for a man—and no life for a woman. A girl like you—you should be taken care of."

She listened to what he was saying, but it really made no sense. Once he had built his fire and stopped trembling, he had become very sure of himself. He seemed to have forgotten that she was doing just fine out there, that she had saved him. He was talking about how she really didn't belong out there in the wilderness. He reminded her of an overconfident pup.

He was toasting the last biscuits when Beka decided that it was time to go. Sarah, having eaten her fill, left with her. "Hey, wait!" she heard the man shout behind her. She didn't stop.

He was, she decided, not one of the dangerous people. Nor was he really a nice person, like Betsy. He fell into another category—not dangerous, friendly, but silly.

OVER THAT WINTER and the winters that followed, she helped other travelers, bringing them food, showing them the way. In Selby Flat, Max heard stories of the Wild Angel, a beautiful savage girl who came to help the unfortunate, then disappeared into the wilderness.

In the summers, when the snow melted, Max went to the mountains. There, he taught Sarah and she taught him, taking him high into the mountains and showing him her world. Each fall, he tried to persuade her to come back with him. Each fall, she refused, preferring her life in the wilderness to what she had seen of human civilization.

PART FOUR

1863

17

PROFESSOR SERUNCA'S WAGON OF WONDERS

"I could easily learn to prefer an elephant to any other vehicle, partly because of that immunity from collisions, and partly because of the fine view one has from up there, and partly because of the dignity one feels in that high place, and partly because one can look in at the windows and see what is going on privately among the family."

—*Following the Equator;* Mark Twain

IN THE SPRING OF 1863, MAX DID NOT COME TO THE LAKE. Each year, Sarah had met him there when the snow melted, before the first spring flowers opened their blossoms. But that year, he did not come. She waited, hunting in the area and returning to the lake every few days to look for him. Beka was with her.

The violets bloomed in the meadow and still Max did not come to the lake. Mountain bluebells bloomed in the moist shade beneath the pines, the wild iris opened its pale blue flowers on the marshy shore of the lake, wild strawberries bloomed in the meadow, and still Max's camp was empty.

Sarah puzzled over his absence—not worrying exactly, but thinking about where he might be. He had rarely talked of what he did when he wasn't with her, and the little that he had said had not made much sense to her. He had said he wrote books and he had showed her one of his books. She had liked the pictures. She had recognized many of the places he had drawn as spots to which she had taken him. She knew he went to Selby Flat, to Sacramento, to San Francisco. But these places were mysterious, distant and unknown.

The meadow was bright with lupine flowers when Sarah grew tired of waiting and decided to look for Max. She and Beka made their way downward into the rolling foothills.

She did not have a plan, exactly. She was hunting as a wolf would hunt, traveling, looking for signs of her quarry. She went to the foothills because that was an area where white men were common. She was looking for his trail, searching for a sign of him. That was how Sarah and Beka came to be resting in the shade on the bank of Rush Creek when the traveling circus came through.

Sarah heard the circus coming long before she saw it. A man's voice, shouting: "Hey, Professor! Are you sure this is the right trail?" The creaking of a wagon and the sound of horses splashing through the stream.

She and Beka moved quietly undercover. A nearby cottonwood tree was overgrown with wild grapevines. Sarah ducked behind the vines, where the lush leaves screened her from casual observation. There, she waited.

The wind shifted, and she caught a strange scent, mingling with the scent of man sweat and horses. An animal, but no animal she had ever smelled before. A grass-eater, by the smell of it—the smell of sweat was accompanied by a faint aroma of hay.

Sarah was staring between the wild grape leaves when a bizarre creature stepped into view. As gray as a granite boulder, as big as a log cabin, it had wide, flat ears that flapped like leaves in the breeze, and an enormous nose that writhed and twisted like a snake. As Sarah watched, the beast dipped its nose in a pool of water, lifted the end, and squirted the water into its mouth, flapping its outlandish ears happily.

A man rode on the strange beast, his leg spread to straddle its thick neck. The rider wore a bowler hat tipped back on his head at a jaunty angle. His neatly trimmed beard and thin mustache gave him a roguish look. As Sarah watched, he patted the beast's neck in a friendly fashion. "What a fine elephant you are, Ruby," he murmured. "A gem of an elephant."

A horse-drawn wagon followed the elephant. It was a wooden-sided wagon, in the tradition of European gypsy caravans. Sarah stared as it passed, fascinated by the pictures that were painted on its wooden sides. In one, a man juggled knives and flaming torches. In another the fantastic beast—the elephant, that's what the man had called it—stood on her hind legs, holding a smiling woman with its amazing nose. In yet another picture, a strange-looking animal—a poodle, though Sarah could not identify it as such—leapt through a flaming hoop. Above and below the pictures, gilt lettering proclaimed this to be PROFESSOR SERUNCA'S WAGON OF WONDERS AND TRAVELING CIRCUS.

Sarah stared. She could not read the words, but she needed no words to realize that these were not ordinary travelers. She squinted at the driver of the wagon. The strange-looking animal painted on the side of the wagon was sleeping on his lap.

PROFESSOR GYRO SERUNCA'S Wagon of Wonders and Traveling Circus was making its way from French Corral to Selby Flat on an extended tour of the mining camps. The elephant's name was Ruby, and she was a good-tempered and well-trained beast. Professor Gyro

Serunca, the man who rode on her back, had transported her from the exotic kingdom of Siam to California at a considerable expense. Professor Gyro Serunca was an animal trainer, a magician, a purveyor of Oriental medicines, and a master of Oriental mysteries.

"Hey, Professor," the wagon's driver shouted again. "I really don't think this is the right trail. It certainly wasn't meant for a wagon."

"Of course it's the trail," the Professor said amiably. "It has to be. We haven't seen anything else that looked remotely like a trail."

The driver shook his head. His name was Cassidy Orton, and he was the juggler depicted on the side of the wagon. Cassidy, who came from an old British circus family, was a man of many talents. In Professor Serunca's show, he juggled knives and torches, threw knives, and performed acrobatics on horseback.

Cassidy was, at that moment, surrounded by the Professor's poodles. He had Snowflake, a white toy poodle in his lap. Two miniature black poodles lay on the boards at his feet, and three standard-sized poodles were in the wagon behind him. All the dogs were sleeping soundly.

Cassidy clicked his tongue to the horses, urging them on as the wagon lurched through the rocky creek bed. "Most of the trails in these parts don't look like trails," he called to the Professor, "but this looks less like a trail than any of them. I think we're lost again."

"I don't agree." Professor Serunca was a confident man. "Remember what that fellow told us. We were to follow the trail down into a valley, then continue on the trail along the creek. . . ."

"But we aren't really following a trail, Professor. We're in the creek itself."

The Professor waved a hand airily. "A minor distinction. I am confident that this is the correct path."

Cassidy shrugged, disturbing the poodle in his lap. Snowflake lifted her head, studied the creek for a moment, then yawned and returned to her nap. She seemed resigned to go wherever the Professor led. Cassidy stroked her head and decided to adopt the same policy.

The Professor's confidence seemed to increase in direct proportion to how far they were off trail. Cassidy had experienced this effect several times during the past month, as they traveled on the poorly marked trails that crisscrossed California's foothills. He wondered how long it would take the Professor's confidence to wear off this time, and guessed that he would start wondering about their location at around suppertime. Then he'd suggest that they make camp, and find the way in the morning.

Cassidy missed the other members of the troupe. Lulu, the young woman in the painting on the side of the wagon had been lured away after the show performed in San Francisco. A wealthy miner had wooed her and won her, marrying her three days after they met. In the mining town of Hell's Half Acre, Charlie, the World's Tallest Man, had tried his hand at gold panning, found a nugget as big as his thumb, and immediately staked a claim. He had tried to talk Cassidy into staying and staking a claim, but Cassidy had decided to stick with the Professor. He didn't feel right abandoning him.

Gyro Serunca was an old family friend. Cassidy's father had traveled with him, many years ago. Professor Serunca had stopped to visit the Orton family on his way to Siam and had, quite casually, asked Cassidy if he wanted to come along and be part of a California tour. "You could meet me in San Francisco a year and a half from now," the Professor said. "After I arrange for an elephant."

During his travels in the States, the Professor said, he had heard a phrase used by those setting forth for California. "I am going to see the elephant," they would say. According to legend, a farmer on his way to town with a wagon of vegetables had encountered a circus parade. Startled by the elephant, his horses had bolted, overturning his wagon and ruining his vegetables. The farmer had reacted with equanimity. "I don't care," he said. "I have seen the elephant."

An exotic adventure with a high price—that was seeing the elephant. "I think it is only appropriate to bring an elephant to California," he told Cassidy. "It seems only fair that those who have gone to see the elephant can truly see the elephant."

When Cassidy told his father of the Professor's plan and asked for advice, Cassidy's father had been unequivocal. "If you have a chance to travel with Gyro, take it," he said. "He is one of the greats. It won't be easy, but it'll be the adventure of a lifetime."

With his father's blessing, Cassidy had left the family show and traveled to California for the adventure of a lifetime. At present, the adventure looked rather bleak. The show was at a low ebb. But Cassidy knew that the Professor would revitalize it somehow. He was as confident in that as the Professor was in the trail.

IT WAS LATE afternoon when the Professor called to Cassidy and said in a tone of great puzzlement, "We seem to have lost the trail."

They had followed the stream into a wide valley. The dry brown grass showed no sign that people had passed that way.

"Yes, I'd say we have," Cassidy agreed. He did not

bother to remind the Professor that he had suggested this some hours earlier.

"Well, perhaps it would be best to camp here." The Professor gazed around him, considering the valley. "It's a beautiful spot, after all. We'll find the way in the morning."

And so Professor Gyro Serunca's Wagon of Wonders and Traveling Circus made camp on the edge of the meadow where the horses could graze, not far from the creek where Ruby could bathe.

SARAH SAT IN a cottonwood tree across the meadow from where the Professor was working with the poodles. She had watched as the dogs leapt from the wagon. She knew that they were dogs by their scent, but they looked nothing like the mangy curs that lived at the Indian village.

As the dogs left the wagon, the Professor had crouched in the grass and greeted each dog individually, scratching this one's ears, rubbing that one's belly, wrestling just a bit with another one. Cassidy hobbled two of the horses, then put them out to graze. He tended to the third horse, a white mare, currying the dust from her coat and talking to her as he did so. The elephant grazed with the horses.

Sarah watched, sorting out the hierarchy in this strange pack. The Professor was clearly the alpha male. All of the dogs deferred to him. So did Cassidy and, as near as she could tell, Ruby. At a guess, she figured that Ruby was the alpha female—she deferred to no one other than the Professor. Among the dogs, the smallest white poodle appeared to be the ranking female.

In the few hours of daylight that remained, the Professor worked with his poodles, who had been misbehaving lately. In the act's finale, the dogs were supposed to form a pyramid, with the three standard poodles as the base, the two miniature poodles in the second tier, and Snowflake at the top. Lately, Pepper, the black standard poodle, had taken to wandering out of place when the pyramid was almost complete. At the last performance, Pepper had decided to lie down without warning and the pyramid had collapsed into a heap of squabbling dogs.

The ensuing dogfight had delighted the miners at French Corral. Betting had been fierce. When Snowflake, with a feistiness that belied her size, chased all the larger dogs out of the ring, a short fellow who had bet heavily on the small dog won the pot. Though the audience had been more than satisfied with the performance, the Professor had not been happy. He was determined to put the dogs through their paces until Pepper behaved.

Meanwhile, Cassidy mounted the white mare and rode at an easy gallop around the perimeter of the meadow. They circled the meadow once, then twice. On the third circuit, Cassidy began to practice his trick riding, striking a series of poses on the mare's back. He started astraddle, then hung off to one side, like an Indian avoiding cavalry fire. He returned to his initial position, then pulled his legs up and easily stood upright, steady as you please. He leaned down and placed his hands on the horse's back, kicked up his legs, and stood on his hands, as relaxed as if he were on the solid ground.

From her perch, Sarah watched him ride. She was aware, as she watched, that he had another observer. When she climbed the tree, she had caught the scent of a mountain lion, sleeping in a tangle of bushes at the edge of the meadow. Sarah's keen eyes caught a flicker of movement—the twitching of a tawny tail—

and she realized the lion was awake. He was watching the horse and rider with great interest.

The mare completed another circuit of the meadow. Cassidy was shifting from a handstand to a headstand when the mare passed the big cat's hiding place. At that moment, the lion leapt out, intending to pull the horse down. The mare shied, dancing to one side as the cat bounded after her. The lion's claws raked the mare's hindquarters, but failed to get a purchase.

Jerked to one side, Cassidy lost his balance, falling as the horse moved beneath him. A trained acrobat, Cassidy tried to get his legs beneath him, but there was too little time for that. He landed awkwardly, catching his full weight on one leg, which twisted beneath him.

Looking down on the scene, Sarah shook her head, scornful of the big cat's hunting technique. The lion had attacked too soon. If the hunter had waited, he would have been just behind the horse, taking the prey by surprise.

The mountain lion yowled in frustration as the mare raced across the meadow faster than the cat could follow. Behind the lion, Cassidy was struggling to his feet. When he put weight on his left foot, he collapsed again. Sarah watched with keen interest to see how the man would deal with the lion.

The lion turned to face Cassidy just as he struggled to his feet again, putting as little weight as possible on his twisted ankle. His uncle, Thaddeus Orton, had been a lion tamer. As a lad, Cassidy had assisted his uncle with the big cats. "Never show them you're afraid," Thaddeus had told his nephew. "That's the key."

Keeping that advice in mind, Cassidy glared at the mountain lion. He had no weapons: His pistol and his buck knife were in the wagon. He struggled to his feet, facing the lion empty-handed.

The lion watched the man through slitted eyes, his tail twitching in the meadow grass. Cassidy watched, helpless, as the lion gathered his hindquarters beneath him, preparing to spring on his prey.

At that moment, Sarah tossed her lariat from the cottonwood tree. Its loop settled neatly over the head of the crouching lion. As the cat pulled forward against the lariat, Sarah looped the rope over the branch where she had been sitting and put her full weight on the rope, pulling the big cat backward as she lowered herself to the ground.

The big cat stood with his hind legs on the ground, his forepaws dangling in midair, held up by the noose. He was choking, fighting for air. Sarah tied the free end of the lariat to a sturdy bush and went to where Cassidy stood unsteadily in the grass.

"Hallo," Sarah said.

Cassidy stared. Sarah had grown from a wild child to become a savage woman of striking beauty. At sixteen years of age, she was slim and graceful and completely unconscious of her own beauty. Her canvas trousers, cut off at the knees, left her slim, muscular legs bare. She wore a red-cotton shirt, stolen from a wagon train, but she had not bothered to button it, the day being warm. As she moved, Cassidy caught tantalizing glimpses of her breasts. Her curly red hair was tied back with a strip of leather.

Sarah stared back. On his last visit, Max had spent some time attempting to teach her manners, telling her that she'd need them when she decided to leave the wilderness. She decided to apply one of Max's lessons now. "How do you do?" She held out her hand.

Cassidy stared at Sarah and the grimy hand the

woman had extended in his direction. "I've been better," he murmured in astonishment. He took her hand, less to shake it than to assure himself that she was real. Holding her hand, he asked, "Who are you? Where the hell did you come from?"

Sarah regarded Cassidy steadily. The man was not following the script, as Max had explained it to Sarah. He was supposed to shake Sarah's hand, and say, "Very well, thank you. How do you do?"

Sarah shrugged, deciding to save Max's lesson in etiquette for someone who responded appropriately. "I am Sarah. I came from that tree." She pointed at the cottonwood. Glancing back, she noticed the mountain lion had slumped, dangling unconscious in the noose. Leaving Cassidy, she went to the rope and untied it, lowering the big cat to the ground. She slipped the noose off the animal's neck. The lion shuddered as she did so, and took a gasping breath.

"What are you doing?" Cassidy shouted from behind her. "That beast will wake up and kill us all."

Sarah shook her head and walked back to Cassidy, coiling the lariat as she did so. "He is a big coward," she said. "He will run away as soon as he wakes up. He will not come back."

Sarah saw no point in killing an animal that she didn't plan to eat—and she knew from experience that mountain-lion meat was stringy and gamy. She had killed a rabbit earlier that afternoon and wasn't hungry.

The lion staggered to his feet. As Sarah had predicted, the big cat slunk toward the trees. He glanced back over his shoulder, then quickened his pace, loping away.

Cassidy heard dogs barking and looked toward camp. It had taken the Professor a few minutes to gather his forces, but now he was hurrying to the rescue, mounted on Ruby. The poodles ran ahead of the elephant, barking in three different pitches: low from the standard poodles, medium from the miniature poodles, and high-pitched yapping from Snowflake.

"Here comes the Professor," Cassidy said. "A little too late, but heroic for all of that." He glanced at the wild woman who had saved him and realized that she might not stick around for this questionable welcoming committee. He reached out and took hold of her hand. "I'm sure the Professor will want to meet you," he said.

Though she could have easily freed herself from Cassidy's grip, Sarah waited. These people and their animals intrigued her. She had never seen a pack of humans and animals traveling together like this. Perhaps they knew something about Max.

The poodles reached them first. The dog raced around and around Cassidy and Sarah, barking and sniffing the places where the lion had been.

Such strange creatures, Sarah thought. They smelled like dogs, but their hair was cut in outlandish patterns. Sarah took her hand from Cassidy's and knelt in the grass to greet them, meeting each approaching dog with a stare that demanded respect. The dogs recognized her look and circled her, maintaining a respectful distance.

Sarah stood up as the elephant approached. Ruby knelt in the grass so that the Professor could climb down. The Professor spoke to Cassidy, but Sarah was staring up at the elephant.

Nothing in the enormous beast's posture indicated that she was a threat. However strange this animal looked and smelled, she seemed relaxed, friendly. The poodles showed no fear of her, romping around her feet in the dry grass.

Sarah took a step toward Ruby, looking the elephant in the eye. Ruby's great gray trunk snaked toward the girl. A puff of grass-scented, elephant breath ruffled her hair. Sarah reached up and patted the trunk that was sniffing her neck. It felt warm and leathery.

"Ruby likes you," the Professor observed.

Sarah glanced at him. He smiled as he met her eyes, then he averted his gaze. Sarah returned his smile. Most humans stared, a threatening expression among the wolves. But the Professor clearly understood the proper way to behave. He was smiling; his hands were open; his stance was relaxed.

He met her eyes again. "Thank you very much for your assistance," he said.

Sarah nodded. Max had, as part of his lesson in etiquette, instructed her on how to deal with thanks. "You are welcome," she said formally. "Think nothing of it."

The Professor nodded, still smiling. His eyes narrowed a bit as he sized her up.

Cassidy spoke up then. "Professor, this is Sarah. Sarah, this is Professor Gyro Serunca."

The Professor tipped his derby hat. "Very pleased to make your acquaintance, Sarah."

Sarah smiled, happy that this man was using phrases for which Max had prepared her. "Likewise, I'm sure."

The Professor studied her for a moment. "Perhaps you would agree to accompany us back to our camp," he suggested. "I would love to talk with you further."

While the poodles romped around them in the grass, Ruby carried Cassidy back to camp with her trunk wrapped around the man's waist, just as she had carried Lulu in past performances.

As they walked, the Professor asked questions of Cassidy. "What happened? I looked up and Lightning was running from a lion and you were on the ground."

Cassidy described what had happened and how Sarah had saved him from the lion. "You were really quite magnificent," Cassidy told Sarah. He was trying very hard not to stare at her legs. Such lovely legs. But their owner seemed rather fierce, and he did not want to give offense.

The Professor studied Sarah as they walked. "So, Sarah, tell me—you live alone in this charming wilderness?"

"I live with the wolves," she said. "Beka is off hunting for quail."

"With the wolves?" The Professor raised his eyebrows, beaming at her. "Beka is a wolf? That's marvelous."

"You're the Wild Angel!" Cassidy said. "I've heard the miners talk about you. You come to rescue people in need."

Sarah regarded him without comment.

"The Wild Angel," the Professor repeated. "That would make a lovely stage name." He nodded. "You must stay to dinner," he told Sarah. "We must talk more. There are so many possibilities."

Sarah hesitated. "Will you have biscuits?" she asked.

"If you want biscuits, I'll make biscuits," Cassidy said quickly.

"I will stay," said Sarah.

It was curiosity that kept her there, as much as the promise of biscuits. She sat by the fire and watched as Professor Serunca ministered to Cassidy's ankle with a Chinese liniment that reeked of strange herbs. He bound the injured joint with strips of linen, torn from a banner that had once said something about the merits of Chinese medicine (the letters had long since faded). While Cassidy made biscuits and fried salt pork, the Professor fetched the white mare (who had only run as far as the other side of the meadow) and treated the horse's wounds with Chinese medicine and muttered words of comfort.

While they ate dinner, the Professor asked her what brought her down from the mountains.

"I'm looking for my friend Max," Sarah told him. "Do you know him?"

"Max," the Professor repeated thoughtfully. "I don't believe I know the fellow." He squinted at her, studying her face. "But perhaps we can help you find him. What does Max do?"

"He draws pictures," she said. "He writes in a notebook."

"I see. An artist, then. What does he do with these pictures?"

"Puts them in a book," she said. "He showed me one."

Cassidy had been listening carefully. Before he had left for California, he had done his best to research the place, gathering several popular accounts of travels in the gold fields. He had brought one of his favorites along. "Hey, Professor, I have a book by a fellow named Max Phillips . . ."

The Professor fetched the book from Cassidy's rucksack. "*In the Diggings,* by Max Phillips," Cassidy said, opening the book.

"There," Sarah cried, pointing to the sketch facing the title page. "That's the lake. Max drew that." She smiled, remembering the sunny afternoon when Max had completed the sketch. She had taken him on a hike high above the valley to a place where the world opened beneath them.

Cassidy nodded, flipping through the pages until he reached the introduction, written by an editor at the publishing house. "Since the publication of *A Young Man's Guide to the Gold Fields,* I have had the great pleasure of corresponding with Max Phillips,"

Cassidy read aloud. "As Mr. Phillips is a man with no fixed address, I send my letters to Selby Hotel in Selby Flat, California. There, Mr. Phillips tells me, Mrs. Selby tucks them behind the barroom mirror to await his next visit. I have not met the redoubtable Mrs. Selby in person, but I have met her in the Mr. Phillips's accounts of life in Selby Flat, and I feel I know her quite well."

"Mrs. Selby!" Sarah was happy now. "Max told me about Mrs. Selby. She makes apple pie."

The Professor nodded. "And she lives in Selby Flat. As it happens, we are on our way to Selby Flat for a performance. Would you like to come with us?"

Sarah hesitated only for a moment. Max had tried many times to persuade her to go with him to Selby Flat. The previous summer, she had promised him that she would accompany him the following year. "Yes," she said. "And we'll find Max."

"If not, we'll find out where he is," the Professor said. "And perhaps, while we are there, you could join us in a performance. As the Wild Angel, I imagine you could be quite an attraction." The Professor smiled at her. "I'm sure you've always dreamed of running away with the circus."

Sarah frowned, confused.

Cassidy shook his head. "Professor, she was raised by wolves. She doesn't know what a circus is."

"She does now," he said. "We are the circus, my child." He lifted his hands in a grand gesture that encompassed Cassidy, the wagon, the animals. "We are the stuff that dreams are made of. The glitter and the glamour and the glory. Not for us the humdrum life of quiet desperation. I invite you to join us, to become a star glittering in the firmament."

Sarah stared at him, wondering what he was talking about. She understood many of his words, but she got lost trying to follow the Professor's rolling sentences. What did the stars have to do with any of this? She glanced upward, where the first stars glittered in the darkening sky. "A star?" she murmured.

"Of course you will be a star!" He leaned back on his elbows, gazing at the sky. "The brightest of all the stars in the heavens."

She liked the Professor, even though she did not know what he was talking about. He reminded her a bit of Rolon—in charge of his pack but relaxed about his power.

"Of course, I can't pay much," he said, cocking his head and dropping his hands. "But surely you don't care about that. A woman like you, a child of nature, doesn't need much money. Do you?"

He paused for her to respond.

Sarah frowned, struggling to come to grips with his meaning. Did she need money? "What is money?" she asked. This was not a word that Max had taught her.

The Professor smiled and raised an eyebrow. "Exactly," he said. "What is money to people like us? Money comes and money goes."

He reached out to Cassidy, smiling, with a hand that was apparently empty. When he took his hand away from Cassidy's ear, it was holding a coin. "Money," he said. "It comes . . ." He closed his hand around the coin, then opened his hand. The coin was gone.

"Where did it go?" she asked.

"It vanished into thin air. It's magic."

She studied his face. He seemed very amused. "You are lying," she said softly, a little puzzled.

"Of course!" His smile broadened. "That's what magic is—a lie that you choose to believe." He snapped his fingers and the coin was back. "Reality and illusion—it's all a sham. And in the end, money is the greatest illusion of all. I remember a time in

Shanghai when I was dead broke, busted, not a nickel to my name. But fate smiles on people like us. . . ."

The Milky Way was twinkling overhead when the Professor finished a series of stories about how fate had smiled on him and his company. "And now we have this! A Wild Angel who comes from nowhere to our aid." He beamed at Cassidy. "It's a wonderful world, is it not?"

Sarah was strangely content. She had understood little of what the Professor had been saying in words, but he treated her like a member of his pack; he welcomed her. That was good.

The fire had died to embers. The air was sweet with pine smoke. A chorus of frogs sang from the nearby creek.

"It is a wonderful world," Cassidy agreed. "And a wonderful life."

Sarah lifted her head. She was not listening to him. She was attending to another voice—the distant howling of a wolf, almost too faint to be heard. While the others watched, she lifted her head and returned the call with a howl that started low and climbed the scale to a high sustained note that sent chills up Cassidy's spine.

"Your friend Beka?" the Professor asked Sarah softly.

Sarah nodded. She stood, listening for Beka's answering howl. There it was again—maybe a mile distant.

She smiled at the Professor. "I really must be going." It was another of the polite phrases Max had taught her.

"Wait," Cassidy said. "You can't . . ."

But Sarah was no longer there to be told what she could not do. She vanished into the night, leaving the circus behind.

18

UP A TREE

"I have always been rather better treated in San Francisco than I actually deserved."

—Mark Twain

AS A LITTLE GIRL, HELEN HARRIS HAD PREFERRED CLIMBING trees to dressing like a young lady and attending church. Her aunt Bridget, who had taken Helen in at age six and adopted her when her mother died, had broken her of this habit. But at age twenty-two, after abstaining from tree-climbing for more than sixteen years, Helen Harris found a use for the skills of her youth.

She was traveling with Miss Paxon. The two women had made camp halfway between Jones Bar and Selby Flat when a hungry black bear lumbered from the bushes and indicated an intense curiosity in the contents of their saddlebags.

Kicking off her shoes and hiking up her long skirts, Helen had scrambled up an oak tree in record time. Miss Paxon had followed, with alacrity. From a safe perch in the branches, the two women watched the bear claw open Helen's saddlebag and thrust its head inside, snuffling loudly. The beast was, Helen suspected, smelling the horehound candy that Helen had secreted in the bottom.

Helen shook her head ruefully. Aunt Bridget would

say that God was punishing Helen for self-indulgence. If Helen had not packed candy in her bag, the bear would not be rummaging through her things. Helen glanced at Miss Paxon. The older woman was watching the bear with interest and showed no signs of intending to blame this incident on Helen. Relieved, Helen returned her attention to the bear.

The bear pulled its head from the bag. Helen's best shawl was now draped around its neck. Ignoring the shawl, the beast continued to claw at the bag, tossing out clothes and pamphlets until it reached a paper sack full of candy. Grabbing the bag in its mouth, the bear shook it vigorously, scattering candy on the ground and looking, Helen thought, as disapproving as her aunt would have looked under similar circumstances.

HELEN'S AUNT BRIDGET was what many would call a God-fearing woman. God was, in fact, the only personage Aunt Bridget feared. Aunt Bridget was wealthy, having outlived a husband who had been a very successful banker. She was stubborn and did not put up with foolishness. She regarded horehound candy as one of many forms of foolishness.

Helen's mother had died of a fever when Helen was six. When Helen remembered her mother, she remembered her laughter first. Her mother had been a happy woman, always laughing and joking. Helen remembered her papa as a pair of arms that held her and scratchy kisses that smelled sweetly of tobacco.

According to Aunt Bridget, Helen's father had been a ne'er-do-well, some sort of criminal. Helen's mother had met and married him against her family's wishes. He had been sent away to the penitentiary when Helen was five, and Helen's mother had come to live with Aunt Bridget.

According to Aunt Bridget, Helen was very lucky

that Aunt Bridget had been there to take her and her mother in, and to keep Helen from the orphanage when her mother died. Helen was not entirely convinced that this was lucky, having wondered at times if the orphanage might not be a cheerier place than her aunt's house, a mansion filled with ancient furniture and equally ancient servants.

Aunt Bridget disapproved of candy. She disapproved of dime novels. She disapproved of fun, and she disapproved of Helen. Aunt Bridget's disapproval was, in a sense, the indirect cause of Helen's current position in a tree.

When the American Temperance Society started a Chicago chapter, Helen's aunt had been one of the first to join. After all, she disapproved of drinking. Aunt Bridget had taken a grim pleasure in the Society's holy war against the demon rum, writing letters to the newspapers, singing hymns outside the local tavern, coercing family friends into signing the Temperance Pledge.

Helen, leading a sheltered life under her aunt's control, had welcomed the Temperance Society activities. They had provided her with an opportunity to leave the house, to sing in the streets, and to catch a glimpse of another world—the dark and intriguing world of saloons and drunkards and the women who consorted with them.

Not long after the formation of the chapter, Miss Paxon, a Temperance lecturer who had letters of introduction from Society chapter presidents in New York and Boston, had come to town. When she arrived, she checked into a respectable downtown hotel, but that lasted only until Aunt Bridget met her. "You'll be my guest for as long as you are in the city," Aunt Bridget insisted.

And so Miss Paxon, a tall blond woman with piercing blue eyes, came to stay in one of Aunt Bridget's many spare rooms. Helen's aunt was very happy about this. Though Aunt Bridget did not say so, Helen knew that this was another skirmish in the ongoing war between her aunt and Mrs. Thompson, the president of the local Temperance Society chapter. By having such an august visitor as her guest, Aunt Bridget had somehow won.

That Friday, Miss Paxon spoke at the Temperance Society's regular evening meeting and told them of her mission. She was going to California, she told the assembled ladies. "The good Lord has called me to do his work and I, his humble servant, have promised to obey. I am called to California on a mission of love, a rescue mission, a holy mission to save the men of California."

Miss Paxon was a powerful speaker, especially when it came to descriptions of drunkenness and depravity. The picture she painted of conditions in California had some women reaching for their handkerchiefs, while others (including Helen's aunt) clenched their fists.

Helen sat at Aunt Bridget's side, watching Miss Paxon exhort the crowd. As she watched, she wondered what it would be like to hear a call. Helen wanted very badly to go to California, that distant land of gold. Was that the same as hearing a call? She would gladly help Miss Paxon with her work. Helen suspected that was not the same as hearing a call, but maybe she just wasn't listening hard enough.

At the podium, Miss Paxon warmed to her subject, speaking of the great work that she could do—if only she had the resolve, if only she had the courage, if only she had the support of the women of the nation. She lingered on this last part. She needed their prayers, but she needed more than that. She needed funding to support her work.

Her audience was greatly moved. They wept; they applauded. Mrs. Thompson passed through the audience with a little basket, and the assembled ladies reached into their purses and donated generously. Then Helen's aunt stood up and said that she would, from her own pocket, match the money collected in Mrs. Thompson's basket.

Miss Paxon thanked them all for their generosity and thanked Helen's aunt in particular. Aunt Bridget smiled in triumph, and the meeting ended with ringing applause.

That evening, Miss Paxon and Aunt Bridget lingered over tea in the drawing room. Helen retired, ostensibly to her bed, but actually to Miss Paxon's room. She wanted to talk to Miss Paxon in private; she wanted to discuss what constituted a call. She wanted to ask Miss Paxon to take her to California.

It was a warm spring evening, and Helen opened the window to let a breath of fresh air into the room. As luck would have it, the breeze from the open window stirred the papers on the small writing desk, sending them fluttering to the floor. Helen hurried to gather the papers, glancing at them as she did so. For the most part, they were pamphlets and flyers related to Temperance Society activities in various cities, but the paper that caught Helen's eye was something else.

"Gitana will tell your future," it proclaimed in bold type. Beneath the type was a picture of Miss Paxon, draped in exotic scarves and smiling mysteriously.

Helen stared at the flyer, mystified. Why would a respectable Temperance lecturer be telling fortunes? Unless she wasn't really a respectable Temperance lecturer.

Helen rummaged through the other papers—the ones on the desk and the ones in Miss Paxon's satchel on the floor. She felt guilty doing it, but she justified her action to herself. This could, she thought, be part of the good Lord's plan. He had sent a breeze to disturb the papers to help Helen in her quest to do his work. It was a bit of a stretch, she realized, but it comforted her some.

Among the papers she found other flyers advertising Miss Paxon's services. The woman was a spiritualist, a dancing instructor, and a professor of mesmerism and phrenology. There were playbills from several theaters advertising "the amazing Gitana." A sketch showed Miss Paxon dressed in a costume made mostly of feathers, holding a large boa constrictor.

When Miss Paxon returned to the room, Helen was sitting in a rocking chair by the window, clutching the flyers. The single candle that burned on the mantelpiece cast a wavering, uncertain light. The shadows shifted and moved around Helen like wild creatures—now running, now lying still.

"Helen," Miss Paxon said softly, "what are you doing here?"

"Please close the door," Helen said. She was not sure what to do. She had, before coming to the room, prepared an earnest speech about her desire to go with Miss Paxon and save the unfortunate drunkards in California. Now that speech no longer seemed appropriate. "I wanted to talk with you," Helen said. "I have to go to California with you."

"I see." Miss Paxon glanced at the papers in Helen's hand and frowned. "You've been looking through my papers?"

"I just came to talk. The wind blew the papers,

and . . ." Helen was flustered, but determined. "I looked at them when I gathered them up."

Miss Paxon seated herself in the straight-backed chair on the other side of the window. "Why do you have to go to California?" she asked calmly.

"I want to get away from this place." Helen waved the hand holding the flyers in a gesture that included the dark-paneled walls that seemed to press closer in the dim light. "I can help you with Temperance lecturing." She glanced down at the flyers. "Or whatever you do. I just want . . ." She struggled for words.

Miss Paxon smiled. "You want to go on an adventure. You want to run away and see the world." She studied Helen. The girl could make trouble by showing those flyers to her aunt. Helen had not threatened to do that just yet, but Miss Paxon knew that the possibility was there.

"Can you dance?" Miss Paxon asked.

"A little," Helen said. "I like music, and I can play the pianoforte."

"Of course you can." Every young woman of means could play the pianoforte. "Can you act on stage?"

Helen's eyes widened. "I've never tried it."

"You don't seem to be shy. Your voice is pleasant enough."

Miss Paxon had been traveling alone for the last year. It had gotten a little lonely. It might be pleasant to have a young companion for a time, if the companion were the right sort of person.

Miss Paxon reached for the deck of tarot cards that she kept in her traveling bag. The cards were wrapped in a scarf of Indian silk. Keeping her eyes on Helen, Miss Paxon unwrapped them and held them out to the younger woman.

"Cut the cards," she said. "I'll make my decision then."

"Why?" Helen asked. "Why should I cut the cards?"

Miss Paxon smiled. "The cards will tell me who you are. Then I will know if I wish to travel with you."

"But you know who I am," Helen said. "I'm Helen Harris."

"Cut the cards." Miss Paxon's voice allowed no disagreement.

Helen reached out. Her hand was shaking as she touched the deck. She had never played with cards; her aunt did not approve of games of chance. She did not know how the cards could tell Miss Paxon anything at all.

She cut, then Miss Paxon took the cards from her hand and studied the card on top. The picture showed a young man in motley clothing, wandering along the edge of a cliff. Over his shoulder, he carried a bag that Helen somehow knew held all his worldly goods. Behind him, a little white dog danced on its hind legs.

"It's the Fool," Miss Paxon said, smiling. "The divine innocent. If he falls, the angels will catch him and set him down safe. He is guided by his foolishness and innocence, but there's no harm in him, and no harm comes to him." She studied Helen for a moment, then said, "Be ready to leave tomorrow."

Helen stared at her as she wrapped the cards in the silk scarf and placed them in her bag. "Will you talk to my aunt?" she said, her voice shaking. "Will you persuade her?"

Miss Paxon shrugged. "Write your aunt a letter explaining that you've decided to go west. Pack a bag—just one bag. Leave the rest to me."

They left at dawn the next day, catching the stage west. When Helen asked Miss Paxon if she had spoken to Aunt Bridget, Miss Paxon just shrugged. "I left your letter on her tea tray. I didn't see there was any need for further discussion," she said.

They went to California, spending a good portion of the money Miss Paxon had collected from the Temperance Society on the trip. By the time they reached San Francisco, Helen had steeled herself to participate in anything Miss Paxon proposed—from stage acting to dancing instruction to mesmerism. But rather than pursuing any of those occupations, Miss Paxon arranged a meeting with the local chapter of the Temperance Society, a group of half a dozen women.

When Helen asked her about this decision, Miss Paxon smiled. "You thought we'd do something more exotic? Maybe a little sinful?" Miss Paxon shook her head. "Plenty of sin in this city already," she said. "But virtue is in short supply."

At the time of Miss Paxon's arrival, San Francisco's chapter of the Temperance Society had not managed to close any saloons. They had all but given up on the cause.

Miss Paxon rallied them. She asked Mrs. Victor, the leader of the group, to take her to the city's most prosperous tavern. Outside that establishment, she asked Mrs. Victor, a woman with a voice deep enough to shake the windows, to lead the group in hymns. There in the street, over the rattle of dicing cups and the laughter of drunks, Miss Paxon shouted prayers. She exhorted the men in the tavern to come out and save themselves.

The owner was one of the first out the door. "Ladies," he said to them, "how long do you intend to keep up this racket?"

Miss Paxon smiled at him. "Until every man in your establishment has signed the Temperance Pledge," she said.

The man shook his head. "You'll wait 'til hell freezes over," he said good-naturedly, and returned to the bar.

The ladies continued their hymns, and Miss Paxon resumed her shouting. A number of drinking men abandoned their posts at the bar and, responding to Miss Paxon's call, joined the ladies for a time, singing "Rock of Ages" with gusto and cheerfully signing Temperance pledges with inebriated scrawls. A man named Harold repented with great zest and fervor, weeping on Helen's shoulder. "Hold my hand to give me courage," he asked Helen, and of course she did. He planted a whiskey-scented kiss on her cheek and thanked her from the bottom of his heart.

The owner came out a second time. A good portion of his clientele was now in the street, singing drunkenly. "Ladies, you are ruining my business," he said. "How can I persuade you to be on your way?"

Miss Paxon smiled again. "Repent and pray with us," she said. "Leave off this evil business."

The owner returned to his establishment, shaking his head. Harold left Helen then and went to stand by Miss Paxon. Mrs. Victor had begun another hymn, so Helen could not hear their conversation. But Harold moved away purposefully through the crowd. He was no longer weeping. In fact, he was grinning. He headed into the tavern.

Not five minutes later, the owner came out a third time. "Ladies!" he shouted. "Your devotion has touched my heart." And he went on at length about how their singing had reminded him of his dear wife, long departed. It was her death that had turned him to drink, he said, and listening to them he had realized how it must pain his wife (who was now among the angels) to see him drinking and selling the demon rum to lead others into the path of wickedness. But he was a changed man; he would sell rum no more; he would change this place of evil into a Temperance hotel, where only tea and healthful beverages were served. And he had them, the ladies of the Temperance Society, to thank for it.

It seemed to Helen that his delivery lacked conviction. Twice, he glanced at Harold, who smiled and nodded and winked, more than once. "Why are you winking?" she whispered to him.

"Winking back tears," he said. "Tears of joy."

Helen had her doubts about this.

"So you can be on your way," the owner said. "Happy that you have done your duty."

Miss Paxon smiled. "I think we'd best stay a time and pray with you."

"You have done so much already," the man cried. "I cannot ask any more."

"You do not have to ask," Miss Paxon said. "We are only too glad to be here in your time of need. We rejoice with the angels in heaven at your salvation. Let us sing together." She turned to Mrs. Victor, who was ready to begin another hymn.

"I must express my gratitude," the man shouted. "How can I help you, who have helped me so much? I know! I can help by spreading the word to others. You must take this message to the hills. As depraved and wicked as we are here in San Francisco, the men in the mine fields are ten times worse. But you good ladies could melt their hearts and get them to mend their ways." He turned to the drunks and the gamblers who had come from his saloon and all the other saloons on the street. "Men!" he cried. "We must take up a collection. We must send these good ladies to the place where they can do the most good. To the mining camps—where men are sorely in need of their assistance."

And the tavern owner took off his hat and took a

hundred-dollar bill from his pocket. "I'll start the collection with this," he said, "for I am the greatest sinner amongst you."

"Let the young lady pass the hat!" Harold cried.

At Harold's insistence, Helen took the hat and walked through the crowd. It seemed to Helen that some of the men were torn between laughter and tears, but they all reached into their pockets and poured dollars and gold into the man's hat, so she supposed that their hearts were moved. Many of them hugged her and thanked her. By the time she returned to Miss Paxon's side, her cheeks were burning—from the scratchy kisses of grateful men and all the attention.

Mrs. Victor led one more hymn, Miss Paxon conferred with Harold, and then all the members of the Temperance Society retired in triumph to Mrs. Victor's parlor for tea.

The next day, on the coach to Sacramento, Helen asked Miss Paxon if she thought the tavern keeper had been sincere in his repentance.

"Sincere? Well, he sincerely wanted us to leave. And he was willing to pay to accomplish that end." Miss Paxon patted her purse. "Now he has a little less money to use for his evil doings."

HELEN HAD COME to California to do the Lord's work. At that moment, looking down at the bear, Helen wondered exactly what the Lord had in mind. The bear was eating the hard candies with great relish, chewing with its mouth open as the candies stuck in its teeth.

"What are we going to do?" she asked Miss Paxon.

"Wait to see what happens next," Miss Paxon said in a tone of great confidence. "It's bound to be interesting."

Helen nodded dubiously. Her aunt Bridget, she was

sure, would have said that they should pray to the Lord for guidance. Hesitantly, she suggested this to Miss Paxon.

Miss Paxon shrugged. "If you like," she said.

Helen bowed her head. "Dear Lord," she began. "We pray for your assistance in our hour of need. We ask . . ." But before Helen could complete her request, she was interrupted by a bloodcurdling howl. "Wolves," she gasped, craning her neck to see if she could find the source of the sound. In the distance, another wolf answered the first. "They're gathering. They're closing in on us."

Staring in the direction of the howling, Helen saw something move: a person. "Hello," she called. She waved, feeling faintly absurd. How does one properly introduce oneself to a stranger in the woods when one is sitting in a tree being menaced by bears and wolves? "Excuse me! We're rather in need of some help. There's a bear eating our luggage, and . . ."

Her explanation trailed off as she got a closer look at the stranger, a young woman who was half-naked, wearing a loose shirt and a pair of men's trousers that had been cut off at the knees, leaving her legs shockingly bare. A bow and a quiver of arrows were slung over her shoulder. A wolf walked at her side.

"Hallo," said the woman. "How do you do?"

Startled, Helen answered automatically. "Very well, thank you. How do you do?"

The woman's smile widened. "Very well."

"Wonderful," said Miss Paxon. "Could you do something about that bear?"

The bear had finished the last of the horehound candy and was idly snuffling through Miss Paxon's things. He nosed a box, and it fell open, spilling lavender-scented face powder on the ground. The bear sneezed mightily, but continued to paw through

Miss Paxon's bag. A glass bottle tumbled from the open bag, breaking against a rock, and the powerful scent of lilac perfume rose from the spill. The bear sneezed again. Sitting back on his haunches, he surveyed the wreckage, shaking his head and sneezing a third time.

The savage woman shrugged. She spoke to the bear then, shouting at the animal in some foreign language. The bear sneezed again, then turned away from the scattered clothes. With a glance at the women in the tree, he shambled away.

"What did you say to him?" Helen asked. "What language was that?"

"I told him that there was a fine rotten log at the bottom of the hill, filled with fat grubs. I told him it was time for him to go." The woman grinned. "But he was going anyway. He did not like that smell." She wrinkled her nose—clearly she did not much care for it either.

"Thank you for your assistance," Miss Paxon said. "Let me introduce myself. I am Miss Paxon, and this is my assistant, Miss Harris. We are on our way to Selby Flat, and I fear we have lost our way. Perhaps you could assist us?"

"There's a circus in the valley," Sarah said. "They are going to Selby Flat. I will take you to them."

Miss Paxon and Helen clambered down from the tree. Miss Paxon shook Sarah's hand and asked Sarah's name. She squatted down to greet Beka, allowing the wolf to sniff her face thoroughly. The wolf sniffed at Helen's skirts in an unseemly fashion.

Sarah found their mule—the beast hadn't gone far—while Helen and Miss Paxon gathered the things that the bear had scattered. The moon was rising, providing enough light to cast shadows, but not enough to reassure Helen that the shadows were harmless. As she repacked the saddlebags, Helen kept a nervous watch on the shadows around her. Sarah and Miss Paxon both seemed quite confident that the bear would not return, but Helen was not so sure.

Finally, the mule was loaded, and they were ready to go. Sarah told the women to follow her and started down the hillside. Miss Paxon led the mule and seemed as confident in her footing as that surefooted beast. But Helen was quite the opposite. After a bit, Sarah let Miss Paxon go ahead, leading the mule. Sarah waited for Helen to catch up.

Sarah was amazed at how slowly Helen traveled. Though the hillside was not terribly steep, and they were following a deer trail that seemed quite wide to Sarah, Helen kept slipping and almost falling. Twice, she started to blunder off the trail, though the way seemed quite clear to Sarah.

Sarah could read fear in the way Helen moved; she held herself stiffly and jerked nervously whenever her dress caught on a branch. She peered nervously at every shadow.

"Come," Sarah said, when Helen finally reached the place where she stood. The woman stopped, obviously startled. She had been watching her feet so carefully that she had not noticed Sarah standing there.

Helen stared at Sarah with wide, frightened eyes. "I keep slipping," she said. "I know I'm going to fall."

"Here, I will help." Sarah held out her hand and led the woman along the trail, walking slowly and showing the woman where to put her feet. Helen clutched Sarah's hand, clinging for dear life.

"Your shoes are not good," Sarah told Helen after observing how they slipped on smooth places in the trail.

"I'm sorry," Helen said. She was still frightened. In the moonlight, Sarah saw tears glistening in her eyes.

Sarah frowned. "You are sorry for your shoes?" she asked.

"I'm sorry I'm so slow."

Sarah shrugged. "You will get faster." She studied the woman's posture. "Do not walk like this," she said, imitating Helen's walk—stiff-legged, back ramrod straight. "Go like this." Sarah relaxed, letting her legs bend so that it was easy to recover from slipping.

Helen giggled nervously. "Aunt Bridget always stressed good posture," she said.

"Who is Aunt Bridget?"

"My aunt. She is very strict."

Sarah frowned. "She is not here."

"You're right. She's not." Helen smiled, relaxing a little. "She'd have nothing good to say if she were. She wouldn't approve of all this. Climbing trees, chasing bears, gallivanting about in the middle of the night."

Sarah studied Helen's face. "I do not think I would like Aunt Bridget."

"Oh, you wouldn't like her at all. And she wouldn't approve of you."

"You do not like Aunt Bridget," Sarah observed.

"Well, I owe her so much." Helen began. Sarah could tell from her tone that she was going to continue. People, Sarah thought, often talked too much.

"But you do not like her," Sarah interrupted before Helen could go on. She studied Helen's face, reading the truth of the matter there. "And she does not approve of you."

Helen laughed suddenly. "You're right. She would be appalled by all this."

"Then why do you care about good posture?" Sarah pronounced the last word carefully, not knowing what it meant, but knowing that it was one reason that Helen could not relax and walk down the hill.

Helen laughed again. "I don't."

"Good. Then follow me."

Helen followed, walking more easily. She started to fall, and rather than stiffening up, she bent her legs and recovered.

"Much better," Sarah said. Helen's grip on Sarah's hand had eased; she was beginning to relax.

"I can see a campfire," Miss Paxon called from the hillside below.

"Not far now," Sarah said to Helen.

"It's not so bad," Helen said. When they reached the meadow, she was smiling, still holding Sarah's hand. "Thank you for helping me," she said. "I could not have done it without you."

Helen could see the light of a distant campfire, flickering through the trees. As Sarah led her across the meadow, Helen saw a bulky shadow move out of the trees and loom closer, following them. She shrieked. "Oh, my goodness!" she cried, her confidence evaporating. "What is it?"

"It is Ruby," Sarah said. "Professor Serunca's elephant."

Helen gaped in amazement as the elephant approached, flapping its ears and lifting its trunk in a salute.

"Professor Serunca!" Miss Paxon exclaimed. "How wonderful!"

"Who's that?" shouted a voice from the campfire.

"Hello, Professor," Miss Paxon called. "It's Gitana. With my traveling companion, Helen Harris."

The Professor stood at the edge of camp, holding a flaming brand from the fire. When he saw the three women, he hurried toward them, beaming when the torchlight fell on Miss Paxon.

"Gitana," the Professor called. "How wonderful to see you again!"

Helen watched in amazement as Professor Serunca

greeted Miss Paxon in the European style, kissing both cheeks. Miss Paxon glanced at Helen and smiled. "The Professor and I were students of the same guru in India. And we have worked together, every now and then."

"Come and sit by the fire," the Professor said. "You must tell me what you've been up to since I saw you last."

Helen sat on a fallen log beside Cassidy, listening to Miss Paxon tell of their experiences in California and the Professor recount the travels of his company to date. Sarah and Beka stood at the edge of the circle of firelight, just behind her.

"This is a fine bit of luck," the Professor said. "You can come with us to Selby Flat, where we will search for Sarah's friend Max. I am quite confident that we will find him."

Sarah sat by the fire, studying their faces in the firelight. Everyone was smiling, happy to be together. A large black poodle leaned against her leg. Snowflake slept in her lap. Helen sat close at her side, glancing at her every now and then, as if for reassurance.

The Professor's confidence was quite persuasive. At that moment, it all seemed quite easy. They would go to Selby Flat. They would find Max. And all would be well.

19

A FORMIDABLE WOMAN

"She was not quite what you would call refined.
She was not quite what you would call unrefined.
She was the kind of person that keeps a parrot."

—*Following the Equator;* Mark Twain

MAX SAT ON A WOODEN CRATE, IDLY SKETCHING THE STEAMSHIP *Discovery* as it chugged slowly toward the dock. For the past two months, he had been at the dock each day that a steamship was due.

He had become a fixture there, known to the longshoremen and the sailors. Just then, he was putting the finishing touches on a panoramic sketch of the derelict ships that filled the harbor, long since abandoned by their crews. Some of them had been converted into floating warehouses, serving as storage for shopkeepers on shore. From where Max sat, he could see the masts of ships that had been run aground and converted to terrestrial use: He had visited a bar in a steamship's belly, a gambling house in an old clipper ship.

It was late June. In March, as he was waiting in Selby Flat for the snows to melt in the high country, he had received a letter from Audrey North.

I have received word that my husband's ship has been lost with all hands. I am a widow now. It is so strange. I loved my husband, but sometimes I felt that I loved the memory of my husband, not the man who returned to this house so rarely, at such great intervals. That man was a stranger to me—a beloved stranger, but a stranger still.

I am grieving, but at the same time, I feel strangely liberated. I am dressed in black, as befits a widow. But I confess that I feel lighter now, as if my husband had been a weight that was dragging me down.

Over the protests of friends and family, I have decided to sell my house in New Bedford and come to California. I will purchase a ticket on a steamship to Panama. I have heard that the journey across the isthmus is not as difficult now as it once was. But that does not matter. Whatever the danger, I am ready for it. Look for me in the spring.

He had hurried to San Francisco to look for her arrival. There, he had waited, fretting that he could not be in the mountains, unable to send a message to Sarah, chafing to be gone, but unwilling to abandon Audrey North to make her way alone.

Each time he met a ship, he inquired of the passengers if they had met Mrs. Audrey North, if they knew her whereabouts. Two days before, a matronly woman, escorting her brood of youngsters ashore, had told him that Mrs. North had been in Panama when she left. "She booked passage on the *Discovery*," the woman assured him. "God willing, she'll be here soon."

The winds that slowed northbound ships were unseasonably strong, he had learned from the sailors. Storms at sea had swamped more than one ship, had delayed others.

"There she is!" cried Tom Jacobs. Jacobs, like Max, had been meeting all the ships for the past month. He was waiting for his wife, whom he hadn't seen in three years. Jacobs bounced on his heels, so excited he couldn't stand still. "With luck, your friend will be aboard, too."

When Jacobs had asked Max who he was waiting for, Max had hesitated. "A friend," he had said, after a pause. He didn't know how to describe his relationship to Audrey North. For more than a decade, they had been corresponding with each other. Over that time they had exchanged views on any number of subjects. Sometimes, those exchanges had been heated.

He was looking forward to meeting Audrey with a mixture of anticipation and apprehension. He had enjoyed corresponding with the woman—with her comfortably far away and no danger that they would ever meet. He was a lonely man, and she had been, in so many ways, the perfect audience for his writings. She had been quite supportive and kind, finding him a publisher, offering words of encouragement.

But he had had so little experience with women over the past decade and a half. He had always been in the company of men, and the thought of meeting a lady made him nervous.

Since he had received the letter saying that she was on her way, he had been trying to imagine meeting Audrey in person. He had no idea what she looked like. A formidable woman, he thought. Broadly built, with a no-nonsense demeanor. She would, he thought, be somewhat reserved. Very respectable, of course.

The steamship was making slow progress. It was surrounded by smaller boats. Agents for the auction houses, eager to know what cargo the *Discovery* carried, had hurried out to bid for scarce items, hoping to purchase the merchandise before the ship even touched ground. Men from some of the city's larger employers were asking whether there were passengers with specific skills: cooks or carpenters or blacksmiths or clerks. One-man ferries, for the traveler in a hurry, met the ship and offered to carry passengers quickly to shore for a mere three dollars. After four months at sea, there were always a few passengers who were willing to pay that extravagant tariff to abandon ship just a few hours sooner than they otherwise would.

Max put away his notebook and left his seat on the crate to join the crowd at the edge of the dock. "There she is!" Jacobs shouted. He waved frantically. "There's my Nancy." A thin blond woman in a calico dress waved back.

Max stared at the passengers who crowded the steamship's railing, scanning their faces. The great throng of weary-looking men, women, and children, Max guessed, had traveled by steerage. Max knew from talking to miners who had come west by steamer that steerage passengers were crowded into a single large compartment in the hull of the ship, sleeping in tiers of berths with no privacy to speak of. It was a beastly, uncomfortable way to travel, particularly in the tropics, where the heat made the sleeping quarters unbearable.

The second-class passengers had it better. Their sleeping chambers held a dozen or more berths, but they usually had portholes, and the passengers ate the same meals as the first-class passengers.

The first-class passengers had small, private cabins, each with two to four berths, a washstand, and a mirror. By the standards of steamships, first-class passengers traveled in luxury.

Nancy, the miner's wife, was among the second-class passengers, a crowd of respectable-looking men and women—shopkeepers, farmers, tradesmen, and the like, by the look of them. One woman stood alone, staring toward the shore. She wore a gray dress of a severe cut. He could not see her hair—it was tucked under a hat. She was frowning at the shore, looking decidedly stern.

Could that be Audrey, he wondered. He could see no other likely candidate. Tentatively, he lifted a hand to wave at her, but she did not wave back. "Mrs. North!" he called, but his voice was lost in the shouting of sailors and longshoremen, the creaking of the dock, and the splash of the waves.

As the ship approached, the dock became a confusion of eager men, each with his own agenda and no one to keep order. Longshoremen pushed forward with their carts, ready to unload the cargo; men who were meeting passengers called up to them. The gangplank was lowered, and the passengers crowded off. Max fought his way through the crowd to the base of the gangplank, just in time to see Nancy rush into the arms of her waiting husband. Then he lost his position for a moment, as a man with a cart full of oranges pushed past, the first cargo to be unloaded. The sweet scent of oranges momentarily mingled with the tang of salt water.

"If I never smell another orange, it will be too soon," said a woman who was stepping off the gangplank. She was a slender woman with auburn curls, wearing a dress the color of new leaves. She seemed to be speaking to him.

"Why is that?" he asked, craning his neck to search for Mrs. North. He couldn't see her anywhere.

"The hold beneath my stateroom was filled with oranges, and I've been smelling them day and night for the past two months," she said. "It was a lovely smell at first, but after two months, I would kill for a peach or an apple, anything but an orange."

Max nodded politely, but did not respond further.

"Are you meeting someone?" she asked.

"Yes, but I seem to have lost her in the crowd," he said, frowning.

"A woman?"

"Yes, yes," Max said, a little impatient now. He was concerned for Mrs. North's well-being. Though she craved adventure, he thought she would be bewildered by the noise and confusion of the dock. He thought the woman who addressed him was being rather brazen. "She was standing by the railing when the boat docked. There she is!" The woman in gray was making her way down the gangplank. "Mrs. North!" he called, waving frantically. "Mrs. North."

She did not look his way.

Max felt someone tap him on the shoulder. The auburn-haired woman again. "That's Miss Hector," she said. "She's come to San Francisco here to manage a school." She smiled. "But as it happens, my name is North. Audrey North."

Max stared, dumbstruck.

"You must be Max."

Max realized his mouth was hanging open and closed it. With an effort, he managed something like a smile. "Mrs. North," he said. "Audrey. My apologies. I didn't think . . . I thought . . ."

She smiled, an expression far more genuine than his own. "What did you think?" she asked.

"I thought you would be older." He spoke without thinking, then colored when he realized how very impertinent he sounded.

But she continued smiling. "I'm forty-four years old," she said. "That's quite old enough, I think."

Her smile widened as she waited for him to respond. He could not think of what to say. He had imagined a plain, solid woman—rather like Mrs. Selby with a literary bent.

"I thought . . ." he hesitated, then continued, "I thought you would be in mourning."

She shook her head. "I wore black all the way to Panama," she said. "That was all I could manage. In the end, the heat decided me. I commissioned this dress from a local seamstress."

Max nodded, but could think of nothing to say. So many men came to California and left their past behind. He supposed it was only fair for a woman to do the same.

"And what else did you think?" she asked.

The last of the passengers was stepping off the gangplank. "I thought you might like to get to a hotel and freshen up," he stammered.

Somehow, despite his confusion, he managed to find her luggage and engage a horse-drawn cab to take them to the hotel where he had been staying, a clean, unpretentious establishment on a quiet street. On the way to the hotel, she asked about Sarah. He told her when he had seen the girl last, how she had been then. "The snow has melted in the high country," he said. "She'll be looking for me, wondering where I am." He asked about her journey, and she told him about Latin American fruit markets and storms at sea.

At last, they reached the hotel. He unloaded her bags and she arranged for a room with Mrs. Price, the proprietress.

"Why don't you take a moment to refresh yourself?" Mrs. Price suggested. "If you would like a bit of tea, I could bring that to the parlor."

"That would be lovely."

An hour later, Max was sitting in the parlor by the front window when Audrey came downstairs. She settled on the horsehair sofa across from him with a sigh.

"Do you know, it feels like the entire city is rolling beneath me," she said. "I can feel every wave and swell."

"You've got your sea legs," Max said, then caught himself. He blushed at having mentioned her legs, something one just did not do.

She stared at him, scrutinizing his face with those intense blue eyes.

"My apologies," he said hastily. "I've been in the hills too long. I . . ."

"Max," she interrupted. "Why are you afraid of me?"

"Afraid of you?" He shook his head. "I don't know what you're talking about. I . . ."

"I've seen it before. I make men nervous."

"My dear lady, you're being foolish. I can't imagine . . ."

"You've been terrified since you met me at the ship. You've been blushing and babbling about nonsense." She considered him with a steady gaze.

He avoided her eyes and started to bluster, knowing he was blustering but unable to stop himself. "Terrified? My dear lady, you've been on that ship too long. You're talking to a man who has faced grizzly bears. Afraid of you? I don't know what you could be thinking. I . . ."

She giggled. No question about it. She definitely giggled. He stopped in mid-sentence, glaring at her.

"Exactly what do you find so amusing?" he asked.

"I was remembering a letter you wrote to me a few years ago. You told me that you had tried to explain to Sarah what lying was. She didn't understand no matter what you said, until she mentioned that you were afraid of Jasper Davis. You told her you weren't. In your letter, you went on at some length about your ability to bluster. And after you had gone on for some time, Sarah said . . ."

"You're lying." He finished her sentence.

Audrey grinned at him. "You certainly didn't exaggerate your ability to bluster," she said.

He nodded. Her eyes were as blue as Sarah's—a brilliant, honest blue that caught the light, sparkling with good humor. "Well, I've had a lot of practice. People expect an author to bluster a bit, I think."

"You do it very well."

"Thank you." He studied her face.

"Remember—we've been corresponding honestly for some thirteen years now."

He leaned back in his chair, still considering her face. "If I'd known we were going to meet, I might have been a little more careful about what I wrote."

She shrugged. "Too late now. I know your secrets."

"Not all of them."

She narrowed her eyes. "Maybe not all, but enough."

"All right, you asked why I'm afraid of you. I'm afraid because you're very pretty and you're very smart and it's been years since I was around a lady." He paused. "I was expecting you to be rather stout and matronly."

"You sound a little disappointed."

"Just surprised. I expected a woman in mourning, and I found a woman who giggles at the first sign of bluster."

She nodded. "You were expecting Mrs. Audrey North, a stout New England matron. But when I crossed the isthmus, I decided that it was time to reinvent myself. I am no longer Mrs. North of New Bedford, grieving widow of Captain North, pillar of her community. Oh, no—I'm simply Audrey North, a woman looking for her niece among the wolves. And I'm certainly not a lady."

Max nodded. "There's a long tradition of men coming west to leave their past behind," he said slowly.

"That's exactly it," she said. "I'm starting fresh."

"All right then," he said. "Let's start again."

She reached out, took his hand, and squeezed it, a gesture of sudden affection. "That's better," she said. "Now I'm not afraid of you, and you aren't afraid of me."

"Were you ever afraid of me?" he asked.

"Terrified," she said steadily. Then she waved her hand, dismissing the past. "Now that all that is settled, let's talk about where we go from here. I understand that we'd best take a riverboat to Sacramento and catch a stagecoach from there to Nevada City. Then perhaps by horse and mule from there to Selby Flat. I am looking forward to seeing my niece as soon as possible."

20

THE CIRCUS COMES TO TOWN

"Clothes make the man.
Naked people have little or no influence in society."

—Mark Twain

MEANWHILE, IN THE CALIFORNIA FOOTHILLS, PROFESSOR Serunca's Traveling Circus was preparing to head for Selby Flat. Before they left, Helen raised the question of Sarah's clothing. She spoke first with Miss Paxon.

"I wonder," she began cautiously. "If Sarah is coming to town with us, I think . . . perhaps we should make sure she is properly dressed."

Miss Paxon glanced over at Sarah. The wild girl was standing beside Ruby, patting the elephant's trunk. Beka sat at Sarah's feet, gazing up at the elephant. The poodles had gathered around them. It looked for all the world like Sarah was introducing Ruby to the wolf. As she watched, Ruby's trunk snaked over to Beka, sniffing at the wolf and being sniffed in return.

Miss Paxon studied Sarah's legs. "Yes, you have a point. No point in starting a riot on our way into town."

"I have a skirt she could wear," Helen said.

"Why don't you ask her if she'd like to do that?"

Sarah caught the scent of Helen's nervousness as the woman approached, clutching a bundle of fabric. Sarah turned away from Ruby and Beka, leaving the two animals to continue getting to know each other, and studied Helen's face. "What is wrong?" she asked Helen.

"I thought you might like to borrow a skirt," Helen said. "So that you will be properly dressed when we get to town." She shook out the bundle in her hands and held up her blue serge traveling skirt. "The length is about right. We'd have to pin the waist in a bit, but otherwise it would be just fine."

Sarah stared at the fabric. "Why would I wear that?"

"Because all the ladies do." Helen paused, gazing at Sarah's exposed legs. "And you really need to cover your legs."

Sarah frowned. "I am not cold."

"You don't wear a skirt to keep warm," Helen said. "You wear it so no one can see your legs."

Sarah looked down at her legs. "Why?" she said.

Helen hesitated. "Well, because . . . because it's not proper." She frowned, realizing how much she sounded like Aunt Bridget. Climbing trees wasn't proper. Eating horehound candy wasn't proper.

Sarah looked puzzled.

Helen touched her own skirt. "It will look quite nice," she said uncertainly. "People will stare if you go to town dressed like that."

Sarah studied Helen's skirt. "Last night," she said, "when you were climbing down from the tree, your skirt got in your way."

Helen nodded. "Yes, well . . . it does get in the way sometimes. But ladies are supposed to wear skirts."

Sarah fingered one side of the skirt that Helen held, examining the material. She tried to imagine running with that fabric rustling around her legs. She smiled, thinking of what it would be like to wear a skirt when she was with the wolf pack. The wolves could have a great tug of war, pulling on it. "It would be difficult to fight in a skirt," she said.

"Ladies don't fight," Helen said.

Sarah stared at her. "They don't?" She shook her head. "I can't be a lady."

Helen looked very distressed. Sarah scratched her head, trying to think of what she might do to make Helen happy. She was already fond of this woman. Sarah glanced at the Professor and Cassidy, who were loading the wagon. "I could cover my legs with trousers," she said.

"Ladies don't wear trousers."

Sarah shrugged. This information seemed irrelevant. "Or I could wear these clothes. I am happy like this."

In the end, after some discussion, Sarah borrowed a pair of the Professor's trousers. Helen buttoned her shirt and instructed her to keep it buttoned. She braided Sarah's hair, which Sarah rather liked, mutual grooming being a common way to show affection in the pack.

Eventually, the wagon was packed, Sarah was dressed, and they were ready to go. Sarah persuaded Beka to ride in the wagon with her and Helen, while Cassidy drove. Miss Paxon and the Professor rode Ruby.

For a time, the wolf was content. She and Sarah had hunted for quail in the predawn hours, and they were both well fed. She slept by Sarah's feet.

As they traveled, Cassidy and Helen chatted about this and that—about the weather, about Cassidy's travels, about how England differed from the States. Sarah listened—having nothing to contribute to the conversation—and watched the two of them. She was aware of another conversation, one of gestures and touches, that accompanied the flow of words. Cassidy touched Helen's hand to get her attention and point to the woodpecker flitting past. Helen tilted her head, looking up at Cassidy as if his comment on the heat were most original. Cassidy put his arm around Helen when instructing her on how to drive the wagon, putting his hands over hers and demonstrating how she should hold the reins. The couple did not comment on this unvoiced conversation, and that puzzled Sarah.

As the day wore on, Beka grew restless, nervously licking her lips and gazing from the wagon with apprehension. Finally, she licked Sarah's hand and stood, making her intention to leave the wagon clear. Taking the loose sleeve of Sarah's shirt in her teeth, she tugged on Sarah's arm, whining low in her throat.

"What's going on?" Helen asked.

"Beka will go," Sarah said. She stroked Beka's ears. She shared the wolf's nervousness, the sense that she was going where she did not belong. But she did not want to turn back now.

Leaning down, Sarah rubbed her head against the wolf's in a gesture of affection, as she gently freed her sleeve from the wolf's grip. Beka licked Sarah's face, then turned away, leaping down from the moving wagon and heading back into the hills.

"Where is she going?" Helen was clearly concerned about the wolf and about Sarah. She took Sarah's hand and squeezed it. "Why is she going?"

"She is going to the hills to hunt," Sarah said. "She is going because she does not belong here."

Holding Helen's hand, Sarah watched the wolf disappear into the brush.

SELBY FLAT HAD changed considerably since Max had led his mule down from Grizzly Hill to report the murders of Sarah's parents. The town now had a blacksmith, a butcher, a baker, a bootmaker, a justice of the peace, a doctor, and a barber, and never mind that the last two were the same man. Though Selby's was still the largest hotel in town, three rival establishments offered rooms as well. The town included a stagecoach stop, four saloons, two general stores, and a school.

Masons had established a lodge in town, as had the Ancient Order of E Clampus Vitus, an equally secret society. The Masons had constructed a fine brick meeting hall near the center of town. The Clampers, as the members of E Clampus Vitus called themselves, met in an old miners' log cabin down by Rock Creek.

The Ancient Order of E Clampus Vitus claimed origins in 4004 B.C. Some spoilsports said that the order had been created in the late 1850s as a drunken response to the Masons, the Odd Fellows, and other fraternal orders. Not so, said the Clampers. Adam, the Clampers said, was the Order's first Noble Grand Humbug, the title given to the leader of a chapter. The society counted among its past members such luminaries as Solomon, George Washington, and Henry Ward Beecher. Since these individuals were conveniently dead, they could neither confirm nor deny their membership in the order.

The Clampers' motto was *Credo Quia Absurdum,* "I believe because it is absurd." Their meeting hall was designated the Hall of Comparative Ovations. Their symbol was the Staff of Relief. Upon initiation, all members were given "titles of equal importance." Their avowed goal was to assist widows and orphans, particularly the widows. Their primary activity was initiating new candidates in extravagant and drunken rituals. They were reputed to do good works, but the truth of that was difficult to ascertain. Since no Clamper could ever recall the events of a meeting on the following day, the activities of the society were assured of remaining secret.

Selby Flat's main street was the same dirt track that

Max had walked along back in 1850—wider to accommodate stagecoaches, but just as dusty in the summer and just as muddy in the winter. The street was occupied by scratching chickens as often as it was by other kinds of traffic.

On the summer day that the circus came to town, a sow and her piglets were asleep in the shade by the barbershop. A couple of hounds had been sleeping there, but the pig had run them off. She outweighed the dogs by a considerable margin and wasn't about to put up with any nonsense. If she wanted a spot in the shade, she took it. She was sleeping soundly when the distant trumpeting of an elephant disturbed her rest.

"What the hell was that?" asked an idler on the porch of Selby's Hotel. "I never heard anything like it."

RUBY LED THE way, carrying Professor Serunca on her back. The Professor shouted as people poured from the saloons and the hotels to stand on the sidewalks and gape. "The show starts an hour before sunset!" he shouted. "Come one, come all! You'll be astounded! You'll be amazed!" An easy promise to make: The crowd was already astounded and amazed by the colorful invasion of their town.

Cassidy was mounted on the white mare. As he rode, he juggled brightly colored balls. The miniature poodles rode on the backs of the bay horses that pulled the wagon. Miss Paxon stood on the wagon seat, and whenever she lifted her hand and shouted "Up!" the poodles stood on their hind legs and waved their paws, dancing to stay balanced.

Helen drove the wagon, clutching the reins and watching the horses nervously. She'd never driven a wagon before. From dime novels, smuggled into her aunt's house and read surreptitiously, she knew that horses were always running off with women so that dashing young men could rescue them. Cassidy had assured her that this would not happen, but she did not quite believe his reassurances. Still, she had enjoyed the time he spent teaching her to drive the wagon.

Sarah sat quietly at Helen's side, not waving or shouting. She watched the people who thronged the streets, examining their faces with grave interest as she passed. No one paid any attention to the quiet figure on the wagon seat.

So many people, all of them talking and shouting. She wondered how she could ever find Max among them.

"You there!" the Professor called to a farmer gaping from the street. "Is there a barn nearby that we could use for the circus?"

The man looked startled to be singled out. "Well, I reckon I have a barn," he said. "You could use that."

"Excellent," shouted the Professor. "Climb aboard and point out the way."

Right there in the street, Ruby knelt and the Professor helped the astonished man climb aboard. The crowd cheered, and the parade continued, escorted by shouting children and barking dogs.

Sarah sniffed the air, fascinated by the smells. Hot iron and smoke from the blacksmith shop; baking bread from the bakery; perfumed pomade from the barbershop; saddle soap from the livery stable; beer and whiskey and tobacco and roasting meat from the saloons and restaurants. And everywhere the scents of people, so many people.

She breathed deeply, sorting through the scents and searching for Max's unique aroma. She could not smell him. So many strangers.

Sarah relaxed a little as they turned off the main street, following a winding track to the man's farmyard and barn. Though a gang of children accompanied them, most of the crowd stayed in town.

The Professor inspected the barn and negotiated with the farmer for its use, discussing how it might best be set up to accommodate the show. "This is simply splendid," he said. "Simply splendid."

Sarah found herself pacing in the barnyard while the Professor made arrangements. In exchange for free admission, he hired three of the older boys to post flyers around the town—in case anyone had missed the parade. "And spread the word," he told them. "We have a special attraction tonight. The Wild Angel will be performing with us. After that, come back and I'll give you another job."

The boys were off in a flurry of noise and dust. The Professor grinned as he turned back to Miss Paxon. "Might as well let them in free," he said. "They'd have been sneaking in anyway." He reached an arm out to Sarah. "Stop your pacing, my dear. Come inside the barn and let's plan tonight's entertainment."

MRS. SELBY RUSHED out of the hotel as soon as she heard that the Wild Angel was with the circus, lingering only long enough to pack a picnic basket. She was sure that Sarah would be hungry.

She was red-faced and out of breath by the time she reached Amos Butterfield's barn. Billy Johnson and two of his friends were standing guard at the door, keeping the other children out, but she bustled past them, not putting up with any nonsense. "Hallo," she called to the people in the barn. "I'm Mrs. Selby. I've come to see Sarah McKensie."

As her eyes adjusted to the dim light inside the barn, she studied the people. She saw Sarah's coppery hair and recognized her delicate features from the sketch Max had shown her years ago.

"There you are!" she cried, her eyes bright with tears. This, at last, was the lost child. A child no longer, she was a young woman. Strangely dressed, to be sure, but Mrs. Selby forgave her that. Mrs. Selby would have forgiven her anything. "Oh, you poor motherless waif."

She hurried to Sarah's side. Sarah tensed, alarmed at the speed of the woman's approach, then relaxed when Mrs. Selby set down her basket and flung her arms open wide, a gesture of such vulnerability that Sarah knew she meant no harm. Sarah did not resist when Mrs. Selby put her arm around Sarah's shoulders and hugged her close. She liked Mrs. Selby's smell, a warm scent that reminded Sarah of biscuits baking.

"Mrs. Selby, I am so glad you found us." The Professor smiled. "Our young friend is eager to find Max, and I thought you might be able to tell us of his whereabouts."

"I certainly can," Mrs. Selby said. "But you must be hungry after all your traveling. I've brought lemonade and a fresh-baked loaf of bread. Max told me Sarah liked the biscuits that he made over the campfire, so I am certain that she will like my bread."

They sat in the barn and had a picnic, while Mrs. Selby told them that Max was in San Francisco, fetching Sarah's aunt. She answered one question and asked half a dozen: How did they meet Sarah? How long were they staying in town? Would they come and stay at Selby's—it would be her pleasure to provide them with rooms.

"You must come and eat at the hotel," Mrs. Selby said to Sarah. "I need to fatten you up. And put some clothes on you, too."

"I have clothes," Sarah said, touching her shirt.

Mrs. Selby shook her head. "You were raised by

wolves, but you are in civilization now," Mrs. Selby said. "We'll get you out of those filthy rags and into a bath and a nice dress. Don't you worry about a thing."

Sarah frowned. She did not like the way that Mrs. Selby had dismissed her clothes. She was fond of the shirt that Max had given her; she liked the way it felt, the way it smelled. She thought the trousers were too long, but she could tolerate them. She glanced at Helen, suspecting that this talk of clothing would lead to another discussion of skirts.

"IT DID MY heart such good to see her," Mrs. Selby told Jasper Davis. "After all those years with the wolves, the poor motherless waif has come back to us at last. She'll be coming to the hotel after the performance. I insisted."

Jasper nodded. He had just ridden in from Nevada City, and stopped by Selby's for a beer to wash the trail dust from his throat. He had missed the excitement of the circus parade, but Mrs. Selby was happy to share all the news—including the news of Sarah McKensie.

"Isn't it wonderful?" Mrs. Selby said.

Jasper agreed that it was wonderful that Sarah McKensie had come down from the wilderness at last. Yes, it would be a fine surprise for Max and Sarah's aunt. He nodded, wondering what the girl remembered, what she had told the circus folks. Clearly, she had said nothing of import to Mrs. Selby, who was reporting with great joy that Sarah had eaten four slices of her fresh bread.

"What is she like?" he asked Mrs. Selby.

"She's the sweetest girl you could meet," Mrs. Selby said stoutly. "A bit shy, but well-spoken. 'Thank you very much,' she said when I buttered her a slice of bread. Just as plain as could be. Max taught her to speak, she said."

"He did?" Jasper narrowed his eyes.

"Oh, yes, he certainly did. Max has been visiting with her in the mountains each summer." Mrs. Selby shook her head, as if reporting on the mischief of a favorite son. "He's been taking care of her all along, without letting us know. But all that doesn't matter, now that she's here. Are you going to the circus tonight?"

"I wouldn't miss it for the world," he said.

The sun was low in the sky when he reached Amos Butterfield's barn. The warm summer day was becoming a balmy summer evening. He made his way through the crowd, smiling and greeting people. He found a place with his cronies, men he knew from the Masons' lodge, on a bench constructed of hay bales and boards.

SARAH PERCHED IN the hayloft on one side of the barn and watched the Professor stroll into the ring, tipping his hat and welcoming the audience to the circus. He talked for a while about reality and illusion and the mysteries of the Orient, but Sarah didn't pay attention to all that.

She was staring down at the audience, the largest gathering of people she had ever seen. She found Mrs. Selby, sitting in the front row, and that reassured her. She saw Helen and Miss Paxon, far in the back.

It wasn't much of a circus, but then, it really didn't have to be. The Professor had a performing elephant, and that was enough in itself to amaze and thrill the people of Selby Flat.

First Cassidy hobbled into the ring and juggled balls and swords and flaming torches, standing carefully on his injured ankle. After he hobbled off, the Professor produced Snowflake, the smallest of the poodles, from his bowler hat. He called the other poodles and they ran out and ran around and around the Professor. At a command, the three big dogs stood still, and the miniature poodles vaulted over them, continuing to run around and around. The Professor put Snowflake down, and she ran with the other, but rather than vaulting the big dogs, she scampered between their legs when the Professor was looking the other way. In the finale, the poodles formed a pyramid with Snowflake standing on her hind legs at the top.

As the dogs ran off the stage, Miss Paxon led Ruby in the door. The elephant ambled into the ring, lifting her trunk as if saluting the Professor. As she strolled around the ring, he talked about her, telling the audience that she weighed five tons and stood nine feet tall at the shoulder. She could win a tug-of-war against a dozen horses. If she decided to charge, she would be unstoppable, trampling everything in her path. (At this, some members of the audience looked somewhat alarmed.)

"I brought Ruby to California from the exotic kingdom of Siam," the Professor said. "We have performed together many times. But tonight, she will not perform under my command. Tonight, we have a special guest. You know her as the Wild Angel of the Sierras. Adopted by wolves when she was just a child, Sarah has lived in the wilderness, surviving by her wits and rescuing those who are in need. Just yesterday, she came to the aid of our humble traveling troupe. When we were threatened by a raging cougar, she came to our rescue. She befriended Ruby, and now she and the elephant will perform together. I present—the Wild Angel."

Sarah hesitated, staring down at the audience. When she had practiced earlier, the barn had been empty. It had been fun to swing down to the floor, fun to ride on Ruby's back. The Professor had been so happy that she would help them.

She took a firm grip on the rope that Cassidy had suspended from the rafters, pushed off her perch, and swung over the heads of the audience into the center of the barn to land beside Ruby. She wore the Professor's trousers and her own flannel shirt, preferring these clothes to the glittery dresses he offered her (all castoffs that Lulu had left behind).

The elephant knelt beside Sarah, and the girl quickly climbed up onto Ruby's back. She rubbed the elephant's head. Ruby smelled pleasantly of warm hay and dust, a comforting smell. Ruby strolled around the ring, swaying gently beneath Sarah.

While Sarah studied the audience, the Professor talked and Ruby went through her paces. She circled the ring, reared onto her hind legs, picked up an American flag and waved it gaily overhead, all in response to the Professor's cues. Sarah was strictly a passenger, with plenty of time to consider the audience as they watched her.

She saw Mrs. Selby, smiling and waving from her front row seat. She saw Helen and Cassidy, standing together at one side of the barn. The rest of the audience was a blur—so many eyes watching, so many hands clapping, so many voices cheering.

At last, Ruby completed her final circuit of the barn. The elephant knelt again. Sarah leapt down and stood beside the Professor. The audience was cheering. "Bow," the Professor told her, and she bowed.

Finally, she left the stage, running up the aisle between the benches to return to the safety of the hayloft. One of the boys that the Professor had pressed into service had already returned the rope to its place, in anticipation of curtain calls. The Professor wanted her to swing down again, saying the audience would enjoy it just as much the second time.

She wasn't thinking about that. She was grateful to

have returned to the shadows of the hayloft, grateful that the audience was watching the Professor now.

The Professor was doing magic tricks with six apparently solid metal rings. First he showed the audience that he had six rings, each one solid metal, each one separate from the others. At least, that's what he said he was showing them. Through all his talk, he kept one ring firmly in his hand. He linked the solid rings by magic, he said, but Sarah noticed that the ring that was in his hand was always the same ring and she suspected that it might not be as solid as the others.

But what she suspected didn't matter. The audience was astounded. He joined the rings together and took them apart, talking all the while. When he was done, the audience applauded.

Miss Paxon brought him a basket for the rings and brought him a rifle. He took the rifle and faced the audience again. "I would like to ask your cooperation in performing my final act. I am going to perform a feat that requires the utmost concentration. In my bare hands, I will catch the bullet, fired from this rifle. If I miss, my life is forfeit. If I succeed, your pleasure is my reward. Now, I need the help of a volunteer, someone who knows how to fire straight and true. A brave man, who will not waver in this task."

There was a great deal of shouting in one section of the audience. A tall man was being pushed forward by three other men. "Here's your volunteer!" shouted one of the men. "Sheriff Davis."

The man shook his head, but the crowd took up the call, shouting for the sheriff. "Hey, Sheriff, if you shoot the magician, who'll take you to trial?" "Come on, Jasper." The man stepped forward.

When the tall man stepped from the crowd, Sarah shivered, struck by a sudden chill. The light of the lantern that hung from the rafters shone on his golden hair. Her heart was pounding.

Professor Serunca handed the man a bullet for his examination. After the man had examined it, the Professor loaded the gun. He handed the rifle to Jasper and walked slowly to the far side of the barn. There he held his hands beneath his chin in a prayerful attitude and closed his eyes. Then he nodded.

The blond man lifted the rifle to his shoulder and fired. In that moment, as Sarah watched, a memory came into sharp focus. A sunny day by a flowing stream; a cold wet stone in her hand. Mama—her mama—was staring down into the valley, an expression of shock and disbelief on her face. In the valley, a man—this man—and lifting a rifle to fire.

Sarah acted without hesitation, her reflexes honed by her years among the wolves. She grabbed the rope and swung down into the ring on a trajectory that would lead her to her enemy.

But Jasper was moving, stepping back and laughing as the Professor displayed the bullet that he had caught in his hands. She landed beside him, her knife drawn, her teeth bared. She was snarling, poised to spring—but for a moment, just for a moment, she hesitated.

What was it that stopped her? She did not hesitate to battle a raging grizzly or face a snarling wolf. From childhood, her reflexes had been trained for fighting. But for a moment, she did not move.

What stopped her? Only this: a scent in the air and the memories that it stirred.

Mingling with the scent of hay, Sarah caught the scent of Jasper Davis, as unique to him as his fingerprints, the aroma that was the essence of the man. A breath and she was transported to another time. She was a child, crouching in a cave among the boulders. She stared from the shadows into the sunlight. There, by a laughing stream, the tall blond man stooped over the fallen body of her mother. The breeze carried his scent—the aroma of terror, of fear, of helplessness. She could not move. She watched as the man stood up, his hands red with blood and overflowing with her mother's coppery curls.

In that moment, Sarah stared at Jasper Davis, frozen in fear. Then she sprang for his throat.

Her hesitation had given him time to prepare. He sidestepped, catching the strike intended for his throat on his arm and swinging the empty rifle as a club. The heavy stock caught her in the temple, sending her slamming backward into one of the heavy timbers that supported the barn. She fell, closing her eyes, tumbling backward into unconsciousness.

JASPER STOOD WITH his hand clamped around his wounded arm, blood welling up between his fingers. "Look to the girl first," he told the doctor. "I can wait." Then he swayed on his feet. The Professor and the juggler helped him to a bench, where he watched the doctor examine the girl.

Cassidy and Miss Paxon were clearing the barn, telling people that the show was over, time to go. The crowd was moving reluctantly. Mrs. Selby stood by the fallen girl, tears on her motherly face. "I don't understand," she said. "Why would she attack the sheriff?"

Jasper shook his head, frowning. "I can't say, Mrs. Selby. But I reckon it was good she attacked me, rather than one of the women or children." He knew that some of those women were close enough to hear. "I hate to think what could have happened then."

"She was always very gentle with us," the Professor said.

Jasper shrugged. “She was raised by wolves,” he said. “Wild animals.”

“She isn’t a wild animal,” Helen said. “She’s a sweet girl, really.”

“Poor child,” Jasper murmured. “I reckon I’ll have to lock her up for the night. In the interests of public safety.”

He shook his head, carefully furrowing his brow in a expression of grave concern.

He watched the doctor kneel by Sarah’s side and thought about how right Mrs. Selby was. It was a wonderful day. Sarah McKensie had tried to kill him in front of a hundred witnesses. He would lock her up immediately. No one could argue with that. He had no choice. And then, when she tried to escape, he would be forced to shoot her. Such a tragedy.

21

HAVE YOU SEEN THE ELEPHANT?

". . . virtue has never been as respectable as money."

—*Innocents Abroad;* Mark Twain

SARAH OPENED HER EYES AND SAW MOONLIGHT SHINING ON A gray wall constructed of roughly fitted stone. She lay on a strawtick mattress on a stone floor. Her mouth was dry. Her head ached, a dull pain that centered in the right temple.

The air reeked of Professor Serunca's Chinese liniment. Carefully, she touched her head and felt a cloth bandage, wrapped like a turban around her temples. She felt for her belt and her knife. Gone. Her lariat. Her bow and arrows. All gone.

Bad stinks clung to this place. The air held the bitter aroma of coffee, the dull scent of gunpowder; the musky smell of the men who had slept on the strawtick mattress before her. The scratchy wool blanket that had been tossed over her reeked of whiskey and tobacco, of old sweat and fear. The nearby bucket stank of urine.

Under all the other smells, through the reek of the liniment, she could smell another scent, one that made her heart pound in fear. It was the scent of the blond man, the sheriff they called Jasper. This was his place—she knew that.

She sat up on the mattress, staring around her. There were three stone walls and a wall of bars that separated the cell from a larger room. In the larger room was a desk, two chairs, some shelves. A jacket hung on the back of one of the chairs. His jacket—she knew by the smell.

She had to get out. His scent brought back memories that made her breath catch in her throat. She had to run. She had to hide.

Her eyes focused on the square of moonlight on one stone wall of her cell. Blinking, she turned her aching head, looking for the source of light. High on another wall, moonlight streamed through a window blocked by steel bars.

She stood up, one hand against the wall for support, cold stone floor against her bare feet. She prowled the limits of her cell, growing stronger with each step. She tested the steel bars that made up the third wall of the cell, but they did not yield to her tugging.

As she turned away from the bars, she heard a sound from outside the window. "Sarah?" a whispered voice said. "Sarah? Are you all right?" Helen's voice.

The window was above her head, but she climbed the rough wall, her bare feet finding tiny ledges on the uneven stone surface of the wall. The opening offered a view of a narrow lane between the jail and a ramshackle building. The bars on the window were fixed securely in the stone wall.

Helen stood in the lane, looking up at the window. "Sarah! I'm so glad to see your face. Oh, your poor head! I tried to tell the sheriff that he didn't need to lock you up. I told him you would stay with me. He wouldn't listen."

Sarah clung to the bars, looking down at Helen. "He is bad," she said. "Very bad."

"Oh, Sarah—what happened? Why did you attack the sheriff?"

Sarah stared at her friend, remembering the things she did not want to remember. "He killed my mama. I remember his scent."

Helen stared at her. "That can't be. Mrs. Selby said that Indians killed your parents."

Sarah's grip on the bars tightened. They were cold in her hands, as cold as the stone beneath her feet when she crouched in the cave, staring out into the sunlight where Jasper Davis stood over her mother. "He shot my mama. He took her hair."

"Took her hair?" Helen's voice was faint.

"With his knife. He cut her—took her hair." She remembered crouching in the darkness and watching as Jasper bent over her mother. The smell of fresh blood mingled with Jasper's scent, and Sarah was afraid. "Run and hide, Mama told me. I hid so he didn't find me."

"He scalped her?"

"I was hiding," Sarah said again. Her voice trembled.

"Why would he do that?" Helen asked. "Why would he kill your mother?"

"I have to get out," Sarah said. "He will come and find me. I have to leave this place." She tugged on the bars, but they resisted her efforts. She reached through the bars, as if she could squeeze through.

Helen reached up and touched Sarah's hand. "I'll get help," she said. "I'll get Miss Paxon. I'll get the Professor. They'll know what to do."

IN THE BAR of Selby's Hotel, Jasper was telling another version of the story to the Professor, Cassidy, Miss Paxon, and a group of his cronies.

"It was a terrible tragedy," he was saying. "Her folks

had made camp on Grizzly Hill, right on Spring Creek. Injuns massacred her parents—scalped them both. I went up there with a half a dozen men from Selby Flat, and we searched for the little girl, but we couldn't find her anywhere."

He shook his head sadly. He started to reach for his whiskey with his wounded arm, then winced and used his other arm. The cut was shallow, but the doctor had insisted on bandaging it. He was glad of that. The bandage reminded everyone of her unprovoked attack. She had set up a perfect situation for him. With care, he could emerge from this as a hero.

"Careful there, Sheriff." Tom Monroe took the bottle and refilled Jasper's glass. "We can't have you out of commission."

Jasper nodded his thanks and continued his story. "Some figured Injuns had taken the girl captive. We searched high and low for Injuns, but never found 'em. Some thought it was Mexicans, making it look like Injuns' work. We didn't find them either." He sipped his whiskey, holding the glass awkwardly in his left hand. "I reckon the story about her being raised by wolves is true. I just wonder how she's going to do in civilization, having been brung up by wild animals."

"She did very well with us," the Professor said.

"She seemed so sweet," Mrs. Selby chimed in. She had gone to fetch another bottle. Now she stood at Jasper's side, frowning. "I really don't see that you had to lock her up."

Jasper looked at Mrs. Selby with a pained look. "You can't imagine I wanted to lock her up." His voice rang with indignation. "Don't tell me you think that, Mrs. Selby!"

Mrs. Selby bit her lip, still frowning.

"I had no choice. She attacked me, and I reckon

that was just as well. I can defend myself. Suppose she had taken after you or one of the women or one of the children?"

Mrs. Selby was shaking her head. "I don't see why on earth she would. Think of all the folks she's rescued from the wilderness. Why on earth would she . . ."

"I can't say," Jasper interrupted her. His tone was that of a man frustrated beyond politeness. "I can't say what goes on in the mind of a wild animal. She's a wild animal, and I reckon that's all you can say about it."

Jasper watched as his friends around the table nodded, looking solemn at this pronouncement. The circus folks looked dubious, but they didn't matter. No one trusted circus folks.

"If only Max were here," Mrs. Selby said. "Can't we just wait until he gets here from San Francisco? He would take responsibility for her."

"I would be willing to take the girl with me," the Professor said. "I will take full responsibility for her."

Jasper shook his head. "Thank you kindly, friend, but I'm afraid she's my responsibility. Tomorrow, I reckon I'll take her on down to Nevada City, where the judge will decide the best thing to do for her."

His cronies were nodding. They liked the idea of sending her to Nevada City, comfortably passing this difficult responsibility on to someone else.

"I reckon in the morning that's just what I'll do," Jasper said.

TIRED OF THE talk in the bar, the Professor and Cassidy had gone out for some air. They were sitting and smoking their pipes on the porch of Selby's Hotel when Helen appeared from the darkness. Her face was pale and she looked frightened.

"Helen, what's wrong? I thought you'd gone to bed," Cassidy said.

"How could I sleep?" Helen said. "How could anyone sleep? We have to help Sarah. We have to . . ." Then she burst into tears.

The Professor smoked calmly as he watched Cassidy comfort her. She was a sweet young woman, but she had not yet learned that it is better to meet crisis with a placid demeanor.

Between her sobs, she managed to tell Sarah's story in its entirety. "That's why she tried to . . . to kill him," she sobbed. "And now, we have to help . . . we have to help her."

"There, there," Cassidy was saying. "Of course we'll help." He looked frantically to the Professor. "The circus takes care of its own."

The Professor puffed thoughtfully on his pipe. "It's obvious that we can't leave her there. I don't trust that sheriff." Throughout the conversation in the bar, the Professor had been studying Jasper. The sheriff had said he was sad when he thought of little Sarah, lost in the wilderness. But his jaw had been set and his eyes had narrowed, signs of anger, not sorrow. When Mrs. Selby had questioned him, the Professor could see the pulse pounding in Jasper's temple. This was a man who did not like to be crossed. "We'll have to spring her from jail and send her to safety."

Cassidy was staring. "You make it sound so easy."

The Professor shrugged. "Helen said the jail had a barred window facing the alley. I imagine that Ruby could yank those bars loose."

Helen nodded enthusiastically.

"Then what?" Cassidy asked.

"Then I would suggest we find her friend Max, who is on his way from San Francisco."

"I'll dress her in my clothes," Helen said. "We can take the wagon to Grass Valley and catch the stage."

Cassidy looked dubious. The Professor smiled. An unlikely approach to a difficult problem—it was the sort of thing he loved. The Professor was a man of extravagant plans. He knew that this one was full of holes, but he didn't mind that. He liked to get a plan rolling—and then see what happened. There was such joy in improvisation.

Cassidy frowned. "How do you plan to lead an elephant through the streets of town without attracting some attention?"

The Professor raised an eyebrow. "I am a master of the Oriental arts of illusion. Leave that to me."

THE PROFESSOR LEFT the hotel alone, following a dirt track that led along Rock Creek toward a log cabin he had noticed earlier. Over the door were the words: "The Hall of Comparative Ovations. E Clampus Vitus."

From outside the door, the professor could hear boisterous laughter and shouting. When he opened the door, he was met with the overpowering reek of whiskey and beer. He stepped inside, doffed his derby, and called in a stentorian voice: "Brethren, I come to you with a great thirst, a heavy purse, and a need for the assistance of my brothers."

The Professor was, of course, a member of the Ancient Order of E Clampus Vitus, and he knew very well how to enlist the aid of the Order. First, he bought a round of drinks. Second, he explained, at the top of his lungs, that an orphan needed their help.

"Pity she ain't a widder," muttered one old Clamper.

"The rescue will involve much noise and confusion," the Professor proclaimed. "And all participating members must feign drunkenness."

"Well," the old Clamper said, downing his whiskey. "I reckon we could lend a hand. One more drink and I might be able to manage that."

"The Noble Grand Humbug has spoken," shouted another man. "We'll lend a hand." He lifted his glass and asked the ritual question, asked at every meeting of the Order. "What say the Brethren?"

From a score of drunken Clampers thundered the ritual answer: "Satisfactory!"

If anything can distract a town from an elephant, it is a mob of drunken Clampers, laughing and shouting through the streets. A well-behaved elephant like Ruby has no need to call attention to herself. She can stroll quietly down the street, the dusty gray of her hide blending with the darkness surrounding her.

The Clampers, on the other hand, do not choose to blend quietly with the darkness. They hoot, they bray, they create every kind of ruckus—smashing bottles (empty ones, of course), singing bawdy songs, dancing in the street.

And so it was that Professor Serunca walked Ruby down the back streets of Selby Flat while the Clampers held an impromptu parade (in honor of a noble feat of Saint Vitis) on the main street. They had decked themselves in their finest ritual attire, with jangling medals fashioned from tin cans and flowing robes made of burlap sacks. The Noble Grand Humbug carried the Staff of Relief and delivered a speech that detailed the accomplishments of Saint Vitis, which seemed to involve much drinking.

Helen, Cassidy, and Miss Paxon met the professor in the alley. "Is it an angry mob, coming to get us?" Helen asked. Her eyes were wide and frightened.

"Oh, no. Those are friends. How are you doing?" the Professor asked Sarah.

In the moonlight, her eyes gleamed through the

barred window. "I am ready to leave this place," she said.

"We're going to get you out, and then you'll dress up in these clothes." Helen held a bundle of clothes, which she had fetched from her room. "Then we'll go to San Francisco and find Max."

The Professor looped a length of sturdy rope, appropriated from the barn, around the bars, fastening the other end to Ruby's harness. Then he urged Ruby forward.

The bars were not designed to withstand the force of an elephant. The sound of the bars tearing loose from the masonry wall was lost in the rattling, crashing, shouting hubbub of a horde of Clampers in full celebration. In a minute, the bars were down. Sarah slipped through the opening.

As soon as her feet touched the ground, she was running—out of the town, back into the wilderness that was her home.

MAX STARED OUT the window of the coach, trying to make out the scenery through the dust. His bones ached from the jolting of the coach. When he smiled at Audrey North, he could feel the gritty layer of dust that coated his face.

"Not my favorite way to travel," he told Audrey, speaking loudly to be heard over the creaking of the coach and the shouts of the driver.

"What is your favorite way to travel?"

"On foot. With a pack mule named after a poet."

"After a poet?" She frowned.

"After a bad poet," he said.

They were nearing the outskirts of Selby Flat. Through the window, Max spotted a man he recognized, riding alongside the coach. "Hello, Buck! What's the news from Selby Flat?"

At that moment, the driver whipped the horses and the coach began to pull ahead. "The Wild Angel has escaped," Buck shouted after the coach. "Jasper Davis has got a posse after her."

"What?" Max stuck his head out the window into a cloud of dust. The coach had left the man behind.

"Escaped?" Audrey said. "That suggests she had been captured."

Max shook his head. "We'll find out when we get to Selby Flat," he said. He had a bad feeling about this.

"MAX! OH, MAX, thank the good Lord you're here!" Mrs. Selby rushed from the kitchen to meet them the moment they stepped into Selby's dining room. Her eyes were red from weeping; even now, she seemed to be fighting back tears. "Sarah is gone," she said. "Run away."

"What happened?" Max asked.

Mrs. Selby held her hands out to Audrey. "You must be the dear child's aunt," she said. "I'm sure you're exhausted from your journey. Sit down, and I will tell you what happened."

Over tea and breakfast, Mrs. Selby recounted the events of the past few days: Sarah's arrival with the circus, her attack on the sheriff, her subsequent escape from jail. "Now Professor Serunca, the owner of the elephant, is locked up in the back of the general store, the elephant is in Mr. Butterfield's barn, and everyone is out looking for Sarah. The sheriff says she's a public menace." Mrs. Selby shook her head.

"Why did she attack the sheriff?" Audrey asked.

"It's all very muddled. The sheriff says she's a wild animal. The circus folks say . . . Oh, here they are. Miss Paxon! Miss Harris! Mr. Orton." Mrs. Selby beckoned to the people who had just stepped in the door. "This is Max. And Sarah's aunt, Mrs. Audrey North."

Max stood, bowing ever so slightly to the ladies, nodding to Mr. Orton. Miss Paxon was a blond woman with regal bearing and piercing blue eyes. Miss Harris was a sweet-faced young woman who looked ever so worried. Mr. Orton had his hand on her shoulder. He seemed to be her protector.

"A pleasure to meet you," Audrey said. "Do you suppose you might join us for breakfast? I understand that you might tell us something of my niece and the crime she's accused of committing."

Max sat back, watching Audrey quiz the three newcomers. She quickly learned their first names: Gitana, Helen, and Cassidy.

"No question that she attacked the sheriff," Cassidy said. "Half the town watched her go after him with a knife."

"I'm so worried about her," Helen said. "She was hurt when the sheriff locked her up, then she ran away."

"We're all worried, dear," said Mrs. Selby. "But now tell them about why she attacked Jasper."

"I talked to her after the sheriff locked her in jail," Helen said. "She said that the sheriff had killed her mama and papa. She said that he killed them and scalped her mama." She frowned, shaking her head. "She was sure of it."

Max stared at the young woman, considering what she had said. "That's why he's been so interested in finding her," he murmured. It explained many things: why Sarah was afraid of Jasper, why Jasper had shot at her, years ago at the lake.

"I just can't believe that of the sheriff," Mrs. Selby said.

"I can," Max said softly. "I certainly can."

Cassidy's eyes met Max's. "You're the only one who

can, so far," he said. "We informed the local justice of the peace . . ."

"That's Tom Monroe," Mrs. Selby added. "He runs the general store."

"A good friend of Jasper's," Max observed.

Cassidy continued. "Mr. Monroe informed us that was impossible. That the girl was clearly deranged, and not a reliable witness."

Max shook his head. "We have to find her before Jasper does," Max said. "We have to protect her."

"Now Max," Mrs. Selby said, "I know you've never liked Jasper, but really . . . why would Jasper do such a thing?"

Max shook his head. "I don't know," he said. "But I believe Sarah. And we need to find her."

Helen was smiling for the first time since she had sat down. There was something familiar about that smile, Max thought, something familiar about this young woman. But Max had no time to wonder about that.

"Even if we find her, the sheriff will put her back in jail." Cassidy was saying. "Is there no greater authority to which we can appeal?"

Mrs. Selby looked at Max. "What about your friend, that nice Patrick Murphy?" She looked at Audrey. "Mr. Murphy is the Marshal in Nevada City and he's an old friend of Max's."

Max shrugged, feeling uncomfortable. "Well, yes, he might help."

"Of course, he will. If you were to send word, I'm sure he'd come along right away." Mrs. Selby glanced at Audrey.

Max noticed the glance, though he knew he was not supposed to. For the past decade, he had spent most of his time in the company of men, but he recognized this look. It was a look that said, "Men! Aren't they foolish?" It reminded him of the mysterious ways in which women seemed to communicate. Put a few women together and soon they knew all about each other. They talked constantly, asking questions, telling about their lives—and that was part of it. But it wasn't the whole story. Perhaps they read signals. They communicated nonverbally, like Sarah's wolves. They knew each other by the cock of the head, the squint of the eyes, the precise tone of voice. They read signals that people didn't even know that they were sending.

"Then don't you think you should send him a message?" Audrey asked.

There was clearly only one correct answer, and Max gave it.

"Now we need to find my niece, that's clear. Where do you suppose she might be?" she asked.

"If I might make a suggestion?" Gitana spoke up for the first time. "When she ran away, she was remembering the murder of her parents, mourning for them. I suggest that she might go to the place of the murder."

"And if there is any evidence of the sheriff's guilt, that's where it will be," Helen added.

"Well, it's been more than a decade since the murder," Max began. "I doubt we'll find anything after all these years."

Helen turned to look at him, her smile fading. He noticed the beginnings of a frown on Audrey's face.

"But you are right in saying that's where we're most likely to find evidence," Max continued, trying to recover from his misstep. "And that's as good a place to look as any."

After that, matters were settled quickly, with Audrey suggesting the roles for various players as efficiently as a general deploying his troops. Max, Audrey, Helen, and Gitana would go to Grizzly Hill. Cassidy would take a message to Patrick Murphy.

Cassidy questioned this division of labor, wondering if it might be wise to include himself in the party searching for evidence and perhaps leave the ladies in the safety of town. His suggestion caused Helen to straighten in her chair and say, in a wounded tone, "Don't you think we can manage, Cassidy?" Max gave him a sympathetic look, and Mr. Orton quickly backed down, accepting his role gracefully.

22

UNEASY MEMORIES

"To believe yourself to be brave is to be brave;
it is the only essential thing."

—Mark Twain

THEY REACHED GRIZZLY HILL ON A BEAUTIFUL SUMMER AFTERnoon. The sky was a pure, unsullied blue; the crimson sun was sinking sweetly behind the oak trees. But for Max, there was a chill in the air, a chill that came from his memories of this valley.

Max remembered Grizzly Hill all too well. The remnants of the McKensies' camp were gone—the tent shredded to tatters and the tatters blown away on the breeze, the boxes crushed for kindling by passing miners. But he remembered where the tent had stood, where he had found Rachel's body, where her husband had fallen. He remembered sitting by the tent and drawing a sketch to send to Audrey, hoping to soothe her grief.

It was a strange place to be and a strange task that had brought him there. All backwards and difficult. There had been a dreadful murder, and he knew who had done the killing. He thought now that he had known it all along, in a deep-down, instinctive sort of way. He had never liked Jasper Davis, and now he knew why.

He knew who had committed the murder, but he

did not know the reason for it. Even Mrs. Selby, who loved Sarah for a long-lost lamb, could not quite bring herself to believe that Jasper Davis had committed this crime. There was no reason for him to commit such a terrible act, and there had to be a reason.

He thought about this as he stood with Audrey by her sister's grave. California poppies had grown on the mound of earth. The brilliant orange flowers nodded in the breeze. An acorn woodpecker flew overhead, a blur of black-and-white feathers, topped by a red cap. The bird watched them from the branch of an oak, then turned to drill a hole in the tree. The woodpecker was busy with its own business, unconcerned with human problems. It did not need to know the reason behind human action. Reasons were irrelevant.

In the distance, a scrub jay shrieked, scolding someone or something in the bushes on the far side of the meadow.

"It's a beautiful spot," Audrey said. "Just as beautiful as the sketch you sent me."

Max studied her face. Her blue eyes were swimming with tears, and that surprised and dismayed him. Since they had set forth on their travels, she had been an intelligent, capable, cheerful companion. She had never complained, never showed a trace of being frail or delicate. When they had learned of the troubles at Selby Flat, she had competently set out to address them, without a moment's hesitation for tears or hysteria.

"Don't cry," he said, realizing as soon as he said it that it was a foolish thing to say. She had every reason to cry if she wanted. He just wished she wouldn't.

"I'm tired, that's all," she said. "I wanted an adventure, but now I'm tired." She wiped her eyes with the back of her hand.

He took his kerchief from his pocket, holding it awkwardly for a moment and then reaching over to dr her tears. "We'll find Sarah. You can be sure of that."

She smiled at him tremulously. "Max, you've been very good friend through all this. Don't start lying t me now. How will we find her in all this?" She waved hand at the valley, the hills beyond it, the mountain beyond that. So much wilderness to search.

"You are right. We won't find her. But she'll find us You can be sure of that."

The scrub jay scolded again, this time from a nearb tree. Max glanced across the valley, wondering wha was bothering the bird. He saw a movement in th grass, then the movement became a gray wolf, calml watching him from beneath the tree.

"That's Beka," he said. "Sarah can't be far away."

"Halloo!" Helen called from the camp. "Max! Au drey! Sarah is here!"

AUDREY FOLLOWED MAX to the camp. She was a few pace behind when Sarah ran to greet him, rushing into hi arms for a hug and then holding his hands and swing ing around him, pulling him with her in an exuberan dance.

The first sight of the girl took her breath away Sarah's hair was exactly the color of her mother's, ragged mop of flaming curls. Her eyes were pure an honest blue. Her face was that of an angel—though this angel had been rather abused of late. There was shadow on her temple, a bruise from the blow tha had struck her down in the circus ring.

Sarah was laughing, an uninhibited peal of joy tha echoed from the hills. Audrey smiled to hear it. Thi was a girl who had never been told to quiet down, t be good, to behave like a lady. Audrey remembered how she and Rachel had behaved as children—the had been tree-climbing tomboys who came home with torn skirts and skinned elbows and no explanation other than they had been playing.

Sarah was strangely dressed—she wore a pair of man's trousers, a red-flannel shirt with a hole torn in the elbow, clothes that Audrey wouldn't have given a tramp back home. But that didn't matter, not a bit. The girl was strong, she was healthy, she was alive.

"Sarah!" Max was saying. "Sarah, stop pulling an old man about. I want you to meet your aunt."

Then those honest, blue eyes were considering Audrey, with an intent, unwavering stare. "Sarah," Max started to say, "it's not polite to stare."

"Hush," Audrey said, waving her hand. "Leave the girl be. Nothing wrong with looking carefully, if that's what you want to do."

Sarah wasn't listening—to Max or to Audrey. The girl circled Audrey like a wolf on the prowl, getting closer with each circuit. Audrey stood very still as Sarah reached out and stroked her hair, delicately touched her cheek.

At last, Sarah stopped in front of Audrey, still studying her. "You look just like your mama at your age," Audrey said softly. "She liked to climb trees, too."

"You smell like Mama." Sarah's voice was just as soft.

"Come here, child." Audrey took the girl in her arms and hugged her close after so many years.

A moment later, Audrey felt someone goose her. She released Sarah and whirled to find Beka sniffing her skirt at crotch level. The goose she had felt had been Beka's inquisitive muzzle.

"Don't worry," Max had said, moving toward them as if to pull the wolf away.

"It's all right," she said quickly. She had dealt with dogs before. She squatted to bring herself nose to nose with the animal. "Hello, Beka," she murmured a Beka sniffed her face. Audrey rubbed Beka's ears, an all was well.

MAX SAT BY the fire, sipping tea and watching Sarah an Audrey. Over dinner, Max had been impressed b Sarah's efforts to use a fork as he had taught her. H was also impressed by Audrey's restraint. When Sara gave up and picked up her salt pork in her hands, sh did not chastise the girl. Rather, she showed Sara how to slice open a biscuit and make a sort of sand wich, then tousled the girl's curls.

It was strange how much alike the two women were Oh, not on the surface of it. Audrey was a well-man nered lady in her forties. Her auburn hair was tie back neatly. She sat on a boulder, her knees togethe her kerchief in her lap as a napkin.

Sarah was a teenage girl with the manners of a sav age. She squatted in the dirt, unconcerned about th arrangement of her legs, content to lick the greas from her hands.

On the surface of it, they could not be more differ ent. But they smiled in the same way. When Audre laughed, he heard echoes of Sarah's unrestraine laughter. They had the same eyes—Audrey's were no as brilliant a blue—time had faded them. But her gaz was just as forthright, just as direct.

Sarah, finished with her dinner, was up and runnin in the meadow, playing a game of chase with Beka. Au drey was watching the girl. Helen was tidying up, wash ing the dishes in the stream. Max found his gaz lingering on Audrey.

"What was that you said earlier about staring?" Au drey asked Max in a cheeky tone.

Max shrugged. "I was just taking your advice t heart. Nothing wrong with looking carefully. I was jus wondering what you were like when you were Sarah's age."

She smiled, shaking her head. "According to my mother, I was a handful. But not as much of a handful as this one."

"Well, being raised by wolves is bound to affect a person. I've done my best to teach her manners, but . . ."

"You've done well." Audrey's tone was warm.

"She doesn't quite have the knack of using a fork yet."

Audrey shrugged. "And I can't bring down a grizzly with a bow and arrow. Seems like using a fork is a minor problem."

For a moment, they watched Sarah chase Beka. The sun had set, but the wolf and the girl seemed unconcerned by the darkness. Max heard Sarah's laughter as she vanished into the night, chasing Beka. A moment later, they reappeared with Beka chasing Sarah. The chase ended in a wrestling match of the sort that had alarmed Max when he first saw it.

"How can we protect her from that sheriff?" Audrey asked. "There must be some way we can bring him to justice."

Max frowned. "If she remembered more about what happened, we might be able to convince people that her memory is right. We might find some reason that Jasper behaved as he did. But I think it frightens her to remember."

"Perhaps I could help with that," Gitana said. She was sitting on the far side of the fire and Max had almost forgotten she was there. "Have you heard of mesmerism? Derived from the work of Franz Mesmer, an Austrian physician and occultist."

Max nodded. "Yes, I've heard of it."

"Under certain conditions, it can be used to assist

someone in remembering events that they have chosen to forget."

"You have some experience in these matters?" Audrey asked.

Gitana nodded. "I spent some time studying in Paris with a student of Mesmer's. I can easily mesmerize a willing subject. If Sarah is willing. . . ."

"We can ask her," Audrey said.

The game of chase was ending. Sarah ran from the meadow to collapse on the ground by Audrey's feet. Max watched as she smiled up at her aunt. Sarah's expression changed as she studied Audrey's face, becoming solemn, concerned. "What is wrong?" she asked.

Audrey stroked the girl's hair. "We have been talking about how we might bring Jasper Davis to justice. Gitana can help you remember what happened to your parents, remember what Jasper Davis did."

Sarah shivered.

"Are you cold?" Helen asked. She had been sitting quietly, listening to the others. "Let me put more wood on the fire."

Sarah shook her head. "I am not cold," she said softly. "I am afraid." So simple. So direct. There was no artifice in her admission.

"What are you afraid of?" Gitana asked.

"I am afraid of Jasper Davis. I remember him, and I am afraid."

"I may be able to help with that," Gitana said. "Mesmerism has been used to assist victims of trauma, to help ease their fears. Do you want me to try to help?"

Sarah was frowning; Max knew she did not understand all the words. She looked up at her aunt, then nodded. "Yes," she said. "I want you to try."

"Sit here beside me," Gitana said. "Audrey, could

you sit on her other side? Now Sarah, look into the fire."

SARAH FELT GITANA gently stroking her hair. The woman spoke in a whisper that rose and fell with the crackling of the fire. "Keep your eyes on the fire, Sarah. Watch the flames and listen to my voice. You are safe here, with your friends. You are safe among us and you can relax."

Sarah listened to the soft voice murmuring about relaxing, about letting go, about listening only to the sound of the voice, about being safe here. She found herself drifting, staring into the fire and listening to the gentle voice that warmed her, comforted her. She let the voice soothe her. Gitana's hand was soft on her shoulder, touching her, reminding her that she was not alone. The touch on her hair calmed her.

She drifted into a trance state, watching the flickering fire.

"Close your eyes, Sarah," the voice said. Obediently, Sarah closed her eyes. "You are very young," the voice said. "Just a little girl. Your mama is with you. Can you see her?"

"Yes," Sarah said. She was with her mama. The crackling of the fire shifted and changed, becoming the babble of water in a rocky stream. The warmth of the fire became the warmth of sunshine on her face. She smiled at her mama. Mama was sitting on a boulder, writing a letter. Little Sarah was playing by the stream.

"Where are you?" the voice asked.

Sarah told the voice where she was, describing the stream and the sunshine and her mama.

"Where is your papa?" the voice asked.

Little Sarah looked around. "Where's Papa?" she

asked her mama. Mama pointed down into the valley below. She could see Papa there. He was waving to two men who rode by on horses. The men didn't stop.

She told the voice this, and the voice asked her if she was sure that there were two men. She watched the men ride up the trail. Yes, two men. She watched them ride away. Little Sarah played in the stream, happy to be with her mama.

"Something bad is going to happen," the voice told her. "But even when that happens, remember you are safe. You are safe with your friends."

Something bad. Little Sarah did not know what that could be. She admired the pretty stones in the water. She reached into the stream, feeling the cold water on her hand, and plucked out a white pebble. "Look, Mama," she said.

Her mama stood, smiling down at Sarah. Then little Sarah heard a sound, like a stick snapping in the fire, a sudden explosion. And Mama's face went pale, white as the stone in Sarah's hand. Sarah looked into the valley, where Mama was looking. She saw the tall blond man with the rifle.

"Mama?" she said, but there was another explosion and Mama fell to the ground. "Mama?"

"Run, Sarah. Run and hide," Mama gasped.

"What is happening, Sarah?" the voice asked.

"Mama has fallen. I have to run and hide. Mama said so. I have to run."

Little Sarah hid among the boulders, her heart beating fast. She watched the tall blond man scalp her mother. The voice asked her what was happening, and she told the voice what she saw. "I am afraid," she told the voice.

"You are safe here," the voice told her. "You don't have to be afraid anymore. Tell me what is happening now."

She told the voice when she crept from the cave in the growing twilight and sat by her mother's body. She told the voice when the wolves came, when Wauna washed her face with a warm tongue, when she sucked rich milk from the she-wolf's teat. She told the voice when Wauna took her into the mountains.

"Listen to me, little Sarah," said the voice. "Keep listening to me. When you grow up, you will remember what happened to your mama and papa. You won't be a little girl anymore. You will be strong. You won't have to run and hide. Do you understand?"

"I will remember," Sarah said. She was sitting beside Wauna in the hills, listening to the wolves howl.

"Yes, you will remember. You will remember that man and what he did. And you will be brave and strong."

Sarah nodded.

"When I say your name three times, you will open your eyes. You will feel warm and rested and very relaxed. And you will remember all that we have done together."

"I will remember," Sarah repeated.

"Sarah. Sarah. Sarah."

Sarah opened her eyes. The campfire had died back to glowing embers. By their ruddy light, she saw that her aunt had been crying; she was wiping her face with Max's handkerchief. Max sat on the ground beside her, his arm around her shoulders. Helen's face was wet with tears.

"How are you, Sarah?" Gitana asked.

"I feel sad," she said. "But I remember."

"That's good. You remember the man who killed your mama?"

"Jasper Davis," she said, remembering the man, remembering his scent, remembering the light on his blond hair.

"And you remember seeing two men ride up the trail. Was Jasper Davis one of those men?"

Sarah nodded. It was strange, but she could think of Jasper Davis now without shivering. She could think of him without being afraid. "Jasper Davis," she said, relishing saying the name without shivering. "Jasper Davis and another man. A short man with dark hair."

"They rode away and only one came back," Max said.

"I am not afraid anymore," Sarah said. She was smiling brilliantly, a smile of joy and savagery. The firelight glittered in her eyes. She took the knife from the sheath at her side. "Now, I can kill Jasper Davis."

23

THE DEAD MAN

"Supposing is good, but finding out is better."

—Mark Twain

MAX STARED AT THE GIRL, AT THE KNIFE IN HER HAND. FOR AS long as Max had known her, Sarah had carried a wooden-handled hunting knife at her side, with a six-inch steel blade that she kept honed to razor sharpness on the granite stones by the river.

"This isn't your knife," he said.

"The sheriff took her knife away when he put her in jail," Helen said.

"Could I take a look at that?" Max asked.

Sarah stared at him, and he could see the savage glint in her eyes.

"Just for a minute, Sarah," he said gently. "I'll give it right back."

Her face relaxed then. She wet her lips, then offered him the knife.

Max turned it over in his hands. This was no a simple hunting blade. Twelve inches long, tapering to a saber point. A knife fighter's blade, patterned after the bowie knife. On the handle, inlaid in silver, was a running wolf with onyx eyes. A matching wolf was etched in the metal of the blade.

"Where did you find this knife?" Max asked.

"On the dead man."

"What dead man would that be?"

Sarah gestured up the hill.

Max studied the blade again. He recognized it, of course. He had only seen the knife itself once, more than a decade before. But he remembered it from the wanted poster that had grown tattered and faded on Mrs. Selby's wall. It was Arno's knife, the one that had disappeared with him after the stagecoach robbery.

"Can you show me where he is?" Max asked.

MAX FOLLOWED SARAH up the hill. Audrey had argued that he should wait until morning, but he had insisted that he go with Sarah right away. He would not be able to sleep without knowing what waited for him up the hill.

The half-moon was rising over the mountains, casting a silvery light that illuminated the narrow trail. The trail was the one he had taken with Jasper Davis so many years before, a track that wound through the brush. Max remembered calling for Sarah until he was hoarse, shouting to the little lost girl and hoping she would hear.

Now he followed that same girl, grown to be a young woman. She paused at a patch of level ground near the top of the hill, beneath an ancient pine tree. There the trail forked. The main branch continued over the hill, heading toward the town that had once been called Humbug and was now known by the more respectable name of North Bloomfield. An even narrower and fainter track wound downward through the bushes, around to the other side of Grizzly Hill.

Max remembered when he had been here with Jasper. Max had rested under the pine. Jasper had offered to look down the faint track. When he returned, he said that he found nothing.

Sarah turned onto the faint trail, and Max followed her on a winding course to a rocky ledge that overlooked the valley. An animal den had been dug into the side of the hill, a narrow cave. In the moonlight, its opening was a patch of darkness. "Over here," Sarah said.

She stood in a hollow beside a clump of bushes. In the tangle of manzanita bushes were the bones of a man, long dead. Scraps of clothing clung to the bones; a leather belt and crossed bandoleers had survived the ravages of time. A few tufts of black hair still clung to the grinning skull, though the flesh had been picked away by jays and other scavenging birds. The grinning mouth revealed a gold tooth, glittering in the moonlight.

"So that's what happened to Arno," Max said. He frowned at Sarah. "How did he die?"

She shrugged. "He has been dead as long as I can remember." She had never troubled herself about the dead man. He could not harm her, and so she ignored him. It was only when she needed a knife that she had remembered that he wore one, and had come to claim it.

"Since your parents' death?"

Sarah nodded.

"Why would he come here?" he muttered to himself.

"He helped carry the box," she said. "His smell was on it."

"The box?"

She nodded in the direction of the den. When Max frowned, she returned to the rock ledge, lay on her belly, and slid headfirst into the opening. Then she wiggled backward, dragging the box out behind her.

A wooden box, bound with steel bands. In the light of the full moon, Max could read the name of the stage company emblazoned on the side.

"I came here with Wauna," Sarah said. "This is where her pups died."

Max nodded, looking down at the box. "People thought that Arno had robbed the stage with a partner. I guess they were right." He stared at the box, piecing together a story. "Suppose Jasper and Arno were partners. They held up the stage, then Jasper killed his partner and hid the loot. But your parents had seen the two men ride up here. He killed them so they wouldn't talk."

Sarah did not seem to be listening. She and Beka were both gazing into the darkness, staring up the hill.

"And now we have some evidence to support your story," Max said. "Now it's not just your word against his. Now . . ."

He did not finish his sentence. Beka growled. Sarah turned and pushed him toward the edge of the ledge. He staggered, his feet sliding on the sand that dusted the smooth rock, and fell into the bushes, joining Arno's bones in the hollow. At that moment, he heard the crack of a rifle from the slope above him.

"Sarah!"

He was tangled in the bones and the bushes. The tough manzanita branches scratched his arms and legs and snagged his clothing. He heard Sarah's feet on the rock above him, then she leapt down beside him, breathing hard.

"Jasper Davis," she said. "I can smell him."

"Are you all right?" Max asked, reaching out to touch the girl in the darkness. His hand brushed her arm and came away sticky with blood. "You're bleeding."

"My arm," she murmured. He could not see her face in the shadows, but her voice was tight with pain.

JASPER WATCHED FROM high on the slope. The girl had pushed Max out of the way, but he thought that he had hit her. Hard to tell. The moon was bright, but they were far away. He reloaded, watching for movement in the darkness below.

"You might as well come out, Max," Jasper called down the hill. "I'll get you anyway. Might as well make it quick."

Max said nothing. Too bad. Jasper had been hoping the man might beg for mercy and give his position away.

"I have to kill the girl." Jasper continued talking as he moved slowly down the hill, picking a path through the brush. He kept his eyes on the ledge below him, watching for any movement. He was ready to fire again. "I have no choice."

He thought he saw one of the bushes below the ledge move, and he casually fired a shot. He listened for a cry of pain, but heard nothing. No luck.

He continued his conversation as he reloaded. "You should have told me you found the girl, Max. I would have taken care of her long ago. Now you know too much. I can't let you go around telling what you know. I've got a position to maintain. You should understand that."

He would kill both Max and the girl. As sheriff, he would discover them here in the hills. He would investigate the crime and find that they had killed each other. That would be easy. And of course he'd have to kill the women down in the valley. It would be quick—a knife to the throat. He'd use the girl's knife. Those were more murders he would blame on the girl. He had warned people that she was dangerous. They should have listened.

"You got in the way, Max. That's all. You should have left well enough alone. I'm rich, and I'm respectable, and that's how I plan to stay. I don't want anyone stirring up old bones."

Still no movement. They were lying low, hiding. He grinned in the darkness. He'd find them. Soon, all the loose ends would be tied up.

The moon was bright. The girl was injured and he knew that Max wouldn't shoot him. Even if the soft-hearted fool happened to have his gun with him, he was a lousy shot.

"Come on, Max," he called. "Talk to me, and I'll make it easy on you. Maybe you and I can work out a deal."

It would be such a pleasure to kill the girl. So unfair that she had escaped him for all these years. And he wouldn't mind killing Max either.

Jasper stood on the ledge now, beside the strong-box. It had been a fine hiding place. No one would venture into a wolf den—except a wolf. No one would have found it—if not for the girl.

He stared down into the bushes, watching for movement. He was patient. He could wait.

PATRICK MURPHY HAD been on his way to Selby Flat to see the wild girl when he met up with Cassidy Orton. The young man had told him some cock-and-bull story about Jasper Davis and the unsolved murders up on Grizzly Hill. "Max asked me to get you," the young man had said. "He said you could help us."

Patrick had shrugged and decided to go along with the young man. He didn't know what Max might be up to, but it seemed likely to be amusing, if nothing else. From their first encounter, Patrick had found Max amusing.

Of course, Max wasn't in camp when Patrick got there. He had headed into the hills following the girl on some kind of wild-goose chase. Something about a dead man, something about a knife. Patrick had left Cassidy Orton by the fire, chatting with a pretty girl named Helen. Orton's motive for participating in this mad scheme was certainly clear.

On foot, Patrick followed the trail the women had pointed out to him. He was up on the main trail when he heard the crack of a rifle shot. He made his way through the brush toward the sound. In a clear patch, he looked down on the ledge where Jasper Davis stood. In the bright moonlight, he recognized the sheriff.

"Hallo, Jasper," he called. "Didn't expect to find you up here. Where's Max?"

The sheriff jerked his head, staring up the hill at Patrick. "Look out behind you," he shouted.

As Patrick turned to confront the unknown danger, he heard another voice. "Look out, Patrick!" That was Max's voice, coming from down below. Patrick turned back just in time to see Jasper lifting his rifle. At that moment, Max popped up over the ledge and threw something round and white at the sheriff. The object struck Jasper in the shoulder, spoiling his aim. Max was on him then.

The fight was over quickly. Max wasn't a fighter. He was a talented artist, an interesting writer, a thoughtful friend—but he wasn't a fighter. As Patrick hurried down the slope, he heard Max swear as Jasper punched him, cursed him, and then ran.

MAX SAT BY the campfire, answering Patrick's questions while Gitana tended to Sarah's wounded arm. She cleaned the wound, ascertained that the bullet had passed through the arm without breaking the bone, and bandaged Sarah with strips of cloth torn from her petticoat. Max's eye ached where Jasper had punched him.

"You're just lucky that's all you got," Patrick told Max. "Lucky he was in such a hurry to get away that he didn't pull his knife." Patrick shook his head. "Never did much like the man," Patrick said. "There was always something a little peculiar about him."

Max nodded wearily, accepting Patrick's need to revise history.

"Not much point in tracking him tonight," Patrick continued. "It'd be too easy for him to set up an ambush and lay for us. Tomorrow, I'll head to Nevada City and gather up a posse. Then I'll head out after Jasper."

"Won't he be far away by then?" Helen asked.

Patrick shrugged. "I reckon that's possible."

"You're saying that he might get away?" Audrey asked.

"I reckon he might. And I'm the first to say that's a pity. I'll get that posse together first thing."

Sarah spoke then. "I will get him," she said. She was standing.

"What was that?" Patrick stared up at her, frowning.

"He will not get away." She smiled, a brilliant smile that brought tears to Max's eyes. Even with her face smeared with dirt, she was beautiful. "I will kill him. I'm not afraid."

"Now, young lady," Patrick began. He sounded like an indulgent father, humoring a child. "You just relax and let us handle this problem."

But he was talking to himself. Sarah and Beka had vanished into the darkness.

SARAH FOLLOWED JASPER. Beka picked up his trail at the rocky ledge and followed his scent to another game trail. That led to the spot where he had tethered his horse. From there, the trail was easy to follow.

Stopping for a moment, she lifted her head and howled, a wailing cry that echoed through the hills. Beka joined in, her deep voice joining Sarah's.

There—an answering howl, far off in the hills. She

howled again. We are hunting, her howl said. Come to me! We are hunting. Again, an answering howl. The pack had heard; the wolves were coming.

Though her arm ached and her body throbbed with injuries sustained over the past few days, she smiled as she ran. The scent of Jasper Davis no longer filled her with unreasoning terror. She knew that somehow, justice—the wolf version of justice—would be served. She smiled, baring her teeth, happy to be on the hunt.

BACK AT THE campfire, Max tried to explain the situation to Patrick, who shook his head in disbelief. "Armed only with a lariat, a bow and arrow, and a knife, she brought down a grizzly," Max told Patrick.

Helen did her best to comfort Audrey. "I'm sure she'll be all right," Helen said. "Cassidy told me she fought off a cougar that was attacking him. She's amazing."

At last, worn-out from worry, Audrey made her bed beneath one of the oak trees. Miss Paxon and Helen spread their blankets nearby. Max and Cassidy found a spot a discreet distance away, giving the ladies their privacy.

Patrick Murphy made his bed by the fire. For a time, he could hear the women murmuring as they prepared their beds. Then they fell silent. He pulled off his boots, made a pillow out of his coat, and pulled a wool blanket up under his chin. He was staring up at the stars, listening to frogs sing in the meadow by the creek when he heard soft footsteps.

"Mr. Murphy," Helen whispered.

Startled, he turned to look at her. "Miss Harris?" he said.

"I wanted to ask you a question," she whispered.

"I see. And you waited until now to do it?"

She bit her lip and sat down on a boulder near his head. "Well, I couldn't ask earlier. You see, it's about Max. You knew Max in Chicago, didn't you?"

"That's right. Max and I go way back."

She wet her lips. "I wonder . . . was Max some kind of criminal?"

Patrick laughed softly. "You could say that."

"He's such a gentle man," Helen murmured. "I can't imagine him as a desperado. What did he do?"

Patrick grinned. "He was an artist."

"There's nothing illegal about that." Her soft voice was puzzled. "Is there?"

"That depends on what you decide to draw. If you draw landscapes or portraits, there's nothing illegal about it. But if you draw banknotes, that's a different story."

In the light of the setting moon, he could see her frowning. "Why would anyone draw a banknote?"

Patrick's smile grew broader. "Few portraits are worth as much as a portrait of a hundred-dollar banknote."

"Counterfeiting," Helen gasped.

Patrick nodded, still smiling. There, by the campfire, while crickets sang beneath the oaks and Sarah stalked a killer, Patrick filled Helen in on a bit of Chicago history. Counterfeiting had been and still was a flourishing business in the town. Each bank issued its own currency; there was no national currency. Since each bank had its own designs, people found it difficult to distinguish counterfeits among the many varieties of legitimate bills. "At one point, we figured that about a third of the bills circulating in Chicago were counterfeit," he told her.

"What about Max?"

Patrick shrugged. "Well, it seems that he fell in love with a lady from a rich family in Boston. He wanted to get married, and so he decided to draw some money. A very small-time operator. He concentrated on large bills—hundreds for the most part—and did a lovely job on them. Passed bills very successfully for a few years."

"Then what happened?"

"Well, he was an artist. In fact, that's what did him in. He couldn't help but improve on the bills as he drew them. One bill had an eagle that looked like it was stuffed and mounted. On Max's bill, the bird looked like it was ready to take flight. Tiny improvements. That's what tipped us off. Otherwise, the bills were perfect."

"You caught him?"

Patrick nodded again. "Caught him and shipped him off to jail. Didn't see him again until I arrived in California. Since gold is the currency in these parts, I wasn't worried about his artistic tendencies. He's a likable cuss, and he seemed to be leading an honest life."

Helen nodded. "I see. Thank you, Mr. Murphy."

"You're welcome, Miss Harris."

She left then, padding off as quietly as she had come. Patrick smiled staring up at the stars. It was always interesting around Max, he thought. Then he closed his eyes.

24

POWER AND MERCY

*"Courage is resistance to fear, mastery of fear—
not absence of fear."*

—Mark Twain

JASPER RODE HARD THAT NIGHT, SPURRING HIS TIRED HORSE UP the ridge of hills that divided the South Fork from the Middle Fork of the Yuba River, following trails that were little better than rabbit tracks. Once, he heard wolves howling in the distance, and he spurred his horse harder.

The moon was overhead when he reached the top of the ridge. He looked back down the trail and saw no sign of pursuit. That was good. He was making good time. It would take a few days for news of his troubles to reach the far northern towns, he figured. He'd have time to liquidate his assets in Downieville before he fled.

He had decided to head east. He could change his name and lose himself among the prospectors seeking silver near Carson City, a territory where civilization had not yet taken hold. He could do well there, he thought. Perhaps he would take up gambling again, refresh the skills that Gentleman Jack had taught him so long ago. He would prosper once again.

His arm ached where the girl had cut him. He was tired, dead tired. He was out of shape from too much drinking, from too much smoking, from living the good life of a prosperous man. He needed a few hours' sleep, he thought, and the horse needed a rest. Then he'd be on his way. He tethered the horse and lay down with his rifle at his side, his pistol in his boot.

JASPER WOKE TO moonlight and eyes. A gray wolf crouched not ten feet from his head, watching him with steady, golden eyes. His campfire had burned down to embers, but the half-moon cast its silver light across the clearing.

Slowly, Jasper reached for his pistol, but it was not tucked into his boot where he had left it. Still moving slowly, still keeping his eyes on the wolf, he sat up, reaching for the rifle at his side. It was not there. As he groped for the rifle, he found his hunting knife and grabbed hold of the handle, pulling it from the sheath.

As he moved, he caught sight of another wolf, smaller than the first, but staring at him with the same intensity. He shifted his gaze and realized that he was surrounded by wolves—an intent and silent circle of watching animals, their eyes gleaming in the moonlight. They were grinning, lips pulled back, tongues lolling past glittering teeth.

Beyond the clearing where Jasper had made his camp, the pines blocked the moonlight, casting dark shadows. Something pale moved in the shadows behind a big gray devil of a wolf with a grizzled muzzle. As Jasper stared, Sarah stepped from the shadows and stood beside the wolf. In her right hand, she held a knife.

Her left arm was bandaged—he'd winged her with that shot. So she was injured, just as he was. That was fair.

"I took the rifle," she said. "I took the pistol."

"Sarah," Jasper said. He smiled, forgetting the wolves that surrounded him. Finally, the girl. So small, so insignificant, and so much trouble. If only he had found her when he killed her parents. He'd have slit her throat, scalped her, and left her with her precious mama, lying in the sun.

Wild Angel indeed. How angelic would she look when he tore off those trousers and spread her legs for his pleasure? He'd take her, then gut her like a rabbit.

He grinned at the thought. He had smiled when he crept up behind his father with the ax. He had smiled when he strangled Gentleman Jack.

"I thought you were too smart to come looking for me," he said. "But I reckon I was wrong. You're just stupid enough. I killed your mama and I'm happy to kill you, too."

"Don't talk," she said. Her gaze did not waver as she stepped past the wolves, into the clearing.

Jasper pulled his legs beneath him, crouching in his bedroll, then kicking the blankets aside. He was wearing only the trousers he had worn to bed.

In his time, Jasper had whittled an opponent or two down to size. In barroom brawls and minor disagreements, a miner was far more likely to pull a knife than a pistol. Though Jasper preferred the pistol, he harbored a certain affection for knife fighting. His long reach gave him an advantage. And a gunfight was over so quickly.

With a knife, it took time to kill a person—and Jasper enjoyed that. It gave his opponent time to realize what was happening, time to realize who was in charge, who held the power. He liked watching his opponent's face when he made the first cut. Start small, slashing off a thumb, slicing the tendons of a wrist. Whittling with short upward strikes, careful not to catch the blade in a rib or some other inconveniently placed bone. Then, as the first wounds bled, he watched the fear grow in his opponent's eyes. His favorite killing stroke was a wide, low, sweep across the belly, a fine way to disembowel his opponent. More than one miner who had the temerity to accuse him of cheating at cards had lost to that blow.

SARAH STUDIED JASPER, looking for weakness. He stood with his knees a little bent, his feet well apart, right foot ahead of left. He held his knife in his right hand, blade angled upward, pointing in her direction.

He was smiling, but that did not bother her. She was smiling, too. His scent filled her nostrils, but she did not feel the terrible fear that had paralyzed her before. She felt as she had before the fight with Marek—alert, alive, her heart pounding with excitement, her senses alert to the smallest change that might give her an advantage.

Her arm ached, but that did not matter. A small ache, a distraction, nothing more. Living among the wolves, she had learned to focus on the hunt, ignoring distractions that might break her concentration.

She caught a glimpse of a movement out of the corner of her eye—a tiny shift in the position of his back leg. She heard a faint sound—his foot moving on the ground—and a fraction of a second later, he lunged forward, his knife slashing through the air.

She was no longer there. At his first movement, she had sprung to one side, reaching out with her knife as she did so to stroke the back of his right wrist with the blade. Not a deep cut—she had to move quickly, no time to put much pressure behind it. Just a sting—and then she leapt away over the firepit, where the embers still burned. From the other side of the clearing, she watched him.

As he turned, she saw a flicker of fear in his eyes,

hidden as quickly as it appeared. In the moonlight, his wound was turning black with blood seeping slowly from the cut. She caught the smell of it in the air and her smile grew wider, the grin of a hunter on the track of her prey.

She was small, a good foot shorter than Jasper. He had the advantage of reach. If she lingered within his range, he could slice her to bits—but she did not linger. She had the fighting reflexes of a wolf—fast, agile, striking without hesitation. By comparison, he was slow, clumsy.

At first, she let him attack, dancing away from each blow and countering with another slash to the wrist, a swipe at his leg, a flick of the knife at his trailing hand. Sometimes, she missed, but often she made contact, each time with a light touch, a small cut.

He swore at her as he fought. "Damn you—you fight like a mosquito. Tiny bites from a tiny girl. You think you can kill me with those? Think again."

She was not listening. Words meant nothing. All her attention was on movement and position. She knew what he was going to do as soon as he did—from a twitch of the foot, a flicker of his eyes, a jerk of his head. Subtle indications—but glaringly obvious to one who had grown up in a wolf pack. The first cut, shallow though it was, distracted him. The cut on his right thigh—not very deep, but deep enough to hurt—caused him to favor one leg.

"I killed your mama. I killed your papa. I'll kill you, too." His smile was gone now. His lips were set in a grim line, no humor left in him.

Still, she waited for his attack, but she began to follow each counter with an attack of her own—a stab, a slash, an upward slice. Always she stayed out of reach, keeping her distance, playing it safe. She concentrated her attacks on existing wounds, slashing again and again at his wrist until he tossed the knife to his other hand. He was bleeding from a dozen cuts.

She fought like a wolf. The pack did not bring down a deer with a single bite. No, it was a long and brutal process. They tore at their prey, allowing no rest, attacking from all sides. She had the patience of a predator—there's no hurry, once your prey is faltering. The air filled with the scent of blood; the fear was in his eyes constantly now.

He was waiting longer between attacks, conserving his strength. She watched him carefully, her eyes never wavering. He held his knife low, as if unable to raise it. She smiled at that. She had known wolves who feigned exhaustion in a fight, hoping their opponent would let his guard down. She would not fall for that.

He stepped backward then—half a step, half a stumble, and she knew from the flicker of his eyes that this was a fake designed to lure her in. For a moment, she let him think he had succeeded, stepping in. In her peripheral vision, she could see the blankets from his bedroll, his boots, the embers of the fire—all obstacles, all potential weapons. His eyes flicked downward and she danced back as he kicked one of his boots into her path, hoping to trip her, holding his knife ready to slash her belly when she did.

When he kicked the boot, he put all his weight on his right leg, which had been weakened by the wound to his thigh. She acted then—springing over the boot, kicking his leg out from under him, slashing his left arm to the bone in a blow that flung his arm to the side. He dropped to his knees, releasing his grip on the knife as she brought her elbow back, striking his temple a solid blow that rocked his head to the side.

She could kill him now. That was clear. In a fight between wolves, this was the moment in which the loser might surrender, submitting to the winner, acknowledging the other animal's superiority.

In that moment, Jasper's eyes met hers. "Mercy," he said. It was a word she did not recognize, a word that Max had not taught her. But she did not need to know the word. His eyes were filled with hatred, and her hand, which gripped his injured arm, felt his muscles tense, ready to strike the moment he saw an opening. This man was not surrendering.

Without hesitation, she struck with the knife, a smooth hard stroke that sliced across the side of his throat, cutting through the carotid artery. Jasper fell, his breath rattling in his throat as hot blood pumped through the slash, flowing down his neck, down his chest.

She stepped back, watching him with the same steady gaze, still smiling faintly, seeing the hatred and fear in his eyes fade as consciousness left him. His breathing stopped.

She left his body there. The wolves would not touch it—human flesh reeking of tobacco and whiskey held little appeal. Other scavengers would find him. Jays would peck out his eyes. Coyotes and foxes would gnaw his bones. Over time, he would nourish the forest, becoming a part of the wilderness.

As Sarah turned away, Beka came to greet her. Sarah reached out to scratch the big wolf's ears. Beka rubbed against her leg, and the other wolves crowded around, grinning. She felt wagging tails strike her, heads butting against her legs.

Beka lifted her head and howled, a low, sweet moan that climbed to echo from the walls of the canyon. The others joined in, a wild chorus of howls. Sarah tipped back her head and lifted her voice, joining the pack in a cry of triumph and completion.

NELLY WAS A LADY

"Apparently there is nothing that cannot happen."

—Mark Twain

THE FLOOR WAS DRENCHED BY THE TIME SARAH WAS DONE WITH her bath. Audrey had started with a basin of water, a washcloth, and a packet of her favorite bubble bath. Sarah had been fascinated by the bubbles, popping them at first, then tossing them in the air. That had led to splashing and entirely too much fun.

Audrey was drenched, too. But she couldn't bring herself to scold Sarah. The girl was so innocent, so happy to be with her, that Audrey just didn't have the heart.

Sarah was wrapped in a towel, sitting on the floor. Audrey had tried to get her to sit on a chair, but that just hadn't worked. Sarah had squatted on the chair, straddled the seat as if it were the branch of an oak, squirmed and wiggled and tried to find a comfortable position, until Audrey finally relented and let her sit on the floor. Audrey had taken the chair and, while Sarah leaned against her leg, had carefully worked out the tangles in Sarah's hair. Now she was brushing the coppery curls with easy, rhythmic strokes.

"Your hair is just like your mother's was," Audrey was saying. "Beautiful and difficult to manage. When it grows out, I'll show you how to tie it up."

Looking down at Sarah, Audrey wondered what had happened, out there in the woods. Sarah and Beka had finally come back to Grizzly Hill where Audrey and Max had waited. Sarah seemed exhausted, but happy. Before she had curled up by the fire to sleep, she told Audrey that Jasper was dead. Though Audrey had asked for details, Sarah did not provide any. She had simply shrugged. "I found him. Now he is dead." The next day, they had brought Sarah back to Selby Flat.

The bruise on Sarah's temple was fading. Audrey had been tending the wound on her right arm, and it was healing well. Soon, the visible traces of her encounters with Jasper would be gone.

Sarah's eyes were half-closed; the rhythmic stroking of the brush had soothed her, relaxed her. She looked so sweet, so delicate. The poor lost lamb, Mrs. Selby called her.

"Hello?" Helen knocked on the bedroom door and poked her head in. "Have you seen Max?"

"He's down on the porch, waiting for us. He offered to help me with Sarah, but I shooed him out. The last thing we need is a man's help."

That night, Professor Serunca's Traveling Circus was putting on a show. The Professor had grown bored while locked in the back room of the general store. Rummaging about for something to read among an assortment of Temperance tracts and battered copies of *Godey's Lady's Book,* he had found a copy of W.H. Smith's classic melodrama, *The Drunkard.* It was the perfect play for a small-town audience, and with a few modifications, he had found the play admirably suited to the players he had available.

The greatest difficulty had been finding a part for Ruby. But he had found a place for her at the end of Act Four, when Edward, the reckless young man who has been lured into becoming a drunkard and a wastrel, is felled by delirium tremens. What better scene for an elephant, the very symbol of delerium tremens? While Edward fell about the stage in convulsions that made the women shiver and the children squeal, Ruby could perform all her usual tricks, and it would fit the play perfectly.

Helen had already dressed for her role as Mary Wilson, the pure, long-suffering heroine. She was wearing her simple traveling dress, a fine costume for her part.

Helen frowned, looking at Sarah. "What's Sarah going to wear?" Helen asked.

Audrey inclined her head toward the dress hanging from a hook on the wall, a simple blue-calico gown with a lovely full skirt. It was Audrey's dress, but she had already taken in the waist. "It may not fit perfectly, but one must make do on the frontier."

Helen nodded, looking a little dubious. "Would you like me to stay and help you get Sarah dressed?" she asked.

"Don't worry, dear," Audrey said. "You just run along and practice your lines. Sarah and I will do just fine."

Helen closed the door, feeling a little guilty. She suspected that dressing Sarah would take longer than Audrey thought.

MAX SAT ON the wooden bench in front of Selby's Hotel. The sun was setting, and the main street was quiet—a few idlers in front of the saloon, chickens scratching in the dust, a mangy dog trotting across the street on very important business. Max could hear the sound of drunken laughter drifting up from the Hall of Comparative Ovations.

"Hello, Max." Professor Serunca stood on the porch, surveying the street. He smiled at the setting sun, the idlers, the chicken, the dog with approval. "What a fine evening!"

Max nodded, but said nothing. The Professor sat on the bench beside him, regarding him quizzically. "You seem thoughtful, my friend."

Max shrugged.

"I suppose it has something to do with Mrs. North," the Professor said. "That would be my guess."

Max frowned. "Well, yes. I've been thinking about . . . well, I've been thinking about what happens now. Audrey came here to find Sarah, and now we've done that. I'm just not sure . . . I want to . . ." His words trailed off. "I can't quite decide what to do."

The Professor nodded. "And by not deciding, you are indeed deciding. After all, every point is a turning point."

"What?"

"Oh, it's a saying where I come from. Every point is a turning point." With his hand, the Professor drew a spiral in the air. "It's usually represented as a spiral. You see, each point along any path is a turning point. You are always making decisions, even if your decision is to stay put."

"I want to talk with Audrey, but there just hasn't been an opportunity," Max said.

"Yes, and the universe just keeps moving on, carrying you along with it." The Professor shrugged. "My friend, sometimes you must make your own opportunity. I wish you luck. But now the universe must take me down to the barn to prepare for the show. I've been told that a reporter from San Francisco has come to cover our performance tonight. I'm most curious to see what he thinks of our efforts."

Max watched the Professor head off to Butterfield's barn, where the show would take place, tipping his bowler to the idlers as he passed. Clearly, he bore the town no grudge for the week he had spent locked up in the back of the store. He was a contented man, at ease with his world. Max wished he could say the same of himself.

In the distance, the Clampers broke into song. It was an old song by Stephen Collins Foster, the same fellow who had written "Oh, Susannah." This song, "Nelly Was a Lady," was a sweet, sad tune about an old slave mourning for his true love Nelly, who had died the night before.

Max sang along, under his breath. He had been married and living in Chicago when the song had first become popular. Hearing it now made him remember that time and think of his wife, long dead. When he had been arrested for counterfeiting, she had returned to her family in Boston.

He had written to her from prison. She had written back—cheerful letters, poking fun at Boston society. He had no clue that she was sick until he received a letter from his wife's sister Bridget, saying that she had died: "Worn down by shame, despondent over her status, she succumbed to a fever."

He wrote to his daughter—but he got that letter back from Bridget. "If you love your daughter, you will let her be," his wife's sister wrote. "I have adopted the child, and she is well taken care of here. Give her a chance to live an honest life, untainted by your past."

He did love his daughter. He did not wish to taint her life. So when he left prison, he had booked passage to California and left his old life behind.

The Clampers stopped singing, but Max continued humming the tune, caught by a sweet feeling of melancholy. For the past few days, he had found himself thinking of the life he had left behind, remembering his wife, wishing he had been able to talk to his daughter before he left.

He heard footsteps behind him and glanced at the doorway. Mrs. Selby stepped out, carrying a lantern. She was hanging it on a hook by the door when Helen came through the door, dressed for her performance. She stopped on the porch, staring at him. More than once in the past few days, he had noticed Helen studying his face, staring when she thought he wasn't looking. "What's that song you're humming?" she asked him.

"An old song." He sang the line that gave the song its title: "Nelly was a lady."

She scowled at him, and he wondered if his rendition of the song was really so bad. She turned away abruptly, hurrying past the idlers. Max stared after her, then glanced at Mrs. Selby, hoping for some clue as to what was going on.

"Poor girl," Mrs. Selby said. "She's very upset. I think you should talk to her."

"You do?" Max shook his head. "I'm sure it has nothing to do with me."

Mrs. Selby frowned and he knew he had given the wrong answer. "Well, I suppose I could."

Mrs. Selby smiled.

Max set out after Helen, aware of Mrs. Selby's eyes at his back. He caught up and fell into step beside her. "Have I done something to offend you?" he asked. "If so, I apologize. I certainly didn't mean . . ."

"My father used to sing that song," she said. Her voice shook. "He called me Nelly."

"He did?" For a moment, the breath seemed to stop in Max's throat. "Who . . . who was your father?"

In the distance, the Clampers hooted and called. Otherwise, the night was very still.

"He went to prison when I was five. I never heard from him again. He was from Chicago. My aunt said he was a gangster." She was walking quickly with her head down, as if she had to watch each step she took.

The drunken singing began again, but Max was not listening. Though the night was warm, he felt a sudden chill. He squinted at Helen, realizing now why her smile had seemed so familiar. Her mother's smile. Her mother's eyes. "Nelly," he said, his voice breaking.

She kept walking, head down, refusing to look at him. She was angry with him, he thought, ashamed to be associated with him.

"I wasn't a gangster," Max said. "I was a foolish young artist, and I was in love with your mother. I had to marry her, and for that, I needed to make money. So I did." He had to hurry to keep up with her. "It was foolish. A terrible mistake. I know that I brought shame on her, shame on you. I'm so sorry for that."

She stopped then, and turned on him. "Why didn't you come see me?" she said. Her face was wet with tears, but her voice was angry. "Why did you leave me there alone?"

"Your aunt said you were better off without me," he stammered. "She said, 'If you love your daughter . . .'" His voice faltered, and he could not finish the sentence. "So I left. You were better off without me."

Suddenly, Max found himself with a young woman in his arms, weeping on his shoulder. "I wasn't better off," she wept. "I hated it there. After Mama died . . ." A new torrent of tears stopped her words.

Max patted her back awkwardly. He had held her in his arms when she was a baby. He had sung her to sleep when she was a toddler. Now she was a young woman, and he did not know what to do. "I'm sorry," he said. "I wouldn't have hurt you for the world. Here . . ." He fumbled in his pocket for a kerchief.

"Helen!" Cassidy stood in the street, glowering at

Max. His hands were in fists. "Are you all right? I was coming up from the barn to get you."

Helen extracted herself from Max's arms and composed herself with an effort. "I'm fine," she managed to say. Max offered her his handkerchief, and she blotted her tears and blew her nose.

"People don't usually weep because they are fine," Cassidy said, eyeing Max with great suspicion. "What's wrong?"

"Max . . ." Her voice faltered. "Max . . ." She could not continue.

"Helen is my daughter," Max told Cassidy. "We just figured it out." He shook his head, watching Helen dry her eyes again. "I should have known it all along. She has her mother's smile. And she's just as beautiful as her mother was. But I'm an idiot, and Helen had to tell me . . ."

Max struggled through a muddled sort of explanation. By the time he was done, Helen had managed a tremulous smile. "We have to go," she told Max. "The show must go on. I . . . we . . . let's talk more later."

Max nodded, and she was gone, her arm linked through Cassidy's. "Tell me what that was all about," Max heard Cassidy say.

"My aunt told me that my father was a gangster," he heard Helen say. "But it turns out that he was Max."

The rest was lost in the distance.

SARAH STARED INTO the mirror. She did not recognize the creature who looked back.

To please Audrey, she had put on the dress. It made her look and feel like a stranger to herself, like one of the white women she had watched from hiding. The full skirt and pinched-in waist gave her body a different shape; the full skirt billowed around her legs. She felt confined, restrained.

But Audrey seemed very happy. "You look lovely," Audrey said. "That color is perfect on you." Her red-gold curls, which Audrey had pinned up so carefully, were already starting to come loose, escaping to curl around her cheeks. "When your hair grows out, it will be much easier to pin it up."

Sarah frowned at her reflection. She was puzzled by Audrey's enthusiasm for the dress, but she was willing to endure it for a time to make Audrey happy.

She turned away from the mirror. Rustling with each step, she walked over to where Audrey had tossed her old clothes. Such a ridiculous garment, she thought. It seemed designed to be as noisy and awkward as possible. Sarah squatted and found her belt in the tangle of clothing.

"What are you doing, Sarah?" Audrey asked. "What could you possibly want . . . oh." Audrey was staring at the knife. "I don't think you'll need that."

Sarah frowned, strapping the belt around her waist. "I always need my knife," she said, in a tone that allowed no room for argument.

Audrey studied her for a moment, then shrugged. "That's fine," she said. "I don't suppose it matters."

26

THE END

". . . there ain't nothing more to write about, and I am rotten glad of it, because if I'd a knowed what a trouble it was to make a book I wouldn't a tackled it and ain't agoing to no more."

—*The Adventures of Huckleberry Finn;* Mark Twain

THE PERFORMANCE WENT VERY WELL UNTIL ACT FIVE. AT THAT point, things got a little out of hand.

Sarah sat between Max and Audrey, watching carefully as the play unfolded. Even though Helen had explained it to her beforehand, it was all a little confusing. Helen was Mary Wilson; Miss Paxon was her widowed mother, and Cassidy was the reckless, but basically good-hearted Edward Middleton. There was another man that Sarah did not know. The Professor had hired him to be the wicked Lawyer Cribbs.

They all walked around the barn, talking loudly and pretending that they were places that they weren't. "Here in our humble home," Helen said—but she wasn't in her home, she was in a barn, and people were calling her Mary.

Lawyer Cribbs leered at Helen as he tried to evict her and her widowed mother from their humble home. Cassidy (though everyone called him Edward) upset this evil plan and won Helen's heart with a ringing affirmation that womanly virtue, not beauty, holds captive the hearts of men.

Sarah thought that the wedding scene between Helen and Cassidy was quite convincing. They liked holding hands; she knew that. But during that scene, Lawyer Cribbs threatened the happy couple: "I shall see them begging for their bread yet. The wife on her bended knees to me, praying for a morsel of food for her starving children. It will be revenge. Revenge!"

Sarah watched him carefully. She did not like that man. She could tell that Helen did not like him either. The audience hissed at him whenever he made one of his speeches. He reminded Sarah of Marek—a bully and a coward.

HELEN STOOD IN the center of the barn, staring defiantly at Lawyer Cribbs, played by Nathaniel Evans. Edward, her hapless husband, had sunk to the depths of drunkeness and depravity, and the evil lawyer had sought out the heroine with lust in mind.

It was easy enough for Helen to feign terror and disgust. Evans's breath reeked of liquor. A professional actor, Evans had recently completed a weeklong engagement at the Nevada City Theatre, performing a one-man show consisting of monologues from Shakespeare. He had bellowed his way through the first half of the play, bringing the fury of King Lear to Butterfield's barn. Now he towered over her, his fist raised against her. He thundered the line, "Nay, then, proud beauty, you shall know my power!"

She took a step back, preparing to deliver her defiant speech, when Helen heard something behind her—the rustling of skirts, the thunder of bare feet on the wooden floor. Then Evans was tumbling backward, propelled by a healthy shove from Sarah, who had rammed her shoulder into his soft belly. The wild girl interposed herself between Helen and Evans. Sarah, Helen realized, had come to rescue her friend.

Sarah held Arno's knife in her hand. Her blue eyes blazed in the lanternlight. She grinned at Evans, a wolfish grin that showed her teeth. "No," she said. "She won't do what you say."

For a moment, the theater was silent, then the audience erupted with cheers and applause. They thought, Helen realized, that it was part of the show. Sarah ignored the outburst, her eyes fixed on the man who was scrambling to his feet.

Helen only had a moment to think. She looked into the audience and spotted Audrey, watching the stage with an expression of disbelief.

"Sarah!" Helen cried out, her voice cracking. "Sarah, my . . . my cousin. Yes, Sarah, my sweet cousin and dear friend." She took a deep breath. "You . . . you . . . you left us many years ago to travel in the West." At the edge of the ring, the Professor was nodding in frantic approval, giving Helen the courage to continue with her improvisation. "But now," she said, "but now you have returned in my hour of greatest need."

Sarah glanced back at her, clearly baffled by Helen's theatrical tone. "Should I kill him?" she asked, gesturing at Evans.

The man had regained his feet. He swayed unsteadily, blinking out at the audience. His attention was torn between the audience and the flashing knife in Sarah's hand. Clearly, he could not decide: remain on stage as part of what was clearly a hit or flee the gleaming blade and the madwoman who talked so coolly of killing him. The audience won. He fell to his knees and bellowed, "Mercy."

"He cries for mercy and we must spare him," Helen said.

"Why?" Sarah asked, her eyes still on the kneeling man. "He is a bad man."

Helen stepped to Sarah's side and took hold of her

hand in a tight grip. "Because . . . because that's what civilized people do."

Sarah frowned. "I am not civilized," she said, and the audience cheered.

A drunken miner in the front row shouted, "You tell 'em. Neither are we."

Helen maintained her grip on Sarah's hand. "We will not stoop to his level. He is a fool and a drunken lout, made wicked by the influence of the demon whiskey. Whiskey steals men's minds and hardens their hearts." Helen was warming up now. That last was taken directly from a Temperance pamphlet, and she delivered it with confidence. Helen did not give Sarah another opportunity to argue. "I would not have your innocent hands stained with his blood."

"You have saved me from a dreadful fate," Helen said, thinking desperately about the rest of the play. In the next act, Edward was supposed to take the Temperance Pledge. Then the play ended with a charming tableau. Mary was back in her sweet cottage, Edward was sober and reading the Bible, and they all sang "Home Sweet Home." Somehow, Helen could not quite see how she could work Sarah and her knife into that tableau.

"I am so happy to see you again, my friend," Helen went on. She could see Cassidy standing by the Professor, conferring feverishly. He looked up and met her eye, pointing at himself. "My only wish is that Edward were here to see you, too. It would make his heart glad."

With that, Cassidy rushed onto the floor. "Begone, old man," he shouted at Evans. He turned to Sarah and placed his hand over Helen's, taking a firm grip on the hand in which Sarah held the knife. "My beloved friend and my beloved wife," he cried. "I have taken the pledge." Sarah frowned at him as he delivered an abbreviated version of his speech on the evils of drink. "And now the time has come for us to go! We will leave this place and go to California to seek our fortune!"

The fiddler that the Professor had hired for the occasion struck up a chorus of "Bound for the Promised Land," the tune they had prepared for the final scene. The Professor urged Ruby onto the floor. She would serve as transportation to California.

Ruby stepped into the ring and knelt beside Helen. Helen waved to the crowd as she mounted the great beast. Sarah looked baffled, but followed Helen's lead.

As the crowd sang, Ruby circled the barn, waving her trunk to the crowd. "Smile and wave," Helen whispered to Sarah. "Just smile and wave."

Sarah did her best to follow orders. They made a spectacular exit, then returned for curtain calls. All in all, it was a bang-up success.

"THANK YOU. I really have no idea whether we will repeat the performance," Helen told the journalist, a bushy-haired fellow who seemed quite full of himself. He had found her and Cassidy tending to Ruby. The Professor had conveniently absented himself, heading for Selby's Hotel. She and Cassidy had been having an interesting conversation about love, when this man had come along and insisted on interviewing her. "The last act was improvised entirely. But I truly like it better than the original. I think Sarah's instinct to attack that nasty man was exactly right." Helen glanced at Cassidy. "I wonder where Audrey and Sarah have gotten to?" she asked him.

"Back to the hotel, I imagine," he said.

"Well, Mr. . . . I'm sorry. I've forgotten your name," Helen said.

"Clemens," said the journalist. "Samuel Clemens."

"Oh, yes. Well, Mr. Clemens, I strongly suggest that you talk with the Professor about his plans for the production."

She watched the young man head off in the direction of the hotel, then she turned to Cassidy and smiled. "I believe we were talking about love," she said.

MAX AND AUDREY took a seat in the back of the bar at Selby's Hotel. The bar was crowded with Clampers who had come to the performance and were continuing the celebration with much drinking and revelry.

"I wonder where Sarah has gotten to," Audrey murmured.

"I'm sure she's with Helen," Max said.

He hailed Mr. Selby and requested two glasses of sherry. Watching the man disappear into the crowd Max had little hope that he would return.

He had to talk to Audrey. He needed to tell her of his discovery that Helen was his daughter. And that revelation required him to tell her of his former profession as a counterfeiter. He had been meaning to talk to Audrey about that, really he had, but the time had never seemed quite right. And of course, he wanted to tell her how much she meant to him.

He fidgeted with his sherry glass nervously. "I'm glad we have some time together," he said. "I've been wanting to talk to you." He hesitated, searching for words. He should tell her about Helen first, he thought, and then about his past. Or should he do it the other way around? "There are some things I need to tell you," he said, speaking loudly to be heard over the noise of the Clampers.

Her eyes were such a beautiful blue. So warm and sweet in the yellow glow of the oil lamps.

"What sorts of things?" she asked. Her voice was warm and encouraging.

"I need to tell you about my past," he began. "We know each other very well, I think, after writing so many letters. But there are some things you should know about me." He reached out and took her hand in his.

Her eyes widened in shock. The Clampers erupted in shouting and applause. He could not hear what she said—the shouting of Clampers drowned her words. But he read her lips. "It's the elephant," she said.

Max turned to follow her gaze. The Clampers had thrown wide the double doors that led into the street, and Ruby was strolling through, following Professor Serunca.

For a time, there was no hope of conversation. The Clampers were toasting the Professor, and the Professor was toasting the Clampers. Ruby was joining in, with earsplitting trumpeting.

About that time, Mrs. Selby slipped out from behind the bar, clutching a bottle of sherry and two glasses. Handing Max the bottle, she took Audrey's arm. Making no attempt to speak above the din, she led Audrey from the room. Max followed, grateful for Mrs. Selby's intervention.

She took them down the hall. "Goodness," she said, opening the door to the parlor that adjoined the rooms that she and Mr. Selby shared. "I think you'd be better off here than in all that noise."

Max could still hear the Clampers shouting, the elephant trumpeting, but the noise was muffled by the walls that separated the parlor from the bar.

"Thank you, Mrs. Selby," he said.

Smiling, Mrs. Selby lit the oil lamps and made sure they were comfortable. It seemed to Max that she gave Audrey a knowing look, but that could have been his imagination. She took the bottle of sherry from Max and poured a glass for each of them.

"I'm sure you need a glass to calm your nerves," she said. "It was such an exciting performance. And the perfect ending, I thought." Then she swept out to help in the bar, leaving the couple alone.

Max took a deep breath, but before he could speak, Audrey was saying, "You know, I've been thinking about what happens next," she said. "I've been thinking that perhaps I will write another book."

Max nodded. "A new book? Another book of poetry. That sounds like a fine idea." He sipped his sherry, trying to think of how he might reintroduce the topic of his past.

"Not poetry," she said. "A book of adventures." Her eyes were sparkling; her face was animated. She set her glass of sherry down on the table by the sofa and leaned forward, taking Max's hand in hers. "The ending was wonderful, because the women leave to go and have an adventure in California. I want to see women off having adventures. So I've decided I will write my niece's story. *Sarah of the Wolves, the Wild Angel of the Gold Fields.* A story of adventure and redemption, in which a tender child makes her way through the wilderness, triumphing over evil." She smiled brilliantly. "You'll have to help me with it, Max. You were a part of it all. An upstanding citizen, trying to save the innocent from the perils of an evil world."

An upstanding citizen? Max shook his head, thinking of his past.

She frowned. "Oh, don't shake your head, Max. You underestimate your appeal as a character. This will be a tale of intrigue and adventure," she said. "At every moment, the reader will be asking—'What happens next?'"

It was an excellent question, he thought. "You must listen to me, Audrey," he said. "I have to tell you . . ."

"Papa?" Helen burst through the door in a flurry

that made the oil lamps flicker. She was smiling, and her cheeks were bright. "I have the most wonderful news. Cassidy . . ." She glanced up at Cassidy, who had followed her through the door. "Cassidy has something to ask you."

Cassidy was holding his hat in his hands. He spoke with careful dignity. "I have come to ask the hand of your daughter in marriage. I am only a poor juggler, but I know that I can make her happy."

Max stared at the young man, then studied his smiling daughter. "Helen, would you like to marry this young man?" he asked, his voice faltering.

She smiled at him, and that was his answer. "I've been a poor father to you up 'til now," he said. "And I am honored that you would consult me in this decision." He looked at Cassidy. "Do you love my daughter?"

"I do."

"Do you promise you will never lie to her? You'll always tell her the truth?"

Cassidy nodded. "I will."

Max nodded gravely, doing his best to appear paternal and feeling like a fraud. "You have my blessing."

Helen leapt from the sofa and flew to Cassidy's side.

"Now, that's settled," Max said. "Perhaps you will excuse us for a moment. I need to have a word with Audrey and . . ."

"Excuse me?" A bushy-haired man knocked on the door and barged into the parlor. The room was very crowded. "Mrs. Selby said I might find Mrs. North here."

"Yes," said Audrey. "I'm Mrs. North."

"My name is Clemens, Samuel Clemens." He smiled at Cassidy and Helen. "I wanted to ask you a few questions about Sarah McKensie. I hope this is a convenient time . . ."

"No," Max interrupted in a tone that brooked no disagreement. "No. This is not a convenient time."

Mr. Clemens stared at Max, taken aback. "And who are you, sir?"

Max straightened up, summoning his dignity and glaring at Mr. Clemens. "I am a counterfeiter from Chicago, and I am an artist," he said. "I am a friend of the Wild Angel, and I am the father of this budding young actress. I am the man who intends to ask the lovely Mrs. North for her hand in marriage, and I am heartily sick of being interrupted." He turned to Audrey and looked her in the eye. "I must tell you the truth: I have not always been an upstanding citizen. I have been a fool. I have been a liar. But I love you, and I want to spend the rest of my life with you. Will you marry me?"

Of course, she said yes. In fact, she exchanged a look with Helen that made Max suspect that she had already known of his intentions—and his career in counterfeiting. Cassidy braved the bar to fetch more glasses, and they drank toast after toast until the sherry was gone. The Clampers, having heard the news from Mrs. Selby (in whom Cassidy had confided when he fetched the glasses) stormed the parlor and insisted that the engaged couples ride Ruby in a triumphant procession down the main street of Selby Flat.

In all the excitement, it was not until the Professor was handing the ladies down from the elephant, that Audrey realized that someone was missing. She turned to Helen and asked, "Where is Sarah? I thought she was with you."

Helen, wide-eyed, shook her head. "I thought she was with you."

"Not to worry, ladies," the Professor said. "Miss Paxon spoke with Sarah right after the show."

"That's correct." Miss Paxon stood by the entrance to Selby's Hotel, smiling. "She indicated that she would be going off to spend some time with her family."

Audrey frowned. "I am her family."

"Of course," Miss Paxon said. "Quite right. I meant her other family. Her pack, so to speak."

"She's returned to the wolves?"

"For a time."

Max put his hand on Audrey's shoulder. "She'll be fine," he said.

FROM HIGH IN the hills, Sarah looked down on the town of Selby Flat. In the distance, she could hear Ruby trumpeting. She smiled. It was good to know that she could visit the town, good to know that she had friends there. But she knew that she did not belong there. She was not civilized, and she did not see any advantage to becoming civilized. Better to return to the wilderness, where she belonged.

She wore the shirt that Max had given her, with the cut-off trousers that left her legs free. The dress that Audrey had insisted she wear had been entirely too confining. She had left that at the hotel. She had Arno's knife at her side. She could make a new lariat, a new bow, a supply of arrows.

Smiling, she tipped her head back and howled, a thin call that carried through the night air. In the distance, she heard an answering howl—a chorus of wolves. Her pack was waiting for her. Without hesitation, she turned her back on civilization.

AFTERWORD—ABOUT TARZAN
BY MARY MAXWELL

"Most writers regard the truth as their most valuable possession, and therefore are most economical in its use."

—Mark Twain

The working title of this novel was *Sarah of the Wolves.* My editor, Beth Meacham, astutely suggested the change to *Wild Angel,* a much more lyrical and compelling title. But for me the book will always retain its original title, a direct allusion to the novel that inspired it.

As a girl, I read *Tarzan of the Apes* and all of Edgar Rice Burroughs's other Tarzan books. My reading of the Tarzan books followed an exhaustive reading of the *Oz* books by L. Frank Baum. As a child, it seemed to me that books were similar. I (quite rightly, as it turns out) regarded Tarzan's Africa as no more real than Dorothy's Oz.

Burroughs knew enough not to let the facts get in the way of a rollicking adventure, and I respect him for that. I admire his willingness to rearrange reality to suit the needs of his story. If he needs a lion, a lion is there. No problem.

With that in mind, I suggest that anyone interested in quibbling with my presentation of reality take their business elsewhere. Yes, Sarah can bring down a grizzly with a bow and arrow and a lariat. After all, if Tarzan can kill a lion with a full nelson, who am I to begrudge Sarah such minor prowess with primitive weapons? This is not an historically and biologically accurate account. For those looking for such a novel, I suggest Pat Murphy's *Nadya—The Wolf Chronicles.* Pat insists on meticulous historical research. I find it only slows me down.

Back when I was reading the *Tarzan* books, I also admired Burroughs' ability to cut out extraneous material. In my memory, one of the most important phrases in *Tarzan* is: "Meanwhile, on the other side of the jungle . . ." And what was happening on the other side of the jungle was never dull.

In the first *Tarzan* book, Burroughs mentions one of Tarzan's more unlikely friendships: "With Tantor, the elephant, he made friends. How? Ask not." I like that. Burroughs took a firm hand with his readers, telling them simply and clearly the way things were. No apology. No explanation.

In this novel, I have adopted some of the traits that I admired in Burroughs's work. I did not manage to incorporate the phrase "Meanwhile, on the other side of the jungle,"—but I employed similar strategies where I could. I did not use the phrase "Ask not," but that was the attitude I chose to adopt. This is the way the world works; do not question it.

Some readers may think that the invention of E Clampus Vitus is one of the ways I have stretched the truth. Think again. The Clampers exist—and they existed at the time of the Gold Rush. They are as I have described them, a secret society dedicated to the protection of widows and orphans, particularly the widows. The Clampers meet in the Hall of Comparative Ovations. Their motto is *Credo Quia Absurdum,* "I believe because it is absurd." Their ritual question is "What say the Brethren?" and their ritual answer: "Satisfactory!"

I was delighted to discover it was unnecessary to invent anything about the Clampers. They are fabulous—in all senses of the word—exactly as they are.

AFTERWORD—ABOUT WOMEN AND WOLVES BY MAX MERRIWELL

"It takes much to convince the average man of anything; and perhaps nothing can ever make him realize that he is the average woman's inferior—yet in several important details the evidence seems to show that that is what he is."

—Mark Twain

If you read Pat Murphy's afterword to the novel, *There and Back Again*, you already know that I not only write fiction under my own name—but also under the pseudonym Mary Maxwell. I enjoy the challenge of writing under a woman's name; it has forced me to attend more closely to differences in the ways that women and men approach the world.

I do not regard myself as an expert on the ways of women—but I do consider myself to be a careful observer. Like Max Phillips, my namesake in *Wild Angel*, I have noticed the glances that women sometimes exchange, looks that comment on the foolishness of men. I have observed the mysterious ways in which women communicate, recognizing signals that men don't know that they are sending—indeed, don't intend to send.

I do not share Max's belief that women have a civilizing influence on men. I also do not agree with Max in his misguided notions that women need to be protected.

I believe that women and wolves have much in common. Both communicate in mysterious ways. Both avoid trouble—but both are fierce when trouble finds them. Both women and wolves are attentive to power relationships. Where men bluster, women and wolves watch, analyzing the situation. When they are ready to act, they act without hesitation.

Far from needing protection, I think young Sarah belongs among the wolves, and I'm happy to have had a hand in putting her there.

AFTERWORD—CLEARING UP THE CONFUSION BY PAT MURPHY

"For business reasons, I must preserve the outward sign of sanity."

—Mark Twain

This book is the second part of a three-part project that combines aspects of a shaggy dog story, a practical joke, and a metafictional opus. Each book stands alone—but they combine to form a whole that is greater than the sum of its parts.

Let me explain: Max Merriwell is a pseudonym of mine. He recently wrote *There and Back Again*, a rollicking space opera published by TOR Books (under my name).

Max is a pseudonym, but he is also a character of sorts. In some alternate universe, he is happily writing many novels—under his own name and under pseudonyms of his own. Each year, Max writes three novels—a science fiction novel under his own name, a fantasy novel under the pseudonym Mary Maxwell, and a mystery under the pseudonym Weldon Merrimax.

Wild Angel is a novel that I wrote as Max Merriwell, writing as Mary Maxwell. (Or you could think of it as a novel that Max Merriwell wrote as Mary Maxwell, in some other universe.) Some characters who appeared in *There and Back Again* reappear here. (If you want to know more about Gyro and his pataphysical friends, read that book.)

Whatever the reality of Max and Mary, I am confident that I, acting alone and in my proper mind, would never have chosen to model a novel on Burroughs's *Tarzan of the Apes.* But it's exactly the sort of thing that Max and Mary would do.

When I began this project, I was delighted to read Gore Vidal's introduction to the Signet Classic edition of *Tarzan of the Apes.* In that introduction, Vidal confesses to reading all twenty-three *Tarzan* books when he was growing up, a confession I find reassuring since I did the same.

As Vidal charitably notes, "Stylistically, Burroughs is—how shall I put it?—uneven. Burroughs's characters speak in unnatural rhythms. In his plotting, Burroughs makes shameless use of coincidence; one can see the long arm of the author reaching in to arrange the characters to his liking."

But back when I was reading *Tarzan,* I wasn't looking for the long arm of the author. When I was reading *Tarzan* as a youngster (and even today, when I can manage to lock the Pat Murphy who writes away from the Pat Murphy who reads), I didn't notice and didn't care. Vidal compares Burroughs's work to a vivid daydream, and I think he's right. When I read *Tarzan* as a girl, the daydream carried me along and I would accept any coincidence that let me go swinging off through the jungle.

Max Merriwell is a pseudonym of mine who knows how to daydream. Mary Maxwell is a pseudonym of Max's who shares his willingness to suspend disbelief and happily swing through the trees, dodging clunky dialogue and ignoring outrageous coincidence and chilling bits of prejudice, accepting the parts of the daydream that worked and disregarding the rest.

As a writer known for my feminist leanings, the doubly layered pseudonym added an interesting aspect to the writing of this novel. Throughout the writing of *Wild Angel*, I was aware that I was a woman, writing as a man, who was writing as a woman. Twisted and confusing, I know, but necessary in a strange way. Max has the confidence to believe that anything he writes is wonderful. Mary shares that confidence—but modifies the subject matter to match a woman's experience.

In his introduction to *Tarzan*, Vidal wrote: "In its naive way, the Tarzan legend returns us to that Eden where, free of clothes and the inhibitions of an oppressive society, a man is able, as William Faulkner put it in his high Confederate style, to prevail as well as endure." Mary felt it necessary to return a woman to that same Eden, and I was glad to share in the dream.

I said at the start that this three-book project is a practical joke. The joke, it seems, is on me. I have created pseudonyms who have become characters who have been writing books that I enjoy—but wouldn't have written without them. It has been a strange and interesting experience.

I will be writing the final book in this project myself, without the assistance of my pseudonyms. That book, *Adventures in Time and Space with Max Merriwell*, deals with Max's adventures when he is writing *There and Back Again*, *Wild Angel*, and a mystery novel (by Weldon Merrimax). The events of the novels that he is writing begin to bleed through into his reality—and his pseudonyms show up and start making trouble.

Ah—that part will be easy to write. They say that you should write what you know. And I've had firsthand experience with that.

ACKNOWLEDGMENTS

Writers Karen Fowler, Angus MacDonald, Daniel Marcus, Carter Scholz, Michael Berry, Richard Russo, Michael Blumlein, Linda Shore, and Ellen Klages took the time to read and thoughtfully comment on all or part of this manuscript. Folks at the Exploratorium understood my need to take a year's leave to work on this three-book project—and helped make that leave possible. Gary Crounse and his colleagues Rupert Peene and Kamishiwa offered advice regarding 'Pataphysics. My editor Beth Meacham provided ongoing support, wise counsel, and careful editing. And my loving husband, Officer Dave Wright, kept me cheerful in times of confusion, having more faith in me than I sometimes have in myself.

THANK YOU ALL,
PAT MURPHY